Praise for Linda Goodnight and her novels

"Linda Goodnight does her protagonists justice with her sensitive writing in *A Season for Grace*."
—*RT Book Reviews*

"*The Heart of Grace*, by Linda Goodnight, is a wonderfully poignant story with excellent character development."
—*RT Book Reviews*

"From its sad, touching beginning to an equally moving conclusion, *A Touch of Grace* will keep you riveted."
—*RT Book Reviews*

"A truly inspiring story of overcoming trying circumstances and discovering personal strength."
—*RT Book Reviews* on *The Last Bridge Home*

LINDA GOODNIGHT
A Season for Grace

&

The Heart of Grace

Love Inspired

Recycling programs
for this product may
not exist in your area.

LOVE INSPIRED BOOKS

ISBN-13: 978-0-373-65156-6

A SEASON FOR GRACE AND THE HEART OF GRACE
Copyright © 2012 by Harlequin Books S.A.

The publisher acknowledges the copyright holder of the individual works as follows:

A SEASON FOR GRACE
Copyright © 2006 by Linda Goodnight

THE HEART OF GRACE
Copyright © 2007 by Linda Goodnight

www.LoveInspiredBooks.com

Printed in U.S.A.

CONTENTS

Books by Linda Goodnight

Love Inspired Books

In the Spirit of...Christmas
A Very Special Delivery
**A Season for Grace*
**A Touch of Grace*
**The Heart of Grace*
Missionary Daddy
A Time to Heal
Home to Crossroads Ranch
The Baby Bond
†*Finding Her Way Home*
†*The Wedding Garden*
The Lawman's Christmas Wish
†*A Place to Belong*
The Nanny's Homecoming
†*The Christmas Child*
†*The Last Bridge Home*

**The Brothers' Bond
†Redemption River

LINDA GOODNIGHT

Winner of a RITA® Award for excellence in inspira-
tional fiction, Linda Goodnight has also won a Book-
sellers' Best Award, an ACFW Book of the Year award
and a Reviewers' Choice Award from *RT Book Reviews.*
Linda has appeared on the Christian bestseller list and
her romance novels have been translated into more than
a dozen languages. Active in orphan ministry, this former nurse and teacher enjoys writing fiction that car-
ries a message of hope and light in a sometimes dark
world. She and her husband, Gene, live in Oklahoma.
Readers can write to her at linda@lindagoodnight.com,
or c/o Love Inspired Books, 233 Broadway, Suite 1001,
New York, NY 10279.

A SEASON FOR GRACE

A father to the fatherless, defender of widows
is God in his holy dwelling.
God sets the lonely in families.
—*Psalms* 68:5, 6

Special thanks to former DHS caseworker
Tammy Potter for answering my social services
questions, and to my buddy Maggie Price for
helping me keep my cop in the realm of reality.
Any mistakes or literary license are my own.
I would also like to acknowledge the legion of
foster and adoptive parents and children
who have shared their insight
into the painful world of social orphans.

Prologue

The worst was happening again. And there was nothing he could do about it.

Collin Grace was only ten years old but he'd seen it all and then some. One thing he'd seen too much of was social workers. He hated them. The sweet-talking women with their briefcases and straight skirts and fancy fingernails. They always meant trouble.

Arms stiff, he stood in front of the school counselor's desk and stared at the office wall. His insides shook so hard he thought he might puke. But he wouldn't ask to be excused. No way he'd let them know how scared he was. Wouldn't do no good anyhow.

Betrayal, painful as a stick in the eye, settled low in his belly. He had thought Mr. James liked him, but the counselor had called the social worker.

Didn't matter. Collin wasn't going to cry. Not like his brother Drew. Stupid kid was fighting and kicking and screaming like he could stop what was happening.

"Now, Drew." The social worker tried to soothe the wild brother. Tried to brush his too-long, dark hair out of his furious blue eyes. Drew snarled like a wounded wolf. "Settle down. Everything will be all right."

That was a lie. And all three of the brothers knew it. Nothing was ever all right. They'd leave this school and go into foster care again. New people to live with, new school, new town, all of them strange and unfriendly. They'd be cleaned up and fattened up, but after a few months Mama would get them back. Then they'd be living under bridges or with some drugged-out old guy who liked to party with Mama. Then she'd disappear. Collin would take charge. Things would be better for a while. The whole mess would start all over again.

People should just leave them alone. He could take care of his brothers.

Drew howled again and slammed his seven-year-old fist into the social worker. "I hate you. Leave me alone!"

He broke for the door.

Collin bit the inside of his lip. Drew hadn't figured out yet that he couldn't escape.

A ruckus broke out. The athletic counselor grabbed Drew and held him down in a chair even though he bucked and spat and growled like a mad tomcat. Drew was a wiry little twerp; Collin gave him credit for that. And he had guts. For what good it would do him, he might as well save his energy. Grown-ups would win. They always did.

People passed the partially open office door and

peered around the edge, curious about all the commotion. Collin tried to pretend he couldn't see them, couldn't hear them. But he could.

"Poor little things," one of the teachers murmured. "Living in a burned-out trailer all by themselves. No wonder they're filthy."

Collin swallowed the cry of humiliation rising up in his stomach like the bad oranges he'd eaten from the convenience-store trash. He did the best he could to keep Drew and Ian clean and fed. It wasn't easy without water or electricity. He'd tried washing them off in the restroom before school, but he guessed he hadn't done too good a job.

"Collin." The fancy-looking social worker had a hand on her stomach where Drew had punched her. "You've been through this before. You know it's for the best. Why don't you help me get your brothers in the car?"

Collin didn't look at her. Instead he focused on his brothers, sick that he couldn't help them. Sick with dread. Who knew what would happen this time? Somehow he had to find a way to keep them all together. That was the important thing. Together, they could survive.

Ian, only four, looked so little sitting in a big brown plastic chair against the wall. His scrawny legs stuck straight out and the oversize tennis shoes threatened to fall off. No shoestrings. They stunk, too. Collin could smell them clean over here.

Like Collin, baby Ian didn't say a word; he didn't fight. He just cried. Silent, broken tears streamed down his cheeks and left tracks like a bicycle through mud. Clad in a plaid flannel shirt with only two buttons and a pair of Drew's tattered jeans pulled together at the belt loops with a piece of electrical cord, his skinny body trembled. Collin could hardly stand that.

They shouldn't have come to school today; then none of this would have happened. But they were hungry and he was fresh out of places to look. School lunch was free, all you could eat.

Seething against an injustice he couldn't name or defend against, he crossed the room to his brother. He didn't say a word; just put his hand on Ian's head. The little one, quivering like a scared puppy, relaxed the tiniest bit. He looked up, eyes saying he trusted his big brother to take care of everything the way he always did.

Collin hoped he could.

The social worker knelt in front of Ian and took his hand. "I know you're scared, honey, but you're going to be fine. You'll have plenty to eat and a nice, safe place to sleep." She tapped his tennis shoes. "And a new pair of shoes, just your size. Things will be better, I promise."

Ian sniffed and dragged a buttonless sleeve across his nose. When he looked at her, he had hope in his eyes. Poor little kid.

Collin ignored the hype. He'd heard it all before and it was a lie. Things were never better. Different, but not better.

The tall counselor, still holding Drew in the chair,

slid to his knees just like the social worker and said, "Boys, sometimes life throws us a curveball. But no matter what happens, I want you to remember one thing. Jesus cares about you. If you let him, He'll take care of you. No matter where you go from here, God will never walk off and leave you."

A funny thing happened then. Drew sort of quieted down and looked as if he was listening. Ian was still sniffin' and snubbin', but watching Mr. James, too. None of them could imagine *anybody* who wouldn't leave them at some point.

"Collin?" The counselor, who Collin used to like a lot, twisted around and stretched an open palm toward him. Collin wanted to take hold. But he couldn't.

After a minute, Mr. James dropped his hand, laid it on Collin's shoe. Something about that big, strong hand on his old tennis shoe bothered Collin. He didn't know if he liked it or hated it.

The room got real quiet then. Too quiet. Mr. James bowed his bald head and whispered something. A prayer, Collin thought, though he didn't know much about such things. He stared at the wall, trying hard not to listen. He didn't dare hope, but the counselor's words made him want to.

Then Mr. James reached into his pocket. Drew and Ian watched him, silent. Collin watched his brothers.

"I want you to have one of these," the counselor said as he placed something in each of the younger boys'

hands. It looked like a fish on a tiny chain. "It's a reminder of what I said, that God will watch over you."

Collin's curiosity made his palm itch to reach out,
but he didn't. Instead, Mr. James had to pry his fingers
apart and slide the fish-shaped piece of metal into the
hollow of his hand.

Much as he wanted to, Collin refused to look at it.
Better to cut to the chase and quit all this hype. "Where
are we going this time?"

His stupid voice shook. He clenched his fists to still
the trembling. The metal fish, warm from Mr. James's
skin, bit into his flesh.

The pretty social worker looked up, startled that he'd
spoken. Collin wondered if she could see the fury, red
and hot, that pushed against the back of his eyes.

"We already have foster placements for Drew and
Ian."

But not for him. The anger turned to fear. "Together?"

As long as they were together, they'd be okay.

"No. I'm sorry. Not this time."

He knew what she meant. He knew the system probably better than she did. Only certain people would take
boys like Drew who expressed their anger. And nobody
would take him. He was too old. People liked little and
cute like Ian, not fighters, not runaways, not big boys
with an attitude.

Panic shot through him, made his heart pound wildly.
"They have to stay with me. Ian gets scared."

The social worker rose and touched his shoulder. "He'll be fine, Collin."

Collin shrugged away to glare at the brown paneled wall behind the counselor's desk. Helpless fury seethed inside him.

The worst had finally happened.

He and Drew and Ian were about to be separated.

Chapter One

Twenty-three years later, Oklahoma City

Sweat burned his eyes, but Collin Grace didn't move. He couldn't. One wrong flinch and somebody died.

Totally focused on the life-and-death scenario playing out on the ground below, he hardly noticed the sun scalding the back of his neck or the sweat soaking through his protective vest.

The Tac-team leader's voice came through the earphone inside his Fritz helmet. "Hostage freed. Suspect in custody. Get down here for debrief."

Collin relaxed and lowered the .308 caliber marksman rifle, a SWAT sniper's best friend, and rose from his prone position on top of the River Street Savings and Loan. Below him, the rest of the team exited a training house and headed toward Sergeant Gerrara.

Frequent training was essential and Collin welcomed every drill. Theirs wasn't a full-time SWAT unit, so they had to stay sharp for those times when the callout would come and they'd have to act. Normally a patrol cop, he'd spent all morning on the firing range, requalifying with every weapon known to mankind. He was good. Real good, with the steadiest hands anyone on the force had ever seen. A fact that made him proud.

"You headed for the gym after this?" His buddy, fellow police officer and teammate, Maurice Johnson shared his propensity for exercise. Stay in shape, stay alive. Most special tactics cops agreed.

Collin peeled his helmet off and swiped a hand over his sweating brow. "Yeah. You?"

"For a few reps. I told Shanita I'd be home early. Bible study at our place tonight." Maurice sliced a sneaky grin in Collin's direction. Sweat dripped from his high ebony cheeks and rolled down a neck the size of a linebacker's. "Wanna come?"

Collin returned the grin with a shake of his head. Maurice wouldn't give up. He extended the same invitation every Thursday.

Collin liked Maurice and his family, but he couldn't see a loner like himself spouting Bible verses and singing in a choir. It puzzled him, too, that a cop as tough and smart as Maurice would feel the need for God. To Collin's way of thinking there was only one person he trusted enough to lean on. And that was himself.

"Phone call for you, Grace," Sergeant Gerrara hollered. "Probably some cutie after your money."

The other cops hooted as Collin shot Maurice an exasperated look and took off in a trot. He received plenty of teasing about his single status. Some of the guys tried to fix him up, but when a woman started pushing him or trying to get inside his head, she was history. He didn't need the grief.

The heavy tactics gear rattled and bounced against his body as he grabbed the cell phone from Sergeant Gerrara's oversize fist, trading it for his rifle.

"Grace."

"Sergeant Collin Grace?" A feminine voice, light and sweet, hummed against his ear.

"Yeah." He shoved his helmet under one arm and stepped away from the gaggle of cops who listened in unabashedly. "Who's this?"

"Mia Carano. I'm with the Cleveland County Department of Child Welfare."

A cord of tension stretched through Collin's chest. Adrenaline, just now receding from the training scenario, ratcheted up a notch. Child welfare, a department he both loathed and longed to hear from. Could it finally be news?

He struggled to keep his voice cool and detached. "Is this about my brothers?"

"Your brothers?"

Envisioning her puzzled frown, Collin realized she had no idea he'd spent years trying to find Ian and Drew. The spurt of energy drained out of him. "Never mind. What can I do for you, Ms. Carano?"

"Do you recall the young boy you picked up last week behind the pawn shop?"

"The runaway?" He could still picture the kid. "Angry, scared, but too proud to admit it?"

"Yes. Mitchell Perez. He's eleven. Going on thirty."

The kid hadn't looked a day over nine. Skinny. Black hair too long and hanging in his eyes. A pack of cigarettes crushed and crammed down in his jeans' pocket. He'd reminded Collin too much of Drew.

"You still got him? Or did he go home?"

"Home for now, but he's giving his mother fits."

From what the kid had told him, she deserved fits. "He'll run again."

"I know. That's why I'm calling you."

Around him the debrief was breaking up. He lifted a hand to the departing team.

"Nothing I can do until he runs."

He leaned an elbow against somebody's black pickup truck and watched cars pull up to a stop sign adjacent to the parking lot. Across the street, shoppers came and went in a strip mall. Normal, common occurrences in the city on a peaceful, sunny afternoon. Ever alert, he filed them away, only half listening to the caller.

"This isn't my first encounter with Mitch. He's a troubled boy, but his mother said you impressed him. He talks about you. Wants to be a cop."

Collin felt a con coming on. Social workers were good at that. He stayed quiet, let her ramble on in that sugary voice.

"He has no father. No male role model."

Big surprise. He switched the phone to the other ear.

"I thought you might be willing to spend some time with the boy. Perhaps through CAPS, our child advocate program. It's sort of like Big Brothers only through the court system."

He was already a big brother and he'd done a sorry job of that. Some of the other officers did that sort of outreach, but not him.

"I don't think so."

"At least give me a chance to talk with you about it. I have some other ideas if CAPS doesn't appeal."

He was sure she did. Her type always had ideas. "This isn't my kind of thing. Call the precinct. They might know somebody."

"Tell you what," she said as if he hadn't just turned her down. "Meet me at Chick's Place in fifteen minutes. I'll buy you a cup of coffee."

She didn't give up easy. She even knew the cops' favorite hamburger joint.

He didn't know why, but he said, "Make it forty-five minutes and a hamburger, onions fried."

She laughed and the sound was light, musical. He liked it. It was her occupation that turned him off.

"I'll even throw in some cheese fries," she added.

"Be still my heart." He couldn't believe he'd said that. Regardless of her sweet voice, he didn't know this woman and didn't particularly want to.

"I'll sit in the first booth so you'll recognize me."

"What if it's occupied?"

"I'll buy them a burger, too." She laughed again. The sound ran over him like fresh summer rain. "See you in forty-five minutes."

The phone went dead and Collin stared down at it, puzzled that a woman—a social worker, no less—had conned him into meeting her for what was, no doubt, even more of a con.

Well, he had news for Mia Carano with the sweet voice. Collin Grace didn't con easy. Regardless of what she wanted, the answer was already no.

Mia recognized him the minute he walked in the door. No matter that the hamburger café was littered with uniformed police officers hunched over burgers or mega-size soft drinks. Collin Grace stood out in a crowd. Brown eyes full of caution swept the room once, as if calculating escape routes, before coming to rest on her. She prided herself on being able to read people. Sergeant Grace didn't trust a soul in the place.

"There he is," the middle-aged officer across from her said, nodding toward the entrance. "That's Amazin' Grace."

Mia fixed her attention on the lean, buff policeman coming her way. With spiked dark hair, slashing eyebrows and a permanent five o'clock shadow, he was good-looking in a hard, manly kind of way. His fatigue pants and fitted brown T-shirt with a Tac-team emblem over the heart looked fresh and clean as though he'd recently changed.

Officer Jess Snow pushed out of the booth he'd kindly allowed her to share. In exchange, he had regaled her with stories about the force, his grandkids, and his plan to retire next year. He'd also told her that the other policemen referred to the officer coming her way as Amazin' Grace because of his uncanny cool and precision even under the most intense conditions. "Guess I'll get moving. Sure was nice talking to you."

She smiled up at the older man. "You, too, Jess."

Officer Snow gave her a wink and nodded to the newcomer as he left.

Collin returned a short, curt nod and then jacked an eyebrow at Mia. "Miss Carano?"

A bewildering flutter tickled her stomach. "Yes, but I prefer Mia."

As he slid into the booth across from her the equipment attached to his belt rattled and a faint stir of some warm, tangy aftershave pierced the scent of frying onions. She noted that he did not return the courtesy by asking her to use his given name.

She wasn't surprised. He was every bit the cool, detached cop. Years of looking at the negative side of life did that to some social workers, as well. Mia was thankful she had the Lord and a very supportive family to pour out all her frustrations and sadness upon. Her work was her calling. She was right where God could

best use her, and she'd long ago made up her mind not
to let the dark side of life burn her out.

Sergeant Grace, on the other hand, might as well be
draped in strips of yellow police tape that screamed,
Caution: Restricted Area. Getting through his invisible
shield wouldn't be as easy as she'd hoped.

He propped his forearms on the tabletop like a bar-
rier between them. His left T-shirt sleeve slid upward
to reveal the bottom curve of a tattoo emblazoned with
a set of initials she couldn't quite make out.

Though she didn't move or change expressions, a
part of her shrank back from him. She'd never understood a man's propensity to mutilate his arms with dye
and needles.

"So," he said, voice deep and smooth. "What can I
do for you, Mia?"

"Don't you want your hamburger first?"

The tight line of his mouth mocked her. "A spoon-
ful of sugar doesn't really make the medicine go down
any easier."

So cynical. And he couldn't be that much older than
she was. Early thirties maybe. "You might actually
enjoy what I have in mind."

"I doubt it." He raised a hand to signal the waitress.
"What would you like?" he asked.

She motioned to her Coke. "This is fine. I'm not
hungry."

He studied her for a second before turning his attention to the waitress. "Bring me a Super Burger. Fry

the onions, hold the tomatoes, and add a big order of cheese fries and a Mountain Dew."

The waitress poised with pen over pad and said in a droll voice, "What's the occasion? Shoot somebody today?"

One side of the policeman's mouth softened. He didn't smile, but he was close. "Only a smart-mouthed waitress. Nobody will miss her."

The waitress chuckled and said to Mia, "I never thought I'd see the day grease would cross his lips."

She sauntered away, hollering the order to a guy in the back.

"I thought all cops were junk-food junkies."

"It's the hours. Guys don't always have time to eat right."

"But you do?"

"Sometimes."

If he was a health food nut he wasn't going to talk to her about it. Curious the way he avoided small talk. Was he this way with everyone? Or just her?

Maybe it was her propensity for nosiness. Maybe it was her talkative Italian heritage. But Mia couldn't resist pushing a little to see what he would do. "So what *do* you eat? Bean sprouts and yogurt?"

"Is that why you're here? To talk about my diet?"

So cold. So empty. Had she made a mistake in thinking this ice man might help a troubled boy?

On the other hand, Grandma Carano said still waters run deep. Gran had been talking about Uncle Vitorio, the only quiet Carano in the giant, noisy family, and she'd been right. Uncle Vitorio was a thinker, an inventor. Granted he mostly invented useless gadgets to amuse himself, but the family considered him brilliant and deep.

Perhaps Collin was the same. Or maybe he just needed some encouragement to loosen up.

She pushed her Coke to one side and got down to business.

"For some reason, Mitchell Perez has developed a heavy case of hero worship for you."

The boy was one of those difficult cases who didn't respond well to any of the case workers, the counselors or anybody else for that matter, but something inside Mia wouldn't give up. Last night, when she'd prayed for the boy, this idea to contact Collin Grace had come into her mind. She'd believed it was God-sent, but now she wondered.

"More and more in the social system we're seeing boys like Mitchell who don't have a clue how to become responsible, caring men. They need real men to teach them and to believe in them. Men they can relate to and admire."

The waitress slid a soda and a paper-covered straw in front of Sergeant Grace.

"How do you know I'm that kind of man?"

"I checked you out."

He tilted his head. "Just because I'm a good cop

doesn't mean I'd be a suitable role model to some street kid."

"I'm normally a good judge of character and I think you would be. The thing here is need. We have so many needy kids, and few men willing to spend a few hours a week to make a difference. Don't you see, Officer? In the long run, your job will be easier if someone intercedes on behalf of these kids now. Maybe they won't end up in trouble later on down the road."

"And maybe they will."

Frustration made her want to pound the table. "You know the statistics. Mentored kids are less likely to get into drugs and crime. They're more likely to go to college. More likely to hold jobs and be responsible citizens. Don't you get it, Officer? A few hours a week of your time can change a boy's life."

He pointed his straw at her. "You haven't been at this long, have you?"

She blinked, leaned back in the booth and tried to calm down. "Seven years."

"Longer than I thought."

"Why? Because I care? Because I'm not burned out?"

"It happens." The shrug in his voice annoyed her.

"Is that what's happened to you?"

A pained look came and went on his face, but he kept silent—again.

Mia leaned forward, her passionate Italian nature taking control. "Look, this may not make any sense to you. Or it may sound idealistic, but I believe what I do makes a difference in these kids' lives."

"Maybe they don't want you to make a difference. Maybe they want to be left alone."

"Left alone? To be abused?"

"Not all of them are mistreated."

"Or neglected. Or cold and hungry, eating out of garbage cans."

Collin's face closed up tighter than a miser's fist. Had the man no compassion?

"There are a lot of troubled kids out there. Why are you so focused on this particular one?"

"I'm concerned about all of them."

"But?"

So he'd heard the hesitation.

"There's something special about Mitch." Something about the boy pulled at her, kept her going back to check on him. Kept her trying. "He wants to make it, but he doesn't know how."

Collin's expression shifted ever so slightly. The change was subtle, but Mia felt him softening. His eyes flicked sideways and, as if glad for the interruption, he said, "Food's coming."

The waitress slid the steaming burger and fries onto the table. "There you go. A year's worth of fat and cholesterol."

"No wonder Chick keeps you around, Millie. You're such a great salesman."

"Saleslady, thank you."

He took a giant bite of the burger and sighed. "Perfect. Just like you."

Millie rolled her eyes and moved on. Collin turned his attention back to Mia. "You were saying?"

"Were you even listening?"

"To every word. The kid is special. Why?"

Mia experienced a twinge of pleasure. Collin Grace confused her, but there was something about him…

"Beneath Mitch's hard layer is a gentleness. A sweet little boy who doesn't know who to trust or where to turn."

"Imagine that. The world screws him over from birth and he stops trusting it. What a concept."

The man was cool to the point of frostbite and had a shell harder than any of the street kids she dealt with. If she could crack this tough nut perhaps other cops would follow suit. She was already pursuing the idea of mentor groups through her church, but cops-as-mentors could make an impact like no other.

She took a big sip of Coke and then said, "At least talk to Mitch."

The pager at Collin's waist went off. He slipped the device from his belt, glanced at the display, and pushed out of the booth, leaving a half-eaten burger and a nearly full basket of cheese fries.

Mia looked up at the tall and dark and distant cop. "Is that your job?"

He nodded curtly. "Gotta go. Thanks for the dinner."

"Could I call you about this later?"

"No point. The answer will still be no." He whipped around with the precision of a marine and strode out of the café before Mia could argue further.

Disappointment curled in her belly. When she could close her surprised mouth, she did so with a huff.

The basket of leftover fries beckoned. She crammed a handful in her mouth. No use wasting perfectly good cheese fries. Even if they did end up on her hips.

Sergeant Collin Grace may have said no, but no didn't always mean absolutely no.

And Mia wasn't quite ready to give up on Mitchell Perez…or Collin Grace.

Chapter Two

"Hey, Grace, you spending the night here or something?"

Eyes glued to the computer screen, Collin lifted a finger to silence the other cop. "Gotta check one more thing."

His shift was long over, and the sun drifted toward the west, but at least once a week he checked and rechecked, just in case he'd missed something the other five thousand times he'd searched.

Somewhere out there he had two brothers, and with the explosion of information on the internet he would find them—eventually. After all this time, though, he wasn't expecting a miracle.

His cell phone played the University of Oklahoma fight song and he glanced down at the caller ID. Her again. Mia Carano. She'd left no less than ten messages over the past three days. He hadn't bothered to return her phone calls. Eventually she'd get the message.

The rollicking strains of "Boomer Sooner" faded away as his voice mail picked up. Collin kept his attention on the computer screen.

Over the years, he'd amassed quite a list of names and addresses. One by one, he'd checked them out and moved them to an inactive file. He typed several more names into the file on his computer and hit Save.

The welfare office suggested he should hire a private search agency, but Collin never planned to do that. The idea of letting someone else poke into his troubled background made him nervous. He'd done a good job of leaving that life behind and didn't want the bones of his childhood dug up by some stranger.

Part of the frustration in this search, though, lay with his own limited memory. Given what he knew of his mother, he wasn't even sure he and his brothers shared a last name. And even if they once had, either or both could have been changed through adoption.

Maurice Johnson, staying late to finish a report, bent over Collin's desk. "Any luck?"

He kept his voice low, and Collin appreciated his discretion. It was one of the reasons he'd confided in his coworker and friend about the missing brothers. It was also one of the reasons the man was one of his few close friends. Maurice knew how to keep his mouth shut.

"Same old thing. I added a few more men with the last names of Grace and Stotz, my mother's maiden name, to the list, but I'm convinced the boys were moved out of Oklahoma after we were separated."

Their home state had been a dead end from the get-go.

"Any luck in the Texas system?"

"Not yet. But it's huge. Finding the names is easy. Matching ages and plundering records isn't quite as simple."

"Even for a cop."

A lot of the old files were not even computerized yet. And even if he could find them, there were plenty of records he couldn't access.

"Yeah. If only most adoption records weren't sealed. Or there was a centralized listing of some sort."

"Twenty years ago record-keeping wasn't the art it is today."

"Tell me about it."

He'd stuck his name and information on a number of legit sibling searches. He'd even placed a letter in his old welfare file in case one of the boys was also searching.

Apparently, his brothers weren't all that eager to make contact. Either that or something had happened to them. His gut clenched. Better not travel that line of thinking.

"Did you ever consider that you might have other family out there? A grandma, an aunt. Somebody."

He shook his head. "Hard as I've tried, I don't remember anyone. If we ever had any family, Mama had long since alienated them."

He'd had stepdads and "uncles" aplenty. He even remembered Ian's dad as a pretty good guy, but the only name he'd ever called the man was Rob.

A few years back he'd tracked his mother down in Seminole County—in jail for public intoxication. His lips twisted at the memory. She'd been too toasted to give false information and for once one of her real names, anyway a name Collin remembered, appeared on the police bulletin.

Their subsequent visit had not been a joyous reunion of mother and son. And, to his great disappointment, she knew less about his brothers' whereabouts than he did.

After that, she had disappeared off the radar screen again. Probably moved in with her latest party man and changed her name for the tenth or hundredth time. Not that Collin cared. It was his brothers he wanted to find. Karen Stotz-Grace-Whatever had given them birth, but if she'd ever been a mother he didn't remember it.

"Do you think they're together?"

"Ian and Drew? No." He remembered that last day too clearly. "They were headed to different foster homes. Chances are they weren't reunited, either."

His mother hadn't bothered to jump through the welfare hoops anymore after that. She'd let the state have custody of all three of them. Collin, who ended up in a group home, had failed in his promise to take care of his brothers. He hoped they had been adopted. He hoped they'd found decent, loving families to give them what he hadn't been able to. Even though they were grown men, he needed to know if they were all right.

And if they weren't...

He got that heavy, sick feeling in the pit of his stomach and logged out of the search engine.

Leaning back in the office chair, he scraped a hand over his face and said, "Think I'll call it a night."

Maurice clapped him on the shoulder. "Come by the house. Shanita will make you a fruit smoothie, and Thomas will harangue you for a game of catch."

"Thanks. But I can't. Gotta get out to the farm." He rose to his feet, stretching to relieve the ache across his midback. "The vet's coming by to check that new pup."

"How's he doing?" The other cops were suckers for animals just as he was. They just didn't take their concern quite as far.

"Still in the danger zone." Fury sizzled his blood every time he thought of the abused pup. "Even after what happened, he likes people."

"Animals are very forgiving," Maurice said.

Collin pushed the glass door open with one hand, holding it for his friend to pass through. Together they left the station and walked through the soft evening breeze to the parking garage.

"Unlike me. If I find out who tied that little fella's legs with wire and left him to die, I'll be tempted to return the favor."

Another police officer had found the collie mix, but not before one foot was amputated and another badly infected. And yet, the animal craved human attention and affection.

They entered the parking garage, footsteps echoing on the concrete, the shady interior cool and welcome. Exhaust fumes hovered in the dimness like smelly ghosts.

Maurice dug in his pocket, keys rattling. "Did your social worker call again today?"

Collin slowed, eyes narrowing. "How did you know?"

His buddy lifted a shoulder. "She has friends in high places."

Great. "The department can't force me to do something like that."

"You take in wounded animals. Why not wounded kids?"

"Not my thing."

"Because it hits too close to home?"

Collin stopped next to his Bronco, pushed the lock release, and listened for the snick.

"I don't need reminders." Enough memories plagued him without that. "You like kids. You do it."

"Someday you're going to have to forgive the past, Collin. Lay it to rest. I know Someone who can help you with that."

Collin recognized the subtle reference to God and let it slide. Though he admired the steadfast faith he saw in Maurice, he wasn't sure what he believed when it came to religion. He fingered the small metal fish in his pocket, rubbing the ever-present scripture that was his one and only connection to God. And to his brothers.

"Nothing to forgive. I just don't like thinking about it."

Maurice looked doubtful but he didn't argue. The quiet acceptance was another part of the man's character Collin appreciated. He said his piece and then shut up.

"This social worker. Her name's Carano, right?"

Collin glanced up, surprised. His grip tightened on the metal door handle. "Yeah."

"She goes to my church."

Collin suppressed a groan. "Don't turn on me, man."

He'd had enough trouble getting Mia Carano out of his head without Maurice weighing in on the deal. The social worker was about the prettiest thing he'd seen in a long time. She emanated a sincere decency that left him unsettled about turning her down, but hearing her smooth, sweet voice on his voice mail a dozen times a day was starting to irritate him.

"Single. Nice family." White teeth flashed in Maurice's dark face. "Easy on the eyes."

Was she ever! Like an ad for an Italian restaurant. Heavy red-brown hair that swirled around her shoulders. Huge, almond-shaped gray-green eyes. A wide, happy mouth. Not too skinny, either. He never had gone for ultra-thin women. Made him think they were hungry.

"I didn't notice."

"You're cool, Grace, but you ain't dead."

"Don't start, Johnson. I'm not interested. A woman like that would talk a man to pieces." Wasn't she already doing as much?

Maurice chuckled and moseyed off toward his car. His deep voice echoed through the concrete dungeon. "Sooner or later, boy, one of them's gonna get you."

Collin waved him off, climbed into his SUV, and cranked the gas-guzzling engine to life. Nobody was going to "get" him. Way he figured, nobody wanted a hard case like him. And that was fine. The only people he really wanted in his life were his brothers. Wherever they were.

Pulling out of the dark underground, he headed west toward the waning sun. The acreage five miles out of the city was a refuge, both for the animals and for him.

His cell phone rang again. Sure enough, it was the social worker. He shook his head and kept driving.

The veterinarian's dually turned down the short dirt driveway directly behind Collin. The six-wheeled pickup, essential for the rugged places a vet had to traverse, churned up dust and gravel.

"Good timing," Collin muttered to the rearview mirror, glad not to be in back of Doc White's mini dust storm, but also glad to see the dependable animal doctor.

If Paige White said she'd be here, she was. With her busy practice, sometimes she didn't arrive until well after dark, but she always arrived. Collin figured the woman worked more hours than anyone he knew.

The vet followed Collin past the half-built house he called home to the bare patches of grass that served as parking spots in front of a weathered old barn.

A string of fenced pens, divided according to species, dotted the space behind the barn. In one, a pair of neglected and starved horses was slowly regaining strength. In another, a deer healed from an arrow wound.

To one side, a rabbit hutch held a raccoon. And inside the small barn were five dogs, three cats and ten kittens. He was near capacity. As usual. He needed to add on again, but he also needed to continue the work on his house. The bank wouldn't loan money on two rooms, a bathroom and a concrete slab framed in wood.

Booted feet first, the vet leaped from the high cab of her truck with a whoop for a greeting.

"Hey there, ornery. How's business?" she hollered as Collin came around the front of his SUV.

"Which one?"

"The only one that counts." She waved a gloved hand toward the barn, and Collin nearly smiled. Paige White, a fortysomething cowgirl with a heart as big and warm as the sun, joked that animals liked her faster, better and longer than humans ever had.

One thing Collin knew for sure, animals responded to her treatment. He fell in step with the short, sturdy blond and headed inside the barn.

Without preliminary, he said, "The pup's leg smells funny."

"You been cleaning those wounds the way I showed you?"

"Every day." He remembered the first time he'd poured antiseptic cleaner on the pup's foot and listened to its pitiful cries.

Doc stopped, stared at him for a minute and then said, "We'll have a look at him first."

Paige White could always read his concern, though he had a poker face. Her uncanny sixth sense would have bothered him under other circumstances.

The scent of fresh straw and warm-blooded animals astir beneath their feet, they reached the stall where the collie was confined.

From a large, custom-cut cardboard box, the pup gazed at them with dark, moist, delighted eyes. His shaggy tail thumped madly at the side of the box.

As always, Collin marveled at the pup's adoring welcome. He'd been cruelly treated by humans and yet his love didn't falter.

Doc knelt down, crooning. "How's my pal today? Huh? How ya doin', boy?"

"I call him Happy."

"Well, Happy." The dog licked her extended hand, the tail thumping faster. "Let me see those legs of yours." She jerked her chin at Collin, who'd hunkered down beside her. "Make sure this guy over here's looking after you."

With exquisite tenderness, she inspected one limb and then the other. Her pale eyebrows slammed together as she examined the deep, ugly wound.

Collin watched, anxious, when she took a hypodermic from her long, leather bag and filled it with medication.

"What's that?"

"More antibiotic." She held the syringe at eye level and flicked the plastic several times. "I don't like the way this looks, Collin. There's not enough tissue left to debride."

"Meaning?"

"We may have to take this foot off, too."

"Ah, man." He scrubbed a hand over his face, heard his whiskers. He knew Paige would fight hard to avoid another amputation, so if she brought up the subject, she wasn't blowing smoke. "Any hope?"

"Where there's life, there's hope. But if he doesn't respond to treatment soon, we'll have to remove the foot to save him. Infection like this can spread to the entire body in a hurry."

"I know. But a dog with two amputated feet…"

He let the thought go. Doc knew the odds of the pup having any quality of life. Finding a home for him would be close to impossible, and Collin only kept the animals until they were healthy and adoptable or ready to return to the wild. He didn't keep pets. Just animals in need.

Doc dropped the empty syringe into a plastic container, then patted his shoulder. "Don't fret. I'll run out again tomorrow. Got Jenner's Feed Store to donate their broken bags of feed to you and I want to be here to see them delivered. Clovis Jenner owes me."

Warmth spread through Collin's chest. "So do I."

Doc was constantly on the look-out for feed, money, any kind of support she could round up for his farm. And she only charged him for supplies or medications, never for her expertise.

"Nonsense. If it wasn't for me and my soft heart, you wouldn't have all these critters. I just can't put them down without trying."

"I know." He felt the same way. Whenever she called with a stray animal in need of a place to heal, Collin took it if he had room. He was stretched to the limit on space and funds, but he had to keep going. "Let's go check on the others."

Together they made the rounds. She checked the cats and dogs first, redressing wounds, giving shots, poking pills down resistant throats, instructing Collin on the next phase of care.

At the horses' pen, she nodded her approval and pushed a tube of medication down each scrawny throat. "They're more alert. See how this one lifts her head now to watch us? That's a very good sign."

One of the mares, Daisy, leaned her velvety nose against Collin's shirtfront and snuffled. In return for her affection, he stroked her neck, relishing the warm, soft feel against his fingers.

The first few days after the horses had arrived, Collin had come out to the barn every four hours to follow the strict refeeding program Doc had put them on. Seeing the horses slowly come back from the brink of death made the sleepless nights and interrupted days worth the effort.

Sometimes the local Future Farmers of America kids helped out. The other cops occasionally did the same. Most of the time, Collin preferred to work alone.

At the raccoon's hutch, Paige declared the hissing creature fit and ready to release. And finally, she stood at the fence and watched the young buck limp listlessly around the pen.

"He's depressed."

"Deer get depressed?"

"Mmm. Trauma, pain, fear lead to depression in any species." She squinted into the gathering darkness, intelligent eyes studying every move the deer made. "The wound looks good though."

"You do good work."

Some bow hunter had shot the buck. He had escaped with an arrow protruding from his hip, finally collapsing near enough to a house that dogs had alerted the owner. Paige had operated on the badly infected hip.

"I do, don't I?" The vet smiled smugly before sobering. "Only time will tell if enough muscle remains for him to survive in the wild, though."

She turned and started back around the barn to her truck. Collin took her bag and followed.

Headlights sliced the dusk and came steadily toward them, the hum of a motor loud against the quiet country evening.

Collin tensed. "Company," he said.

"Who is it?"

"My favorite neighbor," he said, sarcasm thicker than the cloud of dust billowing around the car. "Cecil Slokum."

Collin and his farm were located a half mile from the nearest house, but Slokum harassed him on a regular basis with some complaint about the animals.

The late-model brown sedan pulled to a stop. A man the size and shape of Danny DeVito put the engine in Park and rolled down a window. His face was red with anger.

"I'm not putting up with this anymore, Grace."

The sixth sense that made Collin a good cop kicked in. He made a quick survey of the car's interior, saw no weapons and relaxed a little.

"What's the problem, Mr. Slokum?" He sounded way more polite than he felt.

"One of them dogs of yours took down my daughter's prize ewe last night."

"Didn't happen." All his animals were sick and in pens.

"Just 'cause you're a big shot cop don't make you right. I know what I saw."

"Wasn't one of mine."

"Tell it to the judge." The man shoved a brown envelope out the window.

Collin took it, puzzled. "What is this?"

"See for yourself." With that, Slokum crammed the car into gear and backed out, disappearing down the gravel road much more quickly than he'd come.

Collin stared down at the envelope.

"Might as well open it," Doc said.

With a shrug, Collin tore the seal, pulled out a legal-looking sheet of vellum and read. When he finished, he slammed a fist against the offending form.

Just what he needed right now. Someone else besides the annoying social worker on his back.

"Collin?" Doc said.

Jaw rigid, he handed her the paper and said, "Nothing like good neighbors. The jerk is suing me for damages."

Chapter Three

Mia perched on a high kitchen stool, swiveling back and forth, her mind a million miles away from her mother's noisy kitchen as she sliced boiled zucchini for stuffing.

At the stove, Grandma Maria Celestina stirred her special marinara sauce while Mama prepared the sausages for baked ziti.

The rich scents of tomato and basil and sausages had the whole family prowling in and out of the kitchen.

"Church was good today, huh, Mia?"

"Good, Mama."

At fifty-six, Rosalie Carano was still a pretty woman. People said Mia favored her and she hoped so. She'd always thought Mama looked like Sophia Loren. Flowered apron around her generous hips, Rosalie sailed around the large family kitchen with the efficient energy that had successfully raised five kids.

The whole clan gathered every Sunday after church

for a late-afternoon meal of Mama's traditional Italian cooking, which always included breads and pastries from the family bakery. In the living room, her dad, Leo, argued basketball with her eldest brother Gabe and Grandpa Salvatore. Gabe's wife, Abby, had taken their two kids outside to swim in the above-ground pool accompanied by Mia's pregnant sister, Anna Maria. The other brothers, Adam and Nic, roamed in and out of the kitchen like starving ten-year-olds.

Mia was blessed with a good family. Not perfect by any means, but close and caring. She appreciated that, especially on days like today when she felt inexplicably down in the dumps. Even church service, which usually buoyed her spirits, had left her uncharacteristically quiet.

Collin Grace had not returned one of her phone calls in the past three days, and she'd practically promised Mitchell that he would. She disliked pulling in favors, tried not to use her eldest brother's influence as a city councilman, but Sergeant Grace was a tough nut to crack.

Nic, her baby brother, snitched a handful of grated mozzarella from the bowl at her elbow. Out of habit, she whacked his hand then listened to the expected howl of protest.

"Go away," she muttered.

His grin was unrepentant. At twenty, dark and athletic Nic was a chick magnet. He knew his charms, though they had never worked on either of his sisters.

"You're grumpy."

Brother Adam hooked an elbow around her neck and yanked back. She tilted her head to look up at him. Adam Carano, dark and tall, was eleven months older than Mia. From childhood, they'd been best friends, and he could read her like the Sunday comics.

"What's eating you, sis? You're too quiet. It scares me." He usually complained that she talked too much.

Gabe stuck his head around the edge of the door. "Last time she was quiet, Nic and Adam ended up with strange new haircuts."

Mia rolled her eyes. "I was eight."

"And we've not had a moment of peace and quiet from you since," Adam joked.

"And I," Nic put in, "was scarred for life at the ripe old age of one."

"I should have cut off your tongue."

"Mom," Nic called in a whiney little-boy voice. "Mia's picking on me."

Mia ignored him and set to work stuffing the zucchini boats.

"What is it, Mia?" Mama asked. "Adam's right. You are not yourself."

"It's a kid," Adam replied before she could. "It's always one of her kids."

Mia pulled a face. He knew her so well. "Smarty."

Mama shushed him. "Let her tell us. Maybe we can help."

It was Mama's way. If one of her chicks had a problem, the mother hen rushed in to fix it—bringing with her lasagna or cookies. So Mia told them about Mitch.

"He's salvageable, Mama. There is a lot of good in him, but he needs a man's influence and guidance. I tried getting him into the Big Brothers program but he refuses."

"One of the boys will talk to him. Won't you, boys?" Rosalie eyed her three sons with a look that brooked no argument.

"Sure. Of course we would." All three men nodded in unison like bobble toys in the back window of a car.

Heart filling with love for these overgrown macho teddy bears she called brothers, Mia shook her head. "Thanks, guys. You're the best. But Mitch is distrustful of most people. He'd never agree. For some reason, he zeroed in on one of the street patrolmen and will only talk to him. The cop is perfect, but—"

"Whoo-oo, Mia found her a perfect man. Go, sis." The brothers started in with the catcalls and bad jokes.

When the noise subsided, she said, "Not that kind of perfect, unfortunately. I don't even like the guy."

But she couldn't get him out of her mind, either.

"Mia!"

"Oh, Mama." Mia plopped the last zucchini boat on a pan and sprinkled parmesan on top. "Our first meeting was disastrous. I bought the man a hamburger to soften him up a little, and he didn't even stick around long enough to eat it. And now he doesn't bother to return my phone calls."

"You've lost your charm, sis. Need some lessons?" Nic flexed both arms and preened around the kitchen, bumping into Grandma who, in turn, shook a gnarled finger in his laughing face.

Rosalie whirled and flapped her apron at the men. "Out. Shoo. We'll never get dinner on."

Gabe and Nic disappeared, still laughing. Adam stayed behind, pulled a stool around the bar with one foot, and perched beside Mia.

The most Italian-looking of the Carano brothers, Adam was swarthy and handsome and a tad more serious than his siblings.

"Want me to beat him up?"

"Who? Mitch or the cop?"

He lifted a wide shoulder. "Either. Say the word."

"Maybe later."

They both grinned at the familiar joke. All through high school Adam had threatened to beat up any guy who made her unhappy. Though he'd never done it, the boys in her class had thought he would.

"If I could only convince Sergeant Grace to spend one day with Mitch, I think he'd be hooked. He comes off as cold and uncaring, but I don't think he is."

"Some people aren't kid-crazy like you are. Especially us men types."

"All I want is a few hours a week of his time to save a kid from an almost certain future of crime and drugs." Mama swished by and took the pan of zucchini boats. "The couple of times I managed to get him on the phone, he barely said three words."

Adam swiveled her stool so that her back was to him. Strong hands massaged her shoulders.

"The guy was short and to the point. *No.* The least he could do is explain *why* he refuses, but he clams up like Uncle Vitorio."

Adam chuckled. "And that drives you nuts in a hurry."

"Yes, it does. Human beings have the gift of language. They should use it." She let her head go lax. "That feels good."

"You're tight as a drum."

"I didn't sleep much last night. I couldn't get Mitch off my mind so I got up to pray. And then, the next thing I know I'm praying for Collin Grace, too."

"The cop?"

"Yes. There's something about him...sort of an aloneness, I guess, that bothers me. I can't figure him out."

Adam squeezed her shoulders hard. "There's your trouble, sis. You always want to talk and analyze and dig until you know everything. Some people like to keep their books closed."

"You think so?" She swiveled back around to face him. "You think I'm too nosey? That I talk too much?"

"Yep. Pushy, too."

"Gabe thinks I'm too soft."

"That's because he's the pushiest lawyer in three states."

Didn't she know it? She'd lost her first job because of Gabe, and though he'd done everything in his power to make it up to her in the years since, Mia would never forget the humiliation of having her professional ethics compromised.

Nic stuck his head into the kitchen, then ducked when his mother threw a tea towel at him. "Mia, your purse is ringing. Should I get it?"

Mia slid off the stool and started toward the living room. She might be pushy, but she played fair.

A large masculine hand attached to a hairy arm—Nic's—appeared around the door, holding out the cell phone.

Taking it, Mia pushed the button and said, "Hello."

"Miss Carano, this is Monica Perez."

"Mrs. Perez, is something wrong?" Mia tensed. Today was Sunday. A strange time for calls from a client. "Is it Mitchell?"

The woman's voice sounded more weary than worried. "He's run away again. This time the worthless little creep stole money out of my purse."

Collin kicked back the roller chair and plopped down at his desk. He'd just returned from transporting a prisoner and had to complete the proper paperwork. Paperwork. Blah. Most Sundays he spent at the farm or crashed out on his couch watching ballgames. But this was his weekend to work.

"I need to see Sergeant Grace, please."

Collin recognized the cool, sweet voice immediately. Mia Carano, social worker to the world and nag of the first order, was in the outer office.

"Dandy," he muttered. "Make my day."

Tossing down the pen, he rose and strode toward the door just as she sailed through it. She looked fresh and young in tropical-print capris and an orange T-shirt, a far cry from the business suit and heels of their first meeting.

"Mitch has run away again," she blurted without preliminary.

"Nothing the police can do for twenty-four hours."

"We have to find him. I'm afraid he'll get into trouble again."

"Probably will."

Her gray-green eyes snapped with fire. "I want you to go with me to find him right now. I have some ideas where he might go, but he won't listen to me. He'll listen to you."

The woman was unbelievable. Like a bulldog, she never gave up.

"It's not police business."

"Can't you do something just because it's right? Because a kid out there needs you?"

Collin felt himself softening. Had any social worker ever worked this hard for him or his brothers?

"If I take a drive around, have a look in a couple places, will you leave me alone?"

"Probably not." Her pretty smile stretched wide beneath a pair of twinkling eyes.

She was a pest. An annoying, pretty, sweet, aggravating pest who would probably go right on driving him nuts until he gave in.

Against his better judgment, he reached into a file cabinet and yanked out a form. "Sign this."

"What is it?"

"Department policy. If you're riding in my car, you gotta sign."

The pretty smile grew wider—and warmer.

He was an idiot to do this. Her kind never stopped at one favor.

Without bothering to read the forms that released the police department of liability in case of injury, Mia scribbled her name on the line and then beat him out of the station house. At the curb, she stopped to look at him. He motioned toward his patrol car and she jumped into the passenger's seat. A gentle floral scent wafted on the breeze when she slammed the door. He never noticed things like that and it bugged him.

He also noticed that the inside of his black-and-white was a mess. A clipboard, ticket pad, a travel mug and various other junk littered the floorboards. Usually a neat freak, he wanted to apologize for the mess, but he kept stubbornly silent. Let her think what she liked. Let her think he was a slob. Why should he care what Mia Carano thought of him?

If she was bothered, she didn't say so. But she did talk. And talk. She filled him in on Mitch's likes and dislikes, his grades in school, the places he hung out. And then she started in on the child advocate thing. She told him how desperately the kid needed a strong male in his life. That he was a good kid, smart, funny and kind. A computer whiz at school.

This time there was no Delete button to silence her. Trapped inside the car, Collin had to listen.

He put on his signal, made a smooth turn onto Tenth Street and headed east toward the boy's neighborhood. "How do you know so much about this one kid?"

"His mom, his classmates, his teachers."

"Why?"

"It's my job."

"To come out on Sunday afternoon looking for a runaway?"

"His mother called me."

"Bleeding heart," he muttered.

"Better than being heartless."

He glanced sideways. "You think I'm heartless?"

She glared back. "Aren't you?"

No, he wasn't. But let her think what she would. He wasn't getting involved with anything to do with the social welfare system.

His radio crackled to life. A juvenile shoplifter.

Mia sucked in a distressed breath, the first moment of quiet they'd had.

Collin radioed his location and took the call.

"It's Mitchell," Mia said after hearing the details. "The description and area fit perfectly."

Heading toward the complainant's convenience store, Collin asked, "You got a picture of him?"

"Of course." She rummaged in a glittery silver handbag and stuck a photo under his nose.

Collin spotted the 7-Eleven up ahead. This woman surely did vex him.

He pulled into the concrete drive and parked in the fire lane.

"Stay here. I'll talk to the owner, get what information I can, and then we'll go from there."

The obstinate social worker pushed open her door and followed him inside the convenience store. She whipped out her picture of the Perez kid and showed it to the store owner.

"That's him. Comes in here all the time. I been suspicious of him. Got him on tape this time."

Collin filled out the mandatory paperwork, jotting down all the pertinent information. "What did he take?"

The owner got a funny look on his face. "He took weird stuff. Made me wonder."

Mia paced back and forth in front of the counter. "What kind of weird stuff?"

Collin silenced her with a stare. She widened rebellious eyes at him, but hushed—for the moment.

"Peroxide, cotton balls, a roll of bandage."

Mia's eyes widened even further. "Was he hurt?"

The owner shrugged. "What do I care? He stole from me."

"He's hurt. I just know it. We have to find him."

Collin shot her another look before saying to the clerk, "Anything else we should know?"

"Well, he did pay for the cat food." The man shifted uncomfortably and Collin suspected there was more to the story, but he wouldn't get it from this guy. He motioned to Mia and they left.

Once in the car, he said, "Any ideas?"

She crossed her arms. "You mean, I have permission to talk now?"

Collin stifled a grin. The annoying woman was also cute. "Be my guest."

"I know several places around here where kids hang out."

He knew a few himself. "I doubt he'll be in plain sight, but we can try."

He put the car in gear and drove east. They tried all the usual spots, the parks, the parking lots. They showed the kid's picture in video stores and to other kids on the streets, but soon ran out of places to look.

"We have to find him before he gets into more trouble."

"I doubt he'd come this far. We're nearly to the city dump."

As soon as he said the words, Collin knew. A garbage dump was exactly the kind of place he would have hidden when he was eleven.

With a spurt of adrenaline, he kicked the patrol car up and sped along the mostly deserted stretch of highway on the outskirts of the city.

When he turned onto the road leading to the landfill, Mia said incredulously, "You think he's here? In the city dump?"

He shot her an exasperated look. "Got a better idea?"

"No."

Collin slammed out of the car and climbed to the top of the enormous cavity. The stench rolled over him in waves.

"Ew." Beside him, Mia clapped a hand over her nose.

"Wait in the car. I'll look around."

Collin wasn't the least surprised when she ignored him.

"You go that way." She pointed left. "I'll take the right side."

Determination in her stride, she took off through the trash heap apparently unconcerned about her white shoes or clean clothes. Collin watched her go. A pinch of admiration tugged at him. He'd say one thing for Miss Social Worker, she wasn't a quitter.

His boots slid on loose dirt as he carefully picked his way down the incline. Some of the trash had been recently buried, but much more lay scattered about.

He watched his step, aware that among the discarded furniture and trash bags, danger and disease lurked.

This was not a place for a boy. Unless that boy had no place else to turn.

His chest constricted. He'd been here and done this. Maybe not in this dump, but he understood what the kid was going through. He hated the memories. Hated the heavy pull of dread and hurt they brought.

This was why he didn't want to get involved with Mia's project. And now here he was, knee-deep in trash and recollections, moving toward what appeared to be a shelter of some sort.

Plastic trash bags that stretched across a pair of ragged-out couches were anchored in place by rocks, car parts, a busted TV set. An old refrigerator clogged one end and a cardboard box the other.

Mia was right. The kid had smarts. He'd built his hideout in an area unlikely to be buried for a while and had made the spot blend in with the rest of the junk.

As quietly as he could, Collin leaned down and slid the cardboard box away. What he saw inside made his chest ache.

The kid had tried to make a home inside the shelter. An old blanket and a sack of clothes were piled on one end of a ragged couch. A flashlight lay on an up-turned crate. Beneath the crate, the kid had stored the canned milk, a jar of water, cat food and a box of cereal.

In the dim confines Mitchell knelt over a cardboard box, cotton ball and peroxide in hand.

Collin had a pretty good idea what was inside the box.

At the sudden inflow of light, the kid's head whipped

around. A mix of fear and resentment widened his dark eyes.

"Nice place you got here," Collin said, stooping to enter.

"I'm not doing anything wrong."

"Stealing from convenience stores isn't wrong?"

"I had to. Panda—" Mitchell glanced down at the box "—she's hurt."

Curiosity aroused, Collin moved to the boy's side. A mother cat with three tiny kittens mewed up at him. Mitchell stroked the top of her head and she began to purr.

Collin's heart slammed against his ribs.

Oh, man. Déjà vu all over again.

"Mind if I take a look?"

The kid scooted sideways but hovered protectively.

Collin frowned. The cat was speckled with round burns, several of them clearly infected. "What happened?"

"Some kids had her. Mean kids who like to hurt things. She was their cat, but I took her when they started—"

Collin held up a hand. He didn't need the ugly details to visualize what the kid had saved the cat from.

"You can't stay here, Mitchell. Your mother is worried."

"She's just worried about her ten bucks."

"You shouldn't have taken it."

The kid shrugged, didn't answer, but Collin's own

eyes told him where the money had gone. And if his nose was an indicator, the kid had scavenged a pack of cigarettes somewhere too which would explain the store owner's guilty behavior. He'd probably sold cigarettes to a minor.

"I'm not going back to her house."

"You have to."

"I can't. Panda and her babies will die if I don't take care of her. Archie, too."

"Archie?"

The kid reached behind them to the other couch and gently lifted a turtle out of a shoe box. A piece of silver duct tape ran along a fracture in the green shell.

Emotions swamped Collin. He felt as if he was being sucked under a whirlpool. Memories flashed through his head so fast he thought he was going blind.

At that moment, little Miss Social Worker poked her head through the opening. "I thought I heard voices."

Mitchell shrank away from her, blocking the box of cats with his body.

"I won't leave her," he said belligerently. "You can't make me."

"Maybe your mother will let you keep them," Collin said, hoping Mitchell's mother was better than he suspected.

"I'm not going back there, I said. Never."

"Why not?"

The boy's face closed up tight, a look Collin recognized all too well. Something ugly needed to be said and the kid wasn't ready to deal with it.

As the inevitability of the situation descended upon him, Collin pulled a hand down his face.

After a minute of pulling himself together, he spoke. "Nothing's going to happen to your cat. You have my word."

Mitch's face lightened, though distrust continued to ooze out of him. "How can you be sure?"

"Because," Collin said, wishing there was a way he could avoid involvement and knowing he couldn't, "I'll take her home with me."

The boy's face crumpled, incredulous. The belligerent attitude fled, replaced by the awful yearning of hope. "You will?"

"I know a good vet. Panda will be okay."

Mia ducked under the black plastic and came inside. Her eyes glowed with pleasure. "That's really nice of you, Sergeant Grace."

"Yeah. That's me. Real nice." Stupid, too.

He was a cop. Tough. Hardened to the ugliness of humanity. He could resist about anything. Anything, that is, except looking at Mitch's face and seeing his own reflection.

Like it or not, he was about to become a big brother—again.

He only hoped he didn't mess it up this time around.

Chapter Four

Mitchell sat huddled in the backseat of the patrol car, tense and suspicious. The cardboard carton containing cat, kittens and turtle rested on the seat beside him. The rest of his property was in a battered paint bucket on the floor.

"I told you I'm not going back there."

Mia turned in her seat, antennae going up. "Why not? Is something wrong at home?"

The boy ignored her.

Ever the cop, Collin spoke up. "Juvie Hall is the other alternative."

"Better than home."

The adults exchanged glances.

Collin hadn't said two complete sentences since they'd left Mitch's lean-to. He'd simply gathered up the animals and the rag-tag assortment of supplies and led the way to the cruiser. Mitchell had followed along without a fuss, his only concern for the animals. For some reason that Mia could not fathom, the two silent males seemed to communicate without words.

Right now, though, Collin's words were not helping. Mia stifled the urge to shush him. Something was amiss with the child and he was either too scared or too proud to say so.

She pressed a little harder. "I wish you'd talk to me, Mitch. I can help. It's what I do. If there is a problem at home I can help get it resolved."

Dirt spewed up over the windshield as they bumped and jostled down the dusty road out of the landfill. Once on the highway, Collin flipped on the windshield washers.

"How do you and your mother get along? Any problems there?"

Mitch turned his profile toward her and stared at the spattering water.

Mia softened her voice. "Mitch, if there's abuse, you need to tell me."

His head whipped around, expression fierce. "Leave my mom out of this."

Whoa! "Okay. What about your stepdad?"

Collin gave her a sideways glance that said he wished she'd shut up. She didn't plan on doing that any time soon. Something was wrong in this boy's life. Otherwise, he wouldn't be running away. He wouldn't be shoplifting, and he wouldn't dread going home. She would be a lousy social worker and an even worse human being if she didn't investigate the very real possibility of abuse.

"Mitchell," she urged softly. "You can trust me. I want to help."

The cruiser slowed to a turn, pulled through a concrete drive and stopped. Mitchell jerked upright. His eyes widened in fright.

"Hey. What are we doing here?"

The green-and-red sign of the 7-Eleven convenience store loomed above the gas pumps. Mia recognized it as the store from which Mitch had shoplifted. Facing consequences was an important part of teaching a child right from wrong, but Mia still felt sorry for him. And she felt frustrated to be getting nowhere in their conversation.

Collin shifted into Park and got out of the car.

Mitchell shrank back against the seat. "I ain't going in there."

Mia braced for a strong-armed confrontation between the cop and the kid, prepared to intervene if necessary. But the cop surprised her.

He opened the back door, hunkered down beside the car and spoke quietly, almost gently, to the scared boy. "Everybody messes up sometime, Mitch. Part of being a man means facing up to your mistakes. Are you willing to be a man about it?"

Although Mia was dying to offer to go inside with the boy and talk to the owner, she knew Collin was right. For once, she had to bite her tongue and let the cop do the talking.

Several long seconds passed while Mia thought she would burst. The need to blurt out reassurances and promises swelled like yeast bread on a hot day. Would Mitchell go on his own? Would Sergeant Grace drag him inside if he didn't?

As if in answer to her unasked question, Collin placed one wide hand on the knee of the boy's dirty blue jeans and patiently waited.

The gesture brought a lump to Mia's throat. Her brothers would laugh at her if they knew, but she couldn't help it. There was something moving about the sight of a tough, taciturn cop conveying his trustworthiness with a gentle touch.

The boy's shoulders were so tense, Mia thought his collarbone might snap. Finally, he drew in a shuddering breath and reached for his seat-belt clasp.

"Will you go with me?" Mouth tight and straight, he directed the question to Collin.

The policeman pushed to his feet. "Every step."

And then, as if the social worker in the front seat was invisible, the two males, one tall and buff and immaculate, the other small and thin and tattered, crossed the concrete space and went inside.

The kittens in the backseat made mewing sounds as Panda shifted positions. Mia glanced around to be sure they were staying put. Yellow eyes blinked back.

"Hang tight, Mama," she said. "The abandonment is only temporary."

The poor, bedraggled cat seemed satisfied to stay with her babies and the hapless turtle. So, Mia tilted her forehead against the cool side glass and watched the people inside the store. There were a few customers coming and going, an occasional car door slammed, though the area was reasonably quiet.

She could see Collin and Mitchell moving around inside, see the clerk. Although frustrated at being left behind, for once, she didn't charge into the situation. But she did use her time to pray that somehow the angry shop owner would give the child a break without letting him off scot-free.

Ten minutes later, Collin and Mitch emerged from the building. Collin wore his usual bland expression that gave nothing away. Mitch looked pale, but relieved as he slammed into the backseat.

Mia could hardly contain herself. "How did it go?"

"Okay." Collin started the cruiser and pulled into the lane of slow Sunday-afternoon traffic.

Mia rolled her eyes. That wasn't the answer she was asking for. But since the cop wasn't willing to elaborate, she asked Mitchell. "What was decided? Is he going to press charges?"

Mitch trailed a finger over one of the kittens. "I don't know yet. But he said he'd think about it."

The quiet, gentle boy she usually encountered had returned. The belligerence, most likely posturing brought on by fear, had dissipated. He looked young and small and lost.

Collin spoke up—finally. "We worked out a deal."

"And is this a secret all-male deal? Or can the nosy, female social worker be let in on it?"

Collin glanced her way, eyes sparkling. At least she'd badgered a smile out of him. Sort of.

"Didn't like being left in the car?"

The rat. He had already figured out that she needed to be in the middle of a situation. "This is the sort of thing I'm trained to do. I might have been useful in there."

He didn't argue the point. "We're asking for twenty hours of community service."

That was something she could help with.

"I'll talk to the DA if you'd like." She did that all the time, working deals for the juveniles she encountered. "He's a friend."

"Figures."

"Having friends is not a bad thing, Sergeant."

"It is when you use them to harass people."

Ah, the phone calls to the chief had not pleased him. "I did not harass you."

He lifted an eyebrow at her.

"Well, okay. Maybe I did. But just a little to get your attention."

"You got it."

"Was that a good thing or a bad thing?"

"Time will tell."

Was that a smile she saw? Or a grimace? He was the hardest man in the world to read.

The cruiser pulled to a stop in front of an older frame house in a rundown area of the city. Paint had peeled until the place was more gray than white, and the yard was overgrown. A rusted lawnmower with grass shooting up over the motor looked as though it hadn't been used all summer.

Mia knew the house. She'd been here more than once at the request of the school system, but never could find out anything that justified removing the boy from the home.

"I thought Mitch opted for Juvenile Hall?" she asked.

Collin shut off the engine and opened the car door. "He changed his mind."

A dark-haired woman who was far too thin came out into the yard and stood with her arms folded around her waist.

"Where's my ten bucks?" she asked as soon as Mitch was out of the car.

To Mia's surprise, Mitch reached in his jeans and withdrew a crumpled bill. She looked at Sergeant Grace, suspicious, but the man's poker face gave away nothing. The idea that the tough cop might have bailed the boy out with his mother touched her. Maybe he wasn't so heartless after all.

She listened without comment as Collin apprised Mitchell's mother about the situation. Mrs. Perez didn't seem too pleased with her son, as expected, but her fidgety behavior raised Mia's suspicions. She didn't invite them into the house and seemed anxious to have them gone.

"What's going to happen to him?" she asked. "I don't have no money for lawyers and courts."

"He broke the law, Mrs. Perez. Miss Carano will talk to the DA for him, but at the least he'll do some community service to pay for the things he took from the store."

"He stole from me, too."

Collin's nostrils flared. "You want to press charges?"

Said aloud, the idea seemed harsh even to the fidgety mother. "I don't want him stealing from me anymore. That's all. He'll end up in jail like his old man."

Conversation halted as an old car, the chassis nearly dragging on the street, mufflers missing or altered, rumbled slowly past. Loud hip-hop music pulsed from the interior, overriding every other sound.

Collin turned and stared hard-eyed at the vehicle, garnering a rude gesture in return. Mia had a feeling the car's inhabitants hadn't seen the last of Sergeant Grace.

When the racket subsided, Mia picked up the conversation. "Have you considered counseling?"

Monica Perez rolled her eyes. "Mitchell don't need no shrink. He needs a new set of friends. Them Walters boys down the street get into everything. You oughta go arrest them."

"I could help him meet some new friends if you'd like," Mia said and received a sideways glance from Collin for her efforts.

"Fine with me."

"My church has a basketball league for kids. He could sign up to play."

"I wouldn't mind that, but I ain't got a car. Is it far from here?"

"I'll pick him up. Saturday morning at nine, if he wants to go." She looked at Mitch, stuck like a wood tick to Collin's side. "Mitch?"

"Sure. I guess so."

Collin dropped a hand on the boy's shoulder. "Miss Carano's going out on a limb for you."

Mitch gazed up at the tall cop, his expression a mix of frightened child and troubled youth. "I know."

Mia glimpsed his bewilderment, his failure to understand his own behavior. And as always, something about this kid got to her. A good person was inside there. With God's help, she'd find a way to bring him out.

"Someone will give you a call next week and let you know the DA's decision," Collin was telling Mrs. Perez.

And then with a curt nod, he turned and started back toward the police car. Mia, who preferred long goodbyes with lots of conversation and closure, felt off balance.

Mitch didn't seem to be finished either because he darted after the departing figure.

"Sergeant Grace."

Collin stopped, one hand on the car door.

Suddenly, every vestige of the tough street kid was gone. Mitch looked like what he was, a little boy with nothing and no one to cling to. "You'll take care of Panda?"

"I will."

"Can I come see her sometime?"

The hardened cop studied the small, intense face, his own face intense as if the answer would cost him too much. "She'd be sad if you didn't."

Mia said a quick goodbye to Mrs. Perez and hurried across the overgrown lawn. Now was her chance. Now that Collin had softened just the tiniest bit.

"I could bring Mitch out to your place. Anytime that's convenient for you."

Collin looked from Mitchell to Mia and back again. Mia was certain she must be imagining things because the strong, hardened cop looked more helpless than the boy. Helpless…and scared.

Mia shoved away from the mile-high stack of file folders on her desk and scrounged in the bottom desk drawer for her stash of miniature Snickers. A day like today required chocolate and plenty of it. She took two.

Her case load grew exponentially every day to the point that she was overwhelmed at times. Looking out for the interests of kids was her calling, but on days like today, the calling was a tough one.

She'd made a school visit and six home visits. At the last one, she'd done what every social worker dreads. She'd pulled the two neglected babies and taken them to a foster home. Even now, though she knew she'd made the right choice, she could hear the youngest one crying for his mama. Poor little guy was too young to comprehend that he lived in a crack house.

She nipped the corner of Snickers number one and turned to the computer on her desk. All the reports from today had to be typed up and stored in the master files before she could go home.

"See ya tomorrow, Mia," one of the other workers called as she passed by the open office door.

Mia waved without lifting her eyes from the computer screen. "Have a good evening, Allie."

She reached for another bite of candy. Over the tick-tick-tick of the keyboard, she heard another voice. This one wasn't her coworker.

"Mind if I interrupt for a minute?"

Her head snapped up.

"Collin?" she blurted before remembering he'd never given her permission to call him by his first name. But she had to face the fact. She thought about him, even prayed for him, by his first name.

During the three days since he'd helped her find Mitchell, she'd prayed about him and thought about him a lot. The fact that she didn't know him that well didn't get him out of her mind. She was intrigued. And attracted. More than once, she'd wondered if he was a Christian, but she was afraid she might already know the answer.

Now he stood before her in his blue uniform, patches on each sleeve, shiny metal pins on each collar point and above his name tag. He looked as crisp and clean as new money.

Great. And she looked like a worn-out, overworked social worker whose white blouse was wrinkled and pulling loose from her red skirt. She hoped like crazy there was no chocolate on her teeth.

"Can we talk?"

Collin Grace wanted to talk? Now there was a novel concept.

"Do you know how?" She softened the teasing jab with a smile.

Those brown eyes twinkled but he didn't return the smile. "I want to make a deal with you."

He scraped a client chair away from her desk a little. He might want to talk, but he was still keeping his distance.

Mia rolled back in her own chair to study his solemn face. Whatever was on his mind was serious business. "A deal?"

"In exchange for your help, I'll mentor the kid."

The wonderful thrill of victory shot much-needed energy into her bloodstream. After the day she'd had, this was great news.

"Mitchell Perez? Collin, that's marvelous. He told me on the phone last night that you stopped by after school yesterday. That was so nice of you, and it really made his day. He tried to act all tough about your visit, but he was thrilled. I could tell. And when I told him the DA agreed to community service, he asked if he could work for you. But I had no idea how to answer that without talking to you first and I've just been so busy today...."

Collin lifted one hand to slow her down. "The deal first."

Once she got on a roll, stopping was difficult. But that halted her in her tracks. "Am I going to like this deal?"

"This is confidential. Okay?"

Now her interest was piqued. Very. "Most of my work is confidential. Believe it or not, I can keep my mouth shut when necessary."

He made a huffing noise that sounded remarkably close to a laugh. She got up and moved around the desk past him to close the door even though the office was probably empty by now.

When she sat down again, she had to ask, "Do I have chocolate on my teeth?"

This time he *did* laugh.

"No. You look great."

"Such a smooth liar," she said, and then reached in the file drawer and took out another candy bar. "Want one?"

"No, thanks."

"Oh, yeah. You're the health-food cop. Poor guy. You don't know what you're missing." She unwrapped a Snickers, nibbled the end and shifted into social-worker mode.

"You said you needed my help. What can I do for you, Officer?"

"Collin's okay."

Another thrill, this one as sweet as the caramel, and completely uncalled for, raced through her. Before she could wipe the smile off her face, he did it for her.

"I want you to help me find my brothers."

She blinked, uncomprehending. "Your brothers?"

"Yeah." Collin leaned forward, muscled forearms on his thighs as he clasped his hands in front of him. Steel intensity radiated from him as though the coming confidence was very difficult for him to share. "My little brothers, Drew and Ian, though neither of them are little now."

She got a sinking feeling in the pit of her stomach. "When did you last see them?"

His answer hurt her heart. "More than twenty years ago."

"Tell me," she said simply, knowing for once when to keep quiet and let the other person do the talking. Whatever he had to share, in confidence, about his brothers was important to him.

Over the next fifteen minutes, during which Mia went through three more Snickers bars, Collin told a story all too familiar to a seasoned social worker. Oh, he spoke in vague, simplistic terms about his childhood, but Mia had worked in social services long enough to fill in the blanks. Collin and his brothers had been separated by the social system because of major issues in his family.

"What happened after that day in the principal's

office? Where did you go? Foster care?" she asked, hearing the compassion in her voice and wondering if he would resent it. But she had brothers she adored, too. She knew how devastated she would be if she couldn't find one of them.

"Foster care never worked out for me. I went into a group home," he said simply, and she heard the hurt through the cold retelling. "Ian was so little, not even five. Foster care, maybe even adoption, would be my best guess for him. He was small and sweet and cute. He could have made the adjustment, I think." His nostrils flared. "I hope."

"And your middle brother? Drew? What do you think happened to him?"

He shook his head. The skin over his high, handsome cheekbones drew tight, casting deep hollows in his face. Clearly, talking about the loss of his brothers distressed him. "Drew was a fighter. He would have had a harder time than I did. I remember the social worker that day saying he was headed to a special place or something like that."

"A therapeutic home?"

"Maybe. I don't remember." He pinched at his upper lip, frustrated. "See? That's the problem. I was a kid, too. My memories are more feelings than facts."

And those feelings still cut into him with the power of a chainsaw.

"Did you ever see or hear anything at all about them? Anything that could help us find them?" She didn't

know why she'd said *us*. She hadn't agreed to do anything yet.

"The summer after we were separated, we both
ended up at one of those summer-camp things they do
for kids in the system. We immediately started making
plans to run away together. But, like I said, Drew was a
fighter. He got kicked out the second day. I didn't even
know about the trouble until he was gone."

"And no one told you anything about him?"

"No more than I've told you. Twenty years of searching, of sticking my name in files and on search boards
and registries hasn't found them." The skin on his knuckles alternated white and brown as he flexed and unflexed
his clenched fists. "I've had leads, good ones, but they
were always dead ends."

And it's killing you. All the things she'd wondered
about him now made sense. His chilly reserve. The way
he seemed isolated, a man alone.

Collin Grace *had* been alone most of his life. He'd
been a child alone. Now he was a man alone.

To a woman surrounded by the warmth and noise
and love of a big family, Collin's situation was not only
sad, it was tragic.

"Somewhere out there I have two brothers. I want
them back." And then as if the words came out without his permission, he murmured gruffly, "I need to
know they're okay."

Of course he needed that. Mia's training clicked
through her head. As the oldest of the three boys, he'd

been responsible for the others. Or at least, he'd thought
he was. Having them taken away without a word left
him believing he'd failed them.

Now she understood why he'd been so reluctant to
take Mitchell under his wing. He was afraid of failing
him, too.

The sudden insight almost brought tears to her eyes.

Mia tilted back her chair and drew in a breath, studying the poster on the far wall. The slogan, Social Work
Is Love Made Visible, reminded her why she did what
she did. The love of Christ in her, and through her, min-
istered to people like Collin, to kids like Mitchell. If
she could help, she would.

"Twenty years is forever in the social services system. Do you really think I can find them if you haven't
had any success?"

"You know the system better than I do. You have
access to records that I don't even know exist. Records
that I'm not allowed to see."

Warning hackles rose on Mia's back. She tried not to
let them show. "You aren't asking me to go into sealed
records without permission, are you?"

"Would you?" Dark eyes studied her. He wasn't
pressing, just asking.

"No." She'd done that once for her oldest brother,
Gabe. The favor had cost her a job she loved and a certain amount of credibility with her peers. The bad decision had also cost her a great deal emotionally and
spiritually. God had forgiven her, but she'd always felt

as if she'd let Him down. "I will never compromise my professional or my Christian ethics."

Again.

"Okay, then. Do what you can. You still have access to a lot of records, even the unsealed ones. I've looked everywhere I know, but that's the problem. I don't know how to navigate the system the way you would. I can't seem to find much when it comes to child welfare records of twenty years ago."

"Records from back then aren't computerized."

"I finally figured that one out. But where are they?"

"If they exist, they're still in file cabinets somewhere or they could be piled in boxes in a storage warehouse."

"Like police records."

"Exactly." She crumpled the half-dozen Snickers wrappers into a wad, dismayed to have consumed so many.

"Are you willing to try?"

"Are you willing to be Mitchell's CAP? That's what we call adults who volunteer through our Child Advocate Partners Program." She would help Collin in his search no matter what, but Mitch might as well get a good mentor out of the deal.

"What do I have to do?"

"Some initial paperwork. Being a police officer simplifies the procedure since you already have clearances."

"How much is the welfare office involved?"

"You don't like us much, do you?"

He made a face that said he had good reason.

"Things are different now, Collin. We understand things about children today that we didn't know then."

He didn't buy a word of it. "Yeah. Well."

"If I help you and you become Mitch's CAP, you're going to be stuck with me probably more than you want to be."

"As long as it's you. And only you."

Now why did that make her feel so good? "But you think I talk too much."

The corner of his mouth hiked up. "You do."

"But you're willing to sacrifice?"

"Finding my brothers is worth anything."

Ouch. "Sorry. I was teasing, but maybe I shouldn't have. Finding your brothers *is* serious business."

"No apology necessary." He rose with athletic ease, bringing with him the vague scent of woodsy cologne and starched uniform. "I was teasing, too."

He was? Nice to know he could. "I'll need all the information you can give me about your brothers. Ages, names, dates you can remember, people you remember, places. Any little detail."

From his shirt pocket, he withdrew a small spiral notebook, the kind all cops seemed to carry. "The basics are in here. But I have more information on my computer."

"What kind of information?"

"The research I've done. Names and places I've already eliminated. Group homes, foster parents. I know a lot of places my brothers never were. I just can't find where they are."

He made the admission easily, but Mia read the hopelessness behind such a long and fruitless search. Twenty years was a long time to keep at it. But Collin Grace didn't seem the kind that would ever give up.

And that was exactly the type of person she was, too.

"Everything you've investigated will be useful. Knowing where *not* to look is just as important as knowing where *to* look. The files and the computer will be helpful, but we may have to do some legwork, as well." Now, why did the prospect of going somewhere with Collin sound so very, very appealing? "People are more comfortable with face-to-face questions about these kinds of things."

"Whatever it takes."

"I can't make promises, but I'll do what I can."

"Fair enough."

"Then I guess we have a deal. Will you go out and talk to Mitchell or do you want me to?"

Reluctance radiated from him in waves, but he'd made a deal and he was the kind of man who would keep it. Wasn't he still trying to keep a promise he'd made when he was ten years old? A man like that didn't back off from responsibility.

"I can contact him tomorrow," she offered.

"We could both tell him now. You know what's involved more than I do."

She shook her head, more disappointed than was

wise, considering how little she knew about Collin as a person.

"I'm slammed with extra work tonight. I'll be here until seven at least." And Mitch was a lot more interested in Collin than he was in Mia.

"Too bad," he said. His expression was unreadable as usual so Mia didn't know what to make of his comment. Too bad she couldn't go with him? Or too bad she had so much work to do?

Either way, she watched him turn and stride out of her office and suffered a twinge of regret that she hadn't gone along anyway. She could be dishonest and say she wanted another look at Mitchell's living situation or that she needed to explain the program in more detail. But Mia was not dishonest. Even with herself. She had wanted to spend time with her enigmatic policeman.

And the notion was disturbing to say the least. She hadn't dated anyone in a while. To find her interest piqued by a man who didn't even seem to like her was a real puzzle.

He was a good cop, had a good reputation, and she'd had a sneak peek at the kindness he kept safely hidden. But he also carried a personal history that sometimes meant major emotional issues. Issues that might require counseling and work and, most importantly, healing from God.

And that was the big issue for Mia. Was Collin Grace a believer?

She reached for another Snickers.

Chapter Five

Sometimes Collin felt as if he spent his life inside a vehicle. He'd driven from Mia's office directly to Mitch's place, only to find the little twerp wasn't there. After driving through the neighborhood, he'd spotted him in a park shooting hoops with three other boys.

When Collin got out of the cruiser, Mitchell passed the ball off and headed toward him. The other boys quickly faded into the twilight and disappeared.

"Why are your friends in such a rush?" Collin leaned against the side of the car and folded his arms, watching the shadowy figures with a mixture of amusement and suspicion.

"You scared them off."

"They have reason to be scared of a cop?"

"Maybe."

Which meant yes in eleven-year-old talk.

"It's getting dark. Come on. I'll take you home."

"Am I in trouble?" Mitch asked, climbing readily into the front seat of the cruiser.

"No more than usual."

Streetlights had come on but made little dent in the shadowy time between day and night. This part of town was a haven for the unsavory. Gang types, thugs, druggies, thieves all came sneaking out like cockroaches as soon as the sun went down. No place at all for a young boy.

Collin had to admit Mia was right about one thing. This kid needed a mentor before he fell into the cesspool that surrounded him. Though he still wasn't sure he wanted to be the one, Collin had begun to feel a certain responsibility toward Mitchell. He hated that, but he did. Who better than him to understand what this kid was going through? And that was all he planned to do. Understand and guide. He wasn't letting the kid get to him.

"Why're you here?" Mitch slouched down into the seat and stared out the window at the passing cars with studied disinterest.

"Miss Carano sent me."

Mitch sat up. "No kidding? You gonna be my CAP?"

So, she'd already prepared the kid for this. How had she known he would agree? He hadn't even known himself.

"What do you think about that?"

The kid hitched a shoulder. "I got plenty of other stuff to do."

"Yeah. Including a lot of community service. At least ten hours at the store where you jacked the stuff. The rest is up to you and me and Miss Carano."

"I guess I could come out to your place. Help with the animals. I'm good at that."

"Up to you." Mitch had to make the decision. Otherwise, he'd only resent Collin's interference.

"Panda probably misses me a lot. She doesn't trust many people."

"With good reason." A lot of people had let the cat—and the kid—down. The cruiser eased to a stop at the light. "You work for me, you'll have to lose the cigarettes."

The denial came fast. "I don't smoke."

One hand draped over the steering wheel, Collin just looked at him, long and steady. The boy's eyes shifted sideways. He swallowed and hitched a shoulder. "How'd you know?"

"I have a nose." The light changed. "Gonna lose them or not?"

"Whatever."

"Your choice."

"Why do you care?"

"The animals at my place depend on me."

"What's that got to do with anything?"

"You think about it and let me know which is more important. The animals or the smokes."

Collin slowed and turned into the drive-through of a Mickey D's. "Want a burger?"

He rolled down his window. The smell of hot vegetable oil surrounded the place.

"Miss Carano said you didn't eat junk food."

"She did?" The fact that she'd mentioned him to the boy in any way other than as a court-appointed advocate sent a warm feeling through him. Warm, like her sunny smile.

That warmth, that genuine caring both drew and repelled him. He didn't understand it. But he couldn't deny how good it had felt to dump his burden on her desk and to believe she would do exactly what she promised. Maybe she'd have no better luck than he'd had in finding Drew and Ian. But for the first time in years, he felt renewed hope.

Hanging out with a social worker might not be so bad after all.

Little more than a week later, Collin considered changing his mind.

He stood in the last stall of his barn showing Mitchell how to measure horse feed. The smell of hay and horses circled around his head.

The kid was all right most of the time. The social worker was a different matter.

He did okay on the days Mia dropped Mitch off as planned, said hello and goodbye and drove away in her power suit and speedy little yellow Mustang. The days she climbed out of that Mustang wearing blue jeans and a T-shirt gave him trouble. Regardless that she was here on business to assess the CAP arrangement, dressed like that, she was a woman, not a social worker. It was hard to dislike one and like the other, so he tried to keep his distance.

Trouble was, Mia didn't understand the concept of personal space. She was in his, talking a mile a minute, smile warm, attitude sweet. The more he retreated, the more she advanced.

Over the clatter of horse pellets hitting metal, he could hear her talking in soft, soothing tones to Happy, the pup with the lousy luck and the cheerful outlook.

"How much feed does Smokey get?" Mitch's question pulled Collin back to the horse feed.

"None of the pellets. Just some of this alfalfa."

Mitch frowned, dubious. "He's awful skinny."

"Too much at first can kill him."

"How come somebody let him get like that? I can see his ribs."

The buckskin colt stood quivering in the stall, head down, so depressed Collin wondered if he'd survive.

"Some people don't care."

It was a cold, hard fact that both he and the boy knew all too well. "Yeah."

In the few days Mitch had been here, Collin had ferreted out a few unsavory facts about his home life. The stepdad wasn't exactly father-of-the-year material. And mom wouldn't win any prizes, either, although the kid was loyal to her anyway. Collin didn't press him about his mother. He'd been the same once, until the woman who'd birthed him walked away and never looked back. He hoped that never happened to Mitchell.

Hand full of green, scented hay, the kid knelt in front of the little horse. "Come on, Smokey. It's okay."

The colt nuzzled the outstretched fingers, then nibbled a bit of grass.

Mitch had a way with all the creatures on the farm. Even Doc had commented on that. Like a magnet, he was drawn to the sickest ones, the most wounded, the near-hopeless. Street-kid wariness melted into incredible tenderness when he approached the animals. Not one of them shied away from the boy's tenacious determination to make them all well.

"I promised Happy I'd soak his foot later. Is that okay?" Mitchell was on a mission to save the crippled little collie. Every day, he went to Happy's stall first and last with some extra time in between.

"What did Doc say?"

"She said extra soaks can't hurt nothing."

She was right about that. Happy's foot had reached the point when hope was all but gone. Soaking couldn't make the wound any worse, and any action at all made them feel as if they were doing something. "All right, then."

Collin moved down the corridor, taking care of the menial tasks so necessary for the survival of these wounded creatures who depended on him. Cleaning pens, scooping waste, lining stalls and boxes with fresh straw.

Mia was inside the cat pen.

He frowned at her. "I thought you left." He hadn't really, but he didn't know what else to say.

"You wish." With a laugh, she lifted one of Panda's kittens from the box and draped the fur ball over her shoulder. "What's wrong? Rough day?"

Yeah, he'd had a lousy day, but how did she know? He didn't like having some woman, a social worker at that, inside his head.

"I'm all right." He ducked into Happy's stall to escape her. She followed, but didn't press him about his gray mood.

"Mitch seems to be doing a good job for you, don't you agree?"

"Yeah." The dog wobbled up from his straw bed, tail wagging. The smell of antiseptic and dying flesh was hard to ignore.

"Has he opened up at all about why he runs away so much?"

"A little."

"But you're not going to tell me."

"Confidential."

She rolled her big eyes at him. She had interesting eyes. Huge and almond-shaped, soft and sparkly. He didn't know how a person made her eyes sparkly, but she did.

Mia knelt to stroke the pup while still holding the kitten against her shoulder. Happy, tail thumping a mile a minute, didn't seem to mind having a cat invade his territory. Dumb dog didn't seem to mind much of anything.

"What's going to happen to him?"

"Happy? Or Mitch?"

She gave him another of her wide-eyed looks. He wanted to laugh. "The dog."

"If things don't improve this week, Doc's going to amputate the other foot on Monday."

"Oh, Collin." Her face was stricken. She glanced toward the stall door. "Does Mitch know?"

"No."

"No wonder you're in a bad mood tonight. I thought maybe you'd had to shoot somebody today."

"That would have made me feel better."

She looked up. "Not funny."

"Sorry. Bad cop joke." Using force was the last thing he ever wanted.

"How do you cops do that, anyway? Shoot somebody, I mean."

"We pretend they're lawyers." He shook kibble into Happy's bowl. "Or social workers."

"Ha-ha. I'm laughing." But she did giggle. "When are you going to tell him?"

He crumpled an empty feed sack into an oversize ball. "I don't know."

"Want me to do it?"

"My responsibility." He tossed the sack into a trash bin and knelt beside the pup. "I wish I knew who did this to him."

The little dog licked his outstretched hand, liquid brown eyes delighted by the attention. Anger and helplessness pushed inside Collin's chest. He hated feeling helpless.

"I ran a computer search of the system today on you and your brothers."

His pulse quickened though he told himself to expect nothing. "And came up empty?"

"Mostly."

"Figures." Refusing to be disappointed, he stood and took the kitten from her. The soft, warm body wiggled in protest. As many years as he'd searched he couldn't expect miracles from Mia in a week.

"There's some information about you, but the facts on Drew and Ian seem to be the same that you already have. A couple of foster placements. Some medical records."

He wanted to ask what she'd found on him, but didn't bother. She'd probably tell him anyway. Mia already knew too much about him and she was likely to learn more. Opening his sordid background to anyone always made him feel vulnerable, and nothing scared him like vulnerability.

He led the way out of Happy's stall to take the kitten back to Panda. A glance toward the horses told him Mitch was busy mucking out stalls. A perverse part of him figured that particular job was adequate punishment for shoplifting.

"Collin."

He lowered the tiny tabby to her mother. Panda's burns were healing, but she didn't let anyone except Mitch touch her. Even Doc had had to sedate the cat before treating the wounds, an unusual turn of events.

"Collin," she said again, this time from beneath his elbow.

With a sigh, he turned. "What?"

She wrinkled her nose at him, fully aware her chatter bothered him. She looked cute, and he didn't like it. Social workers weren't supposed to be cute.

"I brought the file of information with me. Do you want to see it?"

"Might as well."

Nothing like cold, hard welfare facts to make a man stop thinking about a pretty woman.

Inside Collin's house for the first time, Mia thought the interior of the unfinished, basically unfurnished house was exactly what she expected of him. Neat and tidy to a fault, one long room served as kitchen, living room, and dining room. The furniture consisted of an easy chair, a TV and a small dining-room set. There were no pictures on the walls, no curtains on the shaded windows, no plants or other decorating touches. Collin lived a neatly Spartan lifestyle.

To Mia, who lived in a veritable jungle of plants, terra-cotta pots and pieces of Tuscan decor jammed into a tiny apartment, the house was sadly bare but filled with potential. A pot here. A plant there.

"I live simply," he said when he caught her looking.

"The place has great potential."

"It's not even finished."

"That's why it has great potential."

He shook his head and pulled out two chairs. "Sit. I'll move the laptop."

She eyed the animated screen saver. "Did Mitchell do that?"

"Yeah. He loves the thing."

Mia knew the boy didn't have a computer at home. "His teacher says he's a regular whiz kid."

"He knows keystroke shortcuts I didn't know existed and can navigate sites I can't get into. I'm afraid to ask if he's ever tried hacking."

"The answer is probably yes."

"I know." With a self-deprecating laugh that surprised her, Collin admitted, "He even offered to teach me keyboarding."

"You should let him. Teaching you would be good for his self-esteem."

"It wouldn't be too good for mine." He wiggled his two index fingers. "Old habits die hard."

A large brown envelope lay on the table beside the computer. She reached for it. "Is that more information about your brothers?"

"No. Just another problem I'm working on."

"Anything I can help with?"

"Not unless you're a lawyer. My neighbor," he said, his lips twisted, "is suing me."

"What for?" She couldn't imagine Collin Grace ever being intrusive enough for any neighbor even to know him, much less be at cross-purposes.

"He claims one of my animals has attacked his prize sheep on more than one occasion."

"They couldn't." All the animals here were both too sick and too well-confined to bother anything.

"Cecil Slokum has found something to complain about ever since I bought this place."

"Why?"

"Don't know. This time though," he waved the envelope in the air, "I ran a background check on him."

"Oooh, suspicious. Remind me never to tick you off."

"Too late."

There was that wicked sense of humor again, coming out of nowhere.

"Have you hired an attorney?"

"No."

"You should."

"And I suppose you just happen to know one. Or two. Maybe you even know the judge."

"Well…" She cupped her hands under her chin and leaned toward him. "As a matter of fact, one of my brothers is an attorney. He's also a city councilman."

Collin leaned back his chair. "So he's the one."

"Don't look like that. If my brother hadn't spoken to the chief, you might never have agreed to mentor Mitch. And you like having him out here. You know you do."

"The kid's all right. He's good for the animals."

She laughed. If Collin wanted to pretend he cared nothing about the boy, fine. But he did.

"You've made more progress with Mitchell in a week than anyone else has made in a year."

The boy basked in the policeman's attention, eager to please him, ready to listen to his few, terse words. According to his fifth-grade teacher, Mitch had even turned in all his homework this week, a first.

Collin set the laptop and the brown envelope on an empty chair. "So, you gonna show me that file you brought or talk me to death?"

"Both." She handed over the manila folder.

His eyes twinkled. "Figures."

"You won't die from a little conversation, Collin. Talking things out might do you some good."

She liked listening to his quiet, manly voice as much as she enjoyed looking at him. He was an attractive man. Mia squelched a stomach flutter. Very attractive.

Less intimidating in street attire, tonight he wore a Tac-team T-shirt neatly tucked into well-worn blue jeans. Muscular biceps, fine-cut by exercise and work, stretched the sleeves snug.

"I keep noticing your tattoo." Among other things. "What is it?"

He looked up from studying the file. For a moment, she thought he wouldn't tell her, but then he pushed the sleeve higher and rotated toward her.

Her heart stutter-stepped. Each leaf of a small shamrock bore, not initials as she'd thought, but a name. "Drew, Ian, Collin," she read.

"I didn't want to forget," he said simply. "Not even for a day."

All her preconceived ideas about tattoos went flying out the door. Without forethought, Mia placed her fingers on his arm just beneath the clover. His dark skin was warm and firm and strong with leashed power.

"What an incredibly loving thing to do."

He slid away from her and stood, closing the file. "Mitch should be up here by now. He has homework."

Helping Mitchell with his homework hadn't been part of the court order but Collin didn't let that deter him.

He crossed the few steps to the door and stood gazing out, his back to her. She felt the uncertainty in him, the discomfort that she'd generated with her comment. Or maybe with her touch. One thing was clear. Collin had a hard time expressing emotions. He might feel them. He just couldn't let them show.

She held back a smile. To an Italian, Collin Grace was a red flag waved in front of a bull. Expression was what she and her family did best. She would either drive Collin crazy or help him heal. She hoped it was the latter. Collin had a lot to offer people if he would only open up and trust a little more.

"Collin?"

He tensed but didn't turn around. "What?"

"My family's having a birthday party on Saturday for Nic, my youngest brother. He's turning twenty-one.

If you'll come, I'll introduce you to Adam. He might be able to help with the lawsuit."

He looked at her over one shoulder. "How many brothers do you have?"

"Three bros, one sister and a lot of cousins, aunts and uncles."

"You're lucky."

"Yes. Incredibly blessed. You'll like them, Collin. They're great people."

He turned all the way around, tilting his head so she would know he teased. "Do they all talk as much as you?"

She grinned. "All but Uncle Vitorio. Come on, Collin. Say you'll be there."

"I wouldn't want to intrude." Which meant he wanted to come.

"No such thing at a Carano gathering. We have a motto. The more the merrier."

"Not too original."

She shrugged. "Who cares? It fits. So what do you say?" She really, really wanted him to come. For professional reasons, of course.

Cocoa-colored eyes holding hers, he considered the invitation for a minute but finally said, "Better not."

Disappointment seeped into her, but disappeared as quickly as the next thought arrived. "You could bring Mitch. He needs to interact with a strong family unit, and even if I do say so myself, mine fits the bill."

Hanging out with the Caranos would be good for Collin, too, but she couldn't say that.

"Proud of them, are you?"

"They're a little crazy, and none of us is perfect by any stretch of the imagination, but yeah, I have a great family."

"Taking Mitch is a good idea, but you don't need me along."

"He won't go without you." And she was glad. Collin needed the warm circle of family around him as much as the child did. A man who'd grown up in the system wouldn't have had too many opportunities to witness healthy family relationships. Besides, the Caranos were a lot of fun and if anyone could melt the ice shield from Collin and Mitchell, her family could.

"Here he comes now," she said at the sound of feet tromping on the porch. "Why don't we ask him?"

Collin held the door open as Mitch, Archie the turtle in hand, came inside. To everyone's astonishment, the turtle with the cracked shell was thriving.

"Ask me what?" The little turtle's claws scratched at the air and found purchase when Mitchell placed him on the table.

"You want to go to a party at my house on Saturday?"

Mitch squinted at Mia and then up at Collin. "You going?"

Mia giggled. Collin slanted his eyes at her in silent warning. She laughed out loud.

"It'll be a great party. Lots of food and games and craziness. My folks have a swimming pool." She let that little bit of enticement dangle.

Scooping Archie against his chest, Mitch plopped into a chair. "A real pool? Or one of them kiddie things?"

"Above-ground, but it's big. Has a slide and everything."

"Are your parents rich?"

Mia laughed. "No. They've run a little family bakery forever, but they know how to save money for the things that matter."

Mitch eyeballed Collin, who had gone to the fridge for boxes of juice. Mia knew avoidance behaviors when she saw them.

"They probably wouldn't want me to come." The boy's voice held a longing that neither adult could miss. "I don't have any trunks."

Collin slammed a straw through the top of a juice box with such force the plastic bent.

"We'll get some," he said gruffly.

"You're going too?" Mitch sat up straight and punched the air. "All right. This will be awesome!"

Collin sent Mia a look that would have quelled anyone but a determined social worker.

And she knew she'd won.

Chapter Six

By the time Saturday afternoon rolled around, the knot in Collin's stomach had grown from the size of a pea to that of a watermelon. Mitchell wasn't in any better shape. The kid, usually mouthy as Mia, had barely said two words on the drive to the Carano place.

Collin knew how the kid felt. Out of place. A misfit. The uncertainty was one of the reasons he avoided hanging out with his police buddy, Maurice. How did a person fit into a family when they didn't know what a family should be?

But Collin had learned about and yearned for the kind of relationships Mia bragged about. Even if he might never have them for himself, he wanted them for Mitch. The kid needed to know there was better out there than a stepdad who knocked your mom around and hung out with thugs. Mitchell needed this, which was exactly why Collin had swallowed his reluctance and put on a show about wanting to meet the Caranos.

When they pulled up in front of the sprawling home in a nice older neighborhood in northwest Oklahoma City, a half-dozen other cars already lined the street out front. Collin did his usual scan of the premises, committing the vehicle descriptions and the entrances and exits to memory, the police officer in him never off duty.

Mitch fidgeted with his seat belt. "You think they'll like me?"

The question bothered Collin but he didn't let his feelings show. The kid already knew that people would judge him by his rough clothes and poor grammar. He might as well have White Trash tattooed on his forehead.

"If Mia likes you, they will, too."

"She likes me because she has to. It's her job."

Collin squeezed the back of Mitch's neck. "You know better."

"Yeah." The boy pumped his eyebrows in silliness. "She likes me 'cause I'm cute."

Collin made a rude noise. Mitch's laughter relaxed them both.

As they started up the hedge-lined walkway, squeals and laughter echoed from the backyard. A football came flying over a wooden privacy fence and landed at Collin's feet. He picked it up just as the gate opened. He expected a kid to come charging after the ball. Instead, a grown man, probably near his age, trotted toward him. His maroon T-shirt was sweat-plastered to his upper body.

Collin held up the ball. "This belong to you?"

"Coulda had a touchdown if I'd been taller." The man stopped in front of them and bent forward, hands on knees to catch his breath. "You must be Collin and Mitch. Glad you're here. Mia's wearing a hole in the carpet."

She was?

"I'm Adam, Mia's favorite brother." He laughed, smile bright in a dark face, and extended his hand to Mitch and then to Collin. "You must be the cop Mia's been telling us about."

She talked about him? "I hope it's good."

"So far."

The man was friendly enough, but Collin knew when he was being checked out. He didn't miss the subtle warning. Mess with a Carano and you have to answer to the whole clan. He admired that. He had been that way with his own brothers, though he was surprised that Adam would feel the need to warn him about anything. He'd come here to help a troubled kid, not because of Mia.

Adam tossed the ball back and forth from one hand to the other. "You play football?" he said to Mitchell.

"I stink at it."

"Awesome." Adam gently shoved the ball into the boy's midsection. "You can be on my team. We all stink at it, too. How about you, Collin?"

"Yeah. I stink at it, too."

Adam laughed and slapped him on the back. "Come

on. I'll take you inside to find Mia. We'll get a game going later."

Adam's friendly greeting took some of the tension out of Collin's jaw. Maybe he could get through this afternoon with a minimum amount of stress.

Collin's first impression of the Carano house was the noise, good noise that came from talk and laughter and activity. Several conversations bounced around the large, crowded living room in competition with a big-screen TV blasting a game between the Texas Longhorns and the Oklahoma State Cowboys. There were kitchen noises too, of pots and pans and cabinets opening and closing.

Through patio doors at the opposite end, the pool was visible, along with the remnants of the touch football game they'd interrupted. He glanced down at Mitch, saw the boy scanning the backyard with typical kid radar. He figured Mitch would be fine as soon as he worked his way outside.

The incredible smell of home-cooked food issued from the enormous area to his left. The kitchen was exactly the kind he had envisioned for Mia, though she no longer lived here. Washed warm with sunlight and the rich earthy colors of brick-red flooring, the room was dappled with overflowing fruit baskets, clear jars of colorful pasta, and copper pots dangling above a center island. He located Mia at the island arranging cheese and fruit on a platter.

The knot in his stomach reacted oddly. He was glad

to see her, whether because she was the only familiar face in the crowd or otherwise, he didn't know. And he wasn't bothering to go there. Two weeks ago, she was a pain in his neck.

She looked so natural here, so much more real than she did in her office and business suits. Home was her element.

She said something to a pretty older woman who could only be her mother. They both had the same large, almond eyes and full mouths. And like her mother, Mia tended to be more rounded and womanly than was currently the trend—a look Collin appreciated.

Today her long hair was down, flowing in soft red-brown waves around her shoulders. Her red T-shirt fitted her to perfection and topped off a pair of white, loose-fitting cropped pants and sandals.

She was talking—no big surprise—as she popped a piece of cheese in her mouth. Suddenly she laughed, clapping one hand over her lips.

"Hey, Mia," Adam hollered over the noise. "You got company."

When she caught sight of him, her face brightened. Hurriedly, she said something over her shoulder, wiped her hands on a towel and rushed in their direction.

"You're here!" For a minute, Collin thought she might hug him. Instead, she grabbed his elbow with one hand, dropped the other arm over Mitch's shoulder, and drew them into the melee.

"I see you've already met Adam, so follow me and we'll try to forge a path to the others."

Adam disappeared into the mix as Mia introduced the newcomers to her sister, parents, grandparents and a number of other people whose connection escaped him.

"I don't expect you to remember everyone the first time," Mia said.

The first time? Collin wasn't sure he could survive a second go-round. Though everyone was as friendly as Mia, he felt like a bug under a microscope.

"This is my baby brother, Nic," Mia was saying. "The birthday boy."

"That's birthday *man* to you, big sister." Across Nic's T-shirt were the words, *What if the Hokey Pokey really is what it's all about?*

Mia laughed and rolled her eyes. "He's twenty-one today and I suspect he will be impossible to live with now that he thinks he's become one of the grown-ups."

Collin shook the younger man's hand. "Good to meet you, Nic. Happy birthday."

"Thanks," Nic answered, his grin wide as he looked from Collin to Mia. Speculation, totally unwarranted, was rife. Just what exactly had Mia told them about him anyway? "You want to hear some secrets about my evil big sister?"

Mia poked a teasing finger in Nic's chest. "No, he doesn't. Not if you want to live to be twenty-two."

Speculation or not, Collin enjoyed the joking exchange between brother and sister.

He leaned toward Nic and spoke in a low voice. "Maybe we should talk later. When Mia isn't around."

Mia pretended horror. "Don't you dare. Nic tells lies about how mean I was to him when he was small."

"They're not lies. Just ask Adam." Nic whipped around. "Hey, Adam. Come help me out."

Adam, the football player in the maroon shirt, popped up from the couch where he was surrounded by kids who fell away like brushed-off dust. Collin was startled to see Mitchell in the mix. At some point the kid had wandered off toward the big-screen TV, and Collin hadn't even noticed. Chalk up one demerit for the Big Brother.

"What's up?" Adam asked, his sweaty T-shirt still damp and dark. "The birthday boy already showing off?"

"Of course," Mia said. "I'm leaving Collin in your mature company so I can help Mom and Grandma get dinner on the table. Do not allow Nic to tell horror stories."

Nic guffawed and Adam struggled to keep a straight face. "Sure, sis. Whatever you say."

"I mean it," she warned with a wagging finger. "Collin, I'll be back to rescue you in five minutes."

Then she returned to the oregano-scented kitchen, leaving Collin with Adam again. The feeling of abandonment came with startling swiftness, that emptiness he despised. Collin bit down on his back teeth, annoyed.

He was a grown-up. He didn't need a babysitter. In fact, he didn't need to be here. He didn't fit.

He shifted uncomfortably and wished for a quiet corner where he could watch and listen without being noticed. Mitchell was probably miserable, too. But one look in the living room told him he was wrong. Mitch was deep in conversation with Mr. Carano and they were both fiddling with a laptop chess game. Give the kid a computer and he was at home anywhere. Collin envied that ease and wondered if he'd ever had it as a kid. If he had, it had been very early in his life. He sure didn't remember.

"You have that shell-shocked look that says Mia didn't warn you about us." Adam's voice broke into his thoughts.

"What? Sorry, my mind strayed."

"No wonder. The noise level in here could rival a landing strip."

"No problem." The noise wasn't what bothered him, though it *was* loud. Loud and enthusiastic. He could see where Mia got her positive energy and upbeat attitude.

"From the look on your face, I'd say your family isn't as big or rowdy as the Carano bunch."

"You'd be right about that." If he had a family.

Adam grabbed a bowl of chips from the coffee table. "Come on, let's head out to the backyard where there's some relative peace. There could be a football game in your future. How about you, Nic? Ready to rumble?"

"Not now. Dana Rozier just pulled up out front with

a carload of babes." He cranked his eyebrows up and down a few times. "Can't disappoint the ladies."

Nic rubbed his hands together and then bounded for the front door.

"Ask them if they want to play football," Adam called and was rewarded with a hyena laugh from the birthday boy. "Oh, well, it was worth a try." He shook his head. "Nic and his girls. I don't see the attraction, do you?"

The Carano brothers were fun. He'd say that for them.

Adam shrugged, hollered at Gabe to organize a team, and then led the way through the sea of people and at least one large dog. The backyard was filled with kids, some swimming, two shooting hoops, and a couple of little ones just running in circles squealing for the joy of it.

Adam set the bowl of chips on the ground and collapsed into a lawn chair. "Grab a chair."

Collin did.

"Man, is this a gorgeous day or what?"

"Yeah." He thought of all the work he could be doing on his house on a day like this. Winter would come soon and he wouldn't be any closer to finishing than he'd been at the beginning of summer.

"Mia says you run a rescue ranch for hurt animals."

"That's right."

"She told me about your problem."

Collin stiffened. Mia had promised to keep his search

for Drew and Ian confidential. "Why would she do that?"

"Mia doesn't keep much from her family. But in this case she thought I could help."

He should have known he couldn't trust a social worker. "I can handle it."

"Sometimes lawsuits, even frivolous ones, can be tricky."

A truckload of tension rushed out of Collin. The lawsuit.

"Mia told me her brother was a lawyer. I didn't realize she meant you."

"I hope you didn't think she meant Nic."

They both chuckled. "Seeing him in a courtroom might be entertaining."

"What about in the operating room?"

"Excuse me?"

"He's applying for medical school. There really is a brain beneath that happy-go-lucky personality."

"I'm impressed."

"Don't be. He hasn't been accepted yet." Adam reached for another handful of tortilla chips and offered the bowl to Collin. "So how can I help you with this lawsuit?"

"I don't want to impose."

"No imposition. A friend of Mia's is a friend of mine."

Were they friends? He hadn't wanted to be, hadn't really thought about it until now. "She's a nice girl."

"A very nice girl." Adam shifted around in the lawn chair so they were face-to-face.

"Sometimes she pushes too hard, comes on too strong, but don't hold that against her. Gabe and I call her a coconut. Tough on the outside, a little nutty when she gets on one of her crusades to change the world, but soft and sweet on the inside."

Collin had seen the sweet side at the ranch. He'd also wrestled with her talkative, pushy side.

"She hounded me for days until I agreed to mentor Mitchell."

"See what I mean? She's so sure she can change the world with love and faith that she never gives up. Sometimes she gets hurt in the process. I wouldn't want to see that happen again."

Mia had been hurt? How? Why? And, most importantly, by whom? Collin, who seldom ate chips, took a handful.

"She's in a tough profession," was all he could think of. "The ugliness burns out a lot of strong people."

"Not Mia. She'll never let that happen. There's too much of God in her. She'll always stay tender and vulnerable to hurt. That's just the way she's made." Adam tossed a chip into the air, caught it in his mouth and crunched. "You know why she's not married?"

He'd wondered. Mia was smart, pretty, personable… though he wondered more that Adam would bring up the subject with a stranger like him. "I figure she's had her chances."

"She has. But Mia is waiting for the right guy. Not just any guy, but the one God sends."

Well, that left him out for sure. Not that it mattered. He wasn't in the market for a woman. Especially a nosey social worker who talked too much and made him think about things and feel things he'd kept buried most of his life.

Adam could relax. Neither he nor his sister had anything to fear from Collin Grace.

Chapter Seven

"He's out in the backyard." Adam jerked a thumb in that direction. "The guy looked like he could use a breather from all of us."

Mia took a fresh glass of tea, sugarless the way she'd seen Collin take it during the meal, and pushed open the patio doors.

The glorious blue sky hung over a perfect early-autumn afternoon. She breathed in a happy breath of fresh air. What a great day this had been. Collin and Mitchell had seemed to have a good time. And her family had risen to the occasion as they always did, wrapping the two newcomers in a welcome of genuine friendliness. Nic had been his usual wild and crazy self, celebrating his twenty-first birthday by shooting videos of all the attendees wearing the Groucho glasses he'd bought for party favors.

This kind of gathering was good for Mitchell. He could learn here, interact with real men and motherly women, learn how to have fun in a clean and healthy way. Though she knew Collin would argue the fact, he needed this kind of thing, too. The protective shell around him kept away hurt, but it also kept away the good emotions.

When he'd walked in the door this afternoon, she'd been almost giddy with pleasure. Later, she'd have to examine that reaction.

In the shady overhang of the house, he leaned against the sun-warmed siding to watch Mitchell splash around in the pool. Was it her imagination or did Collin look isolated, maybe even lonely, standing there apart from the bustle of people? She'd thought a lot about him lately, about his upbringing, about how awful he must feel to be alone in the world, not knowing where his family was, or even if they were alive.

Yes, he was on her mind a great deal.

"You look like you could use this." Ice tinkled against the glass as she held the tea out to him.

"Thanks."

Mia wiped her hand, damp from condensation, down her pant leg. "Overwhelmed?"

He sipped at the tea and swallowed before answering. "A little."

"If a person survives their first dose of Caranos, they're a shoo-in for navy SEALs training or a trip to the funny farm."

He smiled his appreciation of the joke. A day with

her family showed him where she derived her great sense of humor.

"My experience with family gatherings is pretty limited."

"Well, you're a hit. You officially passed inspection by the Carano brothers."

"Carano brothers." He held up his Groucho glasses. "Sounds like a family of mobsters."

"Shh. Don't say that too loud. We are Italian, remember."

They grinned into each other's eyes. From inside the house came a shout of "Touchdown."

The Cowboys must have scored. Here in the yard, the sounds were quieter, the splash of kids sliding into the pool, the occasional yip of the dog.

Though he'd felt out of place all afternoon, Collin liked Mia and her family. A couple of times he'd seen Mrs. Carano, who insisted on being called Rosalie, pat Mitchell's back and ply him with goodies from the family bakery. The kid must be ready to explode, but he'd soaked up the attention like Happy did, as though starved for positive reinforcement.

Had he been like that? He couldn't recall. He'd spent so much time keeping Drew out of trouble and Ian fed and safe that he really didn't remember ever being a child.

Mia swirled the melting ice round and round in her own glass, then pressed the coldness to the side of her neck. Collin's belly reacted to the feminine sight. Mia, with her nice family, her chatterbox ways and her honest concern for people was putting holes in his arguments against social workers. Except for the title and the business suits, she didn't fit the stereotype. Adam hadn't helped any with his innuendoes.

"You won Gabe over when your phone played 'Boomer Sooner.'" A soft smile lifted her pretty mouth, setting a single tiny dimple into relief. He'd never noticed that dimple before.

"I saw the Oklahoma Sooner tag on a couple of cars out there." He didn't bother to say Adam had grilled him about his intentions. No point in embarrassing Mia about a simple misunderstanding. Adam was a good guy. He'd meant well. Even if he was badly misguided.

"We all attended OU. Adam played a little baseball, so we're pretty hard-core Sooner fans. Gabe even has season tickets to the football games."

Collin had never made it to college. "I'm a big football fan myself." Which had made conversation with the Caranos a little easier.

"But not of the Dallas Cowboys. Nic is a little miffed about that, though he thinks he can convert you."

"Want me to lie to him since it's his birthday?"

She punched his arm. "Silly."

"Bully." He rubbed the spot just over his shamrock. A lot of people had asked him about the tattoo before and he'd told them nothing. But Mia was different. She had a way of slipping under his guard, catching him unawares, and the next thing he knew he was telling her way too much.

"I never liked tattoos before. But I like yours," she said as if reading his mind. "When did you have it done?"

"When I was seventeen." He wasn't about to tell her the shape he'd been in when he'd gone to the tattoo parlor.

"Isn't it illegal to get one at that age?"

"I wasn't a cop then."

He'd made the remark to encourage a smile. She didn't disappoint him.

"Well, even if it was illegal, you were very insightful to choose a tattoo that represents so much."

"Yeah. Real insightful." To him the tattoo represented a man, a cop at that, who couldn't find the brothers he'd promised to look after. It represented years of failure. He made a wry face. "I chose a shamrock because I needed space for three words and I like the color green."

Undaunted by his dry tone, she studied the figure. "Three leaves, three brothers. Your names are Irish. And green means everlasting, like the evergreen trees. Everlasting devotion."

He blinked down at the tattoo. Then at her.

She came to his shoulders and he could see the top of her hair. In the bright sunlight, the soft waves gleamed more red than brown. He defeated the sudden and unusual urge to touch her hair.

The tattoo had come about on what would have been Ian's twelfth birthday. Collin had been fighting a terrible depression, and the tattoo seemed like a grown-up, proactive thing to do at the time. Now he looked back on the day with a sense of chagrin and failure.

That had been a tough time for him. His days of being cared for in the foster system had been coming to an end, and he was scared out of his mind. He had no place to go, no training, no family, no money. Only a dim memory of two brothers to cling to and the fish keychain that somehow bound the three of them together. Then as now, every time he smoothed his fingers over the darkening metal, he felt closer to Drew and Ian.

"I can't say I was all that deep and symbolic about a tattoo, Mia. I think I was just hoping for a little good luck." He'd needed all the help he could get in the days following his eighteenth birthday.

"Did it work?"

She tilted her head back against the white siding and stared out at the pool where Mitch splashed with Gabe's ten-year-old son. Abby, Gabe's wife, watched from a lawn chair.

"Nah. Mostly, I think we make our own luck. What about you? Got a rabbit's foot in your purse?"

She smiled, but her eyes remained serious.

"I don't put much stock in luck, either. God, on the other hand, is a different matter. I truly believe He, not luck or coincidence, controls my destiny."

"Like a robot?"

She laughed and shook her head. The reddish waves danced back from her pretty face. "Not like that. People have free will. But if we let Him, God will guide our lives and work everything out for our good."

"You really think that?"

"Yes. I really do."

Well, he didn't. He thought you had to claw and fight and struggle uphill, hoping like mad that some crumb of good would fall in your lap.

"I always figured God was out there somewhere, but He was probably too busy to bother with one person."

"God's not like that, Collin. He's very personal. He cares about the smallest, simplest things in our lives."

"If that's so, why is there so much trouble in the world? Why do kids go hungry and parents mistreat and abandon them?" And why couldn't he find his brothers?

The seed of bitterness he tried to hide rose up like a sickness in his throat.

Mia placed a hand on his arm, a gentle, reassuring touch much like the ones he'd seen Rosalie give to Mitchell. He wanted her to stop. "I hear what you're not saying."

Of course she would. She dealt with people in his shoes all the time. She was trained to read behind the mask, a scary prospect if ever there was one. He didn't want anybody messing around inside his mind.

While his insides churned and he wondered what he was doing here, Collin tossed the remaining ice cubes onto a small bush growing beside the house. When the movement dislodged Mia's hand from his arm, he suffered a pang of loss. Talk about messed up. One minute he wanted her to stop touching him, and the next he was disappointed because she did.

"God can help you find your brothers," she said. "Or at least find out what happened to them."

He kept quiet. Mia had a right to her faith even if he had never witnessed anything much from God.

He rolled the empty glass back and forth between his palms. "Like I said, I don't know much about religion."

"That's okay. Faith's not about religion anyway."

She was losing him again.

"Faith is about having a relationship with the most perfect friend you could ever have. Jesus is a friend who promises to stick closer than a brother."

"Closer than a brother," he murmured softly. And then for some reason, he slid a hand into his pocket, found the tiny fish. The metal was warm from his body heat. "For me that wouldn't be too close."

"Then why can't you stop looking for them? And why is your arm tattooed with their names?"

She had a point there. "I guess I'm trying to keep them close even though they're lost." He pulled the tiny ichthus from his pocket. "See this?"

Her expressive face couldn't hide her surprise. "A Jesus fish?"

"I suppose you want to know why I carry it if I'm not a believer?"

"Yes."

He started to tease and say he carried the fish for luck. But that wasn't true. His feelings were deeper than that though he wasn't sure he had the words to express them.

"The day my brothers and I were separated the school counselor gave us each one of these." He turned the fish over. The bright sunlight caught the faded engraving, *Jesus will never leave you nor forsake you.* He'd thought of that scripture often and hoped it was true. He hoped there was somebody in this world looking after Ian and Drew.

"I wonder if they still have theirs," she murmured quietly.

"Why would they keep a cheap little keychain?" But he hoped they had.

"You kept yours."

He rubbed a finger over the darkened engraving as he'd done dozens of times. This was his link, his connection to Drew and Ian. That link, religion aside, gave him comfort. And if he'd tried to pray a few times as a boy, asking the distant God for help, well, he'd been a kid who just didn't understand the facts of life.

He wished that God could do something about his lost brothers, but he didn't know how to believe in anything but himself. His own strength and determination had gotten him where he was today. He knew better than to rely on anyone or anything else.

Before he could say more, Nic came sprinting around

from the opposite side of the house, an orange plastic water pistol in one hand.

Gabe was right behind him, squirting his own water pistol like mad.

"You're gonna pay, birthday boy," he roared. And from the looks of Gabe's soaked shirtfront, Nic had started the trouble.

With a wild hyena laugh, Nic turned and fired, squirting Gabe as well as the two innocent bystanders. Mia jumped aside with a squeal of laughter.

Oddly disappointed to have his strange conversation with Mia interrupted, Collin brushed a water droplet from his arm.

"And you said your family was functional."

They both laughed as Adam came running past, wearing the Groucho glasses and carrying two squirt guns with another stuck in his shirt pocket.

"Defend yourself," he yelled and tossed a purple plastic pistol in their general direction.

With quick reflexes, Collin caught the squirt gun. As soon as the toy hit his hand, a sudden flashback hit Collin square in the heart.

Drew and Ian armed with water guns they'd gotten somewhere chased him around the trailer. He'd hidden under the house, behind the dangling insulation, and unloaded on them when they'd discovered his where-abouts.

They had all squirted and yelled and chased until the night grew too dark to see each other. As they often did, they'd spent that night without adults, but for once they'd gone to bed smiling.

"Collin?" Mia said, touching the hand that held the water pistol. "What's wrong?"

Even the good memories hurt. All those years he'd missed. All the good times he and his brothers had deserved to have. Though he recognized the irrationality of his emotions, he envied the Caranos. They had what he wanted and would never have. The missing years could not ever be recaptured.

"I gotta go." He handed her the squirt gun and abruptly strode to the pool. "Time to roll, Mitchell."

He felt Mia's gaze on his back.

Mitchell was instantly protesting. "I don't wanna leave yet."

"Sorry. I have to work tomorrow." He did have to work. On his house.

Water sluicing off his hair and shoulders, body language screaming in protest, Mitchell pulled himself slowly out of the pool. He grumbled, "It's not fair."

"Yeah, well, life isn't fair, kid. Get used to it."

Mitch stopped and tilted his head back to look into Collin's face. "Are you mad at me?"

Collin relented the slightest bit. The kid had behaved himself today. No use making Mitch pay for his lousy mood. He hooked an elbow around the boy's wet head.

"I'm not mad."

Trailed by an unusually quiet Mia, they went into the house to bid a civil goodbye to all the Carano clan.

Mitchell dragged through the house like a man condemned, gathered his clothes and shoes for departure. Rosalie bustled into the kitchen and came back with two foil-wrapped plates.

"Leftovers. You two could use a little meat on your bones."

A funny lump formed inside Collin's chest. Was this what a mother did? Just like on television? Did normal mothers fret over the children and make huge family dinners and nag everyone to eat more?

"Take them, Collin," Mia murmured. "Make her happy." She'd protested their departure with all the usual niceties, but his mind was made up. He couldn't be here among this family any longer. It was killing him.

"I hope you'll come back soon, Collin," Rosalie was saying. "And bring this boy." She patted Mitchell's head. "You come anytime you want to, Mitchell. A friend of Mia's is our friend, too."

Finally, when he could bear no more of their kindness, he worked his way out to the sidewalk.

Mia stood in the doorway. She looked uncertain, worried. "Thank you for coming, Collin."

"Our pleasure, huh, Mitch?"

"Yeah." Mitch's bottom lip was dragging the ground. He looped a towel around his neck and sawed the rough terry cloth back and forth.

Collin didn't want to answer the questions in Mia's

eyes, so he turned and started toward his truck. The door behind him didn't close for several more seconds.

He'd gotten himself into this mess with Mia. He'd known from the beginning that a social worker only brought trouble. Now he was knee-deep in this big-brother thing with Mitch and stuck with the constant reminders of everything he and his brothers had missed out on. He knew that sounded selfish and envious. Maybe he was.

Long ago, he'd made peace with who he was as well as who he wasn't. He'd made a decent life for himself and, except for his fruitless search for Drew and Ian, he was happy most of the time.

There was an old adage that said you don't miss what you've never had. He'd always thought it was a lie. Today confirmed his suspicion.

He wished he'd never come here.

Halfway down the sidewalk, Mitch asked, "Can I have Miss Carano bring me out to your house tomorrow afternoon?"

"Miss Carano goes to church. She's not your personal chauffeur."

"I can walk, then. No big deal."

"Five miles?"

"I could borrow a bike."

When Collin didn't answer, Mitchell said, "I guess you don't want me to. That's cool. It's okay. I got plenty of stuff to do."

They walked in silence, Collin feeling like a major

jerk. He didn't want the kid around right now. He wanted to be alone, to sort out whatever was eating a hole in him.

One hand on the truck door, Mitchell said, "Will you soak Happy's foot for me? I promised him, ya know."

That clinched it. The little dog *was* making progress with Mitch's tender, relentless care. "Be ready at one. I'll pick you up."

He was in over his head. He had agreed to mentor Mitchell indefinitely, and he wasn't a man to go back on his word. But Mia's brothers with their camaraderie and craziness stirred up a nest of hornets inside him. The reminders were there, too strong to ignore.

He'd have to set up some ground rules if he was to keep his sanity. Working with Mia was part of the deal but mentoring didn't have to include her family. If she wanted Mitch to experience family relationships she could bring him here herself. He was never coming back to this place again.

Mia sat on the floor of her office surrounded by bent, bedraggled cardboard boxes filled with old files dating back more than twenty years. Three weeks ago she'd hauled these files over from the storage room and had been going through them a few at a time whenever she could break away from her caseload.

So far, dust and an occasional spider were the only things she'd found. The task was, after all, a daunting one that could take years to turn up something. If it ever did.

With the back of her hand she scratched her nose, itchy from the stale smell and dust mites. The Lord had sent Collin Grace her way, and she wouldn't let a little thing like twenty years and a mountain of dusty files stop her from trying to show him that God cared enough to help him find his brothers.

"You busy?"

She looked up to find Adam standing in the doorway. He held out a tall paper cup. "Could you use a break?"

"I hope that's a cherry icy." She took the cup, peeked under the lid and said, "You are the best brother on the planet."

"Does that mean you'll help me clean my apartment this weekend?"

"I knew there was a catch." She sipped the cold drink, let the cool, clean sweetness wash away some of the dust. "New girlfriend coming over?"

He grinned sheepishly. "How did you know?"

Mia chuckled. Every time Adam started dating someone new he went into a cleaning frenzy. Only he wanted Mia to do the cleaning. And the redecorating. And the cooking.

"As long as I don't have to repaint this time."

"We only repainted last time because Mandy isn't a big sports fan."

And Adam's living room had been painted in red

and white with a Red Sox insignia emblazoned on the ceiling. "I knew she wouldn't last long."

"If only I were as wise…." He toasted her with his fountain drink. "Which reminds me, I brought some information by for you to take to your new guy."

She eyed him from beneath a piece of floppy hair. "Excuse me? I haven't had a date in four months. There is no new guy."

"Collin. The cop." He made himself comfortable on the floor beside her. From inside his jacket he extracted an envelope, handing it to her.

"He's a friend, Adam." She read Collin's name on the front of the envelope. "Is this about that lawsuit?"

Adam nodded, but wouldn't be deterred from his original intent of matchmaking. "A few weeks ago you didn't even like the guy. The relationship is progressing pretty fast if you ask me."

"There is no relationship." Even if she wanted there to be, Collin had an invisible shield around him that held others at arm's length. "Ever since the birthday party he's been different. Cooler than usual." And for some-one like Collin, that was as cool as this slush.

"He left soon after we started the water fight. Do you think we scared him off somehow?"

She'd wondered the same thing, though she couldn't imagine anything scaring a tough cop like Collin. "I don't know. Collin's hard to read sometimes. He holds a lot of himself in reserve."

From the bare-bones information Collin had shared

about his childhood, he had every reason to distrust other human beings. But Mia didn't like the idea that he distrusted her, which accounted for her redoubled efforts to find some bit of information for him in these files. Trust had to be earned. And she wanted his.

"I keep wondering if we offended him somehow." He'd been fine while they were talking.

"Anyone who listens to Grandpa tell that story about the nanny goat and doesn't run at the first opportunity is not easily offended. Did he mention anything about why they left so early?"

She'd been out to his farm on a regular basis since the party, but their conversations had mostly been about Mitchell's latest truancy from school and the rescued animals. Once they'd talked about his search and another time he'd shocked her to no end by asking a question about God. She'd been frustrated to have no answer, but thrilled to know he was thinking about spiritual matters.

She rifled through another file, saw nothing related to Collin or his brothers and reached for another.

"Only that he appreciated our hospitality, thought we were a great family. You know, the usual polite stuff. And he thought the afternoon had been good for Mitchell."

Adam took the file folder from her hand and stuck it back in the box. "The boy needs a lot of attention. Did you see Mama plying him with cookies and questions?"

"Mama thinks food is the answer to everyone's problems."

"Isn't it?"

"My hips seem to think so." Every time Mia decided to do something about her few extra pounds, Mama invited her over for pasta and bread or asked her to work a few hours at the bakery. Or she went through a mini-crisis and baked some marvelous creation for herself. Having a family in the bakery business was both a blessing and a terrible temptation.

"So, do you like him?"

"Mitchell? Sure. He's basically a good boy, but he needs a firm hand and a strong role model. He went to Sunday School with me last week."

Adam gave her a look reserved for thick-headed sisters. "I'm talking about Collin."

"And I'm not." Every time a new man appeared on the horizon, her brothers zeroed in like stealth missiles.

"I can hope, can't I?"

"Not in this case." Though there was something about Collin that kept him on her mind all the time, she knew better than to let her feelings take over. She wanted God to choose the right man for her.

"Want me to beat him up? Get things moving?"

She laughed. "You know how I feel about the whole husband-hunting thing. God's timing is always perfect."

"If God is going to send you a husband, He needs to hurry."

"Adam," she admonished. But she had to admit to a

certain restlessness lately. Though her job and her community and church activities kept her life more than busy, she had always planned to be married with a big house filled with kids by now. "You're a fine one to talk. When are you going to find Miss Right and settle down?"

He shrugged a pair of shoulders that had plenty of women interested. "I want what Mom and Dad have. I'm willing to wait as long as it takes to get it."

And she was willing to wait, as well. She only hoped she didn't have to wait forever.

Chapter Eight

An excited Mia jumped out of her Mustang, leaving her jacket behind and hurrying through the cool, windy evening to Collin's front door. In the west the sun was setting, a testament to the shorter days of late autumn.

The hollow sound of a hammer rang through the otherwise quiet countryside. Not once in the months since meeting him had she come to this house and found Collin idle. He was either working on the house, with the animals or helping Mitchell do something. Didn't the man ever lie around on the couch like a slob the way her brothers did?

She waited for a pause in the hammering and then pounded hard on the door. She'd finally found something and she couldn't wait to share the news with Collin.

"Collin, hello."

The hammering ceased. After a minute, she saw movement from the corner of her eye and heard Collin's voice. She spotted him near the side of the house, the area still mostly in skeleton form.

In the fading light, Collin raised the hammer in greeting, a smile lifting the corners of his mouth. Dressed in jeans and a denim shirt, he wore a tool belt slung low on his hips.

"Hey," he said.

She started toward him, her heart doing a weird ker-thumping action. Okay, so she was glad to see him. And yes, he was good-looking enough to make any woman's heart beat a little faster. But she was excited because of the news she had, not because Collin had smiled as if he was glad to see her, too. Mostly.

Adam and his insinuations were getting to her.

"Watch your step." Collin gestured at the pile of tools strewn about on the concrete pad, and then reached out to put a hand under her elbow.

His was a simple act of courtesy, but her silly heart did that ker-thump thing again. Come to think of it, this was the first time Collin had ever intentionally touched her.

A naked lightbulb dangled from an extension cord in one corner to illuminate the work space. The smell and fog of sawdust hung cloudlike above a pile of pale new boards propped beside a table saw.

"I finally have the decking on top," he said with some satisfaction, unmindful of her sudden awareness of him as a man. "Even if the room won't be completely in the dry before the really cold weather sets in, I'll be able to work out here."

Usually Mitchell was under foot, pounding and sawing under Collin's close supervision. She looked around, saw no sign of the boy. "Where's Mitchell?"

Collin placed the hammer on a makeshift table, his welcoming expression going dark. "I caught him smoking in the barn. Took him home early."

"Oh, no. I thought you'd made him see the senselessness of cigarettes."

"Yeah, well that was a big failure, I guess." He sighed, a heavy sound, and ran both hands up the back of his head. "He's been acting up again. Mouthy. Moody. Maybe I'm not doing him any good after all."

"Don't think that, Collin. All kids mess up, regress. But he's come a long way in a short time. The school says he's only missed two days since you spoke to his class on careers in law enforcement. His discipline referrals for fighting are down, too."

He squinted at her. "You know what he's been fighting about?"

"No. Do you?"

"I've got a clue." He turned to the closed door leading into the living area. "Come on in. You're getting cold."

Pleasure bloomed. He'd noticed.

Inside the kitchen, he motioned toward a half-full Mr. Coffee. "Coffee?"

"Sure." She took the offered cup, wrapping her hands

around the warmth. "Are you going to share your insights with me?"

Collin leaned a hip against the clean white counter. If she was a betting woman, she'd bet he'd laid the tile himself. "I think Mitch is under a lot of pressure from some of the other boys."

"What kind of pressure?"

"I haven't figured that part out. There's something though. I have a feeling it has to do with his stepdad. That's a very sore subject lately."

Her caseworker antennae went up. "Anything I need to investigate on a professional basis?"

Over the rim of his coffee cup, Collin gave her the strangest look, a look she'd come to recognize each time she mentioned her job. He took a long time in answering such a simple question.

"I guess it wouldn't hurt to keep your eyes and ears open."

She was already doing that.

"How's Happy?"

"Still happy." He grinned at his own joke and pulled a chair around from the table to straddle the seat. "Doc says the foot is still in danger. It'll kill Mitchell if she has to amputate."

She could tell Collin wouldn't be too happy either, but he wasn't about to say so.

"He's attached."

"Very." Arms folded over the back of the chair, the coffee mug dangled from his fingers.

"You are, too."

He made a face. "Yeah."

And she was glad to know he could form bonds this way, even though they saddened him. Some kids who grew up in the system were never able to love and bond.

"I have a bit of news for you." She laid her purse on the table and pulled out a slip of paper.

"I could use some today. Shoot."

"This may turn out to be nothing, but—" she handed him the note "—this is the address of foster parents who took care of one of your brothers shortly after you were separated. They're not on your list."

The expression on his face went from mildly interested to intense. "Seriously?"

"The address hasn't been updated and there was no telephone, so we may not find anything."

He shoved out of the chair and grabbed a jacket. "Let's go see."

"Collin, wait."

He paused, face impassive.

Suddenly, she regretted her impulsive action to come here first before checking out the address herself.

"I haven't made contact. We don't know if anything will come from this. Don't get your hopes up, okay?"

"It's worth a shot." He shrugged the rest of the way into his jacket. "We'll take my truck."

She had known he'd react this way, pretending not to hope, but grasping at anything. If the foster parents were still around, they might not remember one little boy who passed through their lives so long ago. And if they did, they probably wouldn't remember where the child had gone from there.

"This is the first new piece of the puzzle I've had in a long time," Collin admitted as he smoothly guided the truck around the orange barrels and flashing lights of the ever-present road construction that plagued Oklahoma City. "Dartmouth Drive is back in one of these additions. I've been out here on calls. Not the best part of town."

A bad feeling came over her. She felt the need to say one more time, "Remember, now. This address comes from a very old file."

"I heard you." But she could tell that he didn't want to think that the trip might be futile.

Night had fallen and the wind picked up even more. An enormous harvest moon rose in the east. Mia had a sense of trepidation about approaching a strange house at night.

"Maybe we should have waited until tomorrow."

"I've waited twenty years." The lights of his vehicle swept over a wind-wobbled sign proclaiming Dartmouth Drive. He turned onto a residential street. "Should be right down here on the left."

She could feel the tension emanating from him like heat from a stove. He wanted to find out something new about his brothers so badly. And now that they were nearing the place, Mia was scared. If the trip proved futile, would he be devastated?

"Here's the address." He pulled the truck to a stop along the curb.

She squinted into the darkness. "I don't think anyone is at home, Collin."

"Maybe they watch TV with the lights off."

They made their way up the cracked sidewalk. In the moonlight Mia observed that the grass was overgrown, a possibility only if no one had been here for a long time. Growing season had been over for more than a month.

She shouldn't have let him come here and be disappointed. But she'd been so excited that she hadn't thought everything through in advance. She'd only wanted to give him hope. Now, Collin could be hurt again because of her.

He banged on the front door.

"Collin," she said softly, wanting to touch him, to comfort him.

He ignored her and banged again, harder. "Hello. Anybody home?"

"Collin." This time she did touch him. His arm was like granite.

He stared at the empty, long-abandoned house. In the moonlight, his jaw worked. She heard him swallow and knew he swallowed a load of disappointment.

Abruptly, he did an about-face. "Dry run."

Inside the truck, Mia said, "This was my fault. I'm so sorry."

He gripped the steering wheel and stared at the empty house. "I should be used to it by now."

That small admission, that no matter how many times he came up empty he still hurt, broke Mia's heart. She couldn't imagine the pain and loneliness he'd suffered in his life. She couldn't imagine the pain of being separated from her loved ones the way Collin had been.

When they'd first met, she'd thought him cold and heartless. Now she realized what a foolish judgment she'd made.

Because she didn't know what else to do, Mia closed her eyes and prayed. Prayed for God to help them find Drew and Ian. Prayed that Collin could someday release all his heartache to the only One who could heal him. Prayed that she would somehow find the words to compensate for her bad judgment.

In silence they drove out of the residential area and headed toward Collin's place and her vehicle. Mia was glad she'd left her car at the farm. Collin didn't need to be alone even if he thought he did.

"Are you okay?" she finally asked.

In the dim dash lights he glanced her way, his cop face expressionless. "Sure. You hungry?"

The question had her turning in her seat. "Hungry?"

"As in food. I haven't had dinner."

"Neither have I." She felt out of balance. He had shoved aside what had to be, at least, a disappointment. Was this the way he handled his emotions? By ignoring them?

They parked behind a popular steak house and went inside.

They passed a buffet loaded with steaming vegetables and a variety of meats that had her mouth watering.

"You look confused," Collin said as he held a chair for her.

She was. In more ways than one. "I was expecting a tofu bar with bean sprouts and seaweed."

"I eat what I like."

There went another assumption she shouldn't have made about him.

They filled their plates from the hot bar and found a table. Collin had ordered a steak, as well.

"Comfort food?" she asked gently after the waitress brought their drinks and departed.

He shrugged. "Just hungry. This place makes great steaks."

She squeezed the lemon slice into her tea.

"Want mine?" Collin said, removing the slice from the edge of his glass.

"You're giving up vitamin C?" She teased, but took the offered fruit. "Do you eat out like this all the time?"

"Not that much. Mostly I cook for myself."

She should have figured as much. He'd been self-reliant of necessity all of his life, a notion that made her heart hurt. But that strength had made him good at about anything he set his mind to. She wondered if he knew that about himself and decided that he didn't.

"What's your specialty?" she asked.

"Meat loaf and mashed potatoes. How about you? You live alone, too. Do you eat at your folks' or cook for yourself?"

"For myself most of the time. Although I sneak over to the bakery a little more often than I should."

"You any good?"

"Look at this body." With a self-deprecating twist of her mouth, she held her hands out to the side. "What do you think?"

"I think you look great." His brown eyes sparkled with appreciation.

"That wasn't what I meant." A rush of heat flooded her neck. "I meant—"

He laughed and let her off the hook. "I know what you meant." He pointed a fork at her. "But you still look good."

"Well." She wasn't sure what to say. She got her share of compliments, but she'd never expected one from Collin. He was full of surprises tonight. "Thank you."

The waitress brought his steak and they settled in to eat, making comments now and then about the food. After a bit the conversation lagged and all she could think about was the night's failed trip. Collin might want to ignore the subject, but Mia would explode if she didn't get her feelings out in the open.

"Will you let me apologize for not checking out that address before telling you about it?"

"No use talking the subject to death."

"We haven't talked about it at all." Which was driving her nuts.

"Just as well." He laid aside his fork and took a man-size drink of tea.

"Not really. Talking helps you sort out your feelings, weigh your options." And made her feel a whole lot better.

Collin looked at her, steady and silent. If anyone was going to talk, she would have to be the one.

"I'll keep looking. The information has to be there somewhere. We'll find them."

"You could check the adoption files. See if either of my brothers was adopted."

"I'm checking those."

Attention riveted to his plate, he casually asked, "The sealed ones?"

Her breath froze in her throat. "I won't do that."

He looked up. The naked emotion in his eyes stunned her. "Why not?"

Shoulders instantly tense, she had to remind him, "I told you from the beginning I wouldn't go into sealed files."

"That was before you knew me. Before we were friends."

Friends? "Is that what the compliment was about? To soften me up?"

His jaw tightened. "Is that what you think?"

She leaned back in her chair, miserable to be at odds

with him over this. "No. Not really, but I can't believe you'd ask me to do such a thing."

Anger flared in the normally composed face. His fork clattered against his plate. "Wanting to find my brothers is not a crime. I'm not some do-wrong trying to ferret out information for evil purposes. This is my life we're talking about."

"I know that, Collin. But the files are closed for a reason. Parents requested and were given sealed records because they wanted the promise of privacy. And until those people request a change, those files have to stay sealed."

He crammed a frustrated hand over his head, spiking the hair up in front. "Nearly twenty-five years of my life is down the drain, Mia. I need to find them. They're men now. Opening those files won't hurt them or anybody else."

She shook her head, sick at heart. "I can't. It's wrong. Please understand."

Back rigid, he pushed away from the table and stood. The cold mask she'd encountered the first time they'd met was back in place.

Chapter Nine

Collin was not having a good day. In fact, the last two had been lousy.

He pushed the barn door open, stopping in the entrance to breathe in the warm scents of animals, feed and the ever-present smell of disinfectant. He went through gallons of the stuff trying to protect the sick animals from each other.

Since the night he'd let himself hope, only to be slapped down again, he'd battled a growing sense of emptiness.

After work tonight he'd gone to the gym with Maurice and true to form, his buddy had invited him home for dinner and Bible study. For the first time, he'd wanted to go. But he always felt so out of place in a crowd. And a Bible study was a whole different universe.

Not that he hadn't given God a lot of thought lately. Every time he showered or changed shirts and noticed his shamrock, Mia's words rang in his memory. She had something in her life that he didn't. And that something was more than a big, noisy family. Maurice had the same thing, so Collin figured the difference must be God.

One of the horses nickered as Collin moved down the dirt-packed corridor. These animals depended on him, regardless of the kind of day he'd had. He could take care of himself. They couldn't.

As was his habit, he headed to Happy's pen first. The little dog's attitude could lighten him up no matter what.

Mitchell, whom he hadn't seen since the smoking incident, was already inside the stall.

Irritation flared. The little twerp had some nerve coming back around the animals without permission.

Collin was all prepared to give him a tongue-lashing and send him home when the boy looked up.

What he saw punched him in the gut.

The kid's face was bruised from the eyebrow to below the cheekbone. A sliver of bloodshot eye showed through the swelling.

"What happened?" He heard his own voice, hard and angry.

Mitchell dropped his head, fidgeting with the dog brush in his hands. "I won't smoke anymore, Collin."

"Not what I asked."

Mitchell jerked one narrow shoulder. "Nothing."

With effort, Collin forced a calm he didn't feel. "Home or school?"

The boy was silent for a minute. Then he blew out a gust of air as if he'd been holding his breath, afraid Collin would send him away. "Not my mom."

The stepdad, then. Collin had run a check on Teddy Shipley. He had a rap sheet longer than the road from here to California, where he'd spent a year in the pen for assault with a deadly weapon and manufacturing an illegal substance. A real honey of a guy.

Collin hunkered down beside the boy, rested one hand lightly on the skinny back. "You can tell me anything."

Mitchell developed a sudden fascination with the bristles of Happy's brush. He flicked them back and forth against his palm. "I can't."

And then he dropped the brush and buried his face in Happy's thick fur. Happy, true to his name, moaned in ecstatic joy and licked at the air.

The kid was either scared or he knew something that would incriminate someone he cared about. And the cop in Collin suspected who.

He sighed wearily. Life could be so stinking ugly.

"If he hits you again, I'm all over him."

Mitch's head jerked up. His one good eye widened. "I never told you that. Don't be saying I did."

Compassion, mixed with frustration, pushed at the back of Collin's throat. He clamped down on his back teeth, hating the feelings.

"Did you go to school like this?"

Mitch shook his head. "No."

So that's why he'd shown up here this evening. Things were out of hand at home.

"Does he hit your mom, too?"

Tears welled in the boy's eyes. "She'd be real mad if she knew I told."

"Why?"

"She just would."

What Mitch wasn't saying spoke volumes. Collin had seen this scenario before. He'd also lived it.

Violence. Codependence. Drugs. A mother who preferred the drugs and a violent man to the safety and well-being of herself and her child. He wouldn't be a bit surprised if Teddy was cooking meth again, a suspicion that deserved checking into.

The sound of a car engine had Mitchell scrubbing frantically at his face. Collin turned toward the interruption. He'd know that Mustang purr anywhere. Mia. Just who he did not want to see. A social worker who'd stick her nose into something she couldn't fix. He was a cop. He could handle the situation far better than she could.

Mitch leaped up, recognizing the car, as well. His one good eye widened in panic. "Don't say anything, huh, Collin?"

Like she wouldn't notice an eye swollen shut.

"Go brush down the colt and give him a block of hay," he said, giving the kid an out. If Mia didn't see him, she wouldn't ask questions, and no one would have to lie.

Mitch shot out of the pen, disappearing into the far stall.

Collin picked up an empty feed sack and crushed it into a ball.

His world had been orderly and uneventful until Mia had come barging into it, hounding him, talking until he'd said yes to shut her up. And then her family had gotten in on the deal. First the birthday party. Then Adam's help with the lawsuit. And now Leo, Mia's father, found daily reasons why Collin had to stop by the bakery. Try as he might, Collin couldn't seem to say no.

Man. What had he gotten himself into?

The colt whickered. One of the dogs started barking. And the whole menagerie began moving restlessly.

Collin didn't rush out to greet his visitor. He needed some time to think. Still baffled by Mia's stubbornness over something as simple as looking into a file, he wasn't sure what to say to her.

They didn't share the same sense of justice. He believed in obeying the law, but there was a difference in the spirit of the law and the letter of the law. To him, opening his own brothers' adoption files, if they existed, would fall under the spirit of the law. It was the right and just thing to do.

But he had to be fair to Mia, too. She'd gone above and beyond the call of duty in searching those moldy old files in the first place. And even if she was a pain in the backside sometimes, having her around lightened him somehow, as if the goodness in her could rub off.

After a minute's struggle, Collin decided to wait her out. Mia knew where he was if she had something to say. He'd known from the start he didn't want the grief of some woman trying to get inside his head. He had enough trouble inside there himself.

He went to work scrubbing down a newly emptied pen. The last stray, hit by a car, hadn't made it. He'd been hungry too long to have the strength to fight.

Fifteen minutes later, when Mia hadn't come storming inside the barn, smiling and rattling off at the mouth, Collin began to wonder if he'd heard her car at all. He dumped the last of the bleach water over the metal security cage and went to find out.

Sure enough, Mia's yellow Mustang sat in his driveway but she was nowhere to be seen.

Mitch came to stand beside him, one of Panda's adolescent kittens against his chest. "Where is she?"

"Beats me."

At that very moment, she flounced around the side of the house, her sweater flapping open in the stiff wind. She wasn't wearing her usual smile. Almond eyes shooting sparks, she marched right up to Collin.

"I don't stop being a friend because of a disagreement."

That didn't surprise him. The sudden lift in his mood did. Renewed energy shot through his tired muscles. He hid a smile. Mia was pretty cute when she got all wound up.

She slapped a wooden spoon against his chest.

"I brought food. Home-cooked." She tilted her head in a smug look. "And you are going to love it."

He fought the temptation to laugh. Normally, when a woman pushed too hard, she was history, but with Mia he couldn't stay upset. That fact troubled him, but there it was.

Unmindful of the sparks flying between the adults, Mitch stepped between them. "Food. Cool."

Mia started to say something then stopped. Her mouth dropped open. She stared at Mitchell's bruised face, expression horrified. "What happened to you?"

Mitchell shot Collin a silent plea and then hung his head, averting his battered face.

"I got in a fight."

"Oh, Mitch." And then her fingers gently grazed the boy's cheekbone in a motherly gesture. The tension in Mitch's shoulders visibly relaxed, but his eyes never met Mia's.

Collin let the lie pass for now. Whether Mitch liked the idea or not, a cop was mandated by law to share his suspicions with the proper authorities, and that was Mia. If there was any possibility that a child was in danger, welfare had a right to know. The policeman in him accepted that regardless of his personal aversion.

"I'm starved," he said, knowing his statement would be an effective diversion. Mia's respondent smile washed through him warm and sweet, like a spring wind through a field of flowers. "Cleaning pens can wait until after dinner."

"Not mad at me anymore?" she asked.

Quirking one brow, he started toward the house and left her to figure that out for herself. He wasn't sure he knew the answer anyway.

The early sunsets of November were upon them and the wind blew from the north promising a change in weather. Leaves loosened their tree-grip and tumbled like tiny, colorful gymnasts across the neatly fenced lots housing the grazers. The deer with the bad hip had healed and now roamed restlessly up and down the fence line longing to run free. Collin and Doc had decided to wait until after hunting season ended to give the young buck a fighting chance.

When they reached the house, Collin opened the door and let Mia and Mitchell enter first. The smell of Italian seasoning rushed out and swirled around his nose.

"Smells great. What is it?" Not that he cared—a home-cooked Italian dinner was too good to pass up. Especially one cooked by Mia.

"Lasagna. Wash your hands. Both of you." She shooed them toward the sink. "Food's still hot."

Along with Mitchell, he meekly did as he was told, scrubbing at the kitchen sink. If anyone else came into his house issuing orders and rummaging in his cabinets, he would be furious. Weird that he wasn't bothered much at all.

While Mia rattled forks and thumped plates onto his

tiny table, he murmured to Mitch, "A lie will always come back to bite you. Better tell her."

Mitchell darted a quick glance at Mia and gave his head a slight shake, his too-long hair flopping forward to hide his expression. Collin let the subject drop. For now.

Moments later, they dug into the meal. Collin could barely contain a moan of pleasure.

Lifting a forkful of steaming noodles and melted mozzarella, he said, "If this is your idea of a peace offering, I'll get mad at you more often."

Mia sliced a loaf of bread and pushed the platter toward him. Steam curled upward, bringing the scent of garlic and yeast.

"There are still things I can do to help, Collin. Unlike foster-care files, many of the adoption files have been computerized. I started searching the open ones today."

He took a chunk of the bread and slathered on a pat of real butter. "Are the sealed files on computer, too?"

There was a beat of silence, and then, "It doesn't matter."

She wasn't budging from her hard-nosed stand.

"After all the years I've searched and come up empty, I think the adoption files are the answer. They have to be."

Mitchell was already digging in for seconds. "Why are you trying to get into adoption files?"

Collin started. He never spoke openly about his brothers or his past. He'd never before said a word about them in front of Mitchell. Was this what hanging around with a chatterbox did for a guy? He started to lie to the boy, and then remembered his words only moments before. A lie would always come back to haunt you.

"I'm looking for my brothers," he said honestly. "We were separated in foster care as kids."

Saying the words aloud didn't seem so hard this time.

"No kidding?" Mitch backhanded a string of cheese from his mouth. "You were a foster kid?"

"Yeah. I was." He held his breath. Would the knowledge lessen him in Mitchell's eyes?

Mitch's one unblemished eye, brown and serious, studied him in awe. "But you became a cop. How'd you do that?"

And just that simply, Collin experienced a frisson of pride instead of shame. Mia had been right all along. Mitch needed to know that the two of them shared some commonalities.

"A lousy childhood doesn't have to hold you back."

By now, the boy's mouth was jammed full again, so he just nodded and chewed. He chased the food with a gulp of iced tea and then said, "So where are your brothers? Can Miss Carano find them? Can't the police find them? I'll help you look for them. How many do you have?"

His words tumbled out, eager and naive.

Collin filled him in on the bare facts. "And Miss Carano's helping me search, too. Even though I've been a pain about it."

He gave her his version of an apologetic look. He wasn't sorry for asking her to bend the rules a little, but he was glad to be back on comfortable footing with her. The last couple of days had been lousy without her.

"I've started a hand search of the old records in the storage room of the municipal building," Mia told him. "That's where I found that address the other day."

The police records were warehoused the same way, and he knew from experience that hand searches were tedious and time-consuming. And often fruitless.

"I appreciate all you're doing, Mia. Honestly. But you can't blame me for wanting to investigate every available option."

"I don't blame you." She pushed her plate aside and said, "Anyone for dessert?"

"Dessert?" Both males moaned at the same time.

"You should have warned us." Collin put a hand over his full belly. He looked around the tiny kitchen, spotted a covered container on the bar. "What is it?"

Mia laughed. "My own made-from-scratch cherry chocolate bundt cake. But we can save dessert for later."

"You made it yourself?"

"Yep. The bread and lasagna, too."

The sweet Italian bread *must* have come from her parents' bakery. "No way."

"Way. I didn't grow up a baker's daughter for nothing. All of us kids cut our teeth on the old butcher-block table in the back of the bakery where Mom and

Dad hand-mixed the dough for all kinds of cakes and breads and cookies."

She got up and started clearing the table. Collin grabbed the glasses.

"Let me help with this."

"I can get the dishes. Didn't you say you still have work in the barn?"

"Work can wait."

Mitchell, who looked as if he'd rather be anywhere but in a kitchen with unwashed dishes, piped up. "I'll do the rest of the chores outside. I don't mind."

With a knowing chuckle, Collin gave him instructions and let him go.

"Did you see the look on his face?"

"And to think he prefers mucking out stalls to our esteemed company." Mia feigned hurt.

In the tiny kitchen area, they bumped elbows at the sink. Collin didn't usually enjoy company that much, but over the weeks and months he'd known Mia, she'd become a part of his life. Sometimes an annoying part, but if he was honest, even when they disagreed he depended upon her to see through his anger to the frustration and still be his friend.

He'd never expected to call a social worker "friend."

At times, he could be brooding and moody, and admittedly, he wore a protective armor around his heart. Trouble was, Miss Mia had slipped beneath it at some point and discovered the softer side of him. The idea unhinged him.

"Thanksgiving's coming soon," she said, her voice coming from above a sink of soapy hot water. "We always have a big to-do at Mama's. Turkey, dressing, pecan pie. The works. The Macy's Thanksgiving Day parade on TV and then a veritable marathon of football games afterward."

He knew what was coming and didn't know what to do. Nic's birthday party had stirred up something inside him, a hunger for the things missing in his own life, and he wasn't sure he could go there again.

Mia rinsed a plate under the hot tap. As he reached to take the dish, she held on, forcing him to look down at her.

Green eyes, honey-sweet and honest, held his. "We'd love for you to come. Please say you will."

Steam rose up between them, moist and warm. Her eyes, her tone indicated more than an invitation of kindness to a man who had nowhere else to go. She really wanted him there.

Like most holidays, Thanksgiving was a family occasion. The time or two he'd accepted an invitation, he'd felt like an intruder. "I usually volunteer to work so the officers with families can be off that day."

"Then I'd say you're due a day off this year. Wouldn't you?"

"I'd better not."

Disappointment flashed across her face. Unlike him, she could never hide her feelings. They were there for the whole world to see. And what he saw both troubled and pleased him. Mia liked him. As more than a friend.

She let go of the plate and went back to washing. The air in the kitchen hung heavy with his refusal and her reaction. He didn't want to hurt her. In fact, he couldn't believe she was disappointed. Couldn't believe she'd be interested in him. He didn't belong with her all-American perfect family.

Mia, true to form, rushed in to the fill the quiet, and if he hadn't known better, her chatter would have convinced him that she didn't really care one way or the other. But now he knew her chatter sometimes covered her unease.

Then she mentioned some guy she'd met during the 10-K charity walk last weekend, and his mood turned from thoughtful to sour. If she was attracted to him, why was she having Starbucks with some runner?

He interrupted. "Wonder what's keeping Mitchell?"

Mia stopped in midsentence and gave him a funny look. "He hasn't been gone that long."

"Long enough." He tossed his dish towel over the back of a chair that served as a towel rack, coat rack, whatever.

The water gurgled out of the sink. Mia dried her hands. "If you'll stop scowling, I'll go check. I need to get something out of my car anyway."

"I can go. He's my responsibility."

"Mine, too. You stay here and slice the cake. I have a book in the car for you."

"A Bible?" he asked suspiciously.

Tossing on her sweater, she laughed and opened the door. "You'll see."

Halfway out, she stopped and looked over her shoulder. "I want coffee with my cake."

The door banged shut and Collin found himself grinning into the empty space. Tonight Mia had made this half-finished, scantily furnished, poor excuse for a house feel like a home.

He turned that thought over in his head and went to make the lady's coffee.

Four scoops into the pot, a scream shattered the quiet. Coffee grounds went everywhere. His heart stopped.

"Mia."

He was out the door, running toward the barn before he realized the previously dark sky was lit with bright light. Fire light.

"Mitchell!"

He heard Mia's cry once more and this time he spotted her, running toward the burning barn. Before he could yell for her to stop, to turn back, she disappeared inside.

Collin thought he would die on the spot. Adrenaline ripped through his veins with enough force to knock him down. He broke into a run, pounding over the hard, dry ground.

Flames licked the sky. Sparks shot fifty feet up, fueled by the still wind. The horses screamed in terror. Dogs barked and howled. Several had managed to escape somehow and now scrambled toward him. A kitten streaked past, her fur smoking.

A horrible sense of doom slammed into him, overwhelming. Mia and Mitchell were inside a burning barn along with more than a dozen helpless, trapped, sick and injured animals.

He darted toward the outside water faucet, thankful for the burlap feed sack wrapped around the pipes to prevent freezing. Yanking the sack free, he dipped the rough cloth into the freshly filled trough then rushed into the barn just as Mitchell came stumbling out.

Collin caught him by the shoulders. "Where's Mia?"

Mitchell shook his head, coughing. "I don't know."

With no time to waste, he shoved Mitchell out into the fresh air. "Call 911."

He could only hope the boy obeyed.

And then he charged into the burning building.

Smoke, thick and blinding, wrapped him in a terrifying embrace.

"Mia!" he yelled as he slung the wet sack around his face and head.

Eyes streaming, lungs screaming, he traversed the interior by instinct, throwing open stalls and pens as he called out, over and over again. The animals would at least have a chance this way. Locked in, they would surely die.

He stumbled over something soft and pitched forward, slamming his elbow painfully into a wall. A familiar whine greeted him. When he reached down, the dog licked his hand. Happy.

With more joy than he had time to feel, he scooped the little dog up and headed him in the direction of the open doorway. Even a crippled dog would instinctively move toward the fresh air.

A timber above his head cracked. Honed reflexes moved him to one side as the flaming board thundered to the barn floor. If he stayed too long, he'd never make it out.

Another board fell behind him and then another. Common sense said for him to escape now. His heart wouldn't let him.

"Mia." His voice, hoarse and raspy, made barely a sound against the roaring, crackling fire. Heat seared the back of his hands. His head swam.

If something happened to her. If something happened to Mia.

Suddenly, he heard her coughing. And praying.

Renewed energy propelled him forward.

"I'm coming."

Keep praying, Mia, so I can find you.

With his free hand, he felt along the corridor wall. No longer could he hear animal sounds, but Mia's prayers grew louder.

In the dense darkness he never saw her, but he heard her and reached out, made contact. She frantically clawed at his arm.

"I've got you."

"Thank God. Thank God." A fit of harsh coughing wracked her. "Mitch," she managed.

"He's safe."

Without a thought, Collin stripped the covering from his face and pressed the rough fabric against Mia's mouth and nose. Her breath puffed hot and dry against his fingers.

"This way."

With his knowledge of the barn, he guided them away from the falling center toward the feed room. There, a small window would provide escape.

Though the seconds seemed to drag, Collin knew by the size of the fire that they'd been inside only a few minutes. Thankfully, the flames had not reached this section of the barn yet, but they were fast approaching.

"Hurry," he said needlessly, pushing and pulling her stumbling form.

Inside the feed room, he felt for the window, shoved the sash upward, then easily lifted Mia over the threshold and to safety on the ground.

A roar erupted behind him. The flames, as if enraged by Mia's escape, chased him. Licking along the wall, they found the empty paper sacks and swooshed into the room.

Collin scrambled up and out the window, falling to the ground below. What little air he had left was knocked out in the fall.

Mia grabbed his hand and tugged. "Get up. We have to get away."

Hands clasped, they stumbled around the side of the barn to an area several yards out from the flames. Mia fell to her knees, noisily sucking in the fresh air.

Collin went down beside her, filling his lungs with the sweet, precious oxygen.

"You okay?" he asked when he could breathe again.

"Fine."

But he couldn't take her word for it. By the flickering light of the fire that had nearly stolen her, he searched her face for signs of injury and found none.

"If anything had happened to you—"

And then before his reasonable side could stop him, he pulled her into his arms and kissed her.

She tasted smoky and sweet and wonderful. Emotion as foreign as an elephant and every bit as powerful coursed through him. His world tilted, spun, shimmered with warning.

He pulled back, suddenly afraid of what was happening to him. It was only a kiss, wasn't it? Given out of fear and relief. That was all. Only a kiss.

But he knew better. He'd kissed other women before, but not like this. The others he'd kept at a distance, outside of the armor. Mia was different. Way different.

And the truth of that scared him more than the barn fire.

Chapter Ten

"Here Mitch, take this end down to Adam."

Mia stood in the yard of her parents' home surrounded by large plastic containers filled with Christmas lights and decorations. Twined around her shoulders and across her arms was a tangled strand of frosty icicle lights. Adam worked at the opposite end of the fence attaching the strands as she unraveled them.

The other Caranos were scattered about in the yard and over the exterior of the house in similar activity. Each year on a given Saturday, Rosalie commandeered all available family members to set up outside Christmas decorations while the weather was decent. Today was the day.

Mitch, eager for a promised turkey hunt with Mia's dad, was trying to hurry the process.

"Why are you putting up Christmas lights so early? We haven't even had Thanksgiving yet."

He took the proffered end of the lights and trudged toward Adam.

Mia squinted at him, the November sun bright, the wind light but sharp. "That's the whole point. At the Caranos, turning the lights on for the first time on Thanksgiving night is a big deal. You *are* still coming, aren't you?"

One narrow shoulder jerked. "I guess. Nothing else to do."

Mia recognized Mitch's unique method of saving face. Holidays at his house, from what he'd told her and from what she'd seen, were not festive occasions. And from the latest information Collin had shared, Mia was more concerned than ever. Life at the Perez house grew more troubled with each passing week, and Mitchell spent most of his time on the streets, or with her or her mother and dad to avoid going home. His was a worrisome situation indeed, especially with the added tension between Collin and Mitch since the fire.

"Sure he's coming," Adam hollered. "We're going to finish that computer chess tournament, and I'm going to beat the socks off him."

Mitch handed him the light cord and grinned. "Wanna bet?"

"If I win, you have to wash my car inside and out."

"When *I* win, I get to wear your OU jersey to school."

"No betting around here, boys," Rosalie called from her spot on the front porch. She was winding greenery around the columns.

"Yes, ma'am," Adam replied, his swarthy face wreathed in ornery laughter. He loved to get Mama riled up.

"Yes, ma'am," Mitchell echoed, grinning at Adam.

Mia's dad came around the corner of the house, carrying the last of the nativity pieces that would grace their front yard. "As soon as I put this with the others, I'm going out to Collin's place."

Mia looked up in surprise, her pulse doing the usual flip-flop at Collin's name. "What for?"

Leo, like the other Caranos, had worked overtime to draw Collin into the fold. Though they'd yet to get him back to a large family gathering, he'd started hanging out with regularity at the Carano Bakery—at Leo's insistent invitation.

"Cops and donuts. They're a natural," her dad had said, but she knew he liked the quiet cop.

So did she.

"We need a couple of bales of hay to make the stable scene look authentic," Leo said. "I figured Collin might have some extra."

"Dad," Mia said, stricken at the memory. "Collin won't have any hay."

"Sure he will…" He stopped and set the manger down with a thud. "What was I thinking? All his hay went up with the barn."

"Yeah." Mitch scuffed a toe against the brown grass.

After their escape, while the firefighters drenched the glowing remains of the animal refuge, Collin had asked Mitch if he'd been smoking in the barn again. The question had devastated the boy. He hadn't been to the farm in the days since.

"He doesn't want me out there anymore."

"That's not true. He's upset right now because of the lost animals, but he's not upset with you."

"I could hear the puppies crying."

A heaviness tugged at Mia. They'd discussed this before, but the dying animals haunted him. "I know."

"I tried to find them, but the smoke was so bad."

She slid the lights from her shoulder and signaled Adam with a glance. He touched a finger to his eyebrow in silent agreement, understanding her need to counsel with Mitch. "Let's go sit on the porch and talk."

He followed her, slumping onto the step of the long concrete porch. Rosalie had moved down to the end post to add a red bow to the greenery.

"The investigators are still checking into the fire, but if you say you weren't smoking, I believe you."

"But Collin doesn't."

"I think he does, Mitchell, and he's sorry he hurt your feelings. He just has a hard time saying so."

"He's mad because of the puppies."

"No. He's sad. The same way you and I are."

The young boy stared morosely across the street where two squirrels gathered nuts beneath a pecan tree. "Do you think God cares about animals? Strays, I mean?"

She'd wondered when he'd ask something like that.

Her faith was an open topic with anyone who knew her and the two of them had had more than one deep discussion.

"Sparrows aren't worth much in our eyes, but the Bible says God feeds them and watches over them." She pointed toward the squirrels. "And just look at those guys. God provided all the nuts they could ever want in that one tree. And they don't even have to buy them!"

Her attempt at humor fell flat. Mitchell wasn't in a joking mood.

"I'm going to miss them. Rascal and Slick and Milly and her kittens." Mitchell had named them all, something that had bothered Collin at first.

He gathered a handful of dead grass and tossed the blades one at a time.

"There would be something wrong with us if we didn't grieve over what we care about. But remember this one good thing—God allowed us to love them and give them a nice home in their last days. They hadn't had that before."

"Yeah. That's true." He tossed the remaining grass and wiped a hand down his jeans' leg. "I guess God is okay."

Mia draped an arm across Mitch's shoulders. "God is the best friend you could ever have, Mitchell."

"Is Collin a Christian?"

Something sharp pinched at her heart. "You'll have to ask him about that."

She wanted to believe that Collin would eventually

accept Christ. Especially now. And not just because of Mitch's adoration, though that certainly loomed large. Mitch admired her Christian dad and brothers, too, but he shared a bond with Collin.

"You miss him, don't you?"

"Yeah."

"He misses you, too."

Mitch looked at her, hope as rich as the coffee-colored eyes. "You think?"

"I know. He told me on the phone last night." A phone call she'd instigated. Since the fire, he'd drawn back somewhat, as though he couldn't deal with all the emotions that had come pouring out that night. She was still puzzled and exhilarated by that unexpected kiss. Puzzled even more at how he had seemed to develop amnesia afterward.

"He needs your help out there to get things going again. Let's call him later, huh?"

She would keep on calling until he opened up again.

"I guess so."

"Hey, Mitchell," Mia's dad called. "Are you going to sit around on the porch and suntan or are we going to that turkey shoot?"

"I'm ready." Mitchell leaped up, then caught himself and looked back at Mia. "Okay, Mia?"

After the fire she'd become Mia instead of Miss Carano. That kind of familiarity had never happened before with one of her clients, and she prayed she wouldn't lose perspective. Somehow Mitchell had wound his scruffy self around her heart and that of her family.

"Have fun."

Mitch was gone in a flash.

"You can depend on Dad to interrupt an important conversation," Rosalie murmured, coming to join Mia in Mitch's now-abandoned spot.

"Mitch needs the distraction. He's been pretty down since the fire."

"So have you. Maybe not down so much as too quiet. Want to talk about it?"

"I have a lot on my mind, Mama. That's all. Work, Mitch." She shrugged.

"Collin," Mama concluded.

"Yes. Him, too." She picked at a thread on her knit jacket. "He kissed me the night of the fire."

"Who could blame him? You're beautiful."

Mia laughed. "Oh, Mama, no wonder I love you so."

"You like him?"

"Maybe more than I should. I don't date guys who aren't Christians, Mom. You know that. You taught me that."

"But you're falling for him anyway."

Mia stared morosely at the crystal lights Adam and Nic were tacking in place along the board fence. The brothers argued happily as they worked, the sound of frequent laughs punctuating the air. Two big ol' macho men with marshmallow hearts. How she loved them.

No wonder Collin Grace appealed to her. For all his

outward toughness, he was a softie on the inside just like her brothers.

Two nights ago, he'd lost his hard facade, both with her and then later when he'd found the first of several dead animals. Happy, the little survivor, had saved himself. Mitchell had freed Panda and her remaining kittens, and the large animals were safe in outside pens. But one litter of new kittens and an old sickly dog and her pup hadn't made it out alive. Mia couldn't forget the look on Collin's face: stricken, haunted, guilty.

He'd looked the same in those seconds before he had kissed her. She couldn't get that look or that kiss off her mind.

A kiss shouldn't be such a big deal. She wasn't a teenager. But she had already been fighting her growing emotions and when he'd looked at her, fear and firelight in his eyes, and wrapped her in a hard, protective hug, she'd faced the hard truth. Christian or not, she had strong feelings for Collin Grace. And even if he never admitted it, Collin felt something for her, too. Maybe that's why he was running scared. Collin didn't like to feel.

The wind blew a lock of hair across her face. She pushed the curl behind one ear.

"At first, I thought I was helping Collin. You know, doing the Christian thing, being a witness, going the extra mile, trying to draw him out to a place where he can heal. Collin's a good man, Mama. But he's had so much heartache that he's afraid to trust anybody. Even God."

Mama took Mia's chilled hands in her warm ones. "Then our job is to show him that he can. That God is trustworthy. And so are we. Dad's trying to do that at the bakery."

"I know. After the fire I gave him a book to read, the one about finding your purpose through Christ. We talked about the Lord a little then, but I felt so inadequate in the face of what had happened. I'm not sure I said the right things. I wanted him to know that God cared about him and his animals and his losses."

She yearned to tell Mama about Collin's lost brothers and lean on her wisdom. But she'd promised confidentiality even though telling her mother would help both of them. Rosalie was a prayer warrior who never stopped praying for something until the answer came. Mia wasn't having much success on her own, but God knew where Ian and Drew were.

"How is he handling the fire?"

"The usual way—by pretending he isn't bothered." The fact that he'd retreated into his shell again told her the tough cop with the marshmallow center was mourning the animals and the uninsured barn.

If only she could find some trace of his brothers to cheer him. Some bit of good news. She gripped her mother's hands tighter, giving them a quick bounce.

"Mama. I need you to help me pray about something."

Rosalie's eyes lit up. "Of course. What is it?"

"Well, that's the trouble. I need you to pray. But I can't tell you why."

Her mama looked at her for one beat of time, then smiled a mother's knowing smile. And Mia felt better than she'd felt since the night of the barn fire.

"Thank you, Lord," Mia said as she hung up the telephone. After going through dozens of boxes and hundreds of old records, she'd hit pay dirt two days after the conversation with her mama.

This time, she'd tempered her excitement long enough to make some phone calls and verify that a foster mother named Maxine Fielding not only still lived in Oklahoma City, but also remembered caring for a rowdy eleven-year-old named Drew Grace.

She glanced at the clock. Another two hours before she could head for Collin's place with her news. She thought about calling his cell, but found that unsatisfactory. She wanted to see his face, to watch him smile again. The past week had been a rough one.

A desk laden with paperwork needed her attention anyway, so she went to work there, weeding through files, making calls, setting up appointments. She phoned Mitchell's school to check on his attendance and discipline referrals and to inquire about any further indication of abuse.

Even with the barn fire setback, the boy had held his ground. And after the turkey shoot last Saturday, he'd let her take him out to Collin's where the three of them had spent hours putting together makeshift pens for the remaining animals.

The problems with the stepfather were accumulating though, and all her praying hadn't changed that one bit. The man had been furious when she'd interviewed him about Mitch's black eye, and Mitch hadn't helped by claiming he'd gotten into a fight at school. She wanted to get Mitch out of that house, though she couldn't without substantiated evidence. But now, both she and Collin were watching. Collin had even alerted the drug unit to be aware of possible illegal activities, though nothing had surfaced yet.

At ten after five she rotated her head from side to side, stretching tired muscles. Time to go. She tossed three Snickers wrappers into the trash and then dialed Collin's cell number.

"Grace."

She smiled at the short bark he substituted for a simple hello. And she couldn't deny that her heart jumped at the sound of that strong, masculine voice.

"Your name always makes me think of a song."

"Oh. Hi, Mia," he said. "I didn't recognize the number."

"My office."

"How does my name remind you of a song?"

She'd known he wouldn't let that one pass. With a smile in her voice, she said, "'*Amazing grace, how sweet the sound, that saved a wretch like me.'* It's a song about God's incredible love for us."

"The guys call me Amazing Grace sometimes. I never quite got that."

"Do you know what grace actually means?"

"I'm sure you're going to tell me." She heard the humor behind the gentle jab.

"Unmerited favor. God chooses to love and accept us, not because of what we do or don't do, but all because of His amazing grace."

A moment of silence hummed through the line. Though she hadn't planned to talk about her faith just now, she wanted Collin to understand how much Jesus loved him. She prayed that the truth of amazing grace would soak into his spirit and draw him to the Lord. She also hoped she hadn't just turned him ice-cold to the whole idea.

Finally, his voice soft, Collin said, "I'll never let the guys call me that again."

"Oh, Collin." He'd understood.

"So what's up?" he asked, sidestepping the emotion they both heard in her voice.

"I'm about to leave the office. Are you home?"

"Not yet. Why?"

"I want to talk to you in person."

"News?"

"Maybe." She didn't want to get his hopes up again and have them shattered.

"I'm off duty. Meet me at Braums on Penn. I'll buy you a grilled chicken salad."

"Throw in a hot chocolate and you've got yourself a date."

A soft masculine laugh flowed through the wires and straight into her heart. The memory of their kiss flared to life, unspoken but most definitely not forgotten. Oh, dear.

Mia bit down on the inside of her lip. Why couldn't she ever keep her big mouth shut?

Maxine Fielding had a great memory. The silver-haired woman regaled Collin with the good, the bad and the ugly about his brother's behavior. And the pleasure in Collin's face served as a reward for the lunch hours Mia had spent in the spooky, smelly basement of the municipal building.

"You don't by any chance have some pictures from that time, do you?" she asked the older woman. "Anything that could lead us to some of the boys who might have known Drew?"

"Sorry, hon," Maxine said, her fleshy face sorrowful. "I used to have a lot of pictures of my kids. That's what I always called them. Every one of them that came through here was mine for a while." She gestured with one hand. The knuckles were twisted with arthritis. "Anyways, while I was in the hospital a while back, my daughters decided to clean my house. Threw out all my mementos." She shook her head. "I'm still peeved about that."

Mia wished she hadn't asked, though Collin, sitting on an old velvet couch with his elbows on his knees, showed no emotion. His uniform was still neat after a day's work. And even with a five-o'clock shadow on his normally clean-shaven face, he looked good. A woman could get distracted with him around.

In fact, she *was* distracted. She let Collin do most of the talking, a strange turn of events. She was falling for him, all right, and didn't quite know what to do about it.

In the end, the foster mother recalled two other families that had cared for troubled boys during the same time period as well as a couple of group homes no longer in operation. That information alone gave Mia more names to plug into the computer, some specific files to dig through, and more chances to come up with something solid.

"So what do you think?" she asked when she and Collin were back inside his truck. He cranked the engine and pushed the heat lever to high. As night had fallen, so had the temperatures, and now a light rain spat at the windshield.

"Nice lady. I'm glad Drew was here for a while."

She could hear the unspoken wish that he'd been here, too. "Doesn't that give you hope that your brothers did okay in the system? That maybe they even found a family?"

"Wanna look into those locked files and find out?" A ghost of a smile reflected in the dashboard lights.

"No."

"I knew you'd say that." But his reply held humor instead of animosity, and she hoped he finally understood. There were some things she wouldn't do, even for him.

"Mrs. Fielding liked Drew."

"I've worried about him for so long, thought the worst." He shifted into Reverse and backed the truck onto the street. "Hearing that someone cared about him, even temporarily, felt good."

She was glad. More than glad, she was thankful. Collin had needed this news. He'd needed to leave the tragedy of the barn fire behind for a while. He'd needed to believe something positive had happened to his brothers. As he'd talked with Mrs. Fielding, he'd smiled, even laughed at her fond memories.

Collin's love for his lost brothers was fierce and steadfast, a powerful testament to the way he might someday love a woman. Mia refused to dwell on the lovely thought.

"We're going to find them, Collin."

He reached across the seat and touched her hand. "After tonight, I'm starting to believe you."

Three days before Thanksgiving the weather turned sunny and mild. Collin felt pretty sunny himself as he left the gym with his partner, Maurice, along with

Adam Carano. The other two men argued amiably over which sit-ups worked best, straight knee or bent.

Adam had first come to the gym to discuss the lawsuit, but now he'd become a permanent member along with the two cops. Collin liked the guy. And he also admired the way Adam was handling the lawsuit. When he took on a case, he was a real bulldog. Like his sister.

Collin's smile widened. Thinking about Mia did that to him lately.

"What are you grinning about, Grace?" Adam slapped him on the back. Collin's sweat-damp sweatshirt stuck to his shoulder.

"You talk as much as your sister."

"That's a terrible thing to say to your lawyer."

"When are you going to quit torturing me and get that problem solved?"

"I'm getting close. Did you know your neighbor has a real problem with cops? Especially you?"

Collin sawed a towel back and forth behind his neck. "Tell me something I don't already know."

"Okay, I will." Adam looked pleased with himself. "You remember busting a kid named Joey Stapleton a few years back for breaking and entering?"

"No, but the fire inspector suspects my barn was arson. Not B and E." His good mood evaporated at the memory of the animals Mia, Mitch and he had buried beneath the harvest moon.

Adam held up a hand. "Collin, my man. Lesson one about attorney-client privileges. Never interrupt your lawyer when he's on a roll. You disappoint me. You didn't even ask how Stapleton was connected."

"Okay, I'll bite. Who is he?"

"First of all, Stapleton didn't burn down your barn. He's still serving time. However, his half-brother, who mortgaged his land to defend Stapleton, lives down the road from you. His name is Cecil Slokum."

Now that *was* interesting. But there were plenty of do-wrongs out there with a grudge against him. "You think Slokum could be responsible?" Collin asked.

"Maybe. If Slokum can force you to pay damages for his daughter's ewe and destroy your barn at the same time, he not only gets revenge, he gets back some of the money he spent on his so-called innocent brother."

Collin had entertained the thought before, but a man didn't accuse his neighbor of arson without some kind of evidence. He'd also suspected Mitch of the fire and had lived to regret that mistake. Though his young friend was hanging around the farm once more, Collin could feel a hesitancy in the relationship, as though Mitch feared Collin would turn on him again.

"You got evidence?"

"Circumstantial, but enough to strongly suspect."

Collin's jaw tightened. Though he wanted to grab Cecil Slokum by the neck and shake the truth out of him, he wouldn't. He wasn't that kind of cop.

"Where do we go from here? Anything we can bust him on?"

"I've turned my findings over to the fire marshal and

the DA. If I'm right—" Adam's grin was cocky "—and I usually am, an arrest could come at any time."

"I appreciate it." Although sincere, Collin heard the gruffness in the thanks. He wasn't a lawyer and couldn't do the job Adam could, but he didn't like needing anyone's help either. More and more lately, Adam and Mia and the whole Carano clan made him feel needy. Inside and out. It kept him off balance, edgy, vulnerable.

"I can't believe I didn't figure out Cecil's grudge myself." In fact, he was annoyed that he hadn't dug deeper when the suspicion first sprouted. But work and Mitchell and rebuilding, not to mention Mia and his search, had kept him too busy to think straight.

"That's what friends are for, Collin. To lighten the load."

The words *unmerited favor* flitted through his mind. Was that what Mia meant? He'd thought a lot about that conversation, and the idea that anyone would do something for him without expecting anything in return never would jibe.

"How much do I owe you?" he asked.

Adam looked at him, an odd smile on his face. "My sister would hurt me if I took your money."

A cord of tension wound around inside him. Cool from drying sweat and November air, he shrugged into his hoodie. "I pay my debts."

"There are some debts you can't pay, Collin. The sooner you learn that the better off you'll be. The better off my sister will be, too."

Collin had no clue what Adam meant. And he didn't think he wanted to ask. Especially about the reference to Mia.

They were nearing his truck, and he needed this settled now. "How much, Carano?"

Adam rubbed a hand over his chin as if in deep thought. "Tell you what, Grace. If you really want to repay me, you can do me a favor."

"Name it."

Too late, Collin saw the ornery twinkle.

"Come to Mama's house for Thanksgiving dinner."

Maurice started to laugh. His partner knew his aversion to large family gatherings. He'd also been on Collin's case about Mia.

"I think he blindsided you, partner."

Adam shrugged his wide shoulders and didn't look the least bit sorry. "What do you expect? Lawyers are supposed to be sneaky." He pointed a finger at Collin. "You're going to show up, aren't you?"

"Do I have a choice?"

"Actually, no." Then, with a laugh and a wave, Adam hopped into a sleek SUV and left him standing in the parking lot. To make matters worse, Maurice was still laughing.

Chapter Eleven

Anticipation, sweeter than Christmas morning, filled Mia. She'd had so many failures, but today she felt sure something new would turn up in this stack of records.

With Mrs. Fielding's information, she had located the placement files of the family that had taken Drew after he'd run away from the Fielding home. Surely some mention of Collin's brother would be inside this folder.

She rummaged in her desk for a Snickers, but after a glance at her dusty hands, changed her mind. With the holidays coming up, she'd be fighting more than five pounds if she wasn't careful.

She flipped through page after page, eyes straining at the faded typewritten print until some of her excitement began to fade. The records seemed jumbled, bits and pieces of several files that might or might not relate to Collin's brothers. Then, as if lit by a neon sign, Drew's name leaped out at her.

"Yes!" she whispered, barely able to contain her excitement.

Collin knew she and Mama were praying for a breakthrough, and he'd been politely receptive, but Mia was ready for God to show off a little and prove to Collin that prayer really worked.

She quickly perused the document, found nothing of significance and decided to put the sheet aside while she searched for others. If there was one page about him, perhaps there would be more.

But when she reached the bottom of a rather thick file, two yellowing forms was all she had found. Disappointed, but not disheartened, she settled back to read, hoping for any tidbit to share with Collin.

One was a general report concerning the reasons Drew continued to live in foster care. There was a chronicle of his psycho-social problems, his habit of skipping school, and numerous reports for fighting. He'd been removed from any number of places because of the chip on his shoulder and his propensity for running away.

The other was a social worker's report indicating a placement in a therapeutic group home with six other teenage boys. Her heart fell into her high heels. Drew was fifteen at that point and had been in foster care since age seven. Gone was any hope that he had found a forever family.

She stopped to rub her tired eyes. Thirty was creeping closer and she'd always heard the eyes were the first to go. She needed to schedule a checkup with her optometrist—soon.

After jotting down names and addresses that might prove useful she started to replace the folder in the appropriate box when a newspaper clipping slipped out and filtered to the floor.

The word *fire* caught her attention. Her heart thumped once, hard. The reaction was silly, she told herself. A newspaper article about a fire wasn't necessarily about Drew.

But the clipping *had* been in the same file.

Unable to shake the foreboding, Mia picked up the two-inch column and read. A fire had broken out in a foster home claiming the lives of several teens, though no names were mentioned.

Dread, heavy as a grand piano, came over her. The address matched one of the homes that had cared for Drew. And the timing was perfect.

She rifled through the box, hoping to find something more about the tragedy but came up empty. Finally, she rested her chin in her hand and stared at the clipping, unsure of what to do with this new information. Should she tell Collin right away? Or keep the clipping to herself until she could verify whether Drew had been in that fire?

She rubbed at her eyes again. This time they were moist.

* * *

Collin stood in the doorway watching Mia. Deeply focused on her work, she hadn't heard him come in.

Her dark auburn hair swung forward, brushing her cheek, grazing the top of her desk. He studied her, remembering the silkiness of that hair, the softness of her skin.

He couldn't escape the memory of that night. Especially that insane moment when he'd kissed her and she'd kissed him back. More than once, he'd been tempted to repeat the performance, but caution won out. She pretended nothing incredible had happened. So would he. But that didn't stop him thinking about it.

Her mouth was turned down tonight, unusual for Mia. She rubbed at the corner of one eye and sighed. She was tired.

Her regular workload was always heavy and she was involved in church and the community, but for the past few months, she had been committed to helping him and Mitch. In her spare time, if there was such a thing, she searched the records for his brothers. In the evenings, she was now an active participant, along with Mitch, in rebuilding the barn. He'd asked too much of her.

He was suddenly overcome with a fierce need to take the load off her shoulders. To cheer her up. To make her laugh. Mia had a great laugh.

"Got a minute?"

Mia jumped and slapped one hand over her heart. Her red-rimmed eyes widened. "Collin."

"Didn't mean to scare you." He stepped inside the small office.

"What's wrong?" She didn't smile her usual wide, happy welcome.

"Why does anything have to be wrong?" Man, she was pretty, even with her hair mussed and her eyes red and every bit of makeup rubbed away.

"Because you hate this place. You never come here." She didn't look all that happy to see him.

He frowned. What was going on with her tonight? "Want me to leave?"

She rotated her head from side to side, stretching tight muscles. Collin thought about offering a neck rub, but decided against it. Last time he'd touched her, he'd gone nuts and kissed her, too.

"Don't be silly."

Which was no answer at all. He shifted from one foot to the other and checked out the messy office. Boxes, bent and aging, lined one wall and stacks of manila folders with glaring white typewritten labels were spread here and there.

"Are these the old records you've been searching for me?"

A funny expression flitted across her face. For a second, he wondered if she'd found something. But if she had, wouldn't she be shouting from the rooftops and talking a mile a minute? Instead, she was abnormally quiet tonight.

"These are only a few of the hundreds and hundreds of boxes in that basement," she said.

"Maybe I could help." His offer should have come long before now, but he suspected the files were confidential.

Mia shook her head, long hair swishing over the shoulders of a bright-blue sweater. Blue was definitely her color.

"I was about to stop for the night anyway." She slid some papers into a folder and looked up at him. "So are you going to tell me why you're here or can I assume I'm under arrest?"

This time she offered a smile.

This was the Mia he knew and...appreciated.

"I came with some news." He scraped a straight-backed chair up closer to her desk and sat down. "Unless Adam beat me to it."

Her smile disappeared and she tensed again. "What kind of news? Did something happen?"

Collin waved away her concern. "Nothing bad. At least, I hope you don't think so. Adam invited me to your Mom's for Thanksgiving."

She studied him for two beats. "So did I, but you said no."

That wasn't the reaction he'd anticipated.

"I'm coming now."

"What changed your mind?"

"Your brother is a devious man."

He expected her to laugh and agree. She didn't. She

seemed distracted, not really into the conversation. Earlier he'd felt unwanted, but now he saw what he hadn't before. Something was wrong.

He leaned across the desk to tug at her hand. The bones felt small and fine, and her skin was smoother and softer than Happy's fur. "Let's get out of here. You're exhausted."

"It's not that, Collin. Oh, I am tired, but I'm also upset about something I found in an old file. I need to tell you and I'm not sure how."

That got his attention. The desire to tease her about Thanksgiving dinner disappeared. "Whose old files are we talking about?"

"Drew's. Or at least files associated with Drew. There's some confusion in them. Several files seem to be jumbled together with parts missing. Maybe a box was spilled somehow and hastily repacked. I don't know. But I did find some information that may or may not involve Drew."

He saw the pinched skin around her mouth, the worry around her eyes. And he knew beyond a shadow of a doubt, the news was not going to make him happy.

The day before Thanksgiving Collin unearthed an ancient police report which identified the cause of the Carter Home fire as an electrical short. Better yet, the report listed several witnesses, one of whom turned out to be another former foster kid, Billy Johnson. Collin needed less than thirty minutes to track down the man's name, address and place of employment.

"I'm going with you," Mia said, when he called to tell her of the discovery.

"This is your day off. I thought you and your mom were cooking."

"We are. We still can. But I'm going with you. Don't argue. Come pick me up."

Collin hid a smile. Deep down, he was glad that the bulldog in Mia insisted on going along. Something in him worried that the interview might produce bad news. And though Mia couldn't stop bad news, she was a dandy with moral support and comforting prayers. He'd come to respect that about her. He'd even tried praying a few times himself lately.

Someone had died in that house fire. That's when he'd started praying in earnest. Praying that Drew wasn't the one. He'd even taken to bargaining with God. If Drew was alive, he would believe. If Drew was okay, God must care. He knew such prayers were selfish and unfruitful, but he was a desperate man.

Billy Johnson met them in the grease bay of an auto repair shop on the east side of town, a rag in hand. His blue service uniform was streaked with oil and grease and his fingernails would never see clean, but when he offered his hand, Collin shook it gratefully. This man had known Drew at age fifteen.

"Kinda cold out here," Billy said. "Y'all come inside the office. My boss won't care. I told him you were coming."

They followed the mechanic inside the tiny office stacked with tools and papers and red rags and reeking of grease. A small space heater kept the room pleasantly warm.

"Y'all have a seat." He shoved a car-repair manual off one chair and swiped the red rag over the seat for Mia. Collin settled onto a canvas camp stool. No one sat around this place much.

"I remember Drew." Billy rolled a stool from beneath the desk and balanced on it, pushing himself back and forth with one extended foot. "He was a wiry rascal. Liked to fight."

Collin shot Mia a wry glance. "Sounds like my brother."

"He was okay, though. Me and him, we only punched each other once. After that, we was kinda buddies, ya might say." He grinned. "Foster kids, ya know. We sneaked smokes together. Raided the kitchen. Tormented the house parents. The usual."

"What do you remember about the night of the fire?" Mia asked, and Collin was grateful. His shoulder muscles were as tight as security at the White House. He wanted to get this over with.

"More than I want to," Billy said, scratching at the back of his head. The metal rollers on his stool made an annoying screech against the cement floor. "The house was full, seven or eight boys, I think, so I was asleep in the living room on the couch when the fire broke out."

"But you woke in time to escape?"

"Yes, ma'am. Me and this one other kid." He rolled the stool in and out, in and out, oblivious to the screech.

"Was it Drew?"

"No, ma'am." *Screech. Screech.* "A kid named Jerry. I think he's in the pen now."

Blood pulsing against his temples, Collin leaned forward. "What about Drew?"

Billy hesitated. Collin got a real bad feeling, worse than the time he'd walked into a dark alley and come face to face with a double-barrelled shotgun.

The screeching stopped. "Drew slept in the attic. I'm sorry, officer. Your brother never made it out."

Mia wanted Collin to get angry. She wanted him to cry. She wanted him to react in some way, to show some emotion. But he didn't.

With his cop face on, he thanked Billy Johnson and quietly led the way to the car. The drive back to Mia's apartment was unbearable. She talked, muttered maddeningly useless platitudes, said she was sorry a million times, reminded him that Ian was still out there somewhere, but Collin said nothing in response.

"Why don't you come inside for a while?" she asked when he stopped outside her apartment. "I'll make us something to eat. Better yet, my tiramisu brownies are already baked for tomorrow's dinner. We can sneak one with some fresh coffee. I know brownies and coffee won't change things, but comfort food always makes me feel better."

"I don't think so."

Her heart broke for him. Lord, hasn't he had enough sorrow in his life? Why this?

She pushed the door open, hesitant to leave him alone. "Will you call me later if you need to talk?"

For a minute, she thought he might respond, might even smile. He'd teased her so many times about her tendency to rattle on, but this time he was hurting too much even to tease.

"I'll come out to your place later if you want me to. Or you can come back here. You really shouldn't be alone."

He looked at her and what she read there was clearer than words and so terribly sad she wanted to cry. He'd always been alone.

"I'm here for you, Collin. If you need anything at all, please call me. Let me help. I don't know what to do, either, but I want to do something."

Feeling helpless, she slid out of the truck and stood with one hand holding the door open. Wind swirled around her legs, chilling her. Someone slammed an apartment door and pounded down the metal stairs outside her complex.

"I'm praying for you, Collin. God cares. I care. My family cares. Please know that."

This time he answered, his voice low, and Mia thought she saw a crack in the hard veneer. "I do know."

She couldn't help herself. She reached back inside the cab and touched his cheek. Her heart was full of sorrow and love and the desire to help him heal, but this time she was the one with no words.

Collin reached up and took her hand from his whisker-rough face, gave it a squeeze and let go. "Better get inside. You'll freeze."

She backed away, reluctant to let him leave, but having no other choice.

"We'll see you tomorrow at Mama's, won't we?"

"I don't know, Mia," he said. "I probably wouldn't be very good company."

And then he drove away.

Chapter Twelve

Dead.

The word clattered round and round in Collin's head like a rock in an empty pop can.

Drew, his full-of-energy-and-orneriness brother, was dead. Long dead.

All the years of searching, hoping, gone up in smoke in a house where the kids were throwaways that nobody wanted anyway. Nobody missed them. Nobody mourned them.

He lay on his bed in the darkness, staring up at the shadows cast by the wind-tossed maple outside his window. He had used all the energy in him to drive home and care for the animals. By the time he'd dragged his heavy heart inside, he hadn't had the energy to undress except for his boots.

He'd been alone for years, but tonight he felt empty as if part of him had disappeared. In a way, he supposed it had. The search for his brothers had sustained him since he was ten years old. The hope of reunion had kept him moving forward, kept him fighting upstream when he'd been ready to give up on life in general. The search had given him purpose, made him a cop. Now, half of that hope was gone forever. And with it, half of himself.

He heard the soft shuffle of animal feet on wood floors. The familiar limp and thump that could only belong to Happy.

After the fire, Collin hadn't had the heart to leave the little guy outside with the others. So Happy had moved into a box in the living room, quietly filling Collin's evenings with his sweet presence.

But now, he whined at the bedside, an unusual turn of events.

"What do you want, boy?" Collin said to the dark ceiling.

Happy whined again.

Though his body weighed a thousand pounds and moving took effort he didn't have, Collin rolled to his side and peered down at the shadowy form. The collie lifted one footless leg and pawed at him. When Collin didn't pick him up, Happy tried to jump, a pitiful sight that sent the dog tumbling backward.

Collin swooped him up onto the bed. "Here now."

With a contented sigh, Happy buried his nose under his master's arm and settled down. Collin had never had a dog. Not as a pet. But Happy was getting real close. Both his legs had finally healed after the second amputation, but a dog with two missing feet wasn't likely ever to be adopted.

He smoothed his hand over the shaggy fur, glad for the company of another creature, especially one that didn't talk.

No, that wasn't fair. He liked Mia to talk. He loved her soothing, sweet voice. He loved her enthusiasm for life, her positive take on everything, her belief in the ultimate goodness. She was a light in a dark place.

Mia had been so upset for him. He'd wanted to talk to her, wanted to let her help, but he couldn't. He didn't know how.

Burrowing one hand deep into Happy's thick fur, Collin drew comfort from the warm, loving dog.

A lot of good prayer had done. Not that he expected God to pay any attention to him. But Mia had prayed. And if God was going to listen to anybody, wouldn't He hear someone like her?

With his free hand, Collin dug down into his pants' pocket, felt the metal fish. All this time he'd carried the keychain as a reminder of his brothers. Of that last day together. Of the counselor who'd prayed for them and shown them kindness, given them hope. Had Drew still carried his that fateful night?

A fire. Another fire. He squeezed his eyes shut, but quickly opened them when flames shot up behind his imagination. Drew in a fire. Helpless. Just like the animals in his barn.

All night, he lay there, unable to sleep, unable to

stop picturing the burned animals he'd had to bury. Unable to stop his imagination from making the terrible comparison.

When at last the sun broke above the horizon, heralding the new day, Collin rolled onto his belly and pulled the pillow over his head.

Today was Thanksgiving.

And he wasn't feeling too thankful.

At noon Collin awakened, cold and depressed, to a very urgent demand from Happy to be let outside. Amazed to have slept at all, he stumbled to the front door, bleary-eyed and heavy-headed. The house was cold and the wood floors chilled his bare feet. He'd forgotten to turn on the heat last night.

After cranking the thermostat, he stood at the door to watch the collie hobble around the front yard, tail in motion, sniffing the scent of the resident squirrel as if he had the legs to catch it. Collin had to admit, the little dog's attitude had a positive effect on his own.

When Happy made the choice to stay outside and play, Collin closed the door and went to make coffee.

He felt bad about backing out of dinner at the Caranos'. He didn't like disappointing Mia—or any of the others for that matter. They were a great family. The best. The kind he would have loved to have grown up in. But he didn't belong, especially not today when negative energy was all he had to share.

He hoped Mitch was there, though, instead of at home. The boy needed the Caranos.

While the coffee brewed, the kitchen grew warmer, but Collin's feet didn't. He headed for the bedroom in search of clean socks.

As he opened the dresser drawer, his attention fell to the book Mia had given to him the night of the barn fire. She'd said the contents would encourage him, help him understand his purpose. Until yesterday he'd believed his purpose was to find his brothers. Now he wondered if there had to be more to life than a single-minded effort to accomplish only one thing. He'd found Drew, for whatever good that had done him. What would he do after he found Ian? Once his only purpose was fulfilled, then what? Would his life be over?

Without giving the decision too much thought, he grabbed the book along with a pair of socks and headed for the kitchen and that much-needed cup of coffee. The smell alone was waking him up.

He poured a cup and sat down at the table, flipped the book to a random page, and began to read.

Late that afternoon Happy's excited yip warned Collin that he was not alone. He jammed his hammer into the loop on his tool belt and walked around to the front of the house. For the last few hours, he'd sweated out his depression on the house-in-progress while mulling over the things he'd read in Mia's book.

As he stood in the front yard, chilled by winter wind

on sweat, a caravan of familiar-looking vehicles wound down his driveway, stirred dry leaves and dust and elicited a cacophony of barking from the penned dogs. Happy danced on two feet and a pair of stubs, furry tail in overdrive, mouth stretched into a wide smile.

One fist propped on his hip, Collin blinked in bewilderment at the incoming traffic. Mia's yellow Mustang led the pack, an entire invasion of Caranos.

"Hi, Collin." Mitch jumped out of Mia's barely stopped car, wearing new jeans and an oversize OU jersey. Happy was all over him like honey glaze on ham, wiggling and whining, eyes aglow with love. Mitch laughed in delight and fell to the ground, pulling the dog onto his chest.

Adam bolted out of his red SUV and came charging across the yard, a mock scowl on his face. "Hey, squirt. Don't be desecrating my OU jersey like that."

Mitch leaped up, brushing away the dust. "Sorry, Adam."

Mitchell had come a long way from the defiant kid Collin had picked up for shoplifting.

Adam ruffled his head. "Joking. The jersey is yours. I told you that." He stuck a hand out toward Collin, his dark eyes sparking with the Carano humor. "As your lawyer, I have an obligation to tell you something." He jerked his head toward the rest of the laughing, jabbering group who came toward the house loaded with boxes and dishes. "These women cooked a mega-meal.

And any invited man who doesn't show up to eat it could be in serious danger."

"What is all this?"

"You know the old saying. If Mohammed won't come to the mountain, the mountain will come to him. So, the Caranos have moved Thanksgiving to your place."

"You're kidding." Collin stared in amazement as the whole group trouped inside his house. A waft of incredibly delicious smells trailed them.

Adam clapped him on the back. "Caranos take their food seriously. Especially Thanksgiving food."

The old feelings of inadequacy crowded in with the unexpected company. His house was tiny and his table impossibly small. How would they have a dinner inside there? How would they all even get inside?

But the undaunted Carano clan had thought of everything. From the back of a pickup came folding tables and chairs. He watched, unmoving for several long, bewildered minutes while all around him people laughed and joked and juggled boxes and covered dishes. Why had they done this? Why would Mia and her family go to so much trouble to bring Thanksgiving to a guy who was accustomed to having no holidays at all? Why did they care?

"Close your mouth, Collin," Mia said as she swished past him smelling like sunshine and banana nut bread. "And take this into the house."

Her smile warmed a cold place inside him.

He accepted the foil-wrapped package, still warm from the oven. "You didn't have to do this."

She pointed a finger at him. "Don't say that to Mama."

He didn't understand this kind of family bond. He didn't understand these people. They scared him and nurtured him and made him long to be someone he wasn't. He didn't know whether to run away from them or to them.

For today, he figured he didn't have much say in the matter either way. If this was a game of tag, you're it, he was it. Might as well make the best of the situation.

The twenty-odd people were a tight fit inside Collin's home-in-progress, requiring some creative arrangement, but in no time at all his house smelled of the huge Thanksgiving dinner spread out before them on folding tables. Someone, Mia, he figured, had even thought of brown-and-orange tablecloths and a perky tissue-turkey centerpiece.

Around him, conversation ebbed and flowed. Nic, wearing a sweatshirt that proclaimed *I'm going to graduate on time no matter how long it takes,* wielded a carving knife and fork with a maniacal laugh that had the girls squealing.

As he watched the interaction of people who loved each other, some of the heavy sorrow lifted from Collin. Every time he hung out with the Caranos, he was overwhelmed with both yearning and fear. Yearning to be a part. Fear that he didn't have what it took.

He removed a stack of plates from Mia's hands and began to set them out in long rows.

"I hope you aren't upset with our invasion," Mia said, her sweet eyes seriously concerned that he was angry with her. "I couldn't stand to think of you out here alone on Thanksgiving."

He'd figured Mia was the instigator. She had wanted to be here—with him—and the idea gave him a happy little buzz. Maybe he had it in him after all.

Dinner was over, but the pleasant zing of having Mia and her family in his house didn't go away. The television blared a game between the Lions and the Cowboys which brought occasional shouts of victory from Adam and Nic. Gabe and his wife were deep into a game of Go Fish with their oldest child while the youngest was fast asleep in Collin's bedroom. Mitchell was sprawled with his back against Leo's knees, Happy in his lap. They all looked as full and drowsy and content as Collin felt.

Contentment was not a word he used very often. But something had happened to him today when Mia's family had come onto his turf to draw him into their midst with food and love. If he dwelled on the idea, he'd probably get nervous and back off, so he chose to enjoy. His mind needed their exuberant distraction.

"I'm on KP," he said, gently nudging Rosalie out from in front of his shiny stainless-steel sink. "Cleaning up is the least I can do."

A chorus of groans issued from the Carano men.

"Traitor," Nic grumbled.

"You're starting a terrible precedent," Adam called. "Next year, they'll expect us to cook."

This time the women hooted.

"Anna and I will help Collin, Mama. There's really not room for more than three, anyway. You go sit down. You've cooked for three days."

"Sounds good. I wanted to watch this game anyway." Rosalie untied her apron and hung the starched poplin over the back of a chair. "When these tables are cleared, you boys get them folded and put out in the truck so we have room to play charades or something."

"Will do, Mama."

Rosalie bustled around the tables and squeezed a chair into a tiny space between the wall and Leo. Collin leaned toward Mia and murmured, "Your mom likes football?"

Mia looked up from scraping leftover yams into a container and grinned. He loved the way she always had a smile ready to share. "Mama doesn't know a touchdown from a field goal, but she treasures the time with her boys."

"Your family's lucky to have her."

Mia studied him, expression soft and understanding. "We're very blessed."

Blessed. Yeah, he could see that. But they worked at being a family, too. At this whole togetherness thing. They were a clear picture of how functional families made it happen. Sacrifice, commitment, overlooking each other's quirks. He understood that now in a way he hadn't before.

"I'll wash. You dry. Dish towels in that top drawer." He took a heavy ceramic dish from her and dumped the empty bowl into the soapy water. "You Caranos are great cooks. I can't believe I ate two pieces of pie."

Mia reached for a rinsed glass and their arms brushed. Suddenly, he was remembering that disconcerting kiss.

"There's more for later."

He'd like that a lot. And he didn't mean pie.

They made short work of the kitchen, Anna and Mia whisking dishes and leftovers from the tables while he scrubbed away. While the women carried on most of the conversation Collin listened, comfortable with their chatter.

"I think that's the last one," Mia said, taking a huge stainless pot from his drippy hands.

Collin looked around, saw the tables cleared, and pulled the plug. "Good. The animals are probably thinking I've abandoned them. Can you take over from here?"

"I can," Anna said, her smile a mirror of Mia's. "You two go on. I'll finish up and make some fresh coffee, too."

"I'm not arguing with a deal like that," Mia said.

Nic popped up from his folding chair as Collin and Mia donned their coats. "Need any help?"

"We've got it. Thanks, anyway." As much as he liked

Nic and the other Caranos, he was ready to be alone. Well, almost alone.

Collin pushed the storm door open and waited for Mia to pass through. Her companionship no longer felt like an intrusion. He figured he should worry about that. Later.

Once outside he was tempted, if only for a split second, to take her hand. He settled for a hand under her elbow instead. A man had to form some kind of boundaries with a woman like Mia.

As they fell into step toward the lean-to that now served as shelter for the remaining animals, she glanced over at him. "You didn't get much sleep last night."

"Perceptive." Beneath a narrow slice of silver moon, the air had grown frosty. Collin's breath puffed out beneath the bright yard light. Last night had been one of the worst nights of his life.

"The bags under your eyes gave you away." She slowed her steps to rest one hand on his upper arm. Whether imagined or real, Mia's warmth penetrated the sleeve of his thick coat. "How are you? Really."

"Better now." That surprised him. To know that family not his own could lift his spirits this much.

"I'm so sorry. Deeply, truly sorry. You have every right to be angry and hurt and grief-stricken. I wish I knew what to do to make things better."

She already had. She and her rambunctious family with their big hearts and their open arms.

"Every holiday for more than twenty years, I've

wondered about my brothers. I know what happened to Drew now, but what about Ian? Does he have a family to go home to? A wife and kids? Is he having turkey and dressing and pumpkin pie right this minute with a loving family?"

Or is he as lonely and messed up as me?

"We're going to keep on believing and praying that he's okay and that we are going to locate him. If we found information about Drew, we can find Ian."

"I hope you're right." Maybe then the hole inside him would heal a little.

As they approached the pens, the animals moved restlessly, eager for their own Thanksgiving dinner. The colt whinnied a greeting. A cat meowed, followed by a chorus of kitten mews.

Even after losing six animals to the fire and making the decision to take no more until the barn was rebuilt, he still had too many animals. Caged up this way was no life for them and he hated the arrangement, though there was no other place for the strays to go. He'd ruled out the animal shelter knowing that sick animals wouldn't be adopted and the alternative was euthanasia. Better with him than there. Some were well enough to move around inside a stall but not well enough to be safe from coyotes and other predators if he left them loose. The puppies and kittens were in borrowed cages that opened out to short, makeshift runs. The larger dogs were on chains next to borrowed dog houses. The grazing animals were the lucky ones, unaffected by the fire except for the loss of stall space.

He went to the row of barrels that contained a variety of animal feed. "I have to find a way to get this barn up faster."

At the rate he was going, the barn wouldn't be finished for a year. He had only one stall completed to house the sickest, and a chain-link run for the dogs.

Mia began to distribute dry dog food, stopping to give each animal an ear rub. "I'll feed everyone while you take care of the medications."

He gave her a grateful look. "Good idea."

Panda, who had survived the fire and recovered sufficiently to be adopted, had yet to find a home, though her kittens had. Collin figured he'd never find a place for her. The mama cat allowed Collin or Mia to feed her, but otherwise she feared humans except for Mitchell.

"I thought this was Mitchell's job," Mia said, coming around the shadowy side of the lean-to.

Collin knelt on the ground dabbing antibiotic cream onto a pup's stitches. "He's through serving his time."

"I know. But the responsibility has been good for him."

"He's changed a lot."

"Thanks to you." She handed him a roll of adhesive tape.

"And your family. Sometimes I wonder what will happen to him."

"His stepdad scares me."

Collin looked at her sharply. She'd shoved her hands into her pockets. "Do you mean personally or professionally?"

Even in the halflight, he saw her frown. "Both. Since you told me of your suspicions, I want Mitch out of there, but…"

"But Mitch won't tell you the truth." He put the finishing touches on the bandage and stood. He was as frustrated as Mia over Mitch's reluctance to give them a reason to move him to safety. And for all his watchfulness, Collin couldn't find reasonable cause to pay Teddy Shipley an unexpected official visit.

"I think Mitch won't talk because his mother is using, too. He's afraid of what will happen to her."

In his entire life, including twelve years on the force, Collin had seen nothing but horror come from drugs. He was lucky. Mia would say blessed. And maybe he was. Whichever, he'd somehow escaped the trap of drugs. Too many of the boys he'd known in the group homes were dead, in jail, or living lives of unspeakable despair because of drugs.

"If a meth lab is operating in that house, it's only a matter of time until something bad goes down."

Her voice was stunned. "Do you think that's the case?"

"Maybe." Probably. They were gathering more evidence daily.

A chill of fear trickled down his backbone. "Stay out of there, Mia. You hear me?"

"I'm afraid for him, Collin."

"Me, too," he admitted grimly. Collin knew the reality of Mitchell's situation. Mia was an experienced professional, but she hadn't lived the life. He had.

In silence, his thoughts churning, he put the medical supply box away and doubled-checked the cage latches for security. He couldn't keep the whole world safe, but he could take care of these animals. And Mitchell, too, if the kid would only let him.

Mia tugged on the front of his coat. Her hair blew softly back from her face as she looked up at him. "Stop fretting. You can't always be with him. But Jesus is."

"'He'll never leave you nor forsake you,'" he quoted softly, the words of his keychain making more sense at that moment than they ever had.

"Exactly."

If he was indeed blessed to have avoided the curse of drugs, was Jesus the reason? Had God been with him through everything? "Do you think it's true?"

"I know it is." She pulled her hood up and shivered against a sudden gust of wind.

Collin draped an arm around her shoulders and drew her against his side. She fitted beneath his arm as if curved in exactly the right places for that purpose.

They started back toward the house. Collin reined in his long stride to accommodate her shorter one.

"Mind if I ask you something?" His words were deep and thoughtful.

"Anything." And she meant it.

"I can't believe how much I've laughed tonight."

She bumped him with her hip. "That's not a question."

"After hearing about Drew—" He stopped. Talking about his brother's death was still too fresh and cut too deep.

Mia slipped an arm around his waist and squeezed. She prayed he could feel her compassion and somehow gain comfort. From the time she and Adam had come up with the idea to bring Thanksgiving to him, she'd prayed. Thankfully, he'd responded well to their invasion and had even seemed to enjoy himself in spite of the awful sorrow in his heart.

"I want to ask you something," he said, stopping in a wind break next to the front porch. From inside the house Mia could hear one of the first Christmas commercials of the season.

"Sounds serious."

"It is. I've spent most of my adult life coming to terms with my crazy life, but I'll never understand Drew's death. That's where I'm confused about God. I want to believe He cares but the evidence isn't too strong. I don't mean I'm angry at Him or that I blame Him. But He doesn't seem too involved in my life so far."

His words were not bitter. Instead, they held a yearning, a seeking to understand. Somehow in all the past rejections, Collin had come to see himself as unlovable.

Mia looked up at him, at the strong, manly profile

illuminated by the moon. She admired so much about Collin Grace that he didn't even recognize as good. He'd overcome some incredible odds to become a man with so much depth of character, so much rich emotion that he didn't know how to express all that was inside him.

She shifted against the wall and gazed off into the darkness, praying for wisdom. She'd been a Christian since she was twelve years old. She had a strong, healthy family and many friends. Though she'd had hurts and struggles, nothing in her experience could compare to what this good and decent man had lived through. How could she make him understand that God was here, caring? How could she make him understand that he was loved and loveable?

Her heart filled with realization. Tonight was the night he needed to know.

"I don't have any easy answers. I wish I did. But there's something I want to share with you. Actually, three somethings."

Collin peered down at her, his expression sincere and curious. She saw a trust there that gave her courage.

"First of all, I don't pretend to understand why terrible things happen to innocent people, especially kids. But I do know that God cares. So much that He sent His son to give us hope of a better place than this. A perfect place called Heaven.

"Secondly, He knew Drew's death would devastate you. He kept the news from you until you were ready to handle it. Until you had met a crazy bunch of Caranos who would try their best to help you through the grief."

"Why didn't he just give me back my brother? That's the only thing I've ever wanted."

"I don't know, Collin. I wish He had. But God has a plan for you. And even if Drew isn't a part of your future, he'll always be a part of who you are and what you've become—a good cop, a caring man, a dear and trusted friend."

A gust of wind whipped her hood back. Collin caught each side and tugged the hood up around her face. When she thanked him with a half smile, he moved a fraction closer.

Mia's skin tingled from his nearness. As hard as this was going to be, she had to tell him the truth—all of it.

In the narrow space between them, her breath mingled with his, moist and warm. They really should go inside.

She could see he wanted to kiss her again. And she wanted that too, but she wouldn't follow through. The first time had been unplanned reflex, completely understandable and forgivable. This time would be premeditated.

"Wasn't there a third thing you wanted to tell me?" he murmured, wonderfully, painfully near.

She wasn't scared of the truth, but she didn't know how to predict Collin's reaction. Was she doing the right thing by telling him? She fidgeted with the string on her hood but held Collin's gaze with hers. His expression might not change, but his eyes would tell her what he wouldn't.

"Yes. There is. Something very important. Something that I hope will make you realize how special and valuable you are. At least to me."

Inside the house, Nic's voice shouted "Touchdown!" Neither she nor Collin reacted.

She had his full attention now.

Throat thick with emotion, Mia bracketed Collin's face in her gloved hands. And then, her voice sure, she said, "The third thing is this—I'm in love with you, Collin."

Chapter Thirteen

Collin blinked into her eyes, stunned. She loved him?

A thousand responses thundered through him as wild as mustangs. He didn't know what she expected him to say. He had feelings for her, wanted to kiss her, to be with her, but love? He wasn't even sure what that was.

"You don't have to respond to that." She gave his jaws a final caress and dropped her hands. "I just wanted you to know."

She started to slip under his arm and move away, but he caught her. "No, you don't. You don't drop a bomb like that and walk off."

She stopped and looked up at him, her gaze as clear and honest as a baby's. Something dangerous turned over inside Collin's chest. She was serious. She loved him.

Oh, man. How did he deal with that? And why had she chosen to tell him now in the midst of a conversation about God and Drew?

If her intention was to distract him, she'd succeeded. The idea of kissing her had been on his mind since she'd bopped out of that yellow Mustang and sashayed across his front yard with her family in tow.

Ah, what was he talking about? He'd wanted to kiss her a lot longer than that.

Now that he knew she loved him, he wasn't quite so hesitant to follow through.

Drawing her closer, he lowered his face to hers.

She shrank back against the house and placed a hand on his chest. "I'm sorry, Collin. As much as I'd like to kiss you, I won't."

He frowned. "You love me? But you won't let me kiss you?"

Her eyes filled with tears, confusing him more. He'd made her cry, though he had no idea what he'd done. "I'm sorry. Let me explain."

Reluctantly, he dropped his hands and backed off. Everything in him wanted to hold her more than ever now.

The wind circled in between them. Mia shivered and hugged herself, and he had to fight to keep from taking her in his arms again.

"I could do that for you," he said with a half smile.

But they both knew he wouldn't push the issue.

She rubbed her hands up and down her arms, eyes focused on some distant point in the darkness. "Tonight, I understood something about you, Collin."

"Yeah?" He wished she'd tell him because right now he didn't understand much of anything.

"I realized that you don't know how to receive love. From God or anybody else. You've been hurt and rejected so much in your life that you think you're unlovable."

He didn't much like the idea of anyone poking around inside his head, and he liked it even less when someone thought they knew what made him tick. But he had to admit, there was validity to her words. Normally, he didn't listen to psychobabble, but from Mia—well, Mia was different.

"Love is a gift, Collin, and unless a gift is given away, it has no value. You're valuable to me. I wanted you to understand that. I wanted to give that to you."

"Then why—?" He left the question hanging. She loved him, but she wouldn't kiss him?

He shoved his hands into his jacket pockets.

Her logic didn't make sense.

"Because as much as I love you, I love God more. And I trust Him to know what's best and right for me even when His rules hurt."

Her words were a splash of cold water in the face. One minute she declared her love and the next she shut him out. "And God says I'm not good enough for you?"

"That's not what I mean."

She closed the distance between them and rested her head against his chest. He didn't yield. He'd never let a woman get this close. And now she was telling him she loved him but he wasn't good enough?

But in his heart, he knew she was right. A foster kid from questionable bloodlines could never be good enough for a woman like Mia.

"Will you hear me out?" she asked softly. "This has nothing to do with being good enough."

He relented then, letting her tug one hand from his pocket. He couldn't seem to say no to Mia.

"You have a lot of baggage from the past to deal with, Collin. None of that scares me off. God can heal anything. But that's the key. You have to let Him."

"What does any of that have to do with me kissing you? Does God have rules against a man kissing a woman he cares about?"

Okay, so he cared about her. Maybe a lot, though love wasn't a word in his vocabulary.

Mia's full mouth widened in a characteristic smile. "God's all for kissing. He probably invented it. But he has rules about Christians kissing non-Christians. That's hard for me to accept, but I have to. I'll be your friend. And I won't stop loving you even for a second, but that's as far as we go."

"You mean if I was a Christian, I could kiss you?"

"Yes." She tilted her head to one side and gave him a lopsided smile. "But don't be thinking I go around kissing just anybody, Christian or not."

He already knew that about her.

"Okay, then. Friends. I can do that." Friendship was

all he'd ever expected anyway. Just knowing she was in love with him was burden enough.

Yes, friendship was far better anyway.

Mia dropped the last gaily wrapped gift into her shopping bag and headed out of the mall. The Christmas crowd was thicker than Grandma Carano's spaghetti sauce.

She had met her best girlfriend for a late lunch and they'd talked about Collin. Sharing her concerns with a praying friend had helped. She was thinking about her cop far too much lately and though convinced she'd done the right thing by admitting her love for him, holding to the friendship rule was harder than she'd imagined.

Collin had the uncanny ability to move right on as if nothing had happened. But with a subtle difference. Last night, he'd come to her apartment, bearing a glorious red poinsettia and asked her out to dinner. When she'd refused, he'd wanted to stay and talk about the book she'd loaned him.

Not knowing if she was playing with fire or trying to be a good witness for the Lord, she'd made microwave popcorn and spent the next two hours in an interesting discussion about her faith. Collin was a bright man with a lot of questions and misconceptions about God. He was stuck on the idea that God had abandoned him along with everyone else in his childhood, and nothing she said seemed to help.

But he was seeking the truth, and that alone was a big step.

Upon leaving the crowded mall, Mia picked Mitchell up from school and took him back to her office. They had some things to discuss that couldn't be said at his home. Later, she had his mother's permission to take him Christmas shopping with the money Collin had paid him for working with the animals. No matter that she'd already spent two hours at the mall, shopping was something Mia could always do.

Mitchell looked scruffy and smelled worse. She hoped the odor was normal boy sweat and not cigarette smoke. He'd come too far these six months to regress now.

Once inside her small office, she handed him a stick of beef jerky and motioned to a chair. "Sit down. We need to talk."

He ripped into the jerky. "About Collin?"

That surprised her. "Why do you think this is about Collin?"

One shoulder hitched. He flopped into the chair. "Since we didn't go out to his place, I figure something's up. He said I don't have to come anymore."

"You don't."

"I guess he's tired of me hanging around."

Mia rounded her desk and sat down. "You know that's not true. Your official community service time is completed so nobody will force you to work on the farm anymore. Now the decision to go or not is yours to make."

"Did he and Adam find the guy who started the fire?"

"They think so."

He chewed thoughtfully, then spoke around a wad of jerky. "I don't."

Mia frowned. "What do you mean?"

Mitchell took a sudden interest in the tip of his beef stick. "Nothing."

"Is there something you want to tell me?"

He slouched a little lower in the chair. "No."

Which meant there was.

She sighed and let the subject drop. Mitchell shared confidences according to his timetable, not hers. "Collin needs your help now more than ever."

"It really stinks about his brother. I wish I could do something."

"You already do. You help with the animals. Keep him company. Cheer him up. He depends on you." The boy *was* good for Collin, and the cop was finally at a place where he could realize as much.

Mitchell sat up straighter. "Yeah. I guess he does. He hates mucking out stalls." One tennis-shoed foot banged the front of her desk. "But I meant about his brother."

"We can't do anything about Drew's death, Mitch."

"I meant the other one."

She smiled. "Sooner or later, we'll find Ian."

She let a couple of seconds pass. The subject she

needed to broach wasn't a good one. Muffled voices came and went outside her closed door.

"You want a Coke?" she asked to soften him up.

"Nah."

"Later, then. We'll go to that Mexican place you like."

"Cool." His toe tapped the front of her metal desk over and over again.

Mia picked up a pen. Put it down. Took it up again. "We need to discuss your stepdad."

Mitchell stiffened. The thudding against her desk ceased. He didn't look up.

"I know you're scared of him."

No answer.

"I talked to your mother about going to a women's shelter, but she refuses. She says there's nothing wrong. Frankly, I don't believe her, and I'm worried about both of you." When he didn't respond, she dropped the pen and leaned toward him. She was getting nowhere with this one-sided conversation.

"Mitch, if something should happen, anything at all, if you should ever be afraid, will you call me? Or Collin?"

He thought about her question for several seconds while a telephone rang in another office and a door down the hall slammed shut. Finally, he nodded. "Yeah."

That was the best she was going to get. She rubbed the back of her neck and stretched. "I'll trust you on that."

Her office door opened and another social worker peeked inside. "Mia, could I see you for a minute?"

"Of course." She stood and said to Mitch, "Stay put, okay?" She glanced at the clock. "When I get back we'll head for the mall."

"Can I play on your computer?"

"Sure. And have another beef jerky. I'll be back in a few minutes."

Three days later, Collin bounded up the stairs to the second floor of the Department of Human Services. Mia had said she loved him, but he'd never believed she'd do this.

She looked up from a stack of paperwork, the kind of overwhelming mountain he understood too well. Jammed into one corner of her office, a miniature Christmas tree blinked multicolored lights. A whimsical Santa waved from the wall behind her desk, and Christmas carols issued from her computer speakers.

"Oh, hi, Collin." Mia's face lit up. "I got your note."

"Sorry I missed you." More than sorry. Every day since she'd said those shocking words he'd found an excuse to talk to her, either in person or on the phone. The last couple of days she'd been out of contact and he'd missed her. He'd wanted to surprise her with a special offer that was sure to make her happy. Instead, she'd surprised him.

Somehow the knowledge that she loved him had changed him. He wasn't sure what was happening inside him, but he liked the difference. He felt lighter, happier, freer, which made no sense at all considering the news of Drew's death.

But then today in his mailbox... He slapped the brown envelope down onto her desk. He could never repay her for this.

"This is the best news I've had in a long time."

She grinned at his unusual enthusiasm. "You could use some good news."

He didn't want to think she'd done this out of pity, but if he told the truth, he didn't really care why she'd done it.

"I think this is Ian, don't you?"

She blinked, puzzled. "Excuse me?"

He slid a sheet of paper from the envelope and laid the all-important document in front of her. "I think this is my Ian. I think this is the agency that handled his adoption."

And he hadn't even known Ian was adopted. Part of him rejoiced. At least one brother had found a family.

"Collin, I don't know what you're talking about—" She froze in midsentence as her eyes moved across the confidential document.

All the color drained from her face. Disbelief mixed with hurt, she shot to her feet. Rollers clattered as her chair thunked against the wall behind her. "I can't believe this, Collin. How could you?"

Now he was confused. "How could I what?"

"Break into these confidential files. Compromise me this way. I thought we were at least friends."

They were friends. A lot more than friends. "What are you talking about?"

"You were here in my office while I was gone."

He rocked back, stunned at the unspoken accusation. "You think I broke into your files?"

"What else can I think? This document is from a sealed adoption file. No one, not even me, is supposed to look at those files without express permission or a court order."

He knew how important her professional integrity was. He'd never even considered such a thing. "I wouldn't do that."

"Somebody did."

His jaw grew hard enough to bite through concrete as her accusation hit home. "And you think it was me."

She stared at the twinkling Christmas tree. He sensed a battle going on behind those warm gray-green eyes, but her silence was an affirmation. Finally she said, "Who else would want to?"

He had an idea but if she couldn't figure that one out on her own, he wasn't about to toss out accusations. Not like she'd done. "You'll have to trust me on this, Mia."

She pushed the sheet of paper back into the envelope and handed the packet across the desk. Her hands trembled. "I hope you find him."

"Will you help me?" He needed her. And he wanted her there beside him when Ian was found.

She shook her head, expression bleak. "I'm sorry, Collin. I can't."

She didn't believe him.

All his joy shriveled into a dusty wad. He'd finally let a woman into his heart and she couldn't even give him her trust. Some love that was.

Fine. Dandy. He should have known.

He yanked the envelope from the desk and stalked out.

Mia locked the door of her office and cried. From her computer radio, Karen Carpenter's lush voice sang "Merry Christmas, Darling." She clicked Mute.

How could Collin have done such a thing? He'd been in here two days ago, at her desk while she was at lunch. He'd even left a note. She'd wanted to believe he wouldn't do this to her, but how could she? Hadn't he pressured her more than once to open those files?

Over and over she remembered when Gabe had badgered confidential information from her. Just like Collin he'd said, "Trust me, Mia. You know I wouldn't do anything that could hurt you."

But in the end, her actions on his behalf had hurt her plenty. She'd lost her job and her credibility. And though Gabe had worked hard to make the loss up to her, she couldn't forget the awful sense of betrayal and shame.

Her own flesh-and-blood brother had compromised her for his own gain. How could she believe that Collin wouldn't do the same for a much more worthwhile reason?

Not that she wasn't glad he had the information about Ian. She only wished he'd come by it more honestly.

Collin stewed for two days, hammering away his anger on the barn that didn't seem to be getting any larger.

He hadn't broken into Mia's computer, but even if he had, he wouldn't lie about it. Why couldn't she see that? He'd considered questioning Mitch, but why bother? The deed was done and Mia blamed him.

If he'd known falling for a Christian was this much trouble, he would have run even harder the day she'd bought him a hamburger.

His cell phone rang and he slapped the device from his belt loop. "Grace."

"Mr. Grace, this is the Loving Homes Adoption Agency in Baton Rouge. I think I may have some information for you."

His heart slammed against his rib cage. His hammer dropped to the ground. Happy gazed up at him, puzzled as he grappled in his shirt pocket for a pencil. With shaking fingers, he scribbled the information on a piece of plywood.

His brother's name might be Ian Carpenter.

Everything in him wanted to call Mia, to share the excitement of finally having a concrete lead.

But he wouldn't. She wouldn't want him to.

Chapter Fourteen

The call came in at ten minutes to nine in the morning. A hostage situation. The suspect a convicted felon, armed and dangerous. And probably high on drugs.

Collin donned his gear along with the rest of the Tac-team members as the captain drilled them on the situation. During the serving of a warrant, the suspect had gone ballistic and taken a woman hostage, probably the common-law wife.

Collin exchanged glances with Maurice. He knew his buddy was already praying and he was glad. In situations like this, they needed all the help they could get. The Christmas holidays were high-stress periods. If anyone was going off the deep end, this time of year seemed to bring it on.

As the van approached the neighborhood, Collin grew uneasy. He knew this area.

"This is the Perez house," he said.

Captain Gonzales nodded. "Isn't that the name of the kid you've been mentoring?"

"Yeah. Is he in there?"

"Not anymore. We just got a call from Shipley on somebody's cell phone. There's a social worker inside with him. Not the wife."

Collin's blood ran cold. "Who's the social worker?"

He already knew before the captain spoke. "Adam Carano's sister, Mia. You know her?"

He and Maurice exchanged quick glances.

"We've met." What was Mia doing in there? Hadn't he told her to stay away?

The captain gave him a strange look. He'd told no one except Maurice about his friendship with Mia. If the captain knew he was personally involved he'd send him back to the station. No way Collin was going to leave Mia at the mercy of some doped-up maniac whose last address was the state penitentiary.

Keeping his face passive, he readied his equipment, mind racing with the possibilities. Anything could go down in a situation like this. Anything.

"Why's the social worker involved? Was she there to grab the kid?"

"Bad timing, I think. She was inside when an arrest warrant was served. Shipley flipped out when he saw the cops approaching, and took her hostage."

Dandy.

"Anyone else in the house?"

"We don't know that yet, either. Jeff is working on

getting the floor plans from the rental company that owns the house. Gomez is talking to neighbors to see what they know."

They set up a command post in the parking lot of an apartment complex across the street. Team members quietly dispersed around the property while uniformed officers blocked off the streets and cleared the surrounding area of bystanders.

Collin climbed to the second floor of the apartment building, seeking an advantageous position from which to view the Perez place. Adrenaline raced through his bloodstream at a far greater rate than usual in a call-out. He'd practiced this scenario a thousand times. Had even executed it. But no one he loved had ever been inside the premises.

He squeezed his eyes shut and rubbed a hand over his forehead. Of all the times to realize he was in love, he'd sure picked a doozy.

Through the earpiece in his helmet he heard the captain. They'd made contact with Teddy Shipley. The guy was spewing all kinds of irrationalities, blaming the cops for harassing him, for his inability to get a job, asking for money, a car, amnesty from prosecution.

For the next hour and a half, the negotiator tried to soothe the frenzied suspect. Collin wished like crazy he could hear the conversation but all his information was filtered through the commander. He could hear the other officers, and from his vantage point above the scene he watched the stealth movement of Tac members maneuvering closer to the house, hoping for a chance.

After a while, the suspect moved the hostage into the living room, though even through his scope, Collin could see only their shadowy forms. One of those shadows belonged to Mia. The other much larger form definitely brandished a weapon. And as much as Collin wanted to charge the place and take the guy out with his own hands, right now all he could do was wait.

By noon, the tension hung as thick as L.A. fog. Shipley grew angrier and more demanding by the minute.

Collin, jaw tight, spoke into his mouthpiece. "Has anyone talked to the hostage?"

The answer crackled back. "Yes. She sounded okay. Scared, but pretty calm under the circumstances. We gathered from her subtle answers that Shipley is popping pills on top of meth. He's seriously messed up."

No big surprise there. Collin ground his teeth. No surprise but a really big problem.

At one o'clock, food was brought in. No one bothered to eat it.

At two o'clock, the negotiator still had not established a rapport. The suspect was spewing vitriol with the frequency and strength of a geyser. He was sick of being harassed. He wasn't taking it anymore. He wasn't going back to the pen. And scariest of all, they'd never take him alive.

By three in the afternoon, hope for a peaceful resolution was fading. Shipley came to the dirty window, dragging Mia with him, a nine millimeter at her temple. Collin saw her expression through his scope. Saw the fear in her eyes, the bruises on her face. Hot fury ripped through him.

Collin knew the minute Shipley spotted an officer outside the house. Wild-eyed and crazed, he fired one shot through the picture window. Glass shattered. Shipley shoved Mia toward the opening, screaming threats.

They had an active shooter with a hostage. Things could go south fast. Real fast.

The question came through his earpiece, terse but strong. "Have you got a visual?"

"Yeah." For a man whose knees had turned to water, his voice sounded eerily calm.

He slid down onto his belly, the rough shingles scraping against his vest. He had a visual, but Mia was in the way.

"If you have the shot, take it."

The surge of adrenaline prickled his scalp. His mouth went dry. To his horror, his hands, renowned for their steadiness, began to shake.

In twelve years on the force, he'd never missed, never been scared, not even when he took down a cop killer. But Mia had never been the hostage. Her bright red Christmas sweater and frightened eyes were imprinted in his brain.

What if he hit the woman he loved more than his own life? What if the ice-water-in-his-veins sniper they called Amazing Grace missed?

The December temperature was in the thirties, but sweat broke out all over Collin.

He was the only person standing between Mia and the maniac, and he was terrified.

He couldn't do this. But there was no one else. The other sniper had no shot. Mia's life was in his hands—hands that wouldn't stop shaking.

He needed help. And there was only one place to get it.

Intent on the house, he was afraid to blink and too focused to move. Under the circumstances, he figured God would understand if his prayers weren't too formal. There was no time to close his eyes and bow his head.

"Help me, Lord. I can't handle this one. Steady me. Give me the perfect shot. For Mia."

Then as if God had actually heard him, the strangest thing happened. His hands and guts stopped trembling. The usual cool detachment settled over him. Only the feeling wasn't cool. It was warm, comforting. Something incredible had just happened to him, but he had no time to dwell on it.

"Thanks," he whispered. Later, he'd do a lot better.

His gaze flicked from the felon to Mia. Eyes wide, she stared outward toward the invisible cops. As if in slow motion, Collin saw her mouth move. For a second, he thought she was praying, too, but then through his scope, he read her lips.

"Do it."

She knew he was out here. She knew he was the

sniper on duty. And she trusted him to take care of her. Mia trusted him.

And he wasn't about to let her down.

With exacting skill, he trained the sights on the suspect and waited for the precise moment. No muscle quivered. Not an eyelash blinked.

Suddenly, Mia slumped in a faint.

Collin pulled the trigger. The crack ripped the air, and the suspect crumpled.

In the next few milliseconds that seemed like hours, the Tac-team swarmed the house. Voices screamed in his earpiece.

"Suspect down. Suspect down."

Collin pushed up from the roof. A minute ago, he'd been deadly calm. Now his legs wobbled with such force he wasn't sure he could walk. Rifle in hand, he started down. He made it to the first-floor stairwell and collapsed, sliding down with his back against the hard, block wall.

He could have killed her. He could have hit Mia.

"I will never leave you nor forsake you."

The words entered his head unbidden and he knew they didn't come from him. He shoved one hand into his pocket and withdrew the little keychain.

"Thank you," he muttered. Keychain in his fisted hand, he pressed the little fish to his mouth, dropped his head to his elevated knees, and did something he hadn't done since he was ten years old.

He wept.

* * *

"I don't need an ambulance. I'm okay. Really." Mia struggled against the strong arms of too many paramedics and police officers who wanted her to get into the ambulance. There was only one cop she wanted to see and he was nowhere around.

"Humor us, Mia." Maurice Johnson's familiar face materialized from the crowd. "You're in shock."

Maybe she was in shock. Except for an overriding sense of relief, she felt numb.

A paramedic wrapped a blood pressure cuff around her arm. As she started to resist, her knees buckled. Maurice grabbed her slumping form and helped the paramedic lift her into the back of the ambulance.

"Where's Collin?" she asked. The bruise on her cheekbone started to throb and her head swam.

"Right here."

A tall, lean officer in SWAT uniform pushed through the crowd. His handsome face exhausted, he was the most wonderful thing she'd ever seen.

"Collin," she said, and heard the wobble in her voice, felt the tears in her eyes. She dove out of the ambulance into the strongest arms imaginable. Collin wouldn't let her fall.

"I'm sorry. I was so wrong. I do trust you. I do." The tears came in earnest then.

"I know." His lips brushed her ear. "It's okay. Everything is okay now."

She searched his face and saw something new. A peace she hadn't seen before.

He was still strong and solid and every bit the confident police officer, but something about him had changed.

Later, she'd have to ask. Yes, later, she thought, as she snuggled against his chest and the world went dark.

Collin didn't bother to clean up. Still in uniform, he made one stop before heading to the hospital.

When he walked into the room, Mia was sitting in a hospital bed, chattering at mach speed to convince a young doctor to let her go home.

"Might as well say yes," Collin said.

The blond resident gave him a weary smile. "Persistent, is she?"

"Like a terrier. She'll yap until you give in."

"You sound like a man of experience."

Collin looked at the smiling Mia and his heart wrenched. Her pretty face was swollen and bruised from eye to chin. But that didn't keep her from talking.

"Just trust me on this." He winked at Mia. "And let her go. She'll be well taken care of. I can promise you that."

The doctor scribbled something on the chart and dropped the clipboard into a slot at the foot of the bed. "I'll see what I can do."

As he left, Collin scraped a heavy green chair up to the bedside. "How ya doin'?"

"Better. How are you?"

No one had ever asked him that before except the force psychologist.

"It's part of the job."

"I didn't ask you that." She took the single red rose from him and pressed the bud to her nose. "I knew you were out there today. And I knew you and God would take care of me."

"How?"

She tapped her heart. "I felt you. In here. Just the way I felt God's presence. You saved my life."

Just thinking about what could have happened made Collin want to crush her to him and never let her go. "I've never been that scared."

"You?"

"Terrified," he admitted. "I prayed, Mia. And the strangest thing happened. My hands were shaking and I couldn't do my job. One prayer later, I'm a changed man."

"Oh, Collin." Hope flared in her sweet eyes.

He smiled, the tenderness inside him a scary thing. He had to tell her. He had to say the words no matter how difficult. With Mia, he could be vulnerable.

"I realized that I need God in my life even more than I need you. And I need you more than my next breath. I love you, Mia. Please say you haven't given up on me."

Collin had never seen an angel, but he couldn't imagine anything more beautiful than the expression on Mia's face.

"I don't ever give up, Collin. Don't you know that by now?" She shifted on the bed, grimaced at the IV in her arm. "Mitchell came by with another social worker. He wanted to tell me not to be mad at you anymore."

"He broke into your confidential files?"

"How did you guess?"

"I figured as much all along."

"And said nothing."

"Now don't get your back up. I wanted him to be man enough to own up to mistakes on his own."

"He told us something else, too. Shipley set your barn on fire. Revenge for messing in his business, as he put it. He's just a mean man."

Now that was a stunner. "I guess I owe my neighbor an apology on that at least."

"What about the lawsuit?"

"You brother convinced Mr. Slokum to play nice. He dropped the case when Adam brought up the half brother."

"Adam's a good lawyer."

"What's going to happen to Mitch now?" He hated to ask the obvious. "Foster care?"

She offered a smug smile. "Yes, but I have a plan."

"Which means someone is about to be hit by a bull-dozer named Mia."

"The people I have in mind are used to it."

"If you're thinking who I'm thinking, I approve."

"Mom and Dad love him. He's crazy about them. They're starting the paperwork and foster-care classes, but I think I can pull a few strings so he can live with them now while his mom is in treatment."

"Miss Carano, I love you. Even if you are a social worker."

With a relieved and happy heart, he leaned across the metal rail and kissed her. When she didn't protest, he kissed her again. This time she kissed him back.

Epilogue

The halls were decked with tinsel and garland and rows and rows of white lights. Christmas carols played softly, and the stockings really were hung by the chimney with care.

The Carano Christmas was in full swing. Mia had managed to spirit Collin away from the prying eyes and teasing brothers to give him her gift in private.

"Open your present."

"I don't need presents. I have you, your awesome family and an even more awesome relationship with Christ. What more could a man want?"

He was different since accepting the Lord into his life. Not that his quiet personality had changed, but he was less tense, warmer, freer.

She pressed a small box, wrapped in shiny blue paper and topped with silver ribbon, into his hands. "Don't argue with me, mister. You know I'll win."

Mia watched him, her heart in her throat. He took

his time sliding the ribbon over the corners. Turning the box over and over, he slowly caressed the slick, smooth foil with his fingertips.

Mia bubbled with impatience, but she didn't interfere. He grinned up at her. "I haven't done this many times. Let me enjoy the moment."

The notion that his Christmases weren't filled with good memories stabbed at her. She was determined to make up for lost time, and her family felt the same. They'd finally managed to draw him into the fold and he had begun giving back the banter, though his was still far more reserved than Nic's or Adam's.

Finally, when Mia thought she'd have to rip the gift from his hands and open the box herself, he pulled away the last bit of tape. Tissue paper crinkled as he lifted out the blue-and-white Christmas ornament.

The fragile bulb, held gently in his palm, glimmered beneath the bright light. The old black-and-white photo of three small boys was perfectly centered amidst a snowy Christmas scene. Collin, Drew and Ian in a photo she'd found stuck in a file.

"How did you—?"

The expression on his face was one she would never forget. The cop who hid his feelings couldn't hide them now.

Awe. Yearning. Joy.

With exquisite care, he replaced the bulb and set the box aside to wrap his arms around Mia.

She knew him. Knew he would struggle with the

right words to express his feelings. His heart thundered against her ear. She heard him swallow once. Twice.

"I knew you'd love it."

"Yeah." His chest rose and fell as he continued to press back a tide of emotion. This was one of the things she'd learned to love the most about him. He was so deeply emotional. He felt things so intensely, but all his life he'd stuffed them deeper to avoid hurt.

Finally, he sighed and then with the same sweet tenderness kissed the top of her head. "It's the best present I've ever had."

"Want to hang it on the tree?"

He cast a sideways glance toward the noisy living room. "Dare we go back in there?"

"Actually, I'd rather stay right here with you forever."

"But your brothers would never allow that to happen."

As if on cue, Adam's voice yelled down the hallway. "What's taking you two so long? We got a party going on in here."

"Yeah," Nic hollered. "And I wanna open my presents."

Mia giggled and took Collin's hand. "Be brave."

Such a silly thing to say to a man who had never been anything else in his entire life.

As they entered the living room, everyone quieted. Mitchell stood by the enormous Christmas tree with Nic, Adam and Gabe. Each male wore a Cheshire grin.

"Now you've corrupted Mitchell," she said to them. "What are you up to?"

They all looked at Collin. He, in turn, flicked at glance at her dad who gave a slight nod. Her mother and grandmother, each holding one of Gabe's kids, beamed from the couch. Her very pregnant sister, Anna Maria, waddled across the room and handed Collin a beautiful maroon velvet box topped with a gold plaid bow.

He cleared his throat. "Your present," he said.

Mia got a fluttery feeling in the pit of her stomach. Her gaze ran around the room, saw the intense, excited faces of all the people who loved her best. Gabe aimed the video camera in her direction.

They knew something she didn't.

She lifted the lid and frowned in puzzlement. Lavender rose petals sprang out of the box and fluttered to the floor. She plunged her hands into the velvety petals, releasing the rich spicy scent as she pulled out yet another box. A velvet jeweler's box.

She gasped and looked up at Collin, her mouth open in surprise.

"Look, guys," Nic muttered. "Mia's speechless."

She was too stunned and thrilled to react to the titter of amusement circling the warm, festive room.

"Mia." Collin took the final box from her shaking fingers and went down on one knee in front of her. "I'm not too good with words." He cleared his throat again.

One of the brothers guffawed. Collin slanted him a look. "Give me a break, Nic."

"Want me to ask her for you?"

"Shut up, Adam," Mia said good-naturedly. She touched a trembling palm to Collin's cheek. "You were saying?"

"I love you."

"I love you, too."

"All my life I've distrusted other people. I've kept them on the outside. But you wouldn't let me do that. You forced me to open up, to feel. And I'm so glad you did. To love and know that I'm loved back is an awesome thing."

Mia's heart was about to burst with love. She knew how hard this was for him. For a man of few words, he'd just said a mouthful.

In the background came the soft strains of "I'll Be Home for Christmas."

"Mia." A quiver ran from Collin's hand into hers. He bent his head and placed a whisper of a kiss upon her hand, then slid the ring onto her finger. "Will you marry me?"

Tears sprang into her eyes.

"Yes, I will," was all she could manage as she collapsed against him. Sure and strong, he absorbed the impact and rocked her back and forth, laughing and laughing while she sobbed into his shoulder.

Much later, after Mia's brothers and dad had pounded his back in congratulations and the ladies had kissed his cheek declaring this the most romantic proposal they'd ever witnessed, Collin finally stopped shaking. He'd known how important Mia's family was to her and proposing this way would make her happy. He just hadn't known how nervous he'd be.

Then as if to overwhelm him to the point of no return, Mia's brothers had pledged their time and talents along with that of their church—now his church, too—to help rebuild and expand his animal rehab facility. Their Christmas gift to him and the animals, they'd said. And he was too moved to speak.

"Spiced cider, anyone?" Rosalie manned the large urn that emitted the rich scents of cinnamon and apple.

Standing with his back against the cold patio doors, his new fiancée leaning into him, the fragrance of her perfume embracing him, Collin felt more content than he could remember. He didn't need or want anything else.

Well, perhaps one other thing. "Could I tell you something?" he murmured against Mia's hair.

"Anything." She twisted around to smile at him and he couldn't resist another kiss.

"I followed up on that information Mitchell found."

She was quiet for a moment and he hoped he hadn't rekindled her anger over the unfortunate incident. "I'm glad."

"You are?"

"God turned Mitchell's mistake into something good. How could I be upset about that?"

He should have known she'd say that. "I have a phone number and a name. Someone who may be Ian."

She whirled around, sliding her arms around his waist, her expression joyous. "Collin, that's wonderful! Have you called? What did he say? When are you going to meet him?"

He swallowed a laugh. "Whoa, Miss Bulldog. I have the name and number but I haven't called yet."

"Why not?" But being Mia, she answered her own question. "You're nervous."

"Scared spitless. What if it isn't him?"

"What if it is?" She grabbed his arms and shook him a little. "Collin, you may have found Ian. Come on. Let's call right now. Where is that number?"

He took the slip of paper from his shirt pocket and shared the bits of information. "Ian Carpenter. The dates match. The age matches. I think it's him, but I've had hope before."

"This time, my love, you have something else. You have a family who will always love you and stand with you no matter what. And best of all you have the Lord. He'll—"

"Never leave me nor forsake me," Collin finished with a smile, feeling the truth of her words. He was full to the brim with the kind of love he'd craved all his life. Finding Ian would be icing on his very sweet cake.

He reached into his pocket and took out the small fish keychain, now polished to a pewter gleam.

Mia smiled gently, her face full of love, and stretched

out a palm. Instead of handing her the keychain, he took her hand. "I love you, Mia."

"I love you, Collin."

"Good." He drew in a breath, feeling the strength of his faith urging him on. "Let's go make that call."

* * * * *

Dear Reader,

In my other career, I'm an elementary school teacher. Some years ago my principal asked me to remain in the hallway after school for a few minutes. Social Services was on the way to pick up three of our students. My job was to meet the caseworker and direct her to the office. As long as I live, I will remember the scene inside that room. The three children, one stoic and accepting, one furious and fighting, and the last one silently crying, are imprinted on my memory forever. I've never been able to forget them. I've often wondered what happened to them, where they are now. They haunted me until the only way I could find closure was to create a story for each one, and of course, to give them the happy endings every child deserves. I'm so pleased to bring this heartfelt new series, The Brothers' Bond, to you. I hope you fall in love with each one of "my boys," beginning this month with Collin.

I love hearing from readers. Please visit my website at www.lindagoodnight.com or send an email to linda@lindagoodnight.com.

Blessings to you and yours,

Linda Goodnight

THE HEART OF GRACE

Though you have made me see troubles, many and bitter, you will restore my life again; from the depths of the earth you will again bring me up.
—*Psalms* 71:20

To Gene, with all my love.

Prologue

Drew Grace jerked away from the office door and whirled, poised to run. A social worker was in there. He knew what that meant. It meant trouble.

Heart pounding, he pushed at the teacher blocking his way. A pair of strong hands, those of the school counselor, Mr. James, caught his shoulders and forced him inside the long narrow office.

Fury ripped through Drew, hot and powerful. He doubled up his fist. He might be only seven but he was tough and he could fight. He wasn't ever scared to fight no matter how big the other guy. Anybody that didn't believe that could ask Timothy Wilson. Timothy was in fourth grade but Drew bloodied his nose and made him cry yesterday on the playground. Stupid idiot said Drew stunk. So maybe he did. Big deal. It wasn't none of Timothy's business anyway.

"Sit down, Drew," Mr. James said. "We need to talk to you boys about something."

Talk. Yeah, sure. Drew knew better. They weren't going to talk. They were going to drag him and his brothers off to foster care again.

He wasn't going. Foster parents never liked him. They were mean. They said he was a troublemaker.

Well, he didn't like them, either. If grown-ups would just leave them alone, they'd be okay. Or if Mama would come home. When she was in the chips she brought them presents. That's what she said, in the chips.

His heart hurt a little to think of Mama. And that just made him madder. He slammed the clenched fist into the social worker's gut and pushed past her. Mr. James grabbed him around the waist. Kicking, flailing with all his might, Drew growled like a mad dog as the counselor pushed him into a chair.

Drew gazed frantically around the room looking for escape. He had to get out of here.

His big brother Collin stood beside the counselor's desk, face as cold and hard as ice, arms tight at his sides. Drew knew that look. Collin was mad and probably scared, too, though he always said he wasn't.

His baby brother Ian sat in a chair at the end of the room. Silent tears made dirty streaks on his face. Poor little kid. He was always nice to everybody. He was still in pre-K so what did he know. Ian didn't yet understand all the things that Drew and Collin did. Sometimes you couldn't be nice.

Drew tried to take care of Ian 'cause he was so little.

Well, Drew and Collin together. Collin always knew the best places to find food and stuff.

They had a hiding place, a good one. If he could just get out of here, he'd head there. Maybe the teachers would chase him and give Collin and Ian a chance to escape, too. He was fast. He could outrun them. Then he'd be the hero, and his brothers would give him the biggest share of food. They'd make a fire and build a fort. Just him and his brothers against the world. They could do it.

Sometimes Collin got them out of trouble. But not always. Drew knew he couldn't count on anything when adults were involved. He and Ian and Collin could make it okay by themselves. They always had.

Drew knew how to make a fire. He liked fire. He liked to watch the flames lick up the side of paper and turn it bright orange. He liked the smell of matches.

Just then some nosy teacher walked by and stuck her fat head inside the office. Behind glasses, her eyes bugged out.

"Poor little things," he heard her whisper right before the social worker shut the door in her face. "Living in that old burned-out trailer, that trashy mother gone half the time. No wonder they're filthy."

Drew exploded out of the chair and started toward the door. He'd make her pay for saying that.

But once again, Mr. James caught him. This time he wasn't too gentle. He pushed Drew down into the plastic chair and held him there. Most times Drew liked Mr. James okay, but not today.

"Collin," the social worker said to his big brother. She had a hand on her belly where Drew had punched her. He didn't care. She shouldn't be sticking her nose into his business. That's what Mama said. If welfare would just keep their nose out of her business, everything would be fine. "You've been through this before. You know it's for the best. Why don't you help us get your brothers in the car?"

Collin ignored her. Drew figured his brother was thinking the same thing he was. They had to get out of here.

Ian started sniveling, making hiccuping sounds like he was trying to keep from crying. Drew wanted to go to him and say everything would be okay. But he'd be lying. He didn't want to lie to his brother. Besides, Mr. James was holding him down like a wrestler and wouldn't let him up.

Collin must have noticed Ian, too, because he walked right past that social worker like he didn't even see her and laid a hand on Ian's head. Ian looked up at Collin with wet blue eyes and stopped crying. He kind of shivered like a cold kitten, and Drew got mad all over again. A little kid like that shouldn't have to be scared all the time.

The social worker must have noticed Ian crying, too, because she knelt in front of his chair and told some big lie about taking them to a nice house and buying them all new shoes. Poor kid believed every word. Drew wished it was true, but it wasn't.

Mr. James, who smelled like spearmint gum, loosened his hold the slightest bit and slid to his knees in front of Drew's chair. Drew hoped this was his chance. Mr. James, who coached baseball and was stronger than some of the high school football players, wasn't a dummy. He kept one big hand on Drew's arm and another on his knee.

"Boys," he said, looking around at all three of them. "Sometimes life throws us a curveball. Things happen that we don't expect. But I want you to know one thing." He stared over at the social worker. She was still on her knees in front of Ian. "No matter where you go from here or what happens, you have a friend who will never leave you. His name is Jesus. If you let Him, He'll take care of you."

Something inside Drew quieted. He knew who Jesus was though he'd never been to church. He didn't know how he knew but he did. And even if it was a lie, he liked thinking that there was somebody somewhere that wouldn't leave him and his brothers alone.

"Collin?" Mr. James said and twisted around, holding his hand out. When Collin ignored him, the counselor laid the hand on Collin's worn-out shoe and bowed his head. He started whispering something and Drew knew Mr. James was praying. Praying for Collin and Ian and him.

Drew got a funny lump in his chest, like he might

cry. He squeezed his eyes shut. Mr. James loosened his hold, but Drew didn't try to run. He wasn't mad at Mr. James, not really. He wanted Mr. James to take him home with him and teach him how to play baseball.

When the prayer was over, Drew opened his eyes, curious. The room was real quiet. Even Ian had stopped whimpering.

Mr. James reached into his pocket and pulled out some little key chains and handed them each one. Drew gazed at his, curious about the silver metal fish with words on the back.

He was in second grade. He could read. But not that good.

"I want you to have one of these," the counselor said. He stared at the social worker again in a way Drew didn't understand, like he was daring her to say anything. She looked down and fiddled with the floppy sole of Ian's shoe. "It's a reminder of what I said, that God will watch over you no matter where you go or what you do."

"Where we going this time?" Collin asked, voice hard and mad.

"I have placements for Drew and Ian."

"Together?"

Drew's head jerked up. They always stayed together. They had to stay together.

"Not this time. All the placements are separate."

Blood pounded in Drew's head. He clenched the key chain until the metal bit into his skin.

"Ian gets scared," Collin said, his voice shaky. "He stays with me."

Collin was right. Ian needed his big brothers. They needed each other. All for one, one for all. Like the Three Musketeers movie they saw at a friend's house.

Drew's blood started to heat up again. Separate placements. Places for bad boys. For troublemakers.

He looked frantically at Collin. Why didn't Collin say something? Why didn't he tell her that they couldn't be separated? They'd die if they weren't together.

He opened his mouth to say so, but only a growl came out.

"I'm sorry, boys. This will work out for the best. You'll see." The social worker tried to sound jolly, but Drew was no fool.

They would be separated. Him and Collin and Ian. He would never see his brothers again.

He said a cussword and bolted toward the door. Too late, too late. Mr. James picked him up and carried him out the door, kicking and screaming.

Chapter One

Twenty-three years later, Iraq

Life as he knew it was about to end.

Drew Michaels had made a mistake and now he had to pay the price. No matter how much it hurt, no matter how badly he wanted to hang on, he had to let go of the most important thing in his life—his marriage.

He just hoped he could survive the aftermath.

"Mr. Michaels, take a shot of that."

Camera ever ready, Drew followed the direction of his driver's pointed finger but didn't press the shutter. He was on assignment somewhere outside Baghdad, and if he'd seen one herd of goats he'd seen them all. He wasn't in much of a mood today to take useless photos. Or any kind of photos, come to think of it. The memory of yesterday's telephone conversation with Larissa was too fresh and painful.

He'd finally told her the truth.

Well, not the real truth, but the truth she needed to hear. Their marriage had been a mistake, and he wanted a divorce.

Remembering her reaction made him want to shoot something all right, but not with his camera.

Larissa had cried. He hated himself for that, just as he hated himself for ever thinking he could make a woman like her happy. Any woman, for that matter. Drew Michaels didn't have what it took to settle down and be a husband and father. He wanted to. He just couldn't.

He and Amil, the amiable Iraqi driver, were bumping through another nameless village with the usual string of squat, sand-colored buildings and local citizens going about the normal business of living. Women in long, flowing *abayahs,* children herding goats with a stick, soldiers poised with automatic rifles.

Drew had spent so much time in the Middle East that the military presence had actually started to look normal to him.

Next week he was off to Indonesia. A volcano was on the howl, and disasters were his specialty. Earthquakes, volcanoes, famine, war. You name it, he shot it. Not the usual stuff though. That was boring. He either went for that elusive moment of ambient light or for the people, the human side, the kids. He was good and he knew it. In fact, photography was the only thing he'd ever been good at. If he'd stuck to his work, he wouldn't be in this mess now.

Sand swirled up in front of the jeep and Drew shaded his face. Sunglasses weren't adequate protection against Middle Eastern sand and a photographer couldn't be too careful of his eyes.

Photographic art buffs said he had great artistic vision, an eye for the perfect detail. Able to capture an image that spoke to the consciousness.

He didn't know about all that, but he didn't argue. If they wanted to pay exorbitant prices for his photos, he'd take their money.

The memory of one particular photo exhibition shimmied to the surface. Tulsa. Three years ago.

He'd felt as phony as his last name. All those society types swarming around a display of his work, murmuring things like, "inspired," or "provocative."

He should have known then to cut and run. But he hadn't.

And then Larissa had walked toward him, an artsy diamond choker around her elegant neck, sparkling diamonds dangling from her ears. His eye for detail had served him well at that moment, though he'd wished for a camera to capture her. In a long white fitted gown of some satiny material, chestnut hair pulled up at the sides, one gleaming lock over a bare shoulder, she'd captivated him.

He'd never expected to love anybody, but he'd fallen in love with Larissa on the spot. It was stupid and foolish. Now he had to right the wrong he'd done to her.

"Another week and I'm out of here, Amil," he said to the driver.

"Going home to your woman, huh?"

His woman. The words poked at him like a sticker. He should have known back then that Larissa was too wonderful for a street bum like him. He should have known he didn't have what it took to be a husband.

Attention diverted by a soldier and an Iraqi toddler in a pink dress, Drew didn't bother to answer. Some things hurt too much to discuss.

A G.I., gun slung behind him, had gone down on both knees to tie a little girl's shoe. The contrast was stunning—an innocent toddler and a hardened marine gentled by a child's trust.

Drew pressed the shutter. Now *that* was a picture.

In front of them, two other jeeps bounced along. Though he normally worked alone, he'd been lucky to tag along on this trek into the countryside. They had a meeting with one of the tribal chiefs, and a man never knew what might come of that.

His vest rattled with rolls of film and various lenses as he reached into his inner pocket and removed a photo of Larissa. He'd taken hundreds of the woman who was his wife. She was a photographer's dream, all grace and class and innocence.

He clenched his teeth. His wife. The burning ache in his gut grew hotter. Must be getting an ulcer, a common malady for a disaster photographer.

Larissa was his love, his life, and his wife. But in

three years he'd never been the man she needed. The phone call yesterday had been the hardest call he'd ever made. He hadn't slept more than three hours all week, working up to that call.

Tulsa with Larissa was the only home he'd ever known, but now that was gone, too. He couldn't go back and face her. If he did, he might chicken out. For her sake, he'd remain abroad. And selfish as always, he'd lose himself in the job and leave the dirty work to his lawyer.

His chest pinched tight as he thought of all the things she wanted that he couldn't give her. Himself mostly, but lately she'd mentioned babies.

Even though the temperature outside hovered somewhere around a hundred and ten degrees, Drew shivered. Babies. The idea scared him more than walking through a minefield. Larissa didn't know, didn't understand the dark, secret reasons why he could never, ever father a child.

"She is very beautiful."

"What?" Drew glanced over at Amil. "Oh, Larissa. My wife." The words fell from his lips as if he needed to call her his as long as he could.

"You are a lucky man."

"She wants a baby," he blurted and then wondered why. It was a moot point now.

"So give her one. A fine son to carry on your name."

Which name? he wondered grimly. Michaels? Grace? Another of the reasons he had to let her go. Larissa had no clue she'd married a man who didn't exist. Wouldn't that be a shocker to her rich, politician daddy?

He'd done all right as Drew Michaels, though, and had gained a bit of a reputation with his work. Even if he did feel like a fraud most of the time, he was fine as long as no one else discovered the truth. But he wouldn't pass that legacy of lies on to an innocent child. He knew what happened to kids who came from bad bloodlines.

After making sure Amil's attention had returned to the convoy in front of them, Drew touched the photo to his lips, then slid it back into his vest. Over his heart. She *was* his heart and always would be, long after the ink was dried on the divorce papers, and she was happily married to some nice man who could give her all the babies she wanted.

"You come to Amil's house," the driver was saying. "I will show you sons. Seven of them, I have. They will make you smile and you can—" He lifted one hand from the steering wheel and pretended to snap pictures.

Drew was readying a wisecrack when suddenly, the world exploded.

In a split second of horror, he comprehended the sound and knew what was happening.

Attack. A roadside bomb. God help them all.

The last thing his conscious mind registered was the smile fading from Amil's face and the bizarre experience of flying backward out of the jeep, one hand frantically gripping his Nikon.

He screamed Larissa's name.

* * *

Larissa Stone Michaels sat straight up in bed, heart thundering louder than an Oklahoma rainstorm.

Another bad dream. The third time this week she'd awakened from a terrible nightmare that she couldn't remember. Any time Drew was in the Middle East, she suffered sleepless nights and bad dreams.

Then the memory of yesterday's phone conversation flooded into her consciousness. No wonder she'd had another nightmare. Drew wanted a divorce.

A sob choked out, loud in the silent bedroom. The little Yorkie, Coco, lying at the foot of the bed, raised her tiny head. Larissa pressed a hand to quivering lips, holding back the sorrow that had ended only when she'd finally fallen asleep.

She glanced at the illuminated clock on the curio lamp stand. Four in the morning. Less than three hours since she'd last noted the time.

Many nights she awakened unable to sleep until she'd prayed for Drew's safety. But this night was different. This night, she didn't have that sweet promise that her husband loved her and would be coming home to her.

He was never coming home again.

Tossing back the duvet comforter, she swung both feet to the plush carpet. Her body trembled. The soft whoosh of the heating unit was the only sound in the quiet Southside villa. Weary and heartsick, she went into the bathroom and flicked on the light. After a moment of blindness she found a glass, ran it full of water and drank deeply. The reflection in the mirror looked wild, dark hair tangled around a pale face.

"Oh, Drew," she whispered to the mirror. "What did I do? What happened?"

With grim determination, she swallowed hard against the ache in her throat, pushing back the tears. She couldn't keep doing this. She had to get hold of her emotions long enough to think things through.

She'd had no idea anything was wrong until the phone call. She loved him. Six months ago when he was home, everything had been as good as ever. Before he left for Iraq, he'd held her such a long time and told her how much he loved and needed her.

And now this.

"Jesus. Dear Jesus."

Hands braced on the sink, she squeezed her eyes tight and did the only thing she knew to do. She prayed. For Drew's safety, first and always. For their bewilderingly troubled marriage. For her breaking heart.

But this time the usual sense of peace evaded her. Her emotions were too raw and confused.

She returned to the bedroom, certain she'd slept her last. As she slipped beneath the petal-soft sheets, the phone rang.

A frightful pounding in her temples started up. A call at this time of night could not be good news.

She picked up the receiver and said, "Hello?"

And the nightmare began again. Only this time, she was awake.

Chapter Two

Drew hurt everywhere. His head, his leg, his back, his guts. Even his hair hurt.

He tried to open his eyes but they were too heavy. The drugs, he supposed. Drugs were good, but they didn't eliminate the pain. They only made him stupid, too groggy to form an intelligent sentence, too relaxed to care.

The first time he'd awakened after the blast, he'd been in a helicopter. The whump, whump, whump had sent him into violent tremors. Shock, the docs in Germany said.

Well, yes, he was shocked. Getting blown up wasn't on his list of fun things to do.

He wondered where his cameras were.

"Mr. Michaels." A male voice penetrated the haze. Someone lifted his wrist and felt his pulse. Hard, strong fingers. He wanted the voice to go away but figured he'd slept his allotted quota for the day.

Around this place fifteen minutes was tops before someone else came along to poke, prod or wheel him off to radiology. He'd been scanned and x-rayed so much he probably glowed in the dark. A radioactive photographer.

Funny. He had a brief image of using the glow from his body as available light to snap photos. All good photographers experimented with different light sources. And he was good. Really good. Everybody said so. Especially Larissa. She thought he was wonderful.

Larissa. The sharpest pain yet hit him.

Did she know how much he loved her? Did she know he was hurt? He hoped not. She'd be upset. He'd already caused her enough trouble.

The floaty feeling came back and he leaned into it, ready to go where it led. Thinking of Larissa hurt too much to remain conscious.

"Mr. Michaels."

With an inner sigh, Drew resurfaced and managed to raise his eyelids. Squinting at the bright light and too-white room, he saw his tormenter. A doctor. But he wasn't sure which one. That was one of the problems he'd been having. His memory wasn't as good as it used to be. Things were a little fuzzy. His head hurt. A lot.

"I've never been in a hospital," he grumbled.

"So you told me."

He had?

Eyes wider now, he focused on the physician's name

badge. Dr. Pascal. Neurology. "When can I get out of here?"

The doctor sidestepped the question with one of his own. "How's the vision? Any more problems?"

Drew's gut lurched. He didn't like thinking about the hours of blackness that had surrounded him after the blast. "Twenty-twenty."

"Let's have a look."

Drew wondered who *let's* was. Doctors all seemed to speak as if they were polymorphic. The God complex, he supposed.

His own drug-twisted humor amused him, but in truth, if he looked at the doc too long, he saw more than one. He sobered instantly. There was nothing funny about that.

Two were better than none, but still…

Dr. Pascal's thick fingers stretched Drew's eyelids apart while shining a pin light back and forth. Back and forth. The doc smelled like mouthwash and antiseptic soap.

"No more episodes of blindness? Double vision? Blurriness?"

"Some," he admitted, hating the truth but figuring the doc should know. "How long before it goes away for good?"

"No way to tell. You sustained a pretty nasty concussion, but the CAT scan didn't indicate anything permanent. If you're lucky, this will be gone by the time you are dismissed."

He'd only been lucky once in his life. The day he'd found Larissa. And look how that turned out.

If luck was required to heal his vision, he was in deep trouble.

The jitters in his belly turned to earthquakes. His eyes were everything. A photographer had to see and see clearly.

"Anything you can do for it?"

"Time." The doc fingered something on the bed-side table. "And divine intervention, if you believe in such things."

Drew raised his pounding head ever so slightly and saw the doctor holding the small pewter fish he usually wore on a leather string around his neck. His hand went to his throat. He never liked to be without it. Someone had been thoughtful enough to realize that.

"I'm not a religious man."

He saw no point in explaining to the doc or anyone else that the ichthus was his only link to the past and to the brothers he hadn't seen in more than twenty years. Other than this small reminder, he had nothing. He didn't even know where they were.

Like Larissa, his brothers were gone.

Something deep inside him began to ache. He wished the morphine would kick in again.

The memory of his two brothers, of that last day in the school counselor's office sometimes overwhelmed him, especially when he was weak or sick or overtired.

Times like now. For a few painful seconds, Ian and Collin hovered on the edge of his mind.

Ian, cute and small and loving had probably been adopted. No one could resist that little dude. And Collin. Well, Collin was like him, a survivor. Collin would be okay.

Sometimes he wondered what it would be like to find them again, to be with his brothers, but he couldn't. Never would. He was no longer Drew Grace, pitiful child of a crack queen. He was Drew Michaels, successful photographer. He never wanted anyone, especially Larissa, to discover that he was literally nobody—a nobody with a deadly secret and a gutful of guilt.

Over the years, he'd become a master at forcing his brothers back into the box inside his mind where the past resided.

He did that now, carefully, painstakingly shutting the door on the childish faces of Ian and Collin Grace.

"The brain is an interesting organ," Dr. Pascal said, handing him the necklace without comment.

Drew reclaimed the ichthus, but didn't answer. He didn't know how interesting his brain was and didn't much care. But he couldn't afford to lose the one thing that made him a photographer—his eyes.

"Most visual disturbances resolve as the swelling in your brain returns to normal."

Drew swallowed. His throat was raw and scratchy from what the nurses called intubation. Basically, having a tube stuffed down his throat during surgery.

"And when the problems don't resolve themselves?" he asked.

The doctor patted his shoulder. "No use borrowing trouble. You have enough to think about."

Drew was not comforted. "What happens next?"

"In a few days your surgeons and I will look at dismissal. But you're still weak from the blood loss."

"Tell me about it." He could barely feed himself.

"Losing your spleen is a serious operation. How's the incision?"

"The other docs looked at it this morning. At least, I think it was this morning. They said it was looking good."

"You're fortunate to be healthy and in good physical shape. It probably saved your life."

"I'm a survivor," he said grimly.

"You'll need some rehab on the shattered ankle and heel and plenty of time for the broken ribs to mend."

"So, are you sending me to one of those rehab places?"

The doc's brown eyes crinkled as if he was about to offer Drew the grand prize. "Wouldn't you rather go home?"

The question was a kick in the gut. Sure, he'd like to go home. Wherever that was.

Larissa's knees trembled as she traversed the long white corridor toward Drew's hospital room. For five days, she'd done nothing but pray and make telephone calls and argue with her parents. Even though she was thirty-two years old, they still attempted to run her life. To their way of thinking, she never should have married Drew. And she sure shouldn't run to his bedside after he'd announced his intention to divorce her.

But how could she not? He was her husband and she loved him.

Right now, she refused to deal with the pressure from her parents. Knowing her husband was lying in a hospital bed, seriously injured was all she could handle. The list of injuries was frightening, to say the least. Broken ribs, ankle, heel, a ruptured spleen, and too many cuts and bruises for anyone to tell her about on the telephone. She was terrified to see him.

Her Prada heels echoed in the sterile white environment. She reached room 4723 and stopped, suddenly short of breath, not from the climb but from the uncertainty.

How would Drew look? Would he be conscious? Was he in awful pain?

The new worry crowded in. Would he want her here? Would he be angry that she had come after he'd made it clear that he never wanted to see her again?

During the time Drew was in a military hospital in Germany, she'd called every day. He either hadn't been able or willing to speak to her. Now that he was here in Walter Reed, she'd given up calling. She'd gotten on a plane and come.

The fact that he'd initiated a divorce didn't mean anything at this point. Drew was her husband. He needed her. And she was going to take care of him whether he liked it or not. During his recovery, she would pray every single day for God to change Drew's mind and heal their marriage. A politician's daughter didn't give up without a fight.

Fingers on the handle, she paused to draw in a steadying breath.

"Help me, Lord," she whispered, and then slowly pushed the heavy door inward.

The semi-darkened room was quiet. Drew was alone, eyes closed. A shiver of relief rippled through her. Though bruised and sutured, he still looked like Drew.

She breathed a prayer of gratitude. A roadside bomb often did much worse. From the bits and pieces of information she'd gathered, the rest of the convoy hadn't fared as well.

Given the rhythmic motion of his chest, Drew was sleeping. An IV machine *tick-ticked* at his bedside, and his left leg was elevated on pillows. A medicine scent permeated the small unit. Monitors she couldn't name crowded in around his bed. The whole scenario was surreal and frightening.

Heart in her throat, Larissa tiptoed inside, careful not to wake him. She wanted a minute to drink him in, to love him with her eyes, to remember all the beautiful times they'd had together. And most important of all, to thank God above that he remained alive and would recover. Her husband, her heart. How could he want to end the precious gift God had given them when they'd found each other?

As always, Drew looked larger than life, his tall form too big for the standard issue hospital bed, his skin dark against white sheets. One long, manly hand lay across his chest gripping the necklace he always wore. She'd asked him about the tiny fish more than once, but his vague answers hadn't satisfied. Now that she was a Christian, she wondered even more. Drew tolerated her new faith, but he wasn't interested in sharing it, which made his attachment to the necklace even more curious.

"A friend gave it to me when I was a kid," he'd say. "It's nothing special."

But she didn't believe that. Since he was never without it, she suspected the necklace carried a deeper meaning than he let on. But she had never pressed.

That was part of the problem in their marriage. She never pressed. Drew was dark and brooding at times and she'd learned to tiptoe around the topics that set him off. Part of the attraction from the beginning had been that air of mystery, the things he didn't say or talk about. She wanted to unlock the secrets and see inside his heart. She wanted to know him as he knew her. Drew had never allowed that. For a long time, she'd wondered if he'd ever let her in, if he'd ever let her know the real Drew Michaels. Now she knew he never would.

Once he'd mentioned a "tough" childhood and her hopes had soared that he was about to share his heart. The next day he'd been on the phone about an assign-

ment, and the next day he was gone. She hadn't seen
him again for six weeks. That was the way he was, and
she'd learned to accept it. As long as he'd continued
coming back to her, she'd been happy.

At some point, he'd decided she wasn't enough.

The stabbing pain sliced through her heart again.
What had she done? Why had he stopped loving her?

Drew stirred then and turned his head, emitting a
gentle snore that made her smile. Light from the door
illuminated his face. His cheeks were sunken and he
was much thinner than normal. Beneath his naturally
dark skin existed an unnatural pallor. Pinch lines of
pain encircled his supple mouth. She longed to soothe
them away with her fingertips.

He needed a shave, too, but then Drew had always
gone for the scruffy whiskered look. She'd gone for it
as well, head over heels.

Her eyes lingered for a moment on his face. Her
beautiful, rugged, dangerous Drew. So deep and mysterious, so brilliant and creative and loving. He had
many wonderful traits.

Her thoughts wandered back to the first time they'd
met. After paying an enormous price for a group of his
stunning photographs, she'd been thrilled for the opportunity to meet the man who could portray children
with enough beauty and sensitivity to make her cry.
She'd pictured an equally sensitive artist with a gentle
and unassuming demeanor.

What she'd met was a wild man with a cocky attitude, dark hair tied back with a leather strip, the tiny fish resting in the hollow of his darkly tanned throat. Dressed in tattered jeans, a denim jacket hanging casually from wide, muscular shoulders, the startling photographer had slowly removed his shades and devoured her with wolf eyes. It had been love at first sight.

Three whirlwind weeks later, over the furious protests of her parents, they'd married.

Her parents had been wrong. Drew was wrong. Now she was the only one left who believed in their marriage.

Deep in his sleep-drenched subconscious, Drew smelled Larissa's perfume. Sweet and expensive, just like the wearer. Pleasure washed through him, stronger than the throbbing, incessant pain in his body. Larissa.

Coming slowly out of his latest fifteen-minute nap, he hoped he hadn't been dreaming. He wanted to see her, to hold her. All of the agony of the last few days would disappear as soon as he held her.

Opening his eyes to slits, he saw with relief that she was, indeed, in the room. For a satisfying moment, he looked his fill, unnoticed. She stood at his bedside deep in thought, her attention focused on the wires and tubes dangling around him. She looked stricken, frightened, and he longed to take her in his arms and tell her everything was okay. A fierce protectiveness came over him, laughable because he was too weak to stand up, much less protect anyone.

His Larissa. Classy. Vulnerable. Gorgeous.

He wished for his camera.

Where was his camera anyway? He touched his chest, feeling for the pockets in his vest before realization crept in and he remembered where he was. He also remembered the other thing. He couldn't hold Larissa ever again.

The throbbing in his head reached a crescendo. She would have been so much better off if he'd made her a widow.

As if sensing his wakefulness, Larissa slowly turned, her gorgeous violet eyes liquid with unshed tears. Drew's guts clenched with the need to comfort her. He bit down on the sides of his tongue to hold back the words. Divorce was the right decision, regardless of his physical condition. Maybe because of it, too.

Mustering every bit of courage, he ground out the words, "What are you doing here?"

His hand lay limp across his chest. She reached for it, and her soft, silky fingers soothed more than any medicine. In a minute, he'd pull away, but right now, he just couldn't let go.

"I've come to take you home," she said.

He squeezed his eyes shut against the torment her words brought. *Home.* He didn't have a home.

Through clenched teeth, he said, "We're getting a divorce. I'm not coming home."

"I don't want a divorce, Drew, and you're in no condition at this point to pursue it."

He hardened his heart and his voice, saying as coldly as possible, "It's happening. Get used to it."

Her shimmering tears spilled over then and nearly killed him. Against his own will, he reclaimed her hand.

"Hey, don't do that. I'm not worth crying over."

Face sad, she leaned in and laid her head on his chest. He was sure his heart would explode.

"My ribs," he said, using the injury as an excuse, although her touch made him better instead of worse.

She jerked upright, all concern and contrition. "Oh, sweetheart, I'm sorry. I didn't think. Should I call the nurse?"

Her hands fluttered above him, afraid to touch but needing to comfort. A born nurturer, Larissa's sweet concern was getting to him fast.

Before he became a blubbering idiot, he said, "I don't need a nurse. I need you to leave." He dragged in a painful breath. "Go home to Tulsa and forget me."

"I can't. I won't."

"Sure you will. Marry some great guy and be happy."

"I married a great guy, and I *was* happy."

He turned his face away. If he looked into those suffering eyes much longer, he'd be lost.

"I'm not leaving, Drew," she said gently. "And there really isn't anything you can do about that."

He squelched the grudging admiration for his smart wife. In his pitiful condition, he couldn't do much physically, but he knew how to make her miserable enough to leave. Oh yeah. He knew how to make other people miserable. That seemed to be his specialty. He squeezed down hard on the metal fish in his opposite hand.

Inside, he whispered, *God, if you care about her, make her go away.*

Not that he believed, but Larissa did. And if God was a good God, He'd know Drew was the worst possible choice of husbands for a wealthy socialite whose daddy was a squeaky-clean politician. She was a sweet, loving Christian who had too much to lose by staying hooked up with the likes of him.

But how could he make her go away without being cruel? Her inability to accept the inevitable was exactly why he'd planned to never see her again.

"We'll talk about this later," she said, her voice soft and shaky in the quiet. "Tell me about the accident."

"Accidents are not intentional."

"You know what I mean. What happened over there?"

He noticed how smoothly she'd sidestepped his demand that she leave him alone. All right, then. He'd talk, tell her what she needed to know, and then try again to make her see reason. Right now, his head hurt too much to formulate a battle plan against a smart cookie like Larissa.

He related most of what he could remember, omitting that last horrible experience of flying away from the jeep. He hadn't asked but figured he knew what happened to the rest of the convoy. Not knowing was the better option at this point. He wasn't sure he could handle the truth right now.

"I guess I'm lucky to be alive." A little part of him was scared about that, even though the practical portion thought the world would be better off without him. What if he'd died? Where would he be right now? A near-death experience made a man wonder about things like Heaven and Hell and eternity.

"It's more than luck, Drew."

"Still praying for me?" He knew she was. Every time they spoke on the telephone, even that last time, she ended the call with the same words, "I'm praying for you, Drew."

When she'd first gotten into the religion-thing, he'd thought church was a nice, wholesome hobby to keep her occupied while he was away. But Larissa took her newfound faith very seriously, and he'd noticed the change in her.

"Constantly," she whispered. And one look at her face told him it was true. She was probably praying this very moment. The idea both comforted and disturbed.

Did God even care about a sewer rat like him? If He did, why had life been so ugly? Why was he so filled with garbage that he tainted everything he touched, even his marriage?

But this was where the tainting ended. He'd hurt Larissa enough. He wouldn't damage her more.

"Thanks," he said.

She didn't answer, just sat there looking beautiful and uncertain. He felt like a jerk of the grandest order. The woman who was comfortable with senators and billionaires didn't know what to say or how to act, all because of him.

That he'd ever managed to win her love in the first place still amazed him. He, a nobody from nowhere, had won the heart of the sweetest, kindest, most beautiful girl in Tulsa society. He didn't fit with her kind at all, and they had let him know. Especially her parents.

"I guess your mother and dad were happy to hear about the divorce." The bitterness in his tone surprised even him.

She stared at him, lost for a minute. He was lost, too, his brain tumbling from one topic to the next. The only thing he could think of for very long was the pain in his body and the worse one in his heart.

"Mother and Dad don't run my life."

That was a laugh. She worked for her father, and couldn't say no to her spoiled, whining mother. In the more than three years that he'd known the Stone family, Drew had never done one thing that pleased them. Mostly, he didn't care.

But he did care about Larissa, and the estrangement brought her sorrow.

He'd do anything for Larissa. That's why he had to do this. "I'm tired. Maybe you should leave now."

She stared down at him, biting her bottom lip. "Go ahead and sleep. I'll just sit here beside you."

She wasn't making this easy.

"Go home."

"Not until I can take you with me."

The crashing in his temples grew louder.

"Get this straight, Larissa. I don't want to come home with you. Not now. Not ever."

"You have nowhere else to go."

That hurt. "Sure, I do."

"Where? What else can you do except come home to Tulsa?"

"Rehab. One of those in-patient places. I already talked to the docs." Not quite the truth, but close enough.

"Don't be ridiculous. We have a huge house. I can hire nurses or whatever you need. I can take better care of you than some impersonal rehab facility."

She reached out again, and he shrunk away. If she touched him, he'd lose his courage. With superhuman determination, he stared straight into her movie-star eyes and said, "Let me be clear about this. I can't stand to be in the same house with you anymore. Now, get out and leave me alone."

Abruptly, he closed his eyes and rolled his head to the side.

But not before he saw the stricken expression on his beloved's face.

Chapter Three

Larissa tossed a tiny Gucci bag onto a chair and collapsed on the bed at the nearest hotel. Fat raindrops, like tears, ran in rivulets down the window.

She was too exhausted for tears of her own. Emotionally and physically, she'd gone about as far as she could for now.

The meeting with Drew had been harder than she'd expected, and she hadn't expected an easy time. But she *had* expected him to want to come home to recuperate.

He was badly injured and disturbingly weak. The thought of him alone in an impersonal rehab facility tormented her.

How could he prefer such a place to their lovely, spacious home? The home they'd bought together? He loved that place as much as she did.

He just didn't love her anymore. At least that's what he claimed.

To hold back the cry of despair, she buried her face in a pillow.

Though she'd wanted to question why he had suddenly given up on them, after seeing his injuries, she was too concerned with his health. First, she'd get him well and then she'd fight him. She'd fight and she'd win because, even if it was arrogant, deep down she couldn't believe he'd stopped loving her.

Something was wrong, though. Terribly wrong.

The thought stopped her cold.

Insecurity reared its ugly head. Sometimes men strayed, even strong, steady, decent men like her father. Mother had never guessed, but Larissa had. A politician, like a photographer, traveled widely and alone. Good-looking, charming—both the men in her life would have no problem finding companionship outside the home.

No. She couldn't believe that about Drew. He might be secretive and mysterious in many ways, but he was faithful. She would know if he wasn't.

The other woman in Drew's life had always been his work. Could that be it? Was she cramping his free-wheeling, traveling lifestyle?

No, that didn't make sense, either. He came and went as he pleased already, even though she'd asked him to be home more often. His job had always come first, even before their marriage.

The familiar tune of her cell phone played and she fished the instrument from the bottom of her handbag.

A quick glance at the caller ID brought a groan.

"Hello, Mother."

"Have you seen him?"

With a sigh, Larissa pinched the bridge of her nose. It was always like this—the tug of war between her parents, especially her mother, and her personal choices.

"I had a dreadful flight. Thank you for asking, Mother. And I'm exhausted. Yes, I've seen *him*. His name is Drew."

"I know that," her mother snapped. "Is he all right?"

"Do you care?"

"Larissa! That is no way to speak to your own mother. I have a terrible headache, too, but I wanted to check on my little girl before I took some medication and went to bed. Your happiness is the only thing that ever mattered to me." Her voice took on the whiney, childish quality Larissa had dealt with since childhood. "I wish you were here to make some of your delicious tea. I find it so soothing at times like this."

For Larissa's mother, Marsha Edington Stone, times like this occurred more or less every day.

Her discontented sigh huffed through the telephone lines, and Larissa imagined her sinking into the lush, reclining chair in the vast sitting room, one wrist dramatically tossed across her forehead like some eighteenth-century princess.

"What's upset you this time, Mother?" She'd long ago accepted the fact that Mother's troubles were far more important than her own.

"The luncheon was today. I don't know what possessed me to go without you. I'm not well enough, and now I'm paying for my dedication. All that chatter over who's going to chair next year's art council was too much. You're the logical choice, if they have any sense at all."

Mother had been sick and needy as long as Larissa could remember. Having grown up as the adored only child of a very wealthy oil man, Marsha was spoiled, although she did suffer from migraines and too much time on her hands. Larissa vacillated between pity and annoyance, but like her father, she never refused her mother anything. Larissa steered the conversation away from her mother's health. Marsha was a good person when she wasn't focused on herself.

"I'm sorry," Larissa said, automatically. Say it now, or pay for it later. "Please forgive my selfishness."

"I understand, honey. You've been under so much strain lately. It's no wonder you're edgy. As soon as this thing is over, you can get back to normal."

This *thing,* Larissa assumed, was her marriage. Her mother refused to believe Larissa could be happy married to Drew. She'd long planned a huge society wedding for her only child, and when Larissa and Drew eloped, the die was cast. There was no forgiveness in Marsha Stone for a perceived wrong, and since Larissa was her daughter, Drew remained the focus of the animosity.

Larissa's marriage, to her mother's way of thinking, was a dead horse. No use beating it.

"I do have some lovely news," Mother said. "Did your father tell you?"

Larissa's last conversation with her father had been terse to say the least. "I guess he forgot to mention it."

"We're going on a cruise to Italy. I am so excited. I can hardly believe Thomas has finally agreed to get away from his office long enough to go. We've discussed it for years."

Larissa managed a laugh. "You make it sound as if you've never been out of the house."

Her parents had traveled to enough places to be U.N. ambassadors.

"Oh, you know what I mean."

Actually, she didn't.

"Why don't you come to Italy with us? Oh, darling, it will be such fun. A nice vacation is exactly what you need. We'll go to Venice and let some handsome Italian woo you in a gondola. Then we'll go shopping for the most wonderful wardrobe of Italian leathers. And by the time we return all this unpleasantness will be over."

"Mother." Larissa's anxiety level rose even higher. "I have to be here for Drew."

Silence hummed through the wires. Larissa could imagine the flat line of disapproval on her mother's collagen-injected lips.

"That's ridiculous." This time her mother's tone had a bite to it. "Stop being a doormat to this man. He's never been a husband. Traipsing all over the world and leaving you behind, embarrassed in society. Give him a divorce and move on with your life. Find a good man of our social standing and have a child. You're not getting any younger you know."

"Thanks for the reminder." Her biological clock *was* ticking loudly, and she hungered for children like a starving lioness. But she wanted Drew to be the father of those children, something he flatly refused to discuss. Children, he claimed, were not part of the package.

A headache threatened. She pressed a thumb and forefinger against her eyes. "I can't talk to you about this. I'm sorry." Lately, all she did was apologize.

"We used to talk about everything until you joined that religious group. I suppose they're behind this insane idea of yours to bring Drew home, instead of cutting your losses while you can."

Hoping to avoid a lecture, Larissa said, "I haven't had a chance to talk to anyone at church about this. It's all too fresh. You're my mother. I need you." Boy, was that ever true. "I love you."

"Well," Marsha sniffed. "I love you, too, honey. You're all that matters to me. I'm happy that you enjoy your church friends. Although in my opinion, you take this new religion fad far too seriously. Everybody gets divorced these days. Divorce isn't a sin, you know."

Larissa couldn't agree. According to her Bible, Christians didn't divorce even if they wanted to. And she most certainly did not want to.

But to the Stones, church was strictly a social institution, mostly used to better her father's political career. Though they attended occasionally as a family, especially during election years, they had never discussed personal faith in their home. She hadn't a clue what a relationship with Christ was about until her friend Jennifer had invited her to a Bible study last year after Drew had disappeared on one of his long treks to who-knew-where. Out of boredom and missing Drew so much she was willing to do anything, she'd gone. Within the month, she'd given her life to Christ and become a different person on the inside.

Her mother was still puzzled by her sudden devotion.

Though she'd tried discussing the topic with both her parents, the words had fallen on deaf ears. They said they were Christians "like everybody else" and that was that.

As much as she wanted to revisit the conversation, she didn't want to offend. Mother's sensibilities were so delicate.

"All I ask is that you think about it, Larissa," her mother was saying. "Daddy knows the best divorce lawyers in Oklahoma. Everything can be taken care of while we're in Italy. You won't even have time to be stressed."

"Drew is seriously injured. That's my concern right now."

"Daddy and I are not unfeeling beasts. If you are going to be stubborn about this, we will also arrange for the best rehab care available."

"Just as long as I don't bring Drew back to Tulsa. Right?"

There was a miniscule pause and then, "It's for the best, honey. Let Daddy take care of everything."

Mother made it sound so simple and bloodless. A vacation to Italy. She shook her head, depressed by her parents' lack of understanding. They were wonderful parents, who thought they knew what was best for their child.

Only she wasn't a child anymore.

Thoughts of Drew crowded in. Drew laughing and teasing. Drew charging into the ocean with her on his back. His expression intense when he spoke his love.

No matter what anyone said, she could not forget the beautiful parts of her marriage. They hovered inside her heart and mind like golden butterflies, too rare and special to release into the wild.

Somehow she managed to end the conversation, certain she hadn't heard the end of the Italy cruise. Then she fixed a cup of tea in the hotel coffeemaker. It wasn't her special blend of chamomile and raspberry, but the hot, sweetened drink warmed the chill in her bones.

Outside, a cold rain slashed the windows in incessant sheets. Inside, the hotel room was cozy. She climbed beneath the comforter, pillows propped behind her head, to drink tea and read the Bible.

In her haste, she'd left her own beautiful, Moroccan leather Bible at home. But the bedside table held the familiar Gideon version.

She flipped through the stiff book, finally settling on a page in Corinthians. Much of the Bible was still new to her and this was no different. She read out loud, hoping scripture would soothe her inner tumult. "Love is patient. Love is kind. It does not envy, it does not boast, it is not proud. It is not rude, it is not self-seeking, it is not easily angered, it keeps no record of wrongs. Love does not delight in evil, but rejoices in the truth. It always protects, always trusts, always hopes, always perseveres. Love never fails."

This was what real love was all about. God's kind of love.

As if the ancient words were written just for her, Larissa read them again and again.

"Love is patient," she murmured. "I can be patient with Drew."

And she could also trust and hope and persevere. Because God promised that if she would, love would never fail. She closed her eyes and smiled, ready to sleep now as she hadn't done in days. "Thank you, Lord."

Deep down, she understood what God was telling her. Just keep on loving Drew the way Corinthians stated. Keep loving. Because love would not fail.

The next morning, Drew awakened as soon as the weak winter sun slanted through the gap in the ugly green drapes. He was nervous. Larissa was going to fight him, and right now he was weak. Last night he'd tried to get up and head for the shower on his own. He'd made it to the end of the bed before collapsing like a

Slinky. The nurses had scolded until, chastised, he'd promised to stay put.

He wouldn't necessarily keep that promise. He had to get out of here before he lost all courage.

A nurse arrived, and Drew went through the now familiar humiliation of being treated like a helpless infant. Ah, what was he saying? He *was* a helpless infant.

"Tell the doc I want to see him right away."

"Let's get you cleaned up first. I heard you had a pretty visitor yesterday."

He gave her a look intended to shut her up, but she was a cheeky sort. She pushed her glasses up on her nose and grinned. Drew ignored the insinuation. "Call the doctor."

"I heard you. The doctor will make his rounds soon. Right now he's in surgery."

"Great." He needed to get the rehab arrangements made today and get out of here. His frustratingly weak body was not cooperating. All he could do was wait.

As the nurse administered his morning ablutions, he stared at a painting on the far wall. What was it? A seascape? Mountains?

He squinted, trying to bring the blues and greens into focus. He blinked several times to clear the fog, and just that quick, the picture faded to gray and then to black.

His heart lurched. Cold fear snaked through him. He blinked again and again. Nothing happened.

He dropped his head back onto the pillow, fighting the panic. A groan escaped him.

"Mr. Michaels?" The cheeky nurse's voice held concern. "Did I hurt you? Are you in pain?"

Yes, though not the kind she meant.

For lack of a better excuse, he said, "My side," and grabbed for it.

No way was he telling the nurses about the unpredictable state of his eyesight. They might tell Larissa and then he was done for. If she thought for one minute that he was going blind, she would insist on taking care of him. He wouldn't saddle her with a cranky, worthless, blind photographer.

As professional hands skimmed over the bandage on his belly, Drew fretted. The doc had called the blindness transient. It would go away. It had to.

"There. Is that better?"

Though he had no idea what the nurse had done, he nodded anyway. "Thanks."

"You're welcome." She rattled around his bed and he waited for the sound to disappear before opening his eyes again.

A relieved sigh shuddered through him.

The world had somehow come back into focus.

He looked at his hands. They were shaking.

Outside in the hallway, people passed by talking in low tones. So as not to think about the frightening blindness, he concentrated on the noises and waited for his doctor to arrive.

He didn't have long to wait. In moments, he heard the murmur of a male voice. But there was another voice, too. Larissa. He'd recognize that soft, educated drawl anywhere on earth.

Straining to hear, he caught bits and pieces of the conversation. "Mr. Michaels expressly asked me not to release his information to you, Mrs. Michaels."

Way to go, doc.

"But I'm his wife." Larissa's bewilderment was evident.

"He said you were going through a divorce."

"That's ridiculous. He must have gotten a concussion. We are not getting a divorce."

Drew couldn't hold back a smile of admiration. His woman was gutsy, that was for certain. She'd worked on her father's political campaigns long enough to know how to stand her ground.

The doctor's smooth, professional baritone answered, "He's asked me to make arrangements in a rehab facility here in D.C. I was just stopping by to discuss the particulars with him."

Drew clenched the sheet with both fists, reminding himself that the rehab was his idea. Nevertheless, the thought of going to any institution filled him with dread. He'd been in way too many of them over the years, and probably should have been in others.

Flashes of his early teen years kaleidoscoped behind his eyelids. Boys' homes, therapeutic homes, group homes for troubled kids. He'd battled his way through dozens, fending off bigger, meaner boys, learning to steal and smoke. Learning which illegal drugs manifested what effect.

He'd tried everything and then some but had gone cold turkey after the fire....

He slammed the door right there. Sweat broke out on his body.

Not the fire. He didn't ever think about the fire.

He wasn't that wild, undisciplined kid anymore. He was Drew Michaels, professional photographer. Disciplined, controlled.

Jaw set, he bit down almost hard enough to break a molar. He could do this. He could go to a rehab center for a while and then get back to work where he belonged. And Larissa was not going to interfere.

Larissa stood outside Drew's room, glad to have encountered Dr. Spacey in the hallway so they could speak candidly. According to the nurses, he was the physician in charge of Drew's case.

"As sorry as we are to admit this, Mrs. Michaels," the bespectacled doctor said after listing Drew's many injuries, "our hospital is at capacity. We have to move patients out as quickly as possible—without jeopardizing care, of course. Your husband is well enough for release."

"He can't take care of himself." She stated the obvious.

"Not for some time, I'm afraid. His body has been

through a lot, and he'll need several months of healing to get his strength back."

"That's why I'm here. I'm taking him home."

He cocked an eyebrow at her. "Have you spoken with him about this?"

"Do I have to?"

He looked amused. "Any man that didn't want to go home with you would be crazy, but he has a right to make that decision."

Larissa played the only card she had. She only hoped it worked. "I thought you said he had a severe concussion."

"That's true. He does. It's healing but he's still suffering some aftereffects."

Larissa filed that piece of information away. Maybe the aftereffects were adding to Drew's reluctance. "Then, are you certain he's capable of making the appropriate decisions about his health?"

Dr. Spacey studied her behind black-framed glasses. Graying blond hair peeked out from beneath a green scrub cap. "What do you have in mind?"

"I can charter a plane whenever you say he's ready. We have a large home, easily accessible to the best physicians in the Southwest. I can hire nursing care, physical therapists, whatever you think he needs. No expense will be spared. I can give him much more personalized care than any facility in this country. If his head is giving him trouble, what better place than home and familiar surroundings to help him recover?"

Dr. Spacey rubbed a hand over the back of his neck, thinking. "You have a valid point. The best thing for your husband *would* be home and familiarity. Patients who've been through great trauma usually recover faster and with less psychological effect among family and friends."

Larissa felt a victory coming on. If she could just keep pushing, she might pull this off. "What do I need to do first?"

"Take him home and let him rest. The leg is non-weight bearing for at least six weeks anyway, but a physical therapist will have the details about that after you get him settled. He needs time more than anything else."

She smiled, weary to the bone, but satisfied that she was doing the right thing, whether Drew liked it or not. "I have all the time in the world."

The doctor patted her shoulder. "With that attitude, your husband will get along just fine. Let's go in and talk with him about this."

"But—" She stopped the protest rising in her throat. How did she tell him that her husband preferred a cold, sterile institution to any place with her?

She couldn't. She could only pray that she'd been persuasive enough here in the hall to counteract anything Drew might say in the next few minutes.

Dr. Spacey pushed open the door and went inside the room. There was nothing for her to do but follow, carrying the balloon and box of chocolates picked up at the gift shop.

What would she do if Drew refused to come home with her? How would she manage to convince the doctor that Drew was too ill to know what he was doing?

Whether he wanted to admit it or not, Drew *would* heal more quickly in her care. If she was injured, she would want someone familiar to care for her. She'd want to be home with her family, her friends, and her animals.

Drew had nobody else but her to turn to. Right now he needed her too much to refuse.

The man she'd promised to stand by in sickness and in health had nearly died. And she was not about to abandon him, no matter how much he protested.

Drew was seething. Seething. Larissa and his doctor were conspiring against him.

He stared at the squat surgeon standing over him. "Do you have that rehab set up?"

"Actually, your wife has a better plan."

He refused to look at Larissa, though he could feel her in the room. If he looked, he might weaken.

"I don't like her plan. Send me to rehab."

"You have a healing concussion. I can't be certain you're able to make the best decisions for yourself at this time."

"Meaning?"

"In my judgment, since Mrs. Michaels is your legal

wife, she is the more appropriate decision maker at this time. I'm going to dismiss you tomorrow morning into her care."

Drew shot upright but pain slammed him right back down. He lay back against the pillow, too breathless to speak.

"Everything will be fine, Mr. Michaels. Just be sure to see your doctors in Tulsa. Have them call for your records." He took a card from his shirt pocket and handed it to Larissa. If Drew had been able to get a good breath, he would have complained. This was his life. What was the matter with this crazy doctor?

Giving him a pat on the shoulder, the doctor departed. Drew was furious.

Larissa, her perfume pure torture, moved closer to set her gifts on the nightstand. A teddy bear balloon. Normally, he'd make some wise remark about that, but he was too angry. She was destroying his plan.

"I hope you're not upset." She fiddled with the balloon.

By now, he'd found his breath and his voice. "Just what do you think you're trying to pull?"

"Dr. Spacey and I were discussing your dismissal."

"Yeah, I overheard."

"Good. Then you already know. You are not going to a rehab. You're going home. To our home where you belong."

"What did you do, convince him I'm crazy?"

She found where his fist was clenched against the

bedsheet and tugged his hand into hers. He tried to resist, but for once, a woman was stronger than him. Imagine, too weak to resist a girl.

Violet eyes smiled down at him. "Get used to it, Drew. You married a woman who plans strategy for political campaigns. I outmaneuvered you."

"I'm not going back to Tulsa."

She bent down and kissed his cheek. He thought he'd die of pleasure. "Yes, you are. Tomorrow morning."

With an angry huff, he jerked his hand away. But he was no fool. He knew he'd been beaten.

He was about to spend the next few months convincing the woman he loved more than life, that he couldn't stand her.

This was not going to be fun. His stomach curled in anguish. Not fun at all.

Chapter Four

Drew jangled the tiny bell Larissa had placed at his bedside for that purpose. When no one appeared he threw the blanket aside and sat up. One hand under his cast, he gingerly swung the leg overboard—and then wished he hadn't.

Pain shot from his toes up his leg and into his brain in point-zero-two seconds.

With a hiss, he gritted his teeth to keep from screaming like a baby.

He sat there for a moment, one hand on his ribs, the other on his leg until his breath returned and the pain settled to a piercing howl.

His whole body trembled, a condition that infuriated him. If he could get his strength back, he could be mobile. Having never been dependent on anyone in his life, he hated the helpless feeling.

Five days back in Tulsa and he was still so mad he could spit. How had Larissa managed this? How had she manipulated him into living under the same roof with her again?

To make the situation even more difficult, she had moved him into the downstairs guest room and then surrounded him with luxury. She'd filled it with things he enjoyed, including a plasma TV mounted on the wall and a remote to open and close the drapes. A remote no less, so he could look out onto the backyard at will. She'd put enormous effort into making the room comfortable.

That was the problem. She was killing him with kindness and making him love her more, instead of less. He needed to get out of here and do it fast, but his body wouldn't cooperate.

No matter how much he growled and fussed and acted like a general creep, Larissa kept smiling and bringing him goodies. But he was a detail man. He could see the hurt she tried to hide, and he hated himself for putting it there. But he had to. Someday she'd thank him for it. Someday, when he could get out of her life for good.

Despising himself, he pressed the window remote and opened the drapes to stare broodingly at the yard.

Though Tulsa moved toward winter's end, the weather here was unpredictable. One day would be springlike, the next day snow or ice. Today was sunny, and the television claimed that temperatures were decent enough to be outside.

He'd spent too many years outdoors to appreciate

much time inside a building. No matter how much he hurt, he was as restless as a windshield wiper.

Larissa's backyard, like her house, was pretty, even in winter. Birds pecked at feeders and flitted among the glossy green holly bushes. Wrought-iron benches beckoned him to come out and play around the koi pond.

If only he had his camera equipment he could at least get some shots.

He rang the bell again, more insistent this time. Where was she? The more he annoyed her, the sooner she'd give up and send him to rehab. And he definitely was cranky enough to annoy anyone, even himself.

He'd slept away the first few days back, not caring much about anything. If his information was correct, he'd slept most of the last three weeks. But now he was awake and in a bad mood.

"Larissa!" he yelled and the effort set his ribs to aching.

As if she'd been standing outside the door waiting for him to hurt himself, his wife materialized. Dressed in trendy jeans and a sweater with too-long sleeves that was somehow exactly right on her, she took his breath away. Or she would have if he hadn't already lost it to the rib pain. Coco, the funny little Yorkie he'd bought two years ago to keep her company, trotted in behind.

"Do you need something?" She hovered in the doorway, anxious to help.

She'd been like this since his arrival and he was

pretty tired of it. Sweet and kind and accommodating. Why couldn't she just hate him and get it over with?

"I'm bored." Coco trotted over and sniffed his toes. He wiggled away the tickle, frowning. "Go away, mutt."

Larissa's giggle washed over him as she came in and perched on a chair too close to his bedside. Her perfume came with her and tantalized him. All day long, he had to smell that delicious, irritating perfume.

"Okay. What would you like to talk about?" she asked.

His frown deepened. She was way too chipper. "Your attitude."

Her lush lips quirked at the corners. "*My* attitude?"

Okay, so he was the one in the foul mood. "Yeah, your attitude. Stop behaving like a servant. I don't like it."

Expression mild, she refused to let his crankiness rattle her. "How would you like me to behave? You aren't able to take care of yourself yet."

Like he needed that reminder. "Have the nurse stay longer. I don't want you in here all the time."

The last shot was hateful, so he braced against her inevitable flinch of pain.

It came, then quickly went as she shot back, "Dare I mention that you summoned me like some cranky king?"

Oh, yeah. He had. Lacking a reasonable answer, he did the only thing he could. He glowered.

Larissa got up to retrieve a pillow from against the wall. He'd thrown it earlier in a fit of frustration.

The woman amazed him with her serenity. How could she be calm when he was such a jerk?

"Leave it," he barked. "It's a *throw* pillow."

She picked it up, taking aim in his direction. Eyes narrowed, she said, "Don't tempt me."

His mouth twitched. Mixed with Larissa's grace and class was a good dose of spunk. Sooner or later, she'd get her fill of him.

"If I'm such a pain, send me to rehab. Get me out of here."

"We've had this argument." There was that annoying calm again. "You want to be here. You're just too stubborn to admit I was right. The home health nurses are doing a great job, as is the physical therapist."

So was Larissa.

"None of this changes the inevitable. I want out. You might as well cut me loose now and save us both the stress."

He hadn't planned to blurt that out, but the subject was on his mind most of the time anyway. The longer he stayed here, soaking up her kindness, the more restless he became. He was terrified of falling back into the habit of thinking of this place as his home. It wasn't. It was her house. Her town. Her everything. She deserved it. She belonged. He didn't.

Brocade pillow cradled like a protective shield between them, she refused to rise to the bait. "You need to get well. That's the only thing that matters right now. The rest can wait."

"So, you're saying, as soon as I'm well, you'll agree to divorce."

"That's not what I said." Distress twisted her face. He'd finally upset her. As a result, he felt lower than pond scum.

"Look, Larissa. I'm not trying to be the bad guy here. I'm just being honest." Sort of. He honestly wanted to convince the woman he loved that he didn't love her. How messed up was that? "I wasn't cut out for the married life. You knew it when you first laid eyes on me."

"But I fell in love with you anyway." She came to his bedside and laid a hand on his cheek. Her face softened and grew sad. "You once loved me, too. What happened?"

All it took was one touch from her, and he shuddered like a pathetic puppy. He tried to shrink into the mattress, anything to escape her sweetness. "Give me a break."

"Someone in Iraq did that already." She smiled and stepped back.

Resisting the smile, he deepened his scowl. "Not funny."

"The doctors say depression is natural after trauma this severe. We can call in a counselor if you'd like."

No thanks to that one. He'd had his head shrunk plenty as a teenager, and the results had never been pretty. "I'm not depressed."

"That's why you're so cranky."

"I'm cranky because you won't discuss our situation rationally."

She blinked once, then glanced out the window, teeth sawing back and forth on her bottom lip. When she brought her attention back to him, she looked resigned.

"All right, then. Let's discuss this. I can't even begin to understand what happened, Drew. The last time you were home, things were fine."

"No, they weren't. Things have never been fine. I'm gone all the time. I won't give you a family. Never." He emphasized that part. "I don't fit in your world. Your parents have fought us from the beginning. The pressure from them is killing you. You're miserable. Why can't you admit it and let go? We made a mistake. Let's fix it and move on."

"My parents make me unhappy. You never have."

Nothing like skirting the rest of the issues. "Until now."

She tilted her head in agreement. "Every marriage has ups and downs. If you'd only tell me what's wrong, we can get counseling. We can pray about it. We can talk it out. Work with me, Drew. We're worth it."

He hardened his heart against the sweet words. "You're a great lady, Larissa. You deserve a husband to love you and give you everything you want." *Kids.* "But that guy is not me."

"You could be."

He squeezed his eyes shut against the sorrow in her

beautiful eyes. Through gritted teeth, he said, "I don't want to be. Now leave me alone."

Larissa didn't answer, and he could feel the hurt wafting off her like heat off sheet metal. After a few long, tense seconds, he heard soft footsteps leave the room.

Larissa fought anger for half an hour. Why was she putting herself through this? She should have sent him to a rehab the way he'd wanted. He was impossible. She must be out of her mind to think forcing him to stay here would make him love her again.

She took out a can of chunked chicken and thumped it onto the granite countertop. Tags jingling, Coco danced around her feet. The little Yorkie was great company, but the companionable dog wasn't Drew. Larissa wanted her husband with her all the time. She wanted a family. She wanted Drew.

"Help me know what to do, Lord. I'm so confused." Divorce was not scriptural but how long was a Christian supposed to keep trying when her husband didn't love her anymore?

Despair tugged like lead weight, but she fought away the feeling. The truth was, she'd keep trying as long as she could keep Drew in Tulsa. As awful as it sounded, she was almost thankful for his injuries. Otherwise, she might never have had this chance to make things right.

Larissa pressed her head against the cool cabinet

door and tried to remember the verses she'd read in the hotel. All that came to mind was *Love never fails*.

At the moment love didn't seem to be working at all.

She hated this feeling. The tension between her and Drew could choke an elephant, and she didn't know what to do. Pastor Nelson at church offered counseling services, but until now she'd been unwilling to share her personal problems with anyone except her parents. And they only added to the stress. Maybe she should talk to someone who would listen objectively.

When Drew's sandwich was ready, she took the filled plate and a glass of milk to his room.

Drew had propped the pillows behind his head and was sitting up. The television played an action movie.

She'd expected him to be asleep again. He'd slept a lot since coming home, but he was wide awake. The circles beneath his eyes had lessened and the bruises on his face and arms, once black and yellow, were fading. All were reminders that Drew was not his normal self. Could the trauma be part of the problem? Could the horror of what he'd experienced cause him to behave so wretchedly? The man she'd married had never been like this. He'd been warm and funny, a little cynical and arrogant, but he'd treated her like a queen.

"Hungry?" she asked quietly.

His head rotated in her direction. He looked tired and drawn, as if every conversation stole more of his strength. Guilt pricked Larissa's conscience. He didn't need arguments right now. She'd vowed not to discuss anything troubling until he was better, and she'd already broken that promise. Drew needed to heal, physically, mentally, even spiritually.

Sometimes the line between fighting for his health and fighting for their marriage blurred. She would have to remember that his health came first.

"Not very." He motioned toward the nightstand. "Put it there. I'll eat it later."

Drew normally ate like a horse, but not since the injury.

He extended a hand, then changed his mind, letting it fall to the sheet instead. "Thanks for the sandwich."

As if regretting the earlier outburst, his tone was quiet. Larissa wished she could understand what was going on in that complicated mind of his.

"Will you be all right for a little while?" The nurse had already come and gone for the day. "Mother called."

"Sure." A flicker of amusement flashed in bad-boy eyes. "Give her my love."

"Drew," she admonished, but in truth, the spark of personality pleased her. This was the old Drew.

His face lit with mischief. "Sorry."

He clearly wasn't. The hostility between Drew and her parents had begun the first time they'd met and continued to this day. Drew didn't fit her parents' country-club image of a proper husband for a state senator's daughter. He was far too unpredictable and rough around the edges, and he wasn't impressed by their money and prestige. The very things that appealed most to Larissa were the ones her parents despised.

"I promised to take Mother to the beauty salon."

Drew didn't bother to ask the obvious question because they'd covered this ground before. Her mother seldom went anywhere alone. It made her nervous and brought on migraines.

"Go ahead. I'll be okay." He glanced toward the window with a longing gaze. "I might even run away."

They both knew he could no more run than he could fly.

Larissa smiled. "If you do, be back in time for dinner. I have some fun planned."

His eyebrows lifted in question, but she didn't share her sudden inspiration.

"I've asked Cody from next door to sit with you," she said instead.

"I don't need a sitter."

Too bad. He was getting one.

"Cody's a great kid. You remember him, don't you?" Cody and his sister Kelli, along with several other neighbor kids frequently used her indoor pool. When Drew was away, Larissa enjoyed the company.

"Sure."

"I'm not going to leave you alone."

"I won't really run away." He made an X on his chest. "Cross my heart. Does Cody play video games?"

"All twelve-year-old boys play video games. To hear him tell it, Cody is the king."

"Then, he's my man. Send him over. I hope he has NFL football."

"If you'll promise to be good and stay in bed, I might even bring you a present."

"A present, huh? Let me think." He rubbed his bottom lip. "Considering how bad my ribs hurt today, you got a deal."

Larissa walked out of the room feeling much better than when she'd entered. Now, if she only knew what had caused Drew's sudden mood swing.

Three hours later, ears still ringing from her mother's usual diatribe, Larissa returned to the white villa-style home in south Tulsa. She loved this place. Following an afternoon of listening to her mother's advice, she couldn't wait to get back here to her own little world. She and Drew had chosen this house together shortly after their elopement, and it had become her safe haven.

They had both fallen in love with the house on sight, but for different reasons. She loved the Italian architecture, the koi pond and pool house. He'd been enamored of the spacious open floor plan and the way natural light filled each room with a warm glow. Together they'd added a hot tub, chosen furniture, repainted the living room, and had set up a darkroom in the basement, thrilled with their compatibility in so many important things.

She was sad now to realize that, during their whirlwind courtship, they'd never once talked of children or considered the effect of his travel on their marriage.

Still, those had been wonderful days and this villa was filled with happy memories. If she had her way, there would be many more, including children. But first, she had to change Drew's mind about a lot of things. Starting with the ugly topic of divorce.

Just thinking the word brought on a weight of despair so heavy she could barely keep walking. Her stomach hadn't stopped hurting in days.

Dropping her keys on the hutch, she shucked her coat and wished the ever-present worry would fall away as easily. Putting on an intentionally happy, though false face, she went to check on Drew and Cody.

Cody sat on the floor, video controllers in hand, fighting aliens from outer space. Drew was sound asleep, the lines of fatigue a constant reminder of how weak and ill he was.

The boy looked up and shrugged. "Zonked out."

They kept their conversation low, and Drew didn't stir.

"You must have beaten him."

Cody grinned. "I did."

Ruffling Cody's blond hair, Larissa returned the grin and dropped several bills into the boy's lap. "Drew's not a very good loser."

And neither was she, a trait she'd learned from her father's many election campaigns. No matter how grim the forecast, a Stone never backed down and never quit.

Cody shut down the video machine and stuffed the money into his jeans' pocket. "Drew's pretty fun. Kind of shaky though. He got real tired after a couple of games."

Larissa's heart squeezed. A man who could trek the Congo for days on end had been felled by two video games.

"I appreciate your help, Cody."

"No problem. I'll babysit him anytime you want." He shrugged into his coat. "Well, except when I'm at school. Mom makes me go there no matter what."

Grinning back into the exasperated blue eyes, Larissa saw Cody to the door, watched him run across the wide expanse of her lawn into his yard. Then she headed back to the kitchen to put away the groceries.

Thanks to one of her parent's housekeepers and a gourmet cooking class, Larissa had learned to enjoy cooking. Since bringing Drew home, she'd put that love to good use. His body needed all the help she could give it.

Coco trotted in, looking for a treat. Larissa tossed her a doggie cookie.

From the sick room came the tinkle of Drew's bell. Buoyed by the hope that he'd awakened in the same good mood, she stashed the last box of pasta in the cabinet and headed his way.

When he saw her instead of Cody, he said, "I thought my babysitter had abandoned ship."

"I sent him home. You were out cold."

He scrubbed a hand over his face. "I don't know what's wrong with me."

"Rethink that statement."

"I mean, I know what's wrong. I just don't know why I'm taking so long to recover."

"Well, let me see." She ticked the problems off on her fingers. "You had a concussion, lost several pints of blood, broke your leg in more places than you have bones, lost your spleen, had shrapnel removed from various locations, including your head. Really, Iron Man, I don't know why you don't get out of that bed and run the triathlon."

His grin was adorably sheepish, and she wanted to kiss his scruffy face. She wouldn't, of course. He didn't want her affection and until he did, she would go right on loving him at arm's length.

She was trying hard to believe that love never failed, though, in all honesty, she couldn't understand why her prayers hadn't already been answered. God didn't approve of divorce. So, why didn't he instantly change the situation? She'd asked him to about a thousand times.

"Where's that present you promised?" Drew asked.

She stuck one hand on a hip and teased, "What if I forgot it?"

His eyes narrowed to slits. "You didn't. I know you."

Yes, he did, sometimes better than she knew herself. "And I know you, too, big baby. Here's your present." She handed him the shopping bag. "I hope it's the right one."

He tore into the bag like a kid on Christmas, his face intense with excitement as if a gift were a rare treat. Drew always reacted with the same endearing pleasure that made Larissa want to buy him everything.

"Oh, man." Stunned and pleased, he lifted out the camera. Almost lovingly, he turned it over. "A Nikon. My favorite."

His dark gaze flickered up to hers and held. What she saw in those depths made her heart flutter. Was it only gratitude? Or something more?

"I know," she said, thrilled to please him. He'd loved that camera. Of all the equipment he owned, he preferred this particular one. "And since you lost the other one…" Not wanting to remind him of that terrible day, she let the statement slide.

Already lost in the new camera, Drew checked every detail. "It's perfect, sweetheart," he said, giving her a quick, sweet smile. "Thank you."

Whether intentional or not, the endearment was almost as good as a kiss. Pure happiness zipped through Larissa, a rarity of late.

"I thought you might occupy yourself by snapping some photos around here. Maybe you won't be so grumpy."

His expert fingers quickly readied the camera for use and took aim at her.

Head tilted in mock-annoyance, she was secretly thrilled. Why would he want photos of someone he planned to leave? The little ray of hope glowed brighter.

She opened the drapes so he could try out the zoom.

Then, eyeing the uneaten sandwich on the table, she said, "You play for a while. Then I have another surprise."

Drew grinned. "Two in one day? I may perish from the excitement."

The gleam of white teeth against dark skin was stunning. He should take his own picture. Larissa knew she'd love him even if he were ugly, but he was so wildly beautiful, just looking at him was a pleasure.

Drew didn't know what to do. His wounded body had put him in this spot and his aching heart was dying a slow death. What was wrong with Larissa? Why didn't she hate him yet? It seemed the more he misbehaved, the nicer she became. Surely, she would wake up some morning soon and realize what a loser she had married. If he could convince her of that, he could walk away knowing she would be all right.

Coco hopped upon the bed. Drew aimed the Nikon and snapped. Larissa would get a kick out of a framed photo of Coco, red bows in her ear tufts, toenails freshly painted.

Dismayed at his need to please his wife even now, he tilted his head back and stared at the crown molding. As quickly as that, the world dimmed. The blue wall faded to black. Stunned and scared, he yanked his chin to level and blinked rapidly. The blindness hadn't happened since the hospital. He'd thought he was cured.

Pulse pounding against his temples, he blinked over and over. Slowly the room returned to normal. His pounding heart took a lot longer.

Setting the Nikon aside, he rested back against the pillows to stare around the room. He was afraid to close his eyes again.

An hour later, he was still lying there, listening to his heart beat and soaking up every visual detail when Larissa came sashaying in, a picnic basket on her arm and a big smile on her face. She'd applied fresh lip gloss— a touch of pink. Just enough so Drew couldn't take his eyes off her. She had a beautiful mouth, full and perfectly bowed, and incredibly kissable.

He remembered the last time he'd kissed her. Six months ago.

By sheer force of will he managed to glance away. But there was no real escape.

Larissa climbed onto the side of his rented hospital bed, bringing with her the scent of freshly spritzed perfume and fried chicken. He couldn't decide which smelled better. He was shockingly hungry.

"What are you doing?" he asked. "What is this?"

She set the basket between them. Thank goodness. "A picnic."

He tried to scoot up in the bed away from her, but his ribs screamed in protest. Short of breath, he gave up. "I don't think that's such a good idea."

"Too bad. I want a picnic. We can't go outside, you can't get up, so we're having it right here. A bed picnic." She shot him a cheeky grin. "Don't argue. You're trapped, and I am in charge."

Try as he might, he couldn't keep from grinning, too, although his was grudging. "Who knew you were such a bully?"

As if she did this every day, Larissa opened the basket, flapped a red-and-white checked tablecloth onto the bed, and started setting out an array of colorful plastic wear.

"I'm a campaign strategist. I make a living bullying people—in a nice way, of course." She handed him a chicken leg. "Work on that while I get set up."

His taste buds rejoiced as he bit down on the crispy meat. "I can see why your dad never loses."

She laughed, and the sound was like music. He loved making her laugh. A woman like Larissa should always have a reason to laugh. Thanks to him, she hadn't had much opportunity.

"Potato salad?" she asked.

"The works. I'm starved."

"That's a first."

"So's this picnic."

"Fun, huh? A picnic without ants."

Drew quirked an eyebrow at the tiny dog. "Unless she qualifies."

Larissa laughed again, and Drew was pretty much done for. All men were saps when a woman laughed at their stupid jokes. Larissa was great about that. Ah, what was he thinking? Larissa was great about most things. And right now, he didn't have it in him to hurt her feelings. Not today anyway. Let her have her picnic and her fun. He'd get back to business tomorrow.

For the next half hour, he gave in and let her pamper him. He even let himself enjoy it. The only strained moment had come when she wanted to pray a blessing on the food, but he'd survived that.

She chatted away as if he'd never demanded a divorce or behaved like a jerk, filling him in on details of the people they knew, the changes in Tulsa, the play she'd watched at Christmas without him. Though plays were not part of his bizarre upbringing, he'd come to share Larissa's appreciation of the arts.

At one point during the picnic, he made the mistake of touching her. Without thinking, he'd leaned forward to wipe a cookie crumb from the corner of her mouth. Their gazes locked and held. After a long, aching moment, she turned her cheek into his hand and kissed his palm.

And then she'd backed off, cheeks aflame as if they'd never kissed before.

He didn't know which would kill him first, her sweetness or his guilt.

What had he been thinking when he'd married her, a wealthy, socially accepted politician's daughter who was as good as he was wicked?

Well, there was his answer. He hadn't been thinking at all. He'd been in love, frantically trying to freeze the moment in time, wishing it could last and knowing full well nothing good ever did.

He'd been right, too.

Ah, but he'd loved her so much. Still did, a fact that scared him to pieces and made him vulnerable. He hated vulnerable. Usually, he hit the road when the feelings came. This time he was stuck.

Poor Larissa. She'd been completely innocent to the kind of man he was. And as they always did, the same old lousy things had happened. He'd wanted to be her hero, her everything. Instead, he'd become her absentee husband, a loser who was too afraid of the past to make a decent future with the finest woman on the planet. He'd taken something as good and pure and special as love and found a way to damage it.

Bad blood always told. Change his name. Hide his crime. Deny his past. It didn't matter. Bad blood always told.

If Larissa's God really cared for her, why had He allowed Drew Michaels to ever get near her?

He sat back against the headboard and watched her gather up the remains of their honey-sweet picnic. He was tired, both inside and out, but Larissa's company made him forget the constant pain.

She glanced up a time or two, made a few silly remarks that brought a smile. "There's a good movie on Pay-Per-View tonight. You up for it?"

She wasn't going to let him off easy, was she?

"I think I can fit it into my busy schedule."

As tormenting as it was, he would soak up all the love he could. For the hard times that would come later, long after she had seen the light and cut him loose.

Chapter Five

A wheelchair wasn't a particularly convenient mode of transportation, but Drew had learned to maneuver it like a chariot racer as soon as he had stopped feeling like soft-set Jell-O. The most exciting part of his day was rolling quietly up behind Larissa when her back was turned and waiting for that little startled squeak of awareness.

Pathetic but true. His adventurous life was reduced to photographing black-capped chickadees and begging the kid next door for a game of video NASCAR.

Larissa, on the other hand, was a regular whirling dervish. Constantly in motion, she somehow managed to take care of a crippled, cranky husband, pamper her whining mother, attend church and field dozens of work-related phone calls each day. He'd urged her to go back to work in her father's office, but so far she hadn't.

As long as she was out and about, he was fine. It was when she came home that he was in trouble. Then his steel magnolia of a wife would waft into the room, a fragrant flower to his emotional cesspool, and his inner battle started all over again.

Leg elevated, camera in his lap, he wheeled the chair through the spacious house, careful not to ram his foot into anything. Coco jingled alongside, spoiling his chance for a surprise attack.

Winter was loosening its hold early as it often did here in Tulsa. The first green daffodil shoots were poking up in Larissa's flower garden. Soon, he'd set up a time-lapse camera and see what he could discover.

He found Larissa in the sunny living room arranging fresh flowers on a side table. They had two living rooms, a waste, he thought, because this was the one most used. The family room, she called it, dubbing the other as formal. Here, double French doors opened to a native rock patio and divided walkway leading out to the pool house and down to the koi pond, the hot tub and the gardens. In nice weather, she threw open the doors to meld the outside with the inside.

"I'll be glad when I can get in the pool." He looked longingly through the glass. "Such a shame to have an indoor pool and a hot tub and not be able to use either."

Larissa poked a pink carnation into the vase and reached for a yellow one. "Another few weeks and you'll have the cast off. Be patient."

"Getting blown up forces a man to be patient," he groused.

"And you've fought it every step of the way."

"I'm not good at convalescence. Being stuck in one spot makes me antsy."

She tapped his arm with the flower. The petals felt as soft as the kiss she'd placed in his palm during the bed picnic. He'd laid awake long into the night thinking about that. He should never have allowed the picnic.

"That's an understatement," she said mildly.

He didn't know why, but after a while in the same place, he grew uneasy, as if the world was catching up. After a childhood of constant change, common sense said he'd want roots. Weird that life hadn't worked that way. He wanted to stay put. He just couldn't.

"The living room smells nice."

"Tonight is my turn to host Bible study."

"Oh." Bible study. Like he knew anything about that.

She poked a yellow flower into the vase. After a beat, she glanced at him and said, "You could join us."

There was no missing the hope in her voice, but Drew shook his head. "Not a good idea."

He'd met some of her church pals and they were all right, but he felt out of place in their midst, as if they shared a secret he wasn't privy to. Besides, hanging out with Larissa and her friends wasn't exactly the way to break up a marriage.

Or maybe it was.… Maybe she needed to see how poorly he fit in decent company.

Larissa was an active woman. She had clubs and committees and charities. She biked and golfed and took classes. That's why the whole church-thing baffled him so much. She didn't need the time-filler.

"Finding Christ changed my life, Drew," Larissa said softly. Though she set the flowers in the center of the table, turning them this way and that, Drew knew her real focus was him. Her religion had become that important. "If you'll let Him, He'll do the same for you."

Nothing could change him. Hadn't every social service and therapeutic foster home in Oklahoma tried? He couldn't even change himself.

"I don't know much about God except that a lot of wars are waged in His name."

A fact which had always irked him. People killing people in the name of some deity. Didn't make sense.

"Don't blame God for that. Why do you wear a Christian symbol if you don't believe in God?"

"This?" He touched the ichthus. It felt warm in the hollow of his throat. "I never said I didn't believe."

"You never said you did, either."

She stopped fidgeting with the flowers and came closer to his chair. He had the most foolish urge to pull her down onto his lap and kiss her until she cried uncle. He wanted to make her laugh and get that starry-eyed look that made him feel so strong and powerful and manly. He wanted to nuzzle her neck and hear her say she loved him more than Hershey Kisses. It was their pet phrase, started on their honeymoon. He'd bought six bags of the chocolates and covered her with them while she slept. He'd wanted, he'd told her, to shower her with kisses for the rest of their lives.

What an idiot he'd been to think anything that precious could last.

"I haven't been a Christian very long, Drew, but I wish I could share the experience with you." She tapped her heart. "Something happened to me in here. I don't even know how to explain it, but letting Jesus into my life filled an empty spot."

He knew about empty spots. A hole in his soul, one counselor had called it. Psychic wounds. He'd heard plenty of psychological mumbo jumbo about why he behaved the way he did, but none of their talk had ever filled the gaping emptiness. He couldn't imagine how reading a Bible and singing a few hymns would make any difference.

The only thing that ever helped was going into a dangerous assignment, as if the violence there externalized the powerful emotions raging inside him. Only then could he forget who he really was and where he'd come from. He could forget how much he missed his brothers. Most of all, he could forget the faces of those who had died because of him.

"I'm glad for you, Larissa. If that's what makes you happy."

She touched his arm. A touch, but he soaked her in like the parched deserts of Africa. "He can make you happy, too. He can heal our marriage. If you'll let Him."

"What time are your friends coming over?" he asked, annoyed that his throat was rusty.

"Seven."

He glanced at the huge sunburst clock over the fireplace. "I'd better make myself scarce, then." He started to wheel away. "Any snacks I can steal to take with me?"

"Magic cookies bars. But only if you stay for Bible study."

"You cheat."

She only smiled.

In the end, he'd chickened out and rolled back into his den like some bear in hibernation, lap filled with goodies he'd snitched from the kitchen. She'd prepared enough snacks to feed the whole church and then some.

Her look of disappointment niggled at him.

Ever since her conversion, as she called it, she'd talked too much about religion. Well, not religion really. God. Jesus. The Bible.

He pointed the remote toward the TV and channel-surfed. A hundred and forty channels and nothing worth watching. He pressed Off.

Restless, he ate a few grapes and made a game of catching them in his mouth. A few plunked against the carpet and Coco scurried after them, sniffed and turned up her nose.

"Come here, girl." He patted his lap. The Yorkie obeyed. "Guess it's me and you tonight. Want a cookie?"

Larissa wouldn't approve, but he broke off a bite anyway.

"Don't tell your mom," he said, and grinned when Coco yipped as if she understood.

The little dog was a golden fur ball of pure silk. Red painted toenails matched the bows sprouting from her pointed ears. Larissa thought it was cute. Drew thought it was funny. Coco received better care than some kids.

He knew that for a fact.

He'd never had a dog before unless he counted the strays Collin had tried to keep. Poor mutts never stuck around. There wasn't enough to eat. As an adult, he'd been gone too much to care for an animal.

Sometimes he wondered if he'd bought the dog as much for himself as he had for Larissa.

When the cookies were gone, Coco hopped down and trotted to the door.

"Traitor," Drew said to her departing back. "I know your tricks." She'd sneak into Larissa's party and beg for more treats.

He'd thought about sneaking in there himself. Rather, he'd considered behaving like a jerk, so Larissa would see how unfit he was to be with her friends. In the end, he'd backed out. Even a loser like him couldn't stand to embarrass Larissa that way.

Without the dog for entertainment, he thumbed through a couple of photography magazines and a sports book. Boring. He tossed those aside and flipped through the DVD collection. Most he'd already seen.

He was pretty sick of video games, though he wouldn't tell Cody that. Drew didn't have much experience with kids, but Cody was pretty cool to hang out with on a dismal Saturday while Larissa was off pandering to her mother.

In a few more days, his ribs should be in good enough shape to use the crutches. Then he could drive. He couldn't wait for that day to come. The only place he'd been since arrival was to the doctor's office.

He rolled the chair to the window, looked out. A marbled-white moon dangled overhead but the stars were invisible. Out across the wide expanse of lawn, security lights illuminated an enormous mimosa tree. The breeze wobbled the bare limbs back and forth. He could almost smell the piercing sweet blooms, though they wouldn't come until June.

By then, he'd be gone. He had to be.

Restless, but sick at the thought of leaving, never to return to the only place he'd ever known joy, he wheeled away from the window. He'd known it would be like this if he returned. Agony to be here. Agony to leave. They would both have been so much better off if Larissa had never come after him. But his wife was a politician's daughter. She had trouble accepting that the votes were in and the race was lost.

He spun the chair around. Gray spots speckled the air. The world blurred, fading in and out.

He sucked in a breath.

The spots hovered and wavered. He watched them

as he would a horror movie, with disbelief and a sense of unreality. This couldn't be happening. Not again.

Afraid to touch his eyes, afraid to move, he sat frozen in fear. He could hear the blood pound in his ears.

"God, please don't let this happen."

Whether the words were a prayer, he couldn't say. But he didn't know what else to do.

He was losing his wife. Now he was losing his eyesight, too, and with it, the career that defined him as a human being.

After a few awful minutes, the hazy, tormenting curtain lifted, and he breathed again.

Sweat beaded his upper lip. He turned on every light in the room.

What would he do if the lights went out for good?

Maybe he should tell his doctor, but what was the point? The docs in D.C. had said there was nothing they could do.

He longed to tell Larissa, to share the worry. But he couldn't. If she thought he was going blind, she'd fight the divorce even harder. That's just the way she was. She'd hang on to a useless, worthless photographer out of pity. And he wasn't about to saddle her with a physical *and* an emotional cripple. More than ever, if he was going blind, he had to set her free.

If he was well enough, he'd be out of here tomorrow before she discovered the truth. Not just about his eyes, either. All of it.

Right now, though, he had to get out of this room.

Being alone in the dark had terrified him as a kid. And he and his brothers had been alone in the dark more times than he could count. A few times he'd been locked in a closet for throwing a fit. He hated the dark.

What would it be like to be in darkness forever? A shudder racked him from head to toe.

He shoved the wheels of the chair into motion and rolled to the closet for a pair of aluminum crutches. Previously, the pressure on his ribs and abdominal incision had been too much. But no way was he going in there among Larissa's friends in a wheelchair. This would be a first. If he could do it.

Using the crutches as leverage, he stood on his good foot. Getting up wasn't difficult, but the ribs worried him.

Slowly, he eased down onto the padded rests. A pulling pain rippled beneath his arm and circled his chest. He drew a short breath.

Yep, still hurt.

Teeth gritted, he made his way across the bedroom, stopping at the door to lean and catch his breath. He was weaker than he wanted to be.

After a moment he continued on, hip-hopping on the quiet hall carpeting.

The doorway to the family room seemed a million miles away. Who knew this house was so big?

Arriving in the alcove outside the meeting, he stopped once again to catch his breath. He was panting like a dog, his ribs threatened to come out of his chest, but there was no way he would go back to that empty room.

Voices drifted out of the family room. He eavesdropped for a few minutes until able to enter without making a spectacle. Memories of the child he'd once been, standing on the outside looking in, pushed him forward.

Pasting on a smile that probably resembled a grimace, he thump-thumped into the room. An empty chair waited like an oasis at the end of the couch—if he could get there.

Larissa had prepared a place for him in case he changed his mind. His throat tightened with the sweetness of such a gesture. He never expected anyone to consider him, but Larissa always did.

A momentary hush fell over the conversation. Ten pairs of eyes turned in his direction. Larissa popped up like a jack-in-the-box, long crinkled skirt swirling around her ankles as she rushed to his aid.

"Drew! Honey, what are you doing?" Her expression was a mix of pleasure and concern. "Why didn't you call me? Are you okay?"

He wished she wouldn't have asked him that.

"Great," he muttered through clenched jaws. Even his eyeballs were sweating with the effort.

She stepped closer, lowering her voice, to save his overactive pride. "Do you need help?"

He glared at her. "Not yet. But you'd better get out of my way before I embarrass us both."

Which was exactly what he should do, be rude and crude and obnoxious. But Drew didn't have the strength.

Hovering at his elbow, Larissa followed along as he thumped to the chair. Sweat bathed his face and slicked his palms.

With gratitude and a grunt of triumph, he slithered into the chair.

Larissa watched him for a moment, anxious, and then whirled toward the group. "Most of you know my husband, Drew."

The happiness in her tone almost finished him off. Was it that important that he hang out with a bunch of religious people he barely knew?

Annoyed to feel out of place and uncomfortable, he nodded to the assembly.

A murmur of polite greetings circled around him. Several men offered a handshake. He'd met one of them, Mark Bassett a few times at the country club. Someone asked how he was feeling. He managed a raspy answer, lying through his teeth. He wasn't fine. He was about to die. Every bone in his rib cage hurt. His lungs screamed for air. His body wobbled like a broken hula hoop, and he was sweating like a pig.

But he'd made it. If he was anything at all, Drew Michaels was a survivor. He'd made it in here and he'd make it out. Proof that, when the time came he was still man enough to do what had to be done.

No matter how much it hurt.

As the group settled back into their study, he checked

them out. Though he didn't remember all the names, he remembered details. The blonde with the asymmetrical face, the guy with the pencil mustache who looked like an actor in an old movie, a married couple who could pass for brother and sister. He offered a smile to Larissa's best friend, Jennifer, a red-haired spitfire who had once actually approved of him. Now she glared back as if he was pond scum.

Well, wasn't he?

He was hurting her best friend. He deserved her animosity. No way would she understand that his insistence on a divorce was not intended to hurt Larissa, but to set her free from a lousy future.

He sneaked a peak at Larissa, hovering in the archway between the family and dining rooms. She wore the strangest expression: Surprise, admiration, pleasure, worry. He didn't want her to worry.

Breath returning to normal, he gave her a wink. She smiled.

Suddenly, he forgot about the terrifying blurriness. Forgot about the agonizing journey from the bedroom. He even forgot about the pain in his ribs and all the reasons he shouldn't encourage her.

"We're doing a word study tonight, Drew," Mark said, leaning forward. The dude was a little too preppy for Drew's taste, but he seemed sincere about his faith. Drew pretended interest.

"Jesus is called the Prince of Peace," Mark went on,

"so we wanted to find out what that means to us today, as believers. We're learning about peace."

Drew figured he could use a healthy dose of that.

Though he felt awkward and out of place, no one seemed to notice.

Larissa scooted a kitchen chair right next to his and opened her Bible for him to share. He probably should maneuver away, but moving from this chair now was impossible. Trapped by his own making, he settled in to listen, acutely conscious of his wife's nearness.

From what he could tell, Mark was the leader because he talked the most. "According to the book of John, Jesus' peace is not the kind of peace the world talks about."

"Then what is it?" Jennifer asked.

"I found a place in Philippians," Larissa offered, sounding unusually shy. "I really like it."

Drew had seen her reading the Bible at night. It kind of freaked him out.

"Read it."

She flipped the thin leaves of the Bible, generating a puff of air that stirred her perfume. "Here it is. Philippians 4:7. 'And the peace of God which surpasses all understanding will guard your hearts and minds through Christ Jesus.'" She laid her manicured fingers over the page. "To me, that means no matter what happens or how difficult the situation, you can have peace on the inside, in your heart and mind, knowing that everything is going to work out for the good."

Was she talking about their marriage? Was that why she kept on trying even after he'd made it clear he would not change his mind about a divorce? Was her religion causing all this resistance?

"A peace that passes all understanding," Mark was saying. "Pretty cool."

Peace in any circumstance. Didn't make sense to him. But apparently his wife believed it. His curiosity got the better of him.

The session went on and Drew listened more intently than he'd intended, but he didn't open his ignorant mouth. No way. Though a street kid with little formal education, he'd read widely and traveled enough to pick up a lot of information. He was a quick study at just about anything, but this religion business was uncharted water.

A couple of times he touched the necklace and wondered about the bit of scripture engraved on the back. Someday he might ask someone. But not Larissa and not tonight.

After a while, when Drew's head buzzed with overload, the group broke for refreshments.

The woman with the asymmetrical face, one that would make an interesting photo, came over for a chat. Now he remembered. Her name was Amy.

"We were all sorry to hear about your accident. Our church has been praying for you."

Drew nodded, uncomfortable. "Thanks."

"Could I bring you something to drink?"

After an hour of stress, he was as dry as the Sahara. A bunch of Christians were more nerve-racking than photographing lightning.

"I'm good. Don't trouble yourself."

"No trouble at all. I'm happy to do it." Amy darted off toward the kitchen where Jennifer dug in the refrigerator, handing out Cokes. Drew was aware that Larissa's best friend avoided him like the bird flu.

Larissa, meanwhile, was at the bar, deep in conversation with Mark. Sandy brown hair, blue eyes, laugh crinkles, and a great tan, the guy was all right. Nice. Probably even had blue blood. Much more Larissa's type than a rambling photographer from the back alley.

Drew narrowed his eyes, seeing his wife and the Bible teacher in a new light. Larissa should have married a man like Mark. In fact, Mark might be the right man to step in once Drew was out of the picture. He was a lawyer, part of Larissa's social set, a good Christian, and well able to give Larissa everything she wanted and deserved. If memory served, the guy had lost a wife to an accident some years ago. He was probably ready to settle down and have a few rug rats running around the house.

Drew slid lower in his chair, adjusted the heavily braced leg, and studied the conversing pair.

Yep. Mark was a great candidate to step in once Drew was gone.

"Here you are." Amy returned, bearing a can of pop

and a plate of cookies. He didn't have the energy to admit he'd eaten half a dozen already.

"Thanks."

Amy settled onto Larissa's chair and peppered him with questions. Before long, he was sharing his travels, his photo shoots, interjecting the truth with enough funny comments to make the woman laugh. He laughed once, too, but pain hit his rib cage, so he decided not to do that again.

In spite of his resolve not to, he looked around for Larissa. He couldn't seem to help himself. This time she was chatting up the married couple as they took their leave.

After shutting the door, she turned his way, but before he could catch her attention, Mark said something to her. She laughed. The musical sound sprinkled the air like confetti.

Annoyance zipped through Drew. Larissa was his wife and he should be the man making her laugh. Not some preppy tennis jock with a great tan and a law degree.

He shook his head at the irony. One minute, he wanted to marry her off to the guy and the next he wanted to punch Mark's lights out for making her laugh.

Sheesh.

He took a long, stinging drink of Coke.

He was hopeless.

Chapter Six

As soon as the last guest left, Larissa flipped off the porch light, set the deadbolt lock, then leaned against the door. Her shoulders ached with tension.

The Bible study had gone great, but Drew's unexpected appearance had rattled her nerves. He was barely strong enough to get in and out of the wheelchair. What if he'd fallen and reinjured something?

Most of her friends had no idea that Drew wanted a divorce, but she'd been afraid he might say something. Or worse, that he and Jennifer would get into a confrontation. Jen was a great friend and a good Christian, but her temper sometimes overrode her common sense. Right now, she was furious with Drew.

Larissa glanced toward her husband, still in the straight-backed chair where he'd collapsed two hours earlier. He was staring at her, one knuckled hand to his scruffy cheek.

Even though he looked exhausted, his wolf-eyed gaze gave her butterflies. It always had.

Dear Lord, I love him. Please make him see reason.

She started cleaning up the room, taking the empty pop can and plate from the end table next to him. "What possessed you to get on those crutches tonight?"

He quirked a lopsided smile. "Got to start sometime."

"I nearly had a heart attack when you came wobbling through that archway."

"That makes two of us."

"You're really proud of yourself, aren't you?"

"Yes, ma'am. I'm mobile. Tomorrow, the car."

She harrumphed. "Think again, mister."

He offered an empty glass. When she reached for it, he held on, holding her there while he said, "How do you feel about Mark?"

Where had that come from? "He's a friend."

"That's not what I meant."

He watched her with such intensity that she swallowed, understanding too well what he asked. He was trying to shove his own wife at another man!

She yanked the glass. "I resent that implication."

Drew shrugged, a casual dismissal of her feelings that cut deep. "Mark's more your type."

"You're my husband, Drew, till death do us part."

"In other words, you'd be better off if I'd died in that blast."

She clumped the gathered dishes onto the bar. "Don't do this."

A spray of cookie crumbs fell to the tile. Coco rushed in to clean up the spill. Who cared about Italian tile or cookie crumbs? Her husband wanted a divorce and nothing else mattered. "Why can't you see that we have something beautiful and good, a relationship worth fighting for?"

Drew was silent. She turned and was troubled at the stark yearning in his expression.

"Drew?" she whispered, reaching toward him.

He blinked and the expression was gone, so fast she almost blamed her imagination. Almost.

She moved toward him, tempted to fall against his chest and cry out all her pain and love, to make him admit that he still cared for her. His injured ribs, and the fear of rejection, held her at bay.

She touched his arm, but he shifted away. She squinted at the rock-hard line of his jaw. All this time she'd believed he avoided her touch out of loathing. Now she wondered if the cause was another emotion entirely.

Dropping her hand with a sigh, she said, "It's late. You need to rest."

"Rest won't change the inevitable, Larissa." His voice was cold. "I'm filing for divorce as soon as I can get out of here."

The words still ripped like a chain saw. She held up a hand.

"Let's not have this argument tonight." She couldn't bear it. The Bible study had been so encouraging and now this.

She found a couple of dirty napkins and tossed them

toward the garbage can. Between praying and worrying, she wouldn't sleep again tonight.

"We've never had this conversation at all. Every time I bring it up, you change the subject or run away. Get it through your head, Larissa. I'm out of here. It's over. I'm gone. The only thing keeping me here now is a broken leg."

Her whole body jerked at the vicious assault. Biting back a cry of despair, she asked the inevitable question. "Is there someone else? Is that why you want a divorce?"

She hated the way her voice trembled, but she had to know.

Eyes hot, she watched Drew's face. He wouldn't lie about something this important. She was certain of that.

He stared at her a long time, a muscle over his cheekbone twitching. Finally, he rasped out, "No. Never."

Weak with relief but as confused as ever, she asked, "Then why?"

"I've told you." He gazed toward the fireplace, avoiding her eyes. "I don't want to be married anymore. It cramps my style."

Cramped his style? When had she *ever* done that!

Suddenly, the pressure of the last few weeks came to a head. Like a volcano, she erupted, all the anxiety and fear and hurt boiling over.

"Well, I've got a flash for you, hotshot. Commitment is about sticking with something even when it's not fun anymore." She stabbed a finger at him. "And believe me, you are no fun at all right now. I know you don't want to be here with me. You've made that very clear. But you're still my husband, and I'm not turning my back on you or our marriage."

"But you'd like to, wouldn't you?"

His tone was too quiet and too hopeless. Blasting him wouldn't accomplish a thing.

Exasperated, she went back to cleaning the room. "I can't talk to you."

The room hummed with tension while blood roared in her ears. Drew remained on the chair, but Larissa refused to look at him again. Let him stew. Let him sit there and think up ugly things to say. He could sit there forever for all she cared.

A wadded napkin thunked against her arm.

"Hey."

She whirled on him. "Don't say another word right now."

"I've never seen you so fired up."

"I've never had a husband try to dump me before." At the admission, emotion clogged her throat. With the iron will that helped her deal with a fractious mother and her father's difficult electorate, she swallowed it down. She was not about to cry in front of him again. Never again.

Drew pulled a hand down his face. "Peace?"

She bent and yanked the napkin off the floor. "A little late for that."

"I didn't mean to ruin your Bible study." His tone

had changed from cold and hard to calm and solicitous, and she had no idea why.

"You didn't." *But you're trying to ruin my life. Our lives.* And she refused to discuss it anymore tonight.

She returned the chairs to the kitchen, then straightened the couch pillows. All the while, Drew remained silent, brooding.

Larissa checked the door locks and turned off all the lights except for the family room and hallway. With one last glance at her puzzling, exasperating husband, she started toward the stairs.

"Hey."

One hand on the smooth, golden banister, she stopped but didn't turn around.

Drew didn't speak for another long moment. When he did, she understood his hesitancy. "I think I need some help."

He'd made the trek to the living room, but he couldn't make it back.

Larissa turned around. "You seem to crave independence from me. Why not start now?"

"Smart aleck," he said mildly, his expression soft and troubling. "Come on. Be a sport and help the poor crippled guy."

"In other words, you need me, so you'll put up with my company."

"Something like that."

"You are impossible."

"That's what I've been trying to tell you. I'm a user, Larissa. I'm no good for you."

He was the most bewildering human being on the planet. But she loved him anyway. She'd brought him here to recuperate and for a chance to save their marriage. As much as his cruel words hurt, she wasn't ready to throw in the towel.

With a resigned shake of her head, Larissa went to retrieve the wheelchair.

The trip down the hall to the Bible study must have taken every bit of strength and determination he could muster. When Drew set his mind to do something, he seldom failed, a truth that both comforted and terrified. He would get well, and without divine intervention he would also leave her for good. He was that stubborn.

She wished she could understand why God was letting this happen to her. Wasn't she trying as hard as she could to be a good Christian? Her marriage hadn't deteriorated until after she'd accepted Christ.

"Sit still while I straighten your bed," she said. When the sheets were tightened and the pillows fluffed, she patted the mattress, but kept her distance. There was a limit to the rejection she could tolerate in one night. "I'll bring you some ibuprofen."

"Make that a double," he grunted.

On arms bulging with muscle, he pushed up from the chair to stand on one leg. Halfway up, he started wobbling like a bobble head. His dark skin paled. His upper lip erupted in perspiration.

Larissa's heart twisted with pity—and with sadness for a man who hated to ask for help, especially from his own wife.

Hurrying, she stuck a shoulder under his good arm. "You have *so* overdone."

He was twice her size, but she managed to heave and shove until he tumbled onto the bed. Unintentionally, she fell with him, her arms trapped behind him.

Their faces were inches apart. Larissa's pulse beat a rat-a-tat-tat against her collarbone. Drew's dark, secret eyes searched hers, his manly scent as familiar and wonderful as ever.

As if the sound was torn from deep in his soul, he groaned, "'Rissa."

In that one word, she heard a longing he refused to admit. Though she couldn't understand the source, a battle raged inside him. She waited, hoping for more.

Finally, voice gruff, he said, "Let go."

"I can't. I'm trapped." Not that she was sorry. Nor was she trying to rectify the problem.

"Yes," he answered, sadly. "That's exactly what you are. Trapped."

Then, as if he couldn't stop the action, he stroked her hair back, looped a stray lock over one ear. At the exquisitely tender touch, Larissa melted.

"What are we doing, Drew?" she whispered. "What's happened to us?"

A lump, hot and heavy as a brick, formed behind her breastbone. She leaned closer to kiss him, to reclaim what was hers. He rolled to the side, releasing her, but not before she recognized what he was trying to hide.

She worked in campaigns. She understood better than most what body language and the eyes could say that words didn't.

Drew still cared for her.

Long after the house quieted and Coco abandoned him for Larissa's upstairs room, Drew lay awake staring into the darkness. Tonight had changed him. And he was scared out of his mind. He wished his body would heal faster. He wished to be five thousand miles away.

Most of all, he wished to be upstairs with his wife.

His determination had almost crumbled as she'd leaned over him, warm perfume wrapped around his senses like a cozy blanket.

He was a loathsome excuse for a human being.

Over and over, her wounded expression played in his head. He'd said some hateful things tonight. How much more could she take before throwing him out on the street?

Tossing the cover aside, he slid out of the bed and grappled for the crutches. Painfully, he maneuvered to the stairs and alternately crawled and hobbled to the top. Larissa's room, *their* room, was directly in front of him. Ribs screaming in protest, body distressingly weak, he wobbled to the closed door and rested against it, gathering both his strength and his courage. He didn't even know why he'd come up here.

And then he heard her.

Soft muffled weeping, as if her face were in a pillow. Heartbroken cries of despair. He could hear her voice, too, but couldn't make out the words.

Was she praying?

He squeezed his eyes shut.

Oh, God. And he meant it. Having to hurt her killed him. *Killed him.*

She was the best thing in his life. The only human being, other than his brothers, who had loved him in spite of his failings.

Emotion bubbled up inside, threatening to overflow and drive him to his knees. He longed to offer comfort, to promise her the world and everything in it. Anything to make her happy again.

Perhaps he should go in there, beg her forgiveness, and reveal the whole truth—that he was afraid to let her love him, afraid that he would never be what she needed. Afraid she wouldn't want him once she knew the truth.

He lifted a hand to knock, then let the clenched fist fall to his side.

Leaving her was the most unselfish thing he'd ever do in his life.

He'd come this far. He couldn't back down now.

Tomorrow he'd begin rehab in earnest. In a few weeks, his body would let him leave. If only he could be sure his heart would do the same.

Larissa noticed a change in Drew following the night of the Bible study. Within the week he was hobbling around the house on crutches and by the next his ribs tolerated an outing or two. He still tired easily, but she was relieved to see him healing.

The physical improvements weren't the only changes she noticed, though the others were less subtle. She wasn't foolish enough to think one Bible study had influenced him that much but one never knew. Whatever had happened, he'd mellowed. To her vast relief, he said no more about divorce, though it hovered between them like a bad case of halitosis. She wouldn't complain about the respite even though his silence felt like the calm before the storm.

And now, after that one sweet, aching moment, she believed he still loved her. His words said no, but his eyes said yes. And that alone was enough to keep her going. Though she'd cried herself to sleep that night wondering why he kept a wall between them, something was stirring inside Drew.

She felt him watching her and sometimes when she turned around he would look away, pretending to be otherwise occupied.

If he would only share what troubled him, maybe

they could resolve their issues. But Drew didn't trust her enough for that.

Now that he'd wounded her so deeply, she was afraid of what else he might do. And yet, she couldn't give up hope.

Her mother had called her a fool yesterday. The words cut like a razor, deep and drawing blood.

"Stop catering to a man who doesn't want you. The whole town is talking."

In other words, Mother's friends.

"They wouldn't know my business if you didn't tell them," Larissa had replied, and then she'd left her parents' home, too upset to stay and help with hanging the new drapes. Her mother wouldn't forgive that inconsiderate action for a long time. She'd already phoned twice today, insisting on her daughter's help.

Larissa glanced out on the patio to see Drew maneuvering one crutch at a time down the rock steps to the koi pond. Early spring had arrived, filling her backyard with sweet-scented lilacs and a wild abundance of perennials in need of taming. Camera swaying around his neck, Drew had mentioned feeding the koi while she worked on the flowers. Coco trotted happily along beside him, pausing now and then to gaze up in adoring concern. Her master's slow movement puzzled the little dog.

Now that Drew was mobile, as he called it, he spent considerable time with the fish. Restorative, he said, to sit in the gardens and wait for birds and butterflies to land in sight of his camera lens or to snap action shots of the koi at feeding time. He'd even named the three orange males Groucho, Harpo, and Zippo, after the famous old comedians.

For a man accustomed to erupting volcanoes, civil war, and other wild adventures, watching the fish swim couldn't be too fascinating.

Still, he relieved her of their care as much as possible, for which she was grateful. Cleaning the pool was the downside of enjoying the colorful fish.

Slipping into a hooded jacket, her bucket of gardening tools in hand, Larissa went to join him.

Crutches propped against a chair dragged close to the edge, he tossed food into the water, one piece at a time.

"The irises are taking over," he said, nodding to the tall purple heads around the edge of the pool.

"Spring does that." It occurred to her that Drew hadn't been home long enough to experience their backyard in spring or any other season for that matter. "They start spreading. If I don't divide a few, they'll crowd out the fish."

He bent to the water and pulled one up. Holding the lavender flower next to her face, he shocked her by saying, "This one's the color of your eyes. You have beautiful eyes."

Larissa held her breath as Drew tucked the iris behind her ear and let his hand linger on the fall of hair streaming over her shoulder.

A smile bloomed inside. This was the Drew she knew and loved.

Six months ago, when he was home, he had said those same kinds of romantic things. He'd told her she was beautiful and precious. Then, she'd been confident of his love, though he'd seldom spoken the words. And she had loved him with such fierceness that she'd mourned for days each time he left. What had happened between then and now?

The waterfall tumbling over the flat rock sides of the pool was music. The scent of spring was fresh and moist and promising. She ached for a similar renewal in her fractured marriage but didn't know what else to do.

Except pray. She could always pray, and remember that love never fails. Even though it had so far.

"Some of the neighborhood kids are coming over later to swim," she said, not wanting to move lest Drew's tender mood wither and die with the culled flowers. "Will you keep an eye on them?"

"Rug rats," he said, though his response was harsher than his treatment of the kids. He liked them in a gruff sort of way. "Where will you be?"

"I have some things to do for Mother."

He dropped his hand, disappointing her, his opinion of her errand clear. "What impending disaster is it this time? The patina on her silver spoon needs polishing?"

"Drew," she admonished softly. Sometimes the requests *were* petty excuses for attention. "We didn't finish hanging the new drapes." She didn't mention why. "And she's asked me to interview maid applicants."

"Didn't you do that a few weeks ago?"

"Consuelo didn't iron the way Mother likes."

"Criminal offense. No wonder she's getting the ax." He tossed a grain of feed into the pool. "Don't your mother's demands ever get on your nerves?"

He didn't know the half of it.

"Sometimes," she admitted.

"You don't show it. Even when she calls with some nonsensical crisis that will resolve on its own, you jump and run."

"Wouldn't you have done the same for your mother?"

His expression turned to stone. He lapsed into silence and stared down at Groucho making kissie faces on the surface of the water.

Contrite to bring up an obviously painful topic, but curious, too, at the reaction, Larissa touched his arm. The dark skin was taut beneath her fingertips.

"Why don't you like to talk about your family?"

"They're dead," he said harshly.

"So is my Grandma Sadie, but Dad and I still tell funny stories about her all the time."

"Yeah, well..." He let the topic hang. Forearms on his knees, he flicked a single bit of fish food to Harpo and watched the bubbles send ripples across the surface.

"Surely, you have some good memories." Larissa held her breath. She was pressing again and fully expected Drew to grab his crutches and limp off toward the house. If he was well, he'd head for the telephone and by tomorrow he'd be at the airport. It happened every time she ventured too close.

But why not press? She was losing him anyway.

To her surprise, he didn't back away.

"I had two brothers," he said softly. "Awesome brothers." The words carried the bittersweet ache of love and loss. "All for one and one for all. That was us."

Larissa smiled, thinking of the cute little boy Drew must have been. She would love to have a baby just like him. "Sounds as if you read *The Three Musketeers*."

"I don't remember." His mouth curved in a sad smile. "Collin came up with the idea. He was the smart one."

Collin. Drew had never mentioned any of his family by name before.

She kept quiet, hoping he would go on in that rambling, reminiscent manner. She wanted to know about the fire that took their lives and how he came to be the only one not present at the time. She might even ask.

A breeze ruffled his longish hair and he thrust the dark, loosened locks straight back from his forehead.

"Losing my brothers was the worst thing that ever happened to me."

On her knees beside the pool, Larissa pulled another iris and didn't look at him. Even though her insides tensed with the need to know, she spoke casually as if the answer was really no big deal. "What were they like?"

Asking Drew for personal information was as precarious and unpredictable as playing in the crater of a volcano.

Silence reigned for a few seconds and Larissa figured the conversation was over. She pulled another stray flower, adding it to the bucket for discard.

A pebble of fish food plunked the water in front of her.

"We built a fort. Our secret hiding place in the woods behind the school. Collin brought stray dogs there." He laughed softly, sadly. "They ran off."

Pleased and emboldened, she sat back on her heels to look at him. "And your other brother?"

His eyes flicked to hers, but instead of secret darkness she saw light. "Everybody liked Ian. He was too little to keep up when Collin and I took off for the fort. Collin carried our stuff. You know, kid junk. I carried Ian. He was so skinny, I could put him on my back and run the whole way."

"Most boys would find that pretty annoying, wouldn't they? A tagalong brother too small to carry his own weight."

He twitched one shoulder. "I didn't mind. It was Ian."

"He ain't heavy, he's my brother?" she asked, quoting the old song.

"Yeah, something like that, I guess."

She saw the depth of love he'd had for his siblings and understood a little better why it pained him to discuss them. The loss of those he'd loved so much had left a huge void in his life.

"Once we had this old bike," he went on. "Ian climbed on the handlebars and I peddled like crazy, showing off."

She tapped his bare toes.

"Imagine that. You showing off." His cocky attitude was one of the things that had first attracted her.

He shot her a sideways grin. "I took a bump too fast and Ian went flying. Hit a rock the size of Toledo. Busted his head open." He touched a spot above his temple. "Scared me to death. I thought I'd killed him. Dumb kid wasn't even mad. Instead, he was upset because I was. He kept saying it was okay, it was okay." He shook his head. "Dumb kid."

"Those are good memories, Drew. Memories to cherish."

His gaze found hers and held steady. Something flickered in his expression, a relenting of sorts. After a bit, he said, "In all the bad, I guess I'd let the good get lost."

"I love hearing about your brothers. About you. I like thinking of you as a little boy."

She was no psychologist but any intelligent being with half a heart could see that Drew hid things, maybe even from himself. Arrogant, stubborn, secretive. Did those attributes hide a deeply wounded child?

"You know everything about me that matters," he said.

"No, I don't. You've always held back a part of yourself."

"Why do women have to dig so deep?"

She cocked her head and kept her answer light. "Is that a sexist remark?"

He tossed a grain of fish food at her. "I've never talked to anyone before about Collin and Ian."

The admission sent a ripple of pleasure straight to her heart. She'd longed for this kind of husband-and-wife communication.

"You can tell me anything, Drew. *Anything*."

For a second, he looked bewildered, and then his face hardened as if keeping a distance took great effort.

Grappling for his crutches, he pushed up from the chair. Larissa remained on her knees beside the pool, bucket filled with wayward irises. As Drew maneuvered around her, she stopped him with a hand on his foot.

"Drew." She gazed up into eyes as dark and mysterious as midnight.

"What?"

"Don't run away anymore, Drew. I need you."

He squeezed those mysterious eyes shut, and when he opened them again, he groaned, "Ah, 'Rissa."

Her heart thumped once, hard, before the loud chatter of children's voices shattered the moment.

The neighbor kids, Cody and Kelli, came around the side of the house, followed by three other children in the same age range.

With a beleaguered sigh, Drew turned to greet the newcomers. Larissa's hope filtered to the ground like falling leaves.

"Hey, dudes and dudettes," Drew said to the kids. "What's happening?"

The little girl giggled. She batted long eyelashes. "You said we could swim. Is now okay?"

At eight, Kelli was a fair-haired beauty with eyes as blue as robin eggs. Drew was a sucker for the little girl although he would deny it to the death.

"Sure," Larissa answered. "I have some things to do inside, but Drew will be out here. He won't mind playing chaperone. Will you, Drew?"

She turned in time to catch the roll of his eyes heavenward. "Looking forward to it."

Larissa suppressed a giggle. "I'll bring out some snacks and the cell phone, just in case."

"Yippee," he said wryly, but his eyes sparkled with humor.

Getting faster all the time on his crutches, he followed the gaggle of children. He'd traveled maybe ten yards when he suddenly stopped and wavered.

"Drew?" Pulse in her throat, Larissa dropped the gardening bucket and rushed forward. "What's wrong? Are you okay?"

Leaning heavily on one crutch, he rubbed a hand across his face. "Just a little wobbly. I'm good."

But as he started forward again, Larissa couldn't shake a new awareness.

For one split second before she'd reached him, Drew had looked afraid.

Chapter Seven

Drew prowled his bedroom, restless and worried. Larissa would be back soon. She'd gone into her father's office for a few hours of strategic planning—whatever that entailed. With his cast off and the ribs decently healed, he was well enough the nurses no longer came, and the physical therapist only stopped by every other day.

If he wanted to accomplish anything, now was the time.

A few days ago he'd made a tactical error. He'd talked about Collin and Ian. It scared him that he'd told Larissa so much, as if the few sentences could resurrect his sordid past and ruin his present.

He was getting far too comfortable with Larissa, letting his guard down that way. The trouble had started the night of Larissa's Bible study and hadn't let up.

But he'd been thinking about something she'd said that night. Thinking and wondering.

Larissa was a Christian. Her faith didn't allow for divorce. Now, he wondered if religion was the only reason she wanted to hold on to their crippled marriage.

He'd never planned to marry. Never thought he was capable of loving someone other than himself, considering his lousy childhood. Larissa had changed all that. And now, because of her religion, she believed she was stuck with him forever. He loved her too much to allow that. But unless he made the break soon, he wasn't sure what might happen.

Maybe the concussion had done more than blur his vision.

He'd almost given that away, too. A couple of times he'd been tempted to tell her about the fearful episodes of blindness. But his pride wouldn't let him. He knew her. Out of pity, she'd fight the divorce twice as hard if he went blind.

A shudder wracked his body. A blind photographer.

Time to do something more proactive than beat Cody at video racing. The doc had said the episodes should disappear with time. They hadn't.

He limped to the bedside table and fished around, coming out with a fat phone book. In the yellow pages, he found a long list of ophthalmologists, though he wasn't even sure an eye specialist was the right kind of doctor. He had to start somewhere, but he didn't want Larissa to know. Somehow, he'd find a way to the doctor's office when she was out and about. A cab, he supposed, though the crutches put a crimp in his mobility and wore him out in a hurry. His stamina stunk.

As he lifted the telephone receiver, he flexed his ankle, grateful that the pain was now only soreness. He'd be off the crutches soon.

He heard the front door open and Larissa's voice call, "Drew?"

He slammed the receiver down.

The call would have to wait.

Later that afternoon, Larissa went in to straighten Drew's room. She noticed the open phone book, and out of curiosity glanced at the page. Not surprised to find he was looking up doctors, she *was* surprised at the names circled in pen. All were ophthalmologists.

Eye specialists?

Gnawing on her bottom lip, she wondered.

What else was her secretive husband hiding?

Sunday morning dawned cool and cloudy. Drew awakened with grim determination.

He'd never cared for Larissa's mother, and today he liked her even less. She was to blame for his latest dilemma.

Yesterday, dear Marsha had stopped by. Again. Lately, the woman was underfoot all the time, but yesterday she'd hurt Larissa's feelings, and Drew was still red hot about that. The woman had berated Larissa for spending too much time with her church friends. Like an idiot,

Drew had hobbled into the living room and announced that he was going to church with his wife. Her mother had been so horrified, she'd shut up and left.

Now he had to follow through.

With a determined grimace, he hopped into the bathroom. The things he did to himself.

He showered, shaved and dressed, though he didn't own a suit and wasn't in any shape to go shopping. Larissa's church friends might look down their noses at his attire, but let them. He wasn't interested in impressing anyone anyway.

With more effort than he'd expected, he forced a pair of dark gray chinos over his cast and found a blue shirt Larissa had given him for Christmas. His weight loss made the silky-smooth Italian button-down a little loose, and he needed a haircut, but the mirror said he looked pretty good anyway. He hadn't been this dressed up since their impromptu wedding.

For a few pleasant seconds, he remembered that day. He'd actually been cocky enough to think he could pull off the grand charade and marry a princess without anyone ever knowing he was the frog.

With a self-deprecating laugh, he shook his head.

Delusions of grandeur. But ah, what a great three years they'd enjoyed.

Whether she admitted it or not, Larissa had to know their marriage was an error in judgment. He'd known all along, but hadn't accepted the truth until she'd brought up babies. Then he'd heard the death knell.

Well, whatever. Today, he was going to do one last nice thing for her. And maybe for himself. The whole church/religion thing weighed heavily on his mind lately. He'd even taken to praying about his eyes. Not that it did any good, but he kept thinking God would feel sorry for Larissa and heal him for her sake.

After spritzing on a light dose of cologne, Drew went to find his wife, oddly anxious to see her reaction. He'd looked like day-old roadkill long enough.

The phrase gave him pause. Roadkill.

He'd been lucky. Some of the others in the convoy that day hadn't been. Larissa claimed God was protecting him for some reason known only to Him. Drew didn't know about all that, but he was grateful to be alive. He rubbed an index finger over the little fish around his neck, thinking. Lately, he'd been thinking about a lot of serious things. He supposed a near-death experience had that effect on everyone.

The scent of coffee drew him toward the breakfast nook. Larissa loved the espresso machine and all those exotic types of coffee beans.

He found her standing with her back to him, stirring sweetener into a cup. Her long, dark hair hung in a gleaming sheet from a fancy clasp at the crown. He was suddenly overtaken by the powerful urge to touch the silky hair and to smell its clean, flowery fragrance. He wanted to wrap himself in her presence, in her scent, her warmth and to forget death and destruction, blindness and pain, all the other ugliness that resided outside her arms.

The urge was so powerful he wobbled. To rein in the startling need, he cleared his throat. "Good morning."

She spun around, spoon in hand. Her violet eyes lit up.

"Wow," she said, delighting him.

"You like?" He preened a little. Well, as much as a man with a bum leg could preen.

For one glorious minute, he basked in Larissa's warm honey gaze. Then, quicker than the wink of a shutter, he realized the futility and looked away.

"Are you really going to church with me?"

She hadn't believed him. He should have expected that.

"I said I would." The answer came out gruff and cranky. Thumping up to the bar, he levered onto a stool.

She lifted one finely arched eyebrow. With an inner wrench, Drew remembered the silky feel of that brow beneath his fingertip. With the discipline that made him a patient photographer, he reined in the memory.

"I thought you only said that to upset Mother," she murmured.

He grinned. "Maybe so. But I said it, so I have to do it."

Those glowing, soft eyes sparkled. "Yes, you do. But I wish you'd go for more reasons than to annoy Mother."

"Maybe I am. You said God protected me. I figure I owe Him."

"I might even take you out to lunch afterward."

Uh-oh. "Better not."

Her face fell. He couldn't stand that.

Backpedaling, he said, "What I mean is, I'll take you. Well, technically, you'd be taking me, but..." He offered his cutest grin and shrugged.

Her disappointment lifted instantly. She handed him a cup of coffee. "I know just the place."

"Yeah? Where?" He was trying to be jolly about the whole church thing, but the hint that she might turn this into something more worried him. "Maybe I should just stay home. You can go out with your friends."

She aimed her coffee cup at him. "Oh, no you don't. You are not backing out on me now." She grinned. "I'll tell Mother."

He gave a mock groan. "Sneaky."

"Yeah, well, you should have expected that. Besides, you're all dressed up. Can't waste a good-looking man."

Liking her compliment more than was wise, Drew pointed a finger. "If you're a praying woman, better pray now. I'm driving."

He limped out of the room with the musical sound of her giggle in his ears.

Drew had photographed temples, cathedrals, mosques and shrines all over the world. He'd been in and around any number of churches, but he wasn't prepared for Sunday morning worship service at Larissa's church.

A few people stared. Others introduced themselves.

Most paid him no mind at all. Larissa's klatch of friends, however, gathered around and seemed genuinely glad to see him. Though he found their welcome strange and unsettling, he was also warmed by the friendliness. Even Mark shook his hand and invited him to join an outing next week.

Having considered the church group to be Larissa's friends and not his, Drew had expected to feel left out, like a fifth wheel, but he didn't. His wife's popularity drew him into the circle.

As they entered the sanctuary, choosing a place near the back out of consideration for his disability, Drew couldn't take his eyes off his wife. No wonder she had a bevy of friends. She was beautiful inside and out.

He wondered if he'd ever told her that.

Today, she wore heels with a simple print dress shot with the violet color of her eyes. A single amethyst dangled from a silver choker in the hollow of her throat. Wide silver bracelets adorned one wrist, showing off her long, slim fingers and manicured nails.

He had wanted to please her this morning but, as strange as it sounded, he was the happy one.

The service began and though he was uncomfortable both emotionally and physically, he liked the music. Then the preacher got up, a short dynamo of a guy, and told everyone to open their Bibles to the book of Matthew. He'd never owned a Bible in his life, so Larissa scooted closer to share. He anchored one side of the book on his knee. She anchored the other on hers so that they touched from shoulder to knee, bringing back memories of Bible study. She smiled at him, and her soft perfume danced around his nose.

He hadn't counted on the closeness in the pews. Her nearness was both wonderful and painful. But since he was stuck, he might as well enjoy it. One last, grand gesture. That's why he was here.

He started to sling an arm over the back of the pew, but caught himself in time to refrain, though the warmth of her skin, the silky rustle of her dress, the smell of her hair were all balms for his weary, dry spirit.

At some point, the preacher caught his attention and he managed to focus on the sermon.

At first, the minister talked about laying up treasures in Heaven instead of on earth. Drew had no problem at all with that. Too many people were materialistic. But as the preacher expounded on the verses, Drew read farther down the page.

The eye is the lamp of the body. If your eyes are good, your whole body will be full of light. But if your eyes are bad, your whole body will be full of darkness. If then the light within you is darkness, how great is that darkness!

Drew broke out in a sweat. What was this scripture doing in the same chapter with a discussion of materialism? Any talk about eyes upset him. He still hadn't managed an ophthalmologist appointment. What if his eyes went dark forever? What did a blind photographer without a high school education do for a living?

He wondered if God cared one whit about a man's sight and if praying would do any good. Drew was willing to do about anything to save his vision. For himself as well as for Larissa.

He must have made a sound because Larissa turned her head and whispered, "Are you hurting? Do we need to leave?"

Though he wanted to say yes, he shook his head. "I'm good."

Though unconvinced, she returned her attention to the sermon. Drew went back to the disturbing Bible verse. If God was trying to tell him something, he was definitely listening.

After the service, Larissa wanted to take Drew straight home. The stubborn man wouldn't hear of it.

"You're tired," she insisted as they slowly made their way through the foyer and out into the breezy spring day. "Let me take you home."

"I made reservations."

"You did?" She blinked, surprised.

"Yeah, before church, and I'm hungry. Let's go eat."

"You have that pinched look around your mouth."

"More proof that I'm hungry."

"At least let me get the car and drive up closer." The parking lot was huge and Drew had refused to let her drop him off while she parked. His pride had taken enough of a hit when she hadn't let him drive.

This time she should have saved her breath. With dogged determination, Drew set off across the concrete parking lot. Her heels tap-tapped to the rhythm of his thumpety-thump like some bizarre rap tune. If she thought about it much, the combination would make her laugh.

"Where are these secret reservations you've made?" she asked when they were inside the soft leather interior of the Denali.

A tiny smile tipped the corner of his lips. "Riverside Steakhouse."

A sweet memory danced through her head.

"We don't need a reservation there," she said, puzzled. What was going on?

"We do today." Drew kicked the seat back in reclining position and relaxed.

"You *are* tired," she said. "Let me take you home. We can get lunch at a drive-through on our way." As much as she wanted to go to their special restaurant, his health was more important.

He slanted her a look. "I'm good. Just resting the leg. Drive."

"Would you tell me if you were tired?"

"I'm not."

Okay, then, enough of that. "What did you think of church?"

"I thought you were the most beautiful woman there."

"That's not what I asked."

He slipped on his sunglasses, and then rested his head back, eyes closed. From the side, she could see his lashes against his cheek and the supple curve of his mouth and cheekbones. He was a gorgeous man in a rugged, dangerous, purely masculine way. From the turned heads when they'd entered the church this morning, she wasn't the only one who thought so. Or maybe they were curious about the photographer that married one of their own but few had met. His injury in Iraq held a certain fascination for some people.

Whichever, she was proud to have him by her side. She wished he understood that. How proud she was of him, how happy she felt to show him off and call him hers.

They drove along in silence for a while. She thought he was asleep until out of the blue, he said, "I liked your church."

Her mouth curved in a smile. "Does that mean you'll go again sometime?"

"Larissa."

And just like that the sun went behind a cloud.

"You could attend as long as you're here. It wouldn't hurt anything."

He opened his eyes, head swiveling toward her. "Sneaky."

"I've always wanted you beside me at church. I loved having you there."

She sounded pitiful, begging him. Her mother was

right. She was pathetic to hang on to a man who didn't want to be with her anymore.

Drew removed the sunglasses. "If it's that important to you."

He didn't look too happy about it, but at least he'd agreed.

Hope bloomed as sweet and lovely as the azaleas in Riverside Park. God was at work. She had to keep believing.

They arrived at the Riverside Steakhouse, a small restaurant along the banks of the Arkansas River running through the beautiful park system of Tulsa. They'd come here to the Riverside many times when they were first married, so his choice of restaurants was no surprise.

As they exited the car, he said, "I wish we could take a walk."

"When your leg is well enough, we'll come back and walk all you want."

Leaning on his crutches, he stopped and stared at her from behind the sunglasses but didn't reply.

The silence spoke volumes. He might be nice enough to make lunch reservations, even go to church with her a couple of times, but he hadn't changed his mind. Only the brokenness of his slowly healing body kept him here now. As soon as he was well, he'd be gone again. He was in Tulsa today because he had no choice. He wouldn't allow her to forget that important fact no matter how unwilling he might be to say the hurtful words.

Sometimes she didn't understand God. He commanded Christians not to divorce, but what did he expect her to do in this awful situation? She'd tossed her pride in the Dumpster and practically begged the man to stay her husband. She didn't know what else to do.

Inside the restaurant the scent of sizzling steaks greeted them.

"I love that smell," she said, and was rewarded with one of Drew's smiles.

On the first night they'd met, he'd brought her here after the gallery showing. They'd sat at a window table overlooking the river, the golden moon reflecting off the water. A band played sixties music, people had laughed and talked, and she'd fallen so in love with Drew she could hardly breathe for the wonder of it.

A pretty young woman in sleek black slacks and pristine white shirt greeted them.

"Mr. Michaels," she said with a curiously bright smile. "Your table is ready."

As the hostess led the way to a very familiar table by the window, an odd feeling shifted through Larissa. She glanced at Drew, but his expression was as bland as buttermilk. Why was he doing this?

Even on crutches he managed to hold her chair, and when his fingers brushed the side of her neck Larissa was sure the touch was accidental. But her insides churned with bewilderment.

"Chocolate truffle mousse cake first or last?" he asked, leaning toward her with that disturbing half smile. Yes, he was up to something. Drew had always been unpredictable, but she hadn't seen this coming at all.

"First, of course." She smiled, deciding to give in to whatever game Drew had decided to play.

"That's what I figured." He laughed and put in the order, adding their meal and drink orders, as well. No sooner had the waitress disappeared than the hostess with the big smile came toward them. This time she carried a bouquet of baby pink roses which she handed to Drew. He nodded his thanks and the hostess left.

"For you," he said.

The same restaurant, the same table, even the same dessert. And now roses. "What is all this, Drew?"

He placed a hand over his heart in mock hurt. "Don't tell me you've forgotten the date."

"Of course I haven't. But…" Tears sprang to her eyes.

Four years ago today they had sat at this very table and fallen in love.

"What are you doing?" she whispered.

"I've made you miserable for months. Let me give you this today, before…" He stopped, leaving the rest unsaid. Before he left for good, he wanted to toss out a few conscience-salving crumbs. She should be angry, but she couldn't muster the strength.

Like the pathetic fool her mother said she was, Larissa wanted to play his game, to pretend just for today that Drew still loved and wanted her.

He took her hand. "Remember how happy we were that night?"

Memories flooded in. "We were crazy."

"You wore a white satiny dress," he said. "And I took so many snapshots of you that I ran out of film."

She pointed out the window. "We walked along the water's edge and almost fell in."

"The night was cold."

"And you kept me warm."

Sadness crept back in for all that they'd had and all that was lost.

"No sad faces." He plucked one of the roses and tickled her arm with it. "Today is special, so we are only going to talk about the good things. Deal?"

There was an almost boyish eagerness in him and Larissa couldn't say no. Truth be told, she didn't want to.

They spent most of the afternoon reminiscing. They talked of their first Christmas. Of the hours spent laughing and kissing while they decorated the gigantic Scotch pine Drew had insisted on buying. They laughed about all the times Larissa had tried and failed to teach Drew the game of golf. About the paint she'd spilled on his head when they redecorated the bedroom. About the afternoon they'd spent in his darkroom, photographs completely forgotten. Of the big things and the little things that made their relationship unique. And special.

Long after their plates were cleared away and coffee was served, they talked. It felt so good to relax and laugh again with Drew. When they'd first married, she'd loved those hours of just talking. Mostly she had talked, but Drew was an amazing listener. He listened as though she was the most fascinating speaker in the world. Once he'd even told her that the sound of her voice was a gift he hid inside. And when he was lonely, he took the sound out and listened to her again.

He could say the most romantic things.

Their relationship had been a dream for a while. And even after they'd begun arguing over his constant travel, making up had been incredible.

"You've proved something to me today, Drew," she said, letting her fingers trail across the back of his hand.

"What's that?"

"What we have is worth saving."

He leaned back in his chair and sighed, a heavy, sad sound. The words brought reality crashing painfully down.

"Some things weren't ever meant to be, Larissa. Our marriage is one of those things."

"You picked a crummy time to decide that."

"I brought you here today because I wanted you to remember the good times, to know how special you are, and to understand that this mess isn't your fault. It's mine."

"But that's the problem. I *don't* understand."

"I know you don't and I can't explain." Drew unfolded the maroon napkin and refolded it again and again. "Just remember that you're an incredible woman who will find a good man in no time and marry again. You won't even remember my name."

"Don't be stupid. You're my husband. The only one I'll ever have. The only one I want."

And then, right there in the restaurant, surrounded by waitstaff and customers, Larissa started to cry.

Something inside Drew broke. "Ah, Larissa. Don't do that. Don't cry."

He felt helpless, out of his element. Give him a tornado or a hurricane, he could deal with that. But seeing Larissa cry, knowing he was the cause, was more torture than a thousand scorpion stings. Like the night of the Bible study, when he'd stood outside the master bedroom, he was lost. Only this time, she was within arm's reach.

Before he could reason things out, he pushed back from the table and had her in his arms. "Don't cry, baby. Don't cry. I'm sorry," he whispered against her hair. "Don't cry."

As he held her, loving her as much as he hated himself, Drew knew one thing for certain.

He was going to regret this.

But right now, he couldn't have cared less.

Chapter Eight

The box arrived on Monday morning.

Drew was in the family room, still chiding himself over Sunday's disaster. He'd expected the lunch to make things easier for her, but he'd only hurt her more. And holding her in his arms had nearly ruined him.

He was a wreck. His insides were as tangled as the pasta salad Larissa was making.

If he didn't get out of here soon, he'd ruin her life forever.

All he could think about was being with her, soaking up every smile, every touch, every moment with her.

And when he lay down at night, his dreams were of her. In every one, she learned the truth about his past and hated him, just as he knew she would in real life.

The doorbell played a happy tune and Larissa went to answer it while he limped into the kitchen. The cast was off but the ankle and heel were going to take more rehab time than he'd hoped. He was sick of the crutches and had decided to tough it out without them from now on.

He had an appointment with an eye doctor next week and with the orthopedist on Friday. Somebody had to get him well fast.

Refrigerator door open, orange juice bottle in one hand, he was about to take a big swig when Larissa came back toting a battered cardboard box.

"It's for you," she said. "From Iraq."

She placed the heavy carton onto the breakfast bar, shooting a warning frown toward his orange juice.

Unrepentant, he grinned and chugged the juice just for the fun of it. After backhanding his mouth, he said, "Probably the stuff I left behind at the base camp. Nice of them to send it."

He scooped the box under one arm and limped to the couch in the family room.

Larissa followed, hovering as if worried that he'd sprawl onto the tile floor and break something else.

As much as he hated to admit it, he enjoyed the attention. She was as nurturing and fussy as a mother. Not that he knew anything about mothers but Larissa would be a great one. And someday she'd find a man to make her a mommy as many times as she wanted. Someone other than him. His gut clenched at the thought, though he accepted it as the best thing.

He'd been unfair to her from the start about having kids. He should have told her of his conviction that his kind shouldn't reproduce. Like always, he'd only thought of himself and what made him happy instead of her. He hadn't even considered that she would want children.

Now, he was trying to rectify that selfishness, but she refused to cooperate, and he was losing ground fast.

"Do you suppose some of your equipment is in there?"

"I hope so." He'd left a backpack full of extra cameras, films and lenses behind. "I had rolls and rolls of exposed film back at base camp. Some of the shots should be saleable."

A little part of him was terrified that the markets for his work would dry up while he recouped. Another part was terrified that he'd lose his sight and never work again. He needed to get some shots in the pipeline.

Using the scissors Larissa produced from somewhere, he cut and stripped the tape and opened the box. Larissa lifted out a handful of packing to reveal the backpack along with some clothes and personal effects. In the very bottom, carefully wrapped was a dirty, tattered camera.

"Oh, man." He lifted it out, almost reverently.

"What is it?"

"My Nikon. The one I had in my hand when…" He let the sentence drift away. This was the camera he'd had with him during the attack. "I can't believe it survived."

"And that someone salvaged it for you. How very thoughtful."

"Yeah." Camera in hand, he pushed up from the couch. "I have to see what's on here."

His concussed brain had conveniently dumped most of the activities of that last day. Even though he was more than a little afraid to remember, it was time.

"Do you think the film is still good?"

"Only one way to find out."

Since getting the cast off, he'd been able to spend considerable time in the basement darkroom, though all of his photos lately were of the neighbor kids, the dog, the backyard. This collection of film was the real deal, the kind of stuff he lived for. The kind of shots that paid his bills.

Catching his eagerness, Larissa hefted the backpack of equipment and followed him to the stairs. "I worry when you go down these steep steps."

"I like it when you worry about me," he admitted and then wanted to bite his tongue.

She offered a funny look, but said nothing as she flipped on the lights and walked in front of him down the steps in case he stumbled. Instead of the chemical smell of the basement, he caught the scent of her perfume. Like the fool he was, Drew breathed her in.

The windowless lower level was the perfect darkroom, and he'd outfitted it with all the developing equipment he liked best. Over the years of experimenting, he'd developed techniques that gave his work a unique voice in the photography world. This was the place where the magic happened, and he loved being down here.

"Lights off?" Larissa asked when he'd reached the sink and the film tanks.

He nodded. "You're getting pretty good at this."

She smiled and flipped the switch.

Even in the pitch-black room, Drew could feel Larissa moving next to him. Though accustomed to working in the dark by feel, since the accident the lack of light bothered him.

With practiced ease, he quickly went through the motions to protect the precious film and mix the needed chemicals. When he turned the amber safelight on, Larissa had the thermometer and timer at the ready. Since they'd bought this house, he'd been teaching her about the darkroom. She could probably develop this film as well as he could.

Side by side, they worked as a smooth team. He loved spending time with her down here. The darkroom had been a great place to make out.

Better not follow that train of thought.

"Do you remember any of the pictures you took before the accident?" Her voice was hushed.

"My memory is fuzzy of that day, but I know there were some important shots."

"I thought your memory had all come back. Is the concussion still bothering you?" He knew she fretted.

His heart stumbled a little. "Some."

No use lying about it, though his memory was not the brain injury that worried him most.

After what seemed like an eternity of mixing and

rotating and dipping and rinsing, ghostly images began to form on the negatives.

"We've got something," he said, excited that the film hadn't been devastated by the blast.

Carefully, Larissa helped him pin the negatives to the line over the sink. One by one, he squinted at the tiny, reversed images, his expert eye seeing the potential in each one.

Suddenly, his heart stopped. "Oh, man."

Larissa, clothespin in hand, rotated toward him. "What?"

He handed her the negative.

She squinted at it. "It's a Middle Eastern man with a huge smile."

Drew's head started to spin. He grabbed for the countertop and leaned forward, all the air going out of him.

"Drew, what in the world is wrong?" Sounding panicked, she rushed to his side. "Who is that?"

He'd forgotten. How could he have forgotten the smiling picture of his driver and friend?

"Amil," he whispered. "It was Amil."

Larissa's stomach quivered with concern. Even in the semidarkness of the safelight, Drew's face had drained of all color. She was afraid he might pass out.

Moving close, she slid an arm around his narrow waist. "Are you okay?"

"Yeah. A little dizzy."

"Could I get you something? Some water? Anything?"

He shook his head and took several deep, gulping breaths. "I'm okay. Just shocked for a minute."

Her insides quivered with worry. "Who is Amil?"

"*Was.* Amil was my driver. My buddy. He didn't make it out."

"Oh, Drew. Are you sure?"

"Yeah. I'm sure."

Everything in her ached to wrap her arms around him and pull him close. "I'm so sorry."

"Yeah, me, too. Amil was a good man. I had forgotten about the picture. I snapped it a second before the blast. Seeing his big old friendly smile was quite a shock."

He left the rest unsaid, but Larissa knew what he was thinking. That big old friendly smile was snapped in the last seconds of Amil's life.

She stood next to him, silent, not knowing what to say but also not wanting to move away. Drew had experienced a horror she couldn't begin to comprehend. She'd never had a friend die before her very eyes. Drew, who was usually so self-contained and independent, needed her comfort and her strength. She just wasn't sure he would accept it.

He straightened from the counter and turned toward her, grief emanating from him like heat waves. She hesitated no longer. She walked into his chest and wrapped her arms around his muscled back. Like a drowning soul, he hugged her close.

They stood together for a long time. He didn't cry. Drew never cried, but she felt his sadness on her like a weight. In the nearly four years of their marriage, she couldn't ever remember a time when he'd leaned on her. The thought made her both sad and glad. She had leaned on him when she was upset, but this was the first time he'd let her share his anguish.

"You know what he said to me right before the blast?" Drew murmured against her ear.

"What?" she asked quietly as she rubbed comforting circles on his back. Still too thin, his backbone bumped against her fingertips.

"He asked me to come to his house and take photos of his family. He was so proud of his children. He talked about them all the time." Another ragged breath ruffled the hair above her ear. "Those kids don't have a dad anymore because he befriended an American photographer."

"You can't blame yourself."

"I don't. I'm just sorry that a family lost a good father and provider. And I lost a friend."

Her heart ached for him. War was ugly. He'd seen his share and then some, but she'd never seen him this affected by the tragedies. He usually kept all his emotions locked inside.

She loosened her hold slightly and tilted back, putting a tiny space between them. "Maybe we could do something for his family."

Drew nodded, thoughtful. "He wanted me to take photos of his sons. Seven of them. I'm going to do that."

And if she knew Drew, he'd do more than take pictures.

"You're a good man, Drew Michaels," she said and without pausing to think, she bracketed his face between her hands and kissed him.

It was meant to be a friendly, comforting kiss, but as soon as their lips met, something inside her snapped.

Drew was her husband, and they'd been apart both physically and emotionally for a long time. She'd missed him so very, very much.

Apparently, he'd missed her, too, though he'd been saying just the opposite. When she ended the quick, sweet kiss, he pulled her close again.

His lips found hers and the tenderness was such a surprise Larissa melted against him, confused but jubilant. No matter what he said or how many mixed messages he emitted, Drew cared for her.

When the moment ended, he took her hand and led the way to the basement steps.

Once seated side by side, he pressed her hand between both of his. "We need to talk."

She gave a small laugh. "I don't think they call that talking."

One side of his lips quirked upward. "I need to ask you something important."

She went still. He never wanted to talk about really deep issues. "Okay."

"Tell me about your faith. What made you decide to get religious?"

Larissa blinked twice, trying to follow the sudden switch in topics. She'd expected about any question except this, but then, Drew always did the unexpected.

He wanted to discuss her faith. Amazing. Perhaps God was at work here in the basement of their villa.

"I don't consider it getting religious, exactly," she said carefully, praying all the while. She wanted to say the right things so badly. "I had a religious upbringing, but what I have now is a relationship with Jesus."

"You know I don't understand any of that," he admitted. "I barely know who Jesus is."

"I didn't really know, either, but now I do. God so loved the world that He sent His son to die for us. Jesus is that son. And whoever believes in Him will be saved." Nervous that she'd say the wrong things and drive her husband further away, Larissa fidgeted. "See, that's the part that got me. God loved us that much. He doesn't *need* people. He *wants* us, and He was willing to go to extraordinary lengths to win us. I just couldn't resist that kind of love."

Drew's expression grew thoughtful. "What's it like? To be a Christian, I mean."

After coming to Christ, her first desire had been to share her newfound joy with Drew. She wanted him to experience what she had. At the time, he hadn't been interested. .

"I'm so new at this, Drew. I don't know a lot of Bible verses or have many experiences to share, but I know what happened in my heart when I invited Jesus in. One minute everything seemed dark and hopeless. The next it was as if my whole being was filled with light and hope."

"Light and hope," he murmured. "I like the sound of that."

Larissa recognized his longing because she'd been there.

"He'll do the same for you, Drew, if you ask Him."

Absently, he rubbed the side of his healing ankle and stared into the darkened room. "I'll give it some thought."

That was the best she could ask for.

After a moment of silence, he said, "I'm pretty messed up."

"You're mending. Soon, you can get back to work." She tried to sound chipper but the truth depressed. With his body well, he'd no longer have reason to stay.

"I didn't mean physically," he said. "I meant in here." He tapped his chest. "There are things about me you don't know. I doubt God is too interested."

She'd felt the same way before accepting the Lord. "God can fix anything, Drew. No matter how bad we think we've been." She found his hand. "He can even fix our relationship if we'll let Him."

Drew shook his head. "You're amazing, you know that? I don't understand why you're so good to me."

"Then you really are messed up. I love you, you big goof. When we married," she said, "I wanted forever. I planned my life around you, to have a family with you, to grow old together. I can't give up that dream."

The ache and disappointment was there for him to accept or reject. She dug her fingertips into the rough concrete and waited.

"I'm sorry," he said simply. "The one thing I never wanted was to hurt you, and that's all I've ever done."

He was weakening. She was sure of it.

"Not true."

They grew silent and the gentle mood expanded around them. After a bit, Drew pivoted toward her. But as his head swiveled, his eyes widened in fear.

"Drew? What is it? What's wrong?"

He shook his head and scrubbed at his eyes.

A memory pressed at the back of Larissa's mind. She'd witnessed this behavior more than once. And there was the time she'd seen the phone book open to ophthalmologists.

"Is there something wrong with your eyes?"

He blinked over and over again, the bewildered look slowly disappearing.

"Tell me, Drew. What's going on?"

His head dropped. "I didn't want you to know."

She grabbed his wrist. "Know what? What is it? Did something happen that I don't know about?"

"A lot of things happened over there that I never want you to know."

Her stomach started to churn. Her mind raced through the diagnoses various physicians had rendered. None had mentioned anything about his eyes. But she *knew*.

"What's wrong with your vision?"

He blew out a resigned breath. "Okay. You win. You already know about the concussion. What you don't know is that I lost more than a few memories." She heard him swallow. "Sometimes everything goes black."

"What do you mean, *everything*?"

His bleak expression sent fright bumps crawling over her skin.

"Sometimes I lose my vision. At the most unexpected times, it just goes. One minute I'm seeing, the next a gray fog appears and then the darkness."

"Oh, Drew." She touched the front of his shirt, horrified for him. "Oh, my darling Drew."

He dragged a hand over the aforementioned eyes.

He must be terrified. His eyes were his life.

"What do the doctors say?"

"I don't know."

"Do you mean to tell me that you haven't told your doctor about this?"

"I have an appointment Tuesday."

So that was why the phone book had been open to eye specialists. She moved one step down and turned to look up at him. "When was the last episode?"

"A few days ago while I was playing video pool with

Jake." One of the neighborhood kids who found Drew and his camera fascinating company. "The episodes are getting farther apart, so maybe I'm healing."

He didn't sound too convinced. All the times she'd seen him falter and get that odd, frightened look now made sense. "You're scared out of your mind."

A beat of silence and then a gruff admission. "Yeah. What will I do if I lose my vision? I'm a photographer. I can't do anything else."

He was more than scared. He was like a drowning man whose life raft had sprung a leak. She yanked his hands into hers and gave them a shake.

"You listen to me, Drew Michaels. You are not going to lose your eyesight. We'll get help. And we'll pray. I'll have my entire church pray."

God wouldn't let this happen, would He?

Drew pulled back a little, shaking his head. "I don't want anyone to know. I don't want pity."

Which was probably why he'd chosen to carry this awful secret alone.

"That's too bad. Sometimes you need people, Drew. Right now, we need doctors and we need prayer warriors." She levered up on her knees and leaned toward him. "You're a fighter. I'm a fighter. Together, with God's help, we will find an answer."

Very slowly Drew began to relax. His worried frown eased away and a tiny smile dawned. Her faith and love had given him hope.

"You know, Larissa," he said softly, "if you keep this up, I'm going to start believing in the impossible."

"Nothing, *nothing* is impossible," she said.

And then she kissed him. Hard. He laughed, the maniac. Then she laughed, too. The man had just told her he might be losing his eyesight and they were both sitting in the dark basement laughing.

And she actually felt more hope at this moment than she'd felt in months.

Chapter Nine

Drew sat on the edge of the backyard hot tub, contemplating the mysteries of the universe. Or rather, the mysteries of his beautiful wife.

Coco, the chipper little Yorkie, listened to his mutterings with an attentive ear.

The conversation in the darkroom had changed things between him and Larissa. Well, the conversation and the kiss. He couldn't get the sweetness out of his mind.

Why had she kissed him? Out of pity? Or because she loved him?

She confused him. Or maybe he confused himself. Either way, his insides swirled and spun like the hot tub.

For all her quiet grace, Larissa was a tiger for the underdog and right now, that was him. He found it next to impossible to resist her. In fact, he'd almost given up trying. As long as she was in close proximity, he didn't stand a chance against her constant barrage of unfailing love and support. Resistance would have to take a back burner until he could put distance between them.

Right now, Larissa was love in action. Nobody could resist that.

During the last week she had dragged him from doctor to doctor, she'd researched on the internet, she'd called in her "prayer warriors." None of the specialists had a definitive answer for his visual disturbances, but Larissa subscribed to the proposition that a mix of concussion and mental trauma was the culprit.

Either sounded good to him. He could control his mind and the concussion would heal. He hoped. Other than a couple of incidents of blurriness this week, he'd experienced no total darkness.

Telling Larissa had taken the edge off his fear. Still, he wanted to memorize the world around him, just in case the worst happened. For a man who lived for color and light, the thought that those might disappear forever shook him to the core.

"What would I do, Coco? Not much market for a blind photographer."

Coco jammed a comforting head beneath his hand. Drew stroked the soft, silky fur.

"You look silly with red toenails," he said affectionately. Larissa had the little dog groomed weekly, a waste of time and money, but Coco always smelled good. Not as good as Larissa, of course.

Feet hanging in the swirling waters of the hot tub, he rotated the ankle as the physical therapist had taught him and wrote the alphabet with his toes. He was getting better, stronger. Another week or two.

And then what?

Steam drifted up around him. The air outside was cool with a touch of breeze. He was tempted to slide his whole body into the hot tub, khaki shorts and all.

In his previous times at home, he'd been raring to leave after a few weeks. Now he felt a strange reluctance, as if leaving would be the end of him.

Maybe it would be.

"Would you miss me, Coco?" He'd miss her. He'd miss this house and the grounds. He'd miss the convenience of his own personal darkroom.

Most of all, he'd miss his wife.

Blowing out an exasperated sound, he dragged a hand over his scratchy whiskers.

"God, if you're up there, help me do the right thing for once in my rotten life."

The right thing, to his way of thinking, was still to let her go, let her find someone who could give her all the good things she deserved. But lately, he was weakening. He was tempted to call the whole divorce thing off, to beg forgiveness, and promise Larissa the world. But he knew better than to go that route. When he made a promise, he kept it. Trouble was, he couldn't promise what she wanted, and he would never lie to her. Never. She was the one thing in his life that was clean and pure and devoid of deceit. He might not tell her everything but he had never lied to her, either.

Maybe they could find a compromise. But what kind of compromise could a man offer to a woman who wanted nothing but him and his babies.

He kicked out with his injured foot and splashed his own face.

If he lost his vision, he couldn't even support her or himself. He would be nothing but a parasite.

Beyond photography he had no talents. His repertoire of skills consisted of stealing, fighting and lying, all honed at an early age, but now lying dormant and rusty. As angry as he'd been back then, the fire had served up a warning he'd heeded. With his new identity, he'd shed the troubled skin of teenage Drew Grace in exchange for manhood and a career. He wasn't that person anymore. But the wasted years had left him with nothing worthwhile to fall back on.

"Beyond photography and playing video games, I'm pretty useless," he said to Coco. The dog sidled up closer and grinned, tail wagging. "Oh, yeah and I'm a pretty good ear scratcher."

The dog writhed in ecstasy while he proved the point.

"She loves me, Coco." Coco cocked her head and offered a puzzled frown. "Yeah, I wonder the same thing. Why would an incredible woman like Larissa marry a messed-up dude like me in the first place?"

No sensible reason at all.

"I don't know why, but she does. I feel it." He tapped his chest. "In here. Don't tell anyone, but I love her, too."

She was the only human being in his entire adulthood who had said those words to him. All week, he had felt the power of her love as she'd hounded doctors and encouraged him to keep believing.

He'd given God a lot of thought lately, too. Was Larissa right? Could God fix a messed-up man with so much hidden baggage that he could barely sleep at night?

He had a hard time believing that anyone or anything could erase the tragedies of his past. What was done could not be undone. And yet, he wanted to believe that God could take away the awful guilt.

He sucked in a lungful of moist, heated air, then exhaled very slowly.

He'd never before understood what people got out of religion, but Larissa's explanation of light and dark made perfect sense to a photographer. And the strange scripture from church was starting to make sense, too. Deep down, something was missing inside him. He'd always thought it was a soul, an empty hole brought about by never belonging anywhere or to anyone. Never feeling loved. He'd been such an angry kid and once the anger was under control, he'd filled the void with work. That's what a therapist had once said, but now he wondered. Was the empty place waiting to be filled with the light of God?

It was a topic worthy of serious consideration.

Kids' laughter drifted over the privacy fence. Drew shook his head and laughed with them. The gang must be on the way to entertain him for the afternoon. Weird that he actually looked forward to a bunch of rug rats invading his space.

Larissa stepped out onto the patio. His stomach went south and flip-flopped like a banked koi.

"Your agent called."

He still got a weird rush at the idea of hiring an agent. The last thing he'd ever desired was public notice, given the secret past that could send him to prison. But somehow his photos had taken on a life of their own. He'd wound up with an agent who arranged to have his work hung in galleries and displayed for the art connoisseur to covet. The real work of photo assignments he handled for himself. He'd only hired the agent so he wouldn't have to think about business too much.

Hanging out with rich crowds was a different matter altogether. He hated that part, although his presence at some gatherings was occasionally required. Or so declared his hyperactive agent, Shelby Kates.

"What did she want?" he groused as Larissa swung toward him in a pair of green capris and a fitted blouse that showed off her curves to perfection. His beautiful wife was another reason he didn't want to go blind. He raised his camera and pushed the shutter. She was so accustomed to his constant snapping that she didn't even react.

"Call her back. Something about a showing." She tossed him a fluffy towel that smelled of fabric softener. "Mother will be here soon. Better put on a shirt."

"Great." He made a face, then dried his feet and limped to the phone.

A couple of kids he'd never seen in his life pushed open the French doors. One was a tall, lanky teenage boy with a pearl in his upper lip and a tattoo on his earlobe.

Shaking his head at his wife's eclectic mix of friends, Drew called his agent and discovered he was expected in Charleston on Saturday evening.

Saturday. He'd promised to attend church again on Sunday morning, but Larissa would understand. Duty called.

Soon, the real duty would be calling. What would happen then? Would he follow through with his original plan? Could he?

Right now, he wasn't even sure he could handle a weekend showing. Though his stamina was gradually returning, he couldn't be on the ankle any time without it swelling to the size of a basketball. Most of all, he had a horror of going blind in public.

With a shiver of apprehension, he went to find Larissa and break the news. Before he could, Marsha Stone breezed into his house carrying a stack of decorator portfolios.

"Larissa, darling," she called. The woman hadn't even knocked.

Marsha spotted him. Mouth drawn up as if she smelled a skunk, she was the picture of disapproval. He raised one hand. "Excuse me. I'll find a shirt."

Anything to keep Marsha off Larissa's case. But this was his house and if he wanted to run around without a shirt, he should be able to.

The thought stopped him cold. He'd called this *his house,* not just Larissa's.

Whoa. He really *was* getting too comfortable.

By the time he'd dressed in a pair of familiar old jeans and a time-softened chambray shirt, Larissa and her mother had samples of wallpaper and paint spread all over the family room. Marsha, it seemed, was redecorating again. This was an election year and with Larissa's dad up for reelection, they would do a great deal of entertaining.

The whole idea made Drew tired, primarily because he knew Larissa would end up with the bulk of the work. The effort would be too much for Marsha and his kindhearted wife would never complain. She would just shoulder the load and make her mother happy. She was too good for all of them.

As a diversion from the redecorating schemes, he spent the morning in the darkroom explaining the pros and cons of various chemical mixes to the skinny teenager. Ryan, lip ring and all, turned out to be a camera buff and one of Larissa's tenderhearted attempts to fix the world. More importantly, to Drew anyway, he was a foster kid living with the Ratcliffs down the street.

That alone was enough to get his sympathy.

The boy was interested in photography and filmmaking but not much else.

To tell the truth, the kid kind of reminded Drew of himself back at the beginning when he'd taken that first newspaper job. Only fifteen, he'd lied, claimed to be eighteen, and by the time he needed proof, he'd been on the streets long enough to buy a counterfeit birth certificate, complete with new name, new birth date, and an acceptable, though altogether fake set of parents.

That first job had changed his life. No longer a runaway foster kid, he had learned the fundamentals of photography from a patient veteran.

Ryan displayed a similar intensity when looking through a camera, and Drew found that hard to resist. The kid knew more about digital photography and software than Drew ever wanted to know. To him, photographs were born wet, not inside a computer. The whole digital business, in his opinion, stole the credibility of the work. He'd used the method when time and distance were an issue, but in the end he always returned to the darkroom. In his view and that of other old-school photographers, there was something far more mysterious and artistic and challenging in capturing the perfect shot on site. Digital manipulation seemed like cheating to him.

But he didn't tell the kid that. Not today anyway. He *did* tell him the truth though when the boy lamented his lousy cheap camera. Cameras don't take pictures. Photographers do. And he proved the point by taking Ryan and his lousy cheap camera to Riverside Park for a lesson in light and patience and awaiting the perfect shot.

At noon, he bought the teen a burger and dropped him off at the Ratcliffs' place. Poor joker was stuck in tutoring during spring break after failing ninth grade English. School was one place Drew couldn't offer any assistance. He'd never finished ninth grade English.

"Tomorrow?" Ryan had asked hopefully.

"Sure. Or better yet, show up here about an hour before sunset tonight. We'll have a little fun with color."

The lanky boy hitched one shoulder as if he really didn't care one way or the other, but Drew caught the glint in his eyes. He'd show up.

Back at the house, Marsha was thankfully gone. Larissa had a telephone jammed between shoulder and ear while she scribbled madly on a yellow tablet. She gave him a quick smile that did funny things to his chest. He winked and took her picture. She turned her back and waved him away.

His leg was killing him, but he faked a straight walk to the bedroom, changed into swim trunks and T-shirt, then headed for the hot tub. The heated, churning water gave him more relief than Lortab and left his head a lot less fuzzy.

"Are you out here again?" Larissa called from the back door.

"Why don't you join me?"

The French doors banged shut.

He grinned. Maybe he shouldn't have said that.

With a press of a button, he activated the stereo system. Rascal Flats was singing about a broken road. He could relate. He'd been down a few of those.

The March wind was chilly, an interesting contrast to the steamy tub. Resting his head back in the indention, he floated, letting the ache of standing too long at the park seep out into the water and wishing he knew how to fix the broken road he was on right now.

From the doorway, Larissa watched Drew sleep. Coco lay like a tiny lion on the ledge of the tub, watching, too.

In repose, Drew looked boyish and vulnerable. More than once in their relationship she'd wondered what he'd been like as a child. The dabs of information he'd shared gave her some insight, but she was sad to know all his childhood photos had been lost in the tragic fire that stole his family. He must have been a handsome little boy.

If they had a son, would he look like Drew?

The thought shot an arrow of sorrow into her heart. What if Drew divorced her? What if they never had a child together? Even though he ran scared every time she'd mentioned having a baby, she hadn't given up the dream. Maybe she was a fool and would end up with a broken heart and a broken marriage, but she couldn't stop praying for her husband. Since the day in the basement, he'd become more approachable, less cantankerous, more like the man she'd married. And she had grabbed on to hope with both hands and hadn't let go.

Now here she was standing at the back door staring out at her husband with love and longing.

She'd been watching him a lot lately. Watching him with the neighbor kids, with the dog, with his painstaking perfection in his work, even with her petulant mother. Today she'd admired the patience and respect he had displayed with the troubled Ryan, although from the looks of him, the outing had cost him physically.

Not that he'd ever admit the pain.

There was much about Drew Michaels to admire. Had she ever expressed that to him? Had she ever told him that he was an amazing man with many good qualities? Or had she, as she feared, been too focused on her own agenda for their relationship to let her husband know how special and important he was?

He'd suffered so many hurts and losses, not the least of which was the death of his family. And now the fear of losing his vision hovered over him like a vulture. He'd once confided that he'd learned his trade on the fly, not in college. Yet, he'd risen to the top of his field.

Yes, Drew Michaels was a unique and gifted man, and she was proud to call him husband.

Earlier today, she'd tried talking to her mother, hoping for some advice in mending the troubled relationship. She should have saved her breath.

Seated side by side with a wallpaper book between them, trying to choose between stripes or floral, all

Mother had done was offer for the third time to pay for a divorce. Regardless that Larissa loved the man and never mind that her faith did not allow divorce, her parents thought they knew best.

"It's very clear to everyone that Drew has no intention of ever being a real husband," her mother had said. "If you want a family and a decent man, you have to get a divorce now. You aren't getting any younger, you know."

That little dig had hurt, as it always did.

Now as she gazed out at her husband, heart filled with emotion, Larissa still thought her parents were wrong. Marriage was worth fighting for. God ordained it and she believed it.

With her stomach jumping like a bunch of puppies, she quietly opened the back door and went to join Drew.

He didn't stir at her approach so she sat quietly on the opposite side and enjoyed the view. Coco raised a golden eyebrow in question but didn't move.

Larissa was tempted to snap Drew's photo for a change, but even in sleep, he kept one hand around the camera.

Monarch butterflies flitted among the blooming azalea bushes, a regular stop on their migration route.

Somewhere in the neighborhood a car door slammed and over the hum and slosh of the hot tub motor, she heard the bounce of a driveway basketball game. All her usual visitors had taken off for other interests the minute her mother had appeared, but she figured some would return later.

She dangled her feet in the water, wishing Drew would wake up. She kicked a little. He slept on.

She kicked a wider arc. Still no response.

Finally, orneriness took hold and she flipped a handful of water in his face.

He awakened with a roar. Before Larissa could think or act, Drew heaved his tall, thin but muscular form across the width of the tub and grabbed her feet. Orneriness flashed in dark, gleaming eyes.

Coco leaped to her feet and barked like a Doberman.

Larissa squealed. "Don't you dare. I mean it, Drew."

Of course, that was the wrong thing to say. With a wicked grin, he yanked her heels. Clothes and all, she plunged into the water. The sudden heat stole her breath. She fought to gain her feet but just that quick, two strong arms swooped her up. She emerged spluttering.

Drew was laughing. "How's the water?"

"Hot." She slapped a handful at him.

He dodged to one side and laughed more.

"Could be why they call it a hot tub."

"Har-har. Very funny." She let her body buoy up and down in the deep water. Already wet, she might as well enjoy the therapy. "I came out here to talk to you about something."

Whether he wanted to hear it or not, she was going to tell him straight out.

"Good. I have a couple of things to discuss with

you, as well." He guided her back against the side and stood facing her.

Floating easily, she draped both arms over the outside of the tub as an anchor. "Is this about the call from your agent?"

"Some of my work is being shown in Charleston next weekend. She thinks I need to be there."

She didn't like the sound of that. He hadn't been any farther than downtown Tulsa since the accident, and that exhausted him. "Are you physically ready for a trip like that?"

"I don't know."

"Then, there's your answer. You can't go."

"It's an important opportunity," he said. "I can't pass it up. Especially now that..." He let the thought trail away, but Larissa intuitively caught his meaning.

"Your vision worries me, too. What if—"

"Yeah," he interrupted. Gazing off in the distance, he dipped a hand into the water and slicked back his hair. "What if I suddenly go blind in a strange airport?"

As if startled to have spoken the fear aloud, he faked a grin and tapped her on the chin. "Never mind. I'll be okay."

She caught his hand and gave it a shake. Water sluiced up and around them. "You're not going alone, Drew. I'm going with you."

His heart thumped once, hard, against his rib cage. "I can't ask you to do that."

"You didn't. I offered. And it's a great idea, even if

I do say so myself. I've never been to Charleston, and they say it's a wonderful city."

Yeah, wonderfully romantic. And Larissa was warming to the idea.

Giving her fingers a squeeze, he shook his head. "I don't know, 'Rissa."

"The beach, the history, dinner cruise ships." She lit up with excitement. "Come on, Drew. We'll make it fun. What do you say?"

He wanted to say she was scaring him to death. He wanted to say that a weekend in a romantic city with his beautiful wife sounded incredible. He wanted to say he loved her.

Instead he tried to back off a little to arrange a business deal. "Would you really do that? Go as my Seeing Eye person?"

A little of her excitement dimmed. "No."

But then she smiled, slow and sweet, and Drew knew he was in trouble. She knew exactly what he was up to.

"I will not be your Seeing Eye *person,* Drew. I'm your *wife,* your helpmate, like the Bible says. When one of us is weak, the other is strong. That's what marriage is. That's what I want to be. That's what I am."

He stood staring into violet eyes filled with love he didn't deserve and thought his heart might come out of his chest. "I don't understand you at all."

"Okay, then. Let me be very blunt." She swallowed, a nervous action that belied her assertive words. She was afraid of his reaction, but willing to take a chance, a fact that threatened Drew's resolve in the worst way. "I love you, Drew, more this moment than ever before. I've loved you since the first time I laid eyes on you. And I'm not ever going to stop. No matter what you do or say, I will never, ever stop loving you."

Drew closed his eyes against the blast of pure love flowing from her to him. And along with love came a hope shining brighter than the morning sun over Hawaii.

He was a jerk of the first order, but even he couldn't say no this time. As hard as he'd fought to keep his distance, he wasn't strong enough to battle a force as strong as Larissa's love.

God above knew this was the wrong thing to do, but Drew was lost.

"Ah, 'Rissa," he groaned, barely recognizing his own agonized voice.

She touched him then, pressing fingertips against his lips. "Shh. It will be wonderful, Drew. A chance to make things right, like a second honeymoon. Please, let all this other stuff go, whatever was wrong, and let's be happy again."

The last sentence ruined him. He was done for. He had the power to make his beautiful wife happy for a few days. He had to do it. And as selfish as he was, he wanted one more special memory to cherish. They'd go to Charleston, he'd do everything in his power to give her an amazing time and make her happy.

In the back of his mind, he knew it would never be enough. Whether today, or next week, or three years from now, Larissa would one day wake up and see him as the worst mistake she'd ever made.

But for now, he'd selfishly take whatever she offered.

Chapter Ten

The atmosphere in the gallery was posh. Attending patrons were old Southern money with blue blood flowing back to the Civil War. They spoke in low modulated murmurs, the gentle lilt of South Carolina a real pleasure to listen to. A group of well-dressed men had retired to the outer balcony to smoke cigars and drink something a bit more potent than punch. Briefly, Drew wished to join them, but he couldn't of course, being the center of attention. And he knew Larissa didn't approve or partake.

At present, he held the rapt attention of an attractive woman along with an art reviewer, both of whom eyed him with something other than artistic interest.

Where was Larissa anyway? Or his agent? Someone needed to rescue him from magazine writers and over-zealous ladies with big bank accounts.

In truth, reviewers scared him spitless. What if they delved too deeply into his background? In the back of his mind was the constant terror that his crime would be discovered.

Another reason he shouldn't have given in to Larissa. He'd ignored the most important reason why he had to let her go.

He glanced around, caught a glimpse of his lovely wife making polite conversation with a guy in a tuxedo. She looked stunning as always, and he wondered again why she'd chosen him. That was his wife over there. The most feminine, elegant woman in the room. Her dress and jewelry were understated, her hairstyle simple, and her makeup light. She fit in with these people in a way that he never could, but she loved *him.*

Unbelievable.

He smiled. How could he expect to fit in when he was the only man in the place not wearing a suit?

Getting dressed in the hotel room tonight had been sensory overload. Even now, her soft fragrance and velvet skin lingered in his mind like a love song.

So far, his vision had been fine, but Larissa watched him carefully, never getting too far away.

This second honeymoon idea of hers was more difficult than he'd imagined. Not because he wasn't having a great time. But because he was. Maybe it was the beautiful city or the Southern charm, but here Larissa made him forget all the reasons they were wrong for each other.

Here in Charleston, everything was right.

"Drew," an ultrafeminine Southern voice murmured.

He'd zoned out for a minute and totally missed the woman's question.

"Sorry. My mind strayed." Shelby had threatened to choke him if he was rude to anyone tonight. But with Larissa on his mind, no one else much mattered. They were having a great time and he wanted to soak up every single minute.

"Excuse me," he said as politely as possible. "I need to go find my wife."

Larissa saw her husband slicing through the press of people like a lone wolf whose attention was riveted on his prey. His noticeable limp somehow made him ever more ruggedly attractive.

Pure delight zipped through her veins.

He was coming for her.

Thank goodness.

In thirty seconds flat, he was beside her.

"Excuse us, please," he said to her companion, and then without further explanation, one hand around her upper arm, moved them toward the door.

"What are you doing?" she whispered.

White teeth flashed. "Kidnapping my wife."

"You can't just leave."

"Watch me."

"Drew, there are people in there spending good money for your autographed prints."

"And I appreciate them." One hand to the small of her back, he guided her rapidly down the hall toward the elevators. Once inside, he breathed a loud sigh of relief. "I couldn't take it anymore. When I saw that guy talking to you with that lecherous grin on his face, that was it."

"He wasn't lecherous. Just boring."

"I'm a man. I know lecherous."

She giggled. "I think you were jealous."

"You'd think right." He backed her against the mirrored wall and kissed her. "I'd rather hang out with you than all the checkbooks in Charleston."

Larissa's insides did a happy dance. When he'd finally agreed to this trip, he'd thrown himself wholeheartedly into it. She could scarcely believe this was the same brooding, cranky man who claimed to want a divorce.

Though he'd not said anything, she was almost sure he'd changed his mind. God's word was true. Her steadfast love had won him back. Love hadn't failed.

"Where are we going?" she asked with a smile.

He quirked a teasing eyebrow. "Anywhere but here."

Like two sneaking kids, they hurried out of the gallery. Once outside, Drew grabbed her hand and started to run.

"Drew, you're going to hurt your leg!"

Indeed, he was limping badly, but he didn't let up. She caught his spirit of fun and, in spite of her fitted dress and heels, she ran, too.

By the time they reached the beachfront, they were both breathless and laughing.

"You are crazy," she said when she could breathe again.

The only natural light was a flat white moon, but the condos and hotels above the shoreline illuminated the sand-strewn beach enough for walking. Too early in the season for the usual crush of tourists, the beach was all but deserted. Farther down, she spotted two other couples and a family with a large dog, but their piece of the ocean was romantically empty.

They removed their shoes and strolled. "This place is so beautiful."

A few dinner boats were out on the water. The surf sloshed and pulsed against the shore.

Drew pointed in the distance at a huge light revolving against the night sky. "Don't see too many lighthouses in Oklahoma."

They both grinned at the silly idea of a lighthouse in the landlocked state.

"There's a dock up farther, I think. Want to go sit and make out?"

Larissa bopped him playfully. "I think *you're* the lecher."

"Okay." He sighed in mock defeat. "We can sit and *talk*."

The wooden boards of the dock echoed beneath their bare feet. They walked to the end and sat, dangling their legs over the edge.

"You don't think a shark will jump up and grab my

foot, do you?" Larissa asked, wiggling her hot-pink toenail.

"Are you afraid of some poor little shark?"

"I'm a landlubber. Sharks and big water scare me."

Drew draped an arm around her shoulders and pulled her next to his side. He was warm and solid.

"You're safe with me, darlin'," he said, and Larissa believed that with all her heart. Drew would protect her from anything.

Anything but himself.

They sat for a while, heads touching, as they stared into the vast, black ocean. There was something surreal about sitting in the darkness with the man she loved, the sound of the ocean alive around them.

After a while, Drew said, "Have you ever been to Alaska?"

"No. Why?" Please don't say you're about to run off there on some assignment.

"I'd like to take you there someday," he said, and the words were music to her ears. "The water is so blue and the land still pristine. On nights like this, you can sometimes see the northern lights."

"I remember the pictures you took. Incredible."

"Yeah. I waited for weeks to get those exact shots, waiting for the colors." He chuckled softly. "Do you know how cold a man can get sitting for hours in the dark in Alaska?"

"And you want to take me there?" she asked in pretend horror.

"Ulterior motive. You could keep me warm."

"Oh, you." She bumped his side with her shoulder.

"Ouch. Watch out for the ribs."

"I thought they were healed."

"They are."

She made a face at him.

"I'm glad we came here," he said.

"To the beach?"

The breeze tossed her hair into her eyes. Drew brushed it back, carefully looping it behind her ears. He loved touching her. "I meant to Charleston."

"Me, too," she murmured. "I'm happy, Drew. You make me happy."

The statement both pleased and frightened. Was it possible that they could make this work? That he could change and be the man she wanted?

He wanted to, with all his heart and soul. He'd even told her he would try to stay home more. As long as no one discovered his past, they'd be okay. He had to try, for her sake.

"What did your mother say about us coming here together?" Her parents were going to be livid to know the marriage they'd tried to sabotage was once again gaining ground.

"Oh, you know Mother. She was worried about who was going to help her with the paint contractors while I'm gone."

She hadn't exactly answered his question, but knowing Marsha, the paint contractors *were* more important than her daughter's marriage. Especially since she and Thomas were certain the marriage was dead. Drew had never told Larissa about the time the honorable senator had offered him a lot of money to get lost for good.

"Did you tell your dad?"

"Mother will tell him, I'm sure." She touched his cheek. "Let's not talk about them. Tonight is about us."

The mention of her parents and their ongoing disapproval of him as a husband put a momentary damper on the night.

"Sorry. I promised only happy talk this weekend." He stroked a finger down her forehead, over her nose, and stopped at her lips.

She caught his fingertip between her teeth and nipped gently.

"Ouch." Playfully, he shook the hand as though a shark had bitten him.

"Tell me about your dreams, Drew," she said, with a bemused smile. "What do you see in the future that excites you?"

"The Amazon," he answered without hesitation.

She tilted her head. "The Amazon? I thought you'd been there."

"There are places in the forest that modern man has never seen. I dream of getting those first shots."

He didn't want to think about the other things he dreamed about. He wished he could find his brothers. He wished he could understand God and all the injustices of life better. And he wished he could be the man Larissa deserved.

But he kept all those dreams to himself. Some things were too hard to talk about.

"What about you? What do you dream of, Larissa?"

"Easy one. You and me."

"I like the sound of that." He moved to kiss her, but she stopped him with a hand to his lips.

"Let me finish."

Her soft, luminous eyes were so serious, butterflies invaded Drew's chest. "Okay."

"I dream of you and me—" she hesitated for a nanosecond and then rocked his world "—having a baby."

Everything in him went still. A moment ago he was prepared to kiss her. Now he wanted to run, bad leg and all. Adrenaline shot through his blood vessels and into his brain. His insides started to shake.

Larissa must have felt his reaction because she yanked away.

He reached for her. "Larissa. Honey."

"Don't, Drew. You asked me about my dreams and then you throw them back at me. I want to have a family." Her voice trembled. "That's a perfectly normal dream."

Panic crept up his back and camped on his shoulder. "Before we married you never said anything about wanting kids."

"Everyone wants kids. Why would we have to discuss something so fundamental?"

"Look." At a loss, he stared down at his hands. Telling the truth was impossible. "There are some things a man just knows about himself."

"And you're convinced that you can't be a good father."

"Yeah."

"Drew, that's crazy. Why would you think such a thing?"

The adrenaline shakes grew worse. His mouth was drier than sand. "I've never been around kids. I know nothing about them."

True enough. He never wanted her to know the rest. That he'd come from the bottom of the barrel. From a family so dysfunctional that he'd ended up on the streets without a clue where his mother was or even who his father might be. Dysfunction was in the blood, and he wasn't about to pass it on to some innocent little baby.

They both fell silent, lost in thought. A cruise ship motored past a few hundred yards offshore.

He'd done it again. While trying to make her happy, he'd made her sad.

When Larissa spoke, her voice was soft and tremulous. "You're wonderful with the neighbor kids." The sentiment touched him. The plea nearly killed him. "Will you at least give it some consideration?" She reached out a hand in a gesture of peace. "Please."

Total mush, what else could he do?

"Sure, babe, sure," he murmured, taking her soft hand in his. "I'll think about it."

* * *

Late that night, long after Larissa's soft breathing filled the hotel room, Drew sat on the side of the bed fully dressed. He was thinking about it all right. He couldn't think of anything else.

Head in his hands, he pondered what to do. Larissa made him vulnerable in a way that scared him out of his mind. He was well enough to get back to work. He'd even told Shelby tonight to pass the word around to the right people. At the moment his agent wasn't all that happy with him for abandoning the party, but she was a trooper. She'd be okay.

Larissa stirred behind him, mumbling something in her sleep. He didn't turn to look at her. He was dying inside. Looking at her asleep would finish him off.

Maybe he'd make a few calls when they returned to Tulsa, see what he could get going. He'd hoped to photograph the mysterious purple glow that only appeared at sunset after a volcanic eruption. If he hurried, before the atmosphere in Indonesia cleared, there might still be time.

A baby. He gripped the front of his hair with both hands and pulled. He couldn't be a father. He didn't know how.

Larissa would make a great mother.

"Oh, God," he breathed into the darkness, and just like that he found himself praying. Larissa put a lot of stock in prayer and church and all that. Maybe God would change her mind, make her see reason. God knew

Drew's background and his shortcomings far better than Larissa ever would. "She'll listen to You. Make her see what a dumb idea this is."

He didn't know what he expected but nothing happened.

He tried again.

"Okay, God. I don't know much about You, but I'd like to. For Larissa's sake. It would mean a lot to her. Maybe You could help me out here."

Still nothing. He wondered if there was some kind of password or something that Christians used to get God's attention. To let God know the prayer was from a believer. Maybe that's why God didn't answer. Drew had never been an atheist, but he didn't have what his wife had, either. She shone with an inner light that hadn't been there before.

He, on the other hand, was about as dark inside as an arctic winter.

What did it take for a man to find that light? Church? Prayer? He'd tried both.

The little fish around his neck claimed that God would never leave or forsake him.

"Then why don't You answer me? Why have I never felt Your presence the way Larissa claims to?"

The walls were silent. In the adjacent suite someone flushed a toilet.

Drew shook his head.

Feeling like a fool for talking to the darkness, he rose and went into the bathroom.

It was going to be a very long night.

Chapter Eleven

Larissa hummed a popular praise song as she crossed the parking lot and entered the tasteful reception area of her father's office. God was good. Life was good. She had so much to be thankful for, and on this glorious, sunny Monday morning gratitude overflowed.

The trip to Charleston had been wonderful. Other than the one dark moment when they'd argued, the few days of R & R had revived their relationship. Drew had shown her in a thousand ways that he loved her. They'd had so much fun sightseeing. They'd spent hours talking until she knew her husband better than ever before. And best of all, Drew had promised to consider having a baby.

Please, dear Lord, bring him around to my way of thinking. I want a baby so badly.

She'd left him piddling with chemicals in the darkroom and fully expected to see a new batch of beach photos when she arrived home.

"Hi, Cynthia," she said to the receptionist. "My dad is expecting me."

"You look really chipper this morning," Cynthia said with a smile.

"I am. I had a great mini-vacation to Charleston."

"Lucky you." The receptionist waved toward the inner office. "Go on through. There's nobody with him right now."

Lucky? she thought as she pushed the door open into her father's office. No, not lucky. Larissa didn't believe that way anymore. She believed the Lord had blessed her because she hadn't given up on her marriage during a time when it would have been easier to quit than to stand and fight. She'd followed the Lord's guidance and He hadn't let her down.

Her father, State Senator Thomas Stone, rose from behind a long executive desk, buttoning his suit jacket out of long habit. He was ever the politician, even with his family.

"Larissa, sweetheart."

Larissa hurried around the desk for a hug. Wrapped in the familiar bulk of her father, she leaned for a moment, drawing in the warmth and security of his embrace. As a child, and continuing into adulthood, Dad had been her rock. Even though he strongly disapproved of Drew, he was still her dad.

"How's my girl?"

"Couldn't be better." She pecked him on the cheek and circled back around the desk to a chair.

"Good. It's time to get serious about our strategy, our media blitz, town hall meetings." He reseated himself, automatically undoing the button over his generous middle. "You're the best strategist on the team."

"You always say that, but it's your indefatigable honesty and hard work that keep the voters coming back."

"This year's fight on internet controls may give us some trouble. My opponent is adamantly against censorship of any kind."

"But you're leading the battle against child porn, Dad. The voters know how important it is to protect our most innocent citizens." She was proud to have a father of such integrity.

"Yes, they do, but everyone has a different idea about how to make that happen. It's a very hot topic."

"Along with a dozen others you face all the time." She grabbed a notepad and scribbled some thoughts. "I already have some ideas on this, but Elbert will likely know which direction to take." Elbert was their campaign manager. "Do you want to use that new local company for our campaign ads this time?"

"Stop just a minute, Larissa."

She blinked up at him.

"I didn't ask you here today to work on the campaign."

She laid the pen and pad back on his desk. "You didn't?"

"No." Her father shifted in the leather executive

chair, suddenly looking uncomfortable. "We need to discuss something."

Oh. Now she knew. She sat back.

"Mother must have told you about Drew and me getting back together." If she were a porcupine, her quills would be quivering.

"Yes."

Before he could list all the reasons why she should go through with the divorce, Larissa rushed to defend her marriage.

"Dad, I made a vow before God. Drew is my husband. We're working things out. I love him. Can't you be happy for us?"

Blue eyes never leaving her face, her father fidgeted with a fine ballpoint pen. "Your happiness is all I've ever wanted."

She softened. "I know, Daddy. And I *am* happy. With Drew."

"When this divorce issue first came up, I did something that may upset you. Please believe me when I say I had your best interests at heart. Still do. I simply thought you might need some ammunition."

"Ammunition? For what?" He made her marriage sound like a battle zone. It had never been that.

"You stand to lose a great deal if Drew decided to fight you in court."

"A great deal of money, you mean." Didn't he understand that there was much more at stake here than money? There was her life and her heart.

"Your trust fund is not something to lightly dismiss, Larissa. Men have married women for far less."

Dread and anger pushed at the back of her eyelids. How dare her father insinuate that Drew was after her money!

"Daddy, I can't believe you said that. I can't believe you think I'm that foolish."

"You're not foolish at all. But you are young and trusting."

She laughed bitterly. "I'm not all that young, either, Dad, but I do trust my husband."

"Maybe you shouldn't."

"Do you mind telling me exactly what you're talking about? You've hinted at some subterfuge from the moment we started this conversation. If you know something unsavory about Drew, just tell me."

Her heart was knocking at jackhammer pace.

Please don't let there be anything, Lord.

Her father slid open the top desk drawer and withdrew a large manila envelope.

"It hurts me, honey, to show you this." He pushed the envelope toward her. "But I have to. You're my only child and I'll do anything to protect you."

As soon as her fingers touched the paper, her stomach began to ache. A terrible foreboding kept her from taking the envelope.

"What is it?" Her words came out in a choked whisper.

"I had a private investigator check into Drew's background."

She shot up out of the chair. "You did what?"

"I only want what's best for you, Larissa. Sit down and read the report before you blast me. I'm not the one you should be angry with."

Feeling betrayed by her father's actions, she peeled back the flap on the envelope and slid out a thick file.

Drew's roguish face smiled up at her. She slammed the file down onto the desk. "I don't want to know."

Scared out of her mind, certain that her whole world was about to collapse, she wanted to run home to Drew.

Thomas circled the desk. "Hiding from the truth won't change it."

He was right, of course. Even if she never read the detective's report, she'd always wonder.

Hands shaking, she took up the file again and began to read. After a few pages, she looked up. Her father, love and concern in his eyes, stood waiting to offer moral support.

"There's nothing here that I don't already know about Drew."

"That's exactly the point."

"I don't know what you mean."

"Look closely at the dates. Drew Michaels, successful photographer, world traveler, and the man you married—" he put a hand on her shoulder "—doesn't exist."

Larissa didn't remember leaving the office building. She did recall reading the file over and over again.

Her father was right. Drew suddenly appeared, like a phoenix from the ashes, in Oklahoma City at age eighteen. Before that, he didn't exist. Even the birth certificate was false, unrecorded in the state's vital records.

She pressed the gas pedal of her SUV, driving faster than was prudent. Her chest hurt from the welling sobs.

There had to be an explanation. But the official documents pounded at her. Drew had lied. He had falsified everything he was.

"Oh, Drew, what have you done? Why did you lie to me? Who are you?"

The tears broke then, blurring her vision. She swiped angrily at them. A husband who lied wasn't worth tears.

Her father was right. Only a man with something terrible to hide faked a completely new identity.

Who was Drew Michaels? A fortune hunter? A mass murderer? One of those men with wives strung all over the planet?

She sobbed harder. With all the traveling he did, that's exactly who he could be. She'd seen them on talk shows and news programs. Men who lived double lives.

Or someone worse. The possibilities were endless and frightening.

A traffic light loomed ahead, still green, so she gunned the motor. She had to get home. To confront Drew with this information. Maybe he could explain.

The light turned yellow.

Brakes squealed, and she yanked her head around to see a blue car bearing down on her.

Horns blared.

She screamed.

In the next instant, she cleared the light and the blue car sped past her, the driver's fist raised in anger.

Shaking from head to toe, she drove on, pressing faster and harder to get to Drew.

Her father had pleaded with her to go to her parents' house. He'd offered to call her mother. She laughed wildly. Her mother. Some help she'd be.

Maybe she should call Pastor Nelson. He'd know what to advise or at least pray with her until she was calm again.

But no. This was between her and Drew. She didn't want anyone else to know how stupid and gullible she'd been. She also didn't want to do anything that could hurt Drew. Whatever his reason for the changed identity, she loved him.

"Help me, Lord," she prayed through hot tears and an aching chest. "I don't know what to do."

She turned into the exclusive housing development and drove past the homes of Tulsa's most influential citizens. From the outside, each of them lived perfect lives, but she knew better. They all had problems, some worse than others. The outward trappings were just that—a facade, like her husband.

Who was he? What was he hiding?

As she turned into the driveway, Larissa tried to staunch the racking sobs. Facing Drew would be hard enough; she needed control.

Still, the tears flowed on.

Around the corner of the house, her husband ambled toward her, smiling, the limp less noticeable today. Coco trotted beside him, smiling, too.

Larissa's battered heart threatened to shatter. How could she still love him so much?

For the fraction of a second needed to grab a Kleenex, she took her eyes off the driveway.

As if her day couldn't get worse, she heard a thump and then a terrible scream.

"Coco!" Drew yelled and broke into a limping run.

The world tilted into the bizarre state of slow motion that occurs during an accident. Drew running. Coco screaming in pain. Larissa frozen in horror by the little dog writhing on the concrete.

By the time she fumbled out of the vehicle, Drew had scooped Coco into his hands and was yelling for her to get back inside.

Completely wrung out, she cried, "You drive."

As gently as possible, she took Coco and climbed into the passenger's seat. Drew roared into action.

She had cried all the way home, but now she sobbed and sobbed and sobbed, releasing the pain of Drew's betrayal along with the horror of running over her own dog.

"It's okay, baby," Drew kept saying. "You didn't see her. It's okay."

"She'll die. She'll die. I'll lose her, too." Tears rained down on the moaning, shivering little Yorkie.

"We're not losing her." He set his jaw in grim determination and slammed the accelerator to the floor.

The trip to the animal hospital took ten minutes. Though the detective's report lingered in the back of her mind, Larissa concentrated on her pet. In her out-of-control state, she'd been the one to injure Coco.

No matter what Drew had done or hadn't done, he stood beside her like a rock, arm firmly holding her together. Over and over, he murmured words of comfort and encouragement that only broke her heart more.

He loved her. She loved him. Why couldn't life be that simple?

The vet, after a sedative and x-rays, came into the waiting room. Her first words were the best news Larissa had heard all day.

"Coco will heal," the doctor said. "Her right foot is broken, her shoulder was dislocated and she has a number of bruises. I want to keep her overnight, but if everything goes as I expect, you can pick her up in the morning."

As soon as the verdict was rendered, Larissa fell into Drew's arms and sobbed some more.

"Hey, I told you she'd make it," he said gently, stroking her back and hair as if she were a child. The man had no clue that her tears were a confused mixture of everything that had happened today.

After the trauma of Coco's accident, Larissa had no

strength left to ask Drew about the private investigator's report.

Whatever his secret, it would have to wait.

Two days later, Drew lay on the floor of their bedroom next to Coco's basket unaware that Larissa watched him from the hallway. He'd fried and crumbled bacon and was now patiently hand-feeding the little dog.

"A bum leg is no fun, huh, girl?" he murmured. Coco stared up at him with big, sad eyes. He gently bumped her lips with a piece of bacon. "Your favorite. Come on. Eat for Daddy."

The term tore at Larissa. *Daddy.* Foolish though it be, she wanted Drew to be the daddy of her children regardless of who he was or what he'd done.

Could his secret past be the reason he didn't want to have a baby?

She gripped the door facing, so wrung out with emotion she could hardly focus. She couldn't sleep, couldn't eat, and Drew thought Coco was the reason.

Every time she opened her mouth to ask him about the report, she lost her nerve. As she'd told her father from the beginning, she didn't want to know. She couldn't *bear* to know.

This was the Drew she knew and loved. The one who had slept on the floor next to her dog for the last two nights. The Drew who had told her over and over that the accident was not her fault. The Drew who kept trying to cheer her up with silly jokes, hugs, and even a bouquet of flowers.

She trusted him. As dumb as that sounded, she couldn't believe that *her* Drew had done anything terrible. There had to be a good reason why he kept his background a secret.

"Cody and Kelli want to know if Coco can have visitors," she said, trying to pretend that everything was normal.

He looked up and smiled. Her stomach did a somersault.

"What do you think?"

"They know to keep her calm and quiet."

"Then I say yes, maybe this afternoon after her nap."

Larissa rolled her eyes. "She naps all the time."

Drew dusted bacon crumbs from his fingers and sat up. He patted the carpet next to him, and she joined him.

"What have you been doing?"

She'd been on the phone with her father, making sure he didn't interfere again. If she was ever to know the truth, Drew would have to tell her himself.

"Talking to my dad."

"Campaign stuff?"

She nodded and scooted back against the wall. Drew came with her and they sat together watching their pet doze. When he leaned forward, the fish necklace swung out.

She touched his throat. "Tell me again when you got this necklace."

"A friend."

If she asked the right questions, perhaps the truth would come out on its own.

"You've told me that. But who was the friend?"

He gave her a curious look. "A teacher, when I was a kid."

"Can teachers do that?"

"I guess they can. Anyway, he did. He was a counselor. A Christian guy, real nice."

"Why did he give it to you?"

Drew got quiet. Had she struck a nerve?

"He gave them to lots of kids, not just me." He peered down at her, quizzical. "Why the twenty questions?"

"Just curious." She shrugged as if the answer didn't matter. "You've told me so little about your childhood. I don't know your parents' names or even where you went to school. You know those things about me."

She held her breath, hoping to glean some simple, sensible explanation for his empty past.

"That's because you're interesting and I'm not."

"That is so not true. You must have been an adorable little boy."

"Of course I was. Almost as adorable as I am now."

She bumped his arm. "Be serious."

"What else is there to know? I was a pain-in-the-neck kid with two great brothers. I lived in Oklahoma City. I had my first photography job at the big daily newspaper. A guy named Dwayne taught me everything about taking pictures. What else is there?"

You tell me, she wanted to say. Instead she asked, "Where did you go to school?"

"Would you believe me if I said Harvard?"

"Only if it's true."

He laughed. "It's not." He hooked an elbow around her neck and tugged. "Did I ever tell you how much I like that little freckle right there?" He kissed the spot beside her lip.

"Don't try to distract me." She pushed him away. "Where did you go to school?"

"Oklahoma City," he said, frustrating her. She wanted place names, people names.

"Which school?"

"Several of them." His face darkened. "We moved a lot. I was such a rotten student I've tried to forget my school days."

In an intentional avoidance maneuver Drew twisted away to focus on Coco. The dog was sound asleep.

Her questions were obviously making him fidgety.

She placed a hand in the center of his tense back. Softly, she asked, "Was your childhood that bad, honey? Is that why you get this way when I ask?"

Over one shoulder he gazed at her, expression bleak. In a harsh whisper, he said, "Yeah. It was. Can we drop the subject, please?"

Whatever had happened to Drew had cut deep and left scars. As much as she wanted to know, Larissa backed off. Someday perhaps he'd trust her enough to reveal his inner torment. Even if he never did, she would love the Drew he was now. And pray with all her heart that the secret wouldn't someday destroy their marriage and shatter her heart.

Chapter Twelve

Coco's road to recovery was shorter than Drew's although the little dog played her injury to the hilt. Neither of her owners could refuse her anything, from hand-feeding to endless games with her squeaky toy.

"She's using your guilt against you," Drew said.

"And you're just a big pushover." Larissa lay on a patio lounger in the bright sunshine catching some rays. Coco, splinted foot aloft, lay on her back in Larissa's lap.

Since Coco's accident, Drew had felt different. Or perhaps the change had begun in Charleston. He wasn't sure. But he was strangely content these days, the constant pressure to be on the move lessened.

He still believed he wasn't good enough for Larissa, but for some unfathomable reason, he made her happy. He'd battled long and hard to help her see how worthless he was, but he'd lost. Somehow she'd turned the tables on him, and now he was scared of losing her.

The ironic notion made him laugh.

So, he'd come to a decision. If he could convince his lovely bride to raise dogs instead of children, maybe they had a chance. Maybe he could pretend to be the man she wanted. Maybe she would never have to know about his past. He'd do just about anything for her, so why not go on living the lie if that pleased his beautiful wife?

First, though, he'd make sure she wouldn't be stuck with a blind photographer who couldn't pay his own bills.

"I think I'm jealous," he said. "Coco's getting all the attention now."

Larissa pushed a pair of sunglasses onto her head and sat up, careful not to upset the dog.

"You're as spoiled as she is."

"I like it, too." He hunkered down beside the chair. "Not counting the stiff ankle, though, I'm close to one hundred percent. Well, maybe seventy-five."

In other words, he no longer felt as weak as a wet noodle.

"What about your vision? You've said nothing about it since Charleston."

"No more blackouts." Though the double vision came and went a lot. It stressed him. No use stressing her.

She stroked the side of his face with her fingertips. "I'm glad."

Basking in the glow of her love, he pressed a kiss to

her palm. "But just in case, my agent and I have been doing some business on the phone."

"What do you mean, just in case?" She sat up and glared at him. Coco awakened and stretched. "You are not going to lose your sight, Drew. Too many people are praying."

He hoped prayer worked, but he wasn't counting on it.

"Hear me out. Shelby had an interesting proposition." His ankle started to throb, so he moved to the end of Larissa's lounger. "She thinks we should do a book, one of those coffee table things."

"That's a magnificent idea."

He thought so, too. Even if the lights went out for good, he had enough photographs on hand to sell individually or in books to make a living for a long time.

"A couple of publishers have expressed interest in a book of my kid shots. If that does well, we could do more." And then he'd know he could support his wife.

"Oh, it will. I just know it." She folded her long, elegant legs under her and leaned forward to grab his hand. "Your photos of children are stunning. Some of them move me to tears. Others make me smile. They're powerful, Drew. The public will love them."

He laughed, thrilled by her enthusiasm. "You're my best cheerleader."

"That's because I've seen the pictures. I don't think you realize how special they are. But when the public sees them, you may end up doing book tours and talk shows."

"That's what Shelby said, too." The whole idea of publicity made him nervous, though, so he planned to pass on that little perk. Someone out there might recognize him, then all his deception and planning would be for naught. Husband of a senator's daughter, famous photographer of children arrested for killing a bunch of kids.

Not good.

The dark cloud of doubt descended.

"I'll have to give the idea more thought."

"Go with it. It's a wonderful concept. And you wouldn't need to travel all the time."

"I've thought of that, too."

"Would you mind?"

He recognized the pinch of worry and knew his restless wandering had caused it. All during their marriage, Larissa had taken a backseat to his work. A woman like her, who deserved the world. The ugly truth of his neglect grieved him.

Slowly, he shook his head. "You know, as surprising as this may be, I wouldn't." He tickled the bottom of her foot. "Hanging out with you is kinda fun."

She wiggled her toes. "Told you."

"The city is doing a building demolition late this afternoon," he said. "I promised Ryan we'd go down after school and see what we can shoot."

"You've captivated that kid. The Radcliffs say he's even doing better in school."

"That's because I told him if his grades didn't improve, he couldn't use my darkroom."

"Ah, bribery."

"It works. Now what must I bribe you with to get a kiss before I leave?"

Her perfect mouth bowed in a smile. "Chocolate is good. Or roses."

He removed his shades and leaned in. The scent of coconut lotion filled his senses. "Sorry, all out. Anything else you want?"

A look flickered across her violet eyes, but she didn't answer. Instead, she grabbed his shirt collar and pulled him to her for a mind-numbing, blood-rushing kiss.

Drew was certain his eyes, blurry before, were now crossed.

When she released him, he leaned back, bemused. "Wow."

She took the dog from him. "Too bad you have to run off."

"No kidding," he said and started toward the door. "Why did I tell Ryan I would pick him up from school?"

His wife's delicious giggle followed him into the house.

Larissa stroked Coco's silky fur, her heart singing as Drew left. Every day she fell more in love with him.

Whoever Drew Michaels had been before, he was a good man now. Let the past remain buried.

When he'd jokingly asked what she wanted, she'd almost said a baby, but that particular subject hadn't been broached since Charleston. Drew had promised to think about it and she wanted to give him plenty of time.

Taking her lotion and her dog, she went into the house.

Why was she lying to herself? She didn't mention a baby because she was afraid of his reaction. Things had been going so smoothly. Drew was attending church and asking very astute questions, most of which she couldn't answer. Fortunately, Mark and Drew had become friendly enough to spend a little time together. According to her husband, Mark was pretty smart about the Bible.

She could only keep praying that the little fish around Drew's neck would soon come to have real meaning.

After a quick shower, she grabbed a bottle of water from the fridge and turned on the television. The local news had interviewed her dad about a government scam he'd uncovered and the piece had gained national attention. According to his office, the interview would air today. She shoved a tape into the recorder. As part of her father's campaign team, she routinely gathered tidbits and sound bites for his ads.

As her dad's familiar baritone filled the living room, pride swelled in Larissa's chest. Thomas Stone was the best congressman in the state, even if she did say so.

Though unhappy about the investigation, she knew her father had only been trying to protect her.

She settled back against the couch cushions, letting her wet hair dry naturally while the news ran.

Later, she and Drew had tickets for a touring Broadway play at the Performing Arts Theater, but she had plenty of time to get ready.

The sun had made her lazy. Curling her feet onto the sofa, she stretched out and thought about what she'd wear tonight. The news played on but she paid it no mind.

Last week, she'd purchased a pair of strappy heels that would look great with a short cocktail dress. Maybe the blue one Drew liked so much.

Suddenly, an image on the television caught her attention. Two male hands each holding a small, pewter key chain in the shape of a Jesus fish.

"Separated as boys, reunited as men," the narrator's voice intoned. "Connected by one brother's memory and the Christian symbol that each carried in his pocket. Coincidence? Or divine intervention?"

The poignantly beautiful shot faded to black.

A tingle went down Larissa's spine. She sat straight up, lazy no more.

Drew wore an ichthus exactly like that.

She tried to blow off the strange sensation. Lots of people had Jesus fish these days.

The eerie feeling wouldn't go away.

To satisfy her curiosity, Larissa rewound the tape to the beginning of the piece, the section she'd missed.

The reporter started the story, introducing the two brothers, one a cop in Oklahoma City, the other a street minister in New Orleans.

Larissa listened with rapt attention. Something about the tall, dark brother was familiar. His sculpted cheekbones, square jaw and darkly intense eyes reminded her so much of Drew. It was weird. Too weird.

With expert skill, the narrator wove a heartbreaking story of three brothers, separated by foster care as children.

She frowned. Three brothers? But there were only two in the story.

"Collin Grace would not give up the search," the reporter said. "For more than twenty years he searched for his brothers, only to discover that Drew had died in a fire at age fifteen."

Collin and Drew!

Blood rushed through her ears with such force, she could hardly hear the program. But she tried not to jump to conclusions. There were lots of men in the world named Collin and Drew.

"Ian Carpenter, the youngest of the three brothers had been adopted by a Louisiana family."

Now she was shaking all over. Drew had told her his brothers' names. Ian and Collin.

But that made no sense. According to her husband, his brothers had died in a fire. According to this news report, Drew had died in a fire. They couldn't be the same set of brothers. Could they?

As the news story drew to a close, Larissa once more glimpsed the image of the men's hands, each bearing the fish symbol. A symbol that Drew also carried.

She hit Rewind again, playing the tape over and over until her heart hammered so hard she wondered if she might pass out.

All three of the names were the same. The fish symbol, given to each boy by a school counselor, was the same. And even though the fire story was convoluted, it was still part of the story. Something was going on here. Could the missing brother, the one purported to have died in a fire, be her husband? Could something about this separation be the cause of Drew's secretiveness?

Trembling all over, but more excited than she'd been in ages, Larissa grabbed the telephone. As a congressman's daughter, she had a certain amount of clout. Someone at CNN could put her in contact with the original reporter of that story.

Within ten minutes she had the name of Gretchen Barker, a journalist with Channel Eleven news in New Orleans. She called the station only to discover that Ms. Barker was not working that day. After breathlessly explaining the situation, she was relieved to hear that the producer would give the reporter a message and ask her to contact Larissa ASAP.

She hung up the phone, nervous as a cat on diet pills. If the reporter called back while Drew was here, what would she do? She couldn't lie to him, but if this was true and he was the missing brother, she wasn't sure how he would handle the news. After all, he'd hidden the truth for years. There must be a reason.

Coco's fluffy head moved back and forth as Larissa paced from one side of the room to the other.

"Your daddy has brothers," she said, chewing on the side of her nail. "He needs them. They need him."

The memory of Collin Grace's face, so sorrowful for the lost brother and so overjoyed with the reunion, was imprinted on her mind. If Drew was his brother, the man deserved to know he was alive.

She paced to the window and looked out, praying that Drew wouldn't return before Gretchen Barker called.

Throat dry with nerves, she gulped down the rest of her water.

Still no call. She played the tape again.

Halfway through, the phone chirped.

Punching Pause, she vaulted from the chair and ripped the receiver from the hook. "Hello."

A woman's smooth, professional voice said, "This is Gretchen Barker with Channel Eleven News in New Orleans. May I speak with Larissa Michaels?"

"This is she."

"I understand you may have some information about the reunion story I did on two brothers."

"Ms. Barker, this may sound crazy, but I think the third brother, Drew, may still be alive."

She quickly apprised Gretchen of the evidence, delighted when the reporter concurred.

"Larissa," she said. "I hope you don't mind if I call you that. You see, we may be relatives soon. I'm engaged to Ian Carpenter."

"Oh, my goodness." Larissa's head swam with emotion and excitement. "This is amazing."

"I think you may be on to something. At least I hope you are. But we can't be sure until you to talk to Collin. He remembers more about the boys' childhood than anyone, which isn't pretty, by the way, so prepare yourself. I told him about your call to the station. He said if there was even the most remote chance that you had information on Drew he wants to talk to you. I'm a skeptical reporter, but from what you've told me, I think there's more than a remote chance."

Larissa's hand trembled as she grabbed for a pencil. "Do you have his number?"

A thousand questions raced through Larissa's mind, but she saved them for Collin. If he and Drew were brothers, he would know.

"Not only do I have his number, I have the man himself. He's in the next room."

"Oh. Oh, my goodness. I can't believe this is happening." Adrenaline rushed to her head. She took a deep breath to clear the powerful jumble of nerves.

"I can't, either, but it's wonderful. Can you hold on or would you like for him to call you back privately?"

"Actually, I could use a minute to gather my thoughts. If you'll give me his number, I'll call him right back."

"Sure. He'll probably feel the same way." Gretchen rattled off an area code right there in Oklahoma and then added her own cell number.

Somehow, Larissa thanked Gretchen properly and rang off. Her hands shook.

After checking the front window to be sure Drew had not returned, she drew in a deep, shaky breath and punched in Collin's number, throat so full of emotion she wasn't sure she could even speak.

He answered on the first ring. "Grace."

Unsure of how to begin, she blurted, "This is Larissa Michaels. I think I'm married to your brother."

A sharp inhale and then, "Tell me why you think so."

Collin's voice was tense and steel-edged. He was trying hard to be an unemotional cop. He was failing. The hope zinging through the wires ripped at Larissa. This mattered even more to him than it did to her.

"His name is Drew, and he's told me he had two brothers, Ian and Collin, in Oklahoma City, but he says they died in a fire along with the rest of his family."

"The names fit but not the fire."

"He wears a Jesus fish on a necklace that looks exactly like yours and Ian's. He never takes it off and acts funny whenever I ask about it."

"Funny? In what way?"

"Secretive. Dark. Almost depressed. He's shared very little with me about his past."

"Why?"

"I was hoping you could help me clear up the mystery."

"I'm a police officer who deals in facts and evidence. Any of this could be coincidence, but…" His voice trailed off, lost in thought.

Larissa picked up on his longing. "But you want your brother to be alive."

He drew a ragged breath. "Yeah. Tell me everything he's ever mentioned. Any little detail."

She did, including the story of the hiding place in the woods and carrying Ian on his back. It sounded like such a small amount.

"I'm embarrassed to know so little about the man I've been married to for more than three years."

"It's enough." Collin's words were tight with excitement. "He's my brother. That's Drew. Everything fits except the fire."

Larissa's heart lurched. "But why has he lied about you? Why has he kept his childhood a secret?"

"Shame. Pride. I don't know."

"He has nothing to be ashamed of." But she knew it was exactly the kind of thing Drew would do. He was a proud man.

"What about the fire? Why would he lie about that?"

"I don't know. There *was* a fire and several people died, but the records list Drew as one of the dead."

"I can't figure out what could have happened, can you? According to a private investigator, Drew Michaels suddenly began to exist at the age of eighteen. There's no record of him before that."

"You had him investigated?" Ice dripped from the words, accusing her.

"No. My father did. And Drew has no idea, so please keep this between us."

Silence hummed over the line. She'd upset him.

"Mr. Grace, please. I love my husband. I mean him no harm, ever. I only want to help him. Why else would I be calling you?"

Finally, he relented. She could almost hear his cop brain working as he put together all the evidence.

"What date did the P.I. first encounter a record of your husband's existence?"

She named the year. "Why?"

"You've just sealed the case. That's the same year my brother supposedly died in a fire."

"But it brings me right back to the same question. Why all the secrecy?"

"Drew is the only one who can explain what happened, but in my line of work I've encountered stranger occurrences. Sometimes people want a change, want to start over. Considering the kind of childhood we led, it would be understandable."

"Would I be out of line to ask about your childhood?"

After a moment of hesitation, he said, "I've hidden my background all my life, too. Not in the way Drew apparently has, but it's not something I like to talk about. I'd rather Drew told you."

"So would I, but he hasn't."

"Just suffice it to say, we lived a hard life. Our mother was a crack addict who left us for days at a time. When she was home, she wasn't always nice. Drew knows what it is to be hungry and scared and helpless. Getting separated from each other was the worst thing that ever happened to us. To me anyway."

"Oh, Collin." Pain tore a hole in her heart. "I'm so sorry. So, so sorry." The pieces of her husband's puzzle began to fall into place. "I understand now why he didn't tell me."

And why he was so reluctant to have a baby. He must be terrified of repeating the ugly cycle. *Oh, my precious husband.* The love inside her tripled. What an admirable, resilient man she'd married.

"I don't know how to thank you," Collin said. "I searched for such a long time and now to find both my brothers in the space of a few months. God is awesome."

"Yes, He is." A smile bloomed. "I take it you're a Christian, too."

"A new one, thanks to my fiancée and her family. I never put much stock in God before, but now I know the Bible verse on this key chain is true." He jiggled something against the receiver. "In all these years God has never forsaken us. We've had rough times, but God has always worked things for our good."

"Now I realize God used Drew's accident as a way to reunite the three of you." She didn't add that the accident had also given her and Drew time to mend their marital problems. After all, Collin was a stranger.

"What accident? Is my brother okay?"

She briefly filled him in on Drew's line of work, the explosion, and his recovery.

When she finished, Collin said, "I'm only a couple of hours away. How about if I drive up there tonight? Or tomorrow, if that's better?"

Larissa felt his eagerness over the phone, but she was not ready for this. Drew had no idea what she'd done.

She put a hand to her forehead. "I'm not sure that's a good idea. I haven't had time to absorb all this, much less break it to Drew. I only saw the news clip about a half hour ago."

"Lady, I've been waiting for more than twenty years. I want to see my brother."

"I understand that, but I need time to gauge how he feels, what he wants. He's hidden his past for a reason. He may need some time."

"I want to talk to him. To see him. He's my brother."

"Soon. I promise."

Collin's yearning was getting to her in a hurry. More rattled now than ever, she said a quick goodbye and hung up.

Both thrilled and terrified, she sat on the sofa, telephone receiver clasped to her chest and prayed. All the while, her mind raced.

How was Drew going to react to this news? Had he ever tried to find his lost siblings? Did he even want to?

Worse yet, what if Collin told him about the private investigator? Without a doubt, Drew would not react well to that little piece of information.

She pinched her lips together, thinking.

Tonight was the play, but perhaps they should cancel. She was too overwrought at the moment to enjoy an evening out. She needed time alone with her husband. A revelation of this proportion required exactly the right time and the right mood.

But she couldn't cancel. She'd looked forward to this play for months and Drew knew it. He'd ordered the tickets as a sweet surprise for her. If she canceled now, he would know something was amiss. And his feelings would be hurt.

"Lord, please help. I don't know what to do. I fear I've opened a can of worms that will only make matters worse. If Drew wanted me to know, he would have told me."

The fact that he hadn't trusted her enough sliced deeply.

How in the world would she ever find a way to tell him that she knew about his secret past? The past he'd tried so hard to leave behind?

Would he be angry? Would he hate her for prying?

A thousand thoughts swirled in her head, fast and confusing.

With an anxious groan, she went to the bedroom to fix her hair for the play.

Chapter Thirteen

"What's wrong, sweetheart?"

Drew watched his wife remove a pair of long, glittering earrings and drop them on the dresser. She'd been super quiet tonight, her thoughts a thousand miles away. "You haven't been yourself. Didn't you like the play?"

"I have a headache."

"Why didn't you say something earlier?" The artsy play scene wasn't all that important. He would have brought her home.

She shrugged, saying nothing, as distracted now as she had been all evening.

"Are you sure that's all?"

He stood behind her, watching her beautiful face in the mirror. Her gaze rose to meet his, then quickly shifted away. A tiny furrow pinched her eyebrows together.

Drew couldn't help wonder if he'd done something to upset her.

He placed his hands on her bare shoulders and began to massage, breathing in the sweet, clean smell of her hair.

"Tension?"

She nodded, letting her head tilt from side to side. After a minute, she reached back and patted his hands. "I think I'll take some aspirin and go to bed."

A faint twinge of disappointment hit him. Usually she loved his massages. He dropped his hands and watched her head for the bathroom to change.

The play was one she'd anticipated for months, but she'd barely said a word about it.

Something more than a headache was bothering his wife. And it worried him for more reasons than one.

Tossing his jacket onto the back of a chair, he went to check on Coco. When he returned with the dog and her basket, Larissa was already in bed, her back turned. Only the lamp on his side burned.

As quietly as possible, he prepared for bed, then snapped off the light.

Larissa didn't stir.

After a few seconds, he whispered, "I love you."

There was no answer. She must have been asleep already.

He lay in the darkness wondering. Was it the baby thing again? One of the couples they'd met for coffee during the intermission had announced a baby on the way. Larissa had not been the same since.

No, there was something else. He could feel it. She

was keeping something from him. Tomorrow, after she was rested and the headache cured, he would ask.

Drew awakened to the sound of Coco's insistent whine. Scrubbing both hands over his sleepy face, he sat up. Daylight flooded the room.

"What time is it?" He twisted around to ask Larissa.

Her side of the bed was empty.

"Uh-oh. We've overslept again, Coco. Mommy's already up." He scratched at his chest and looked around. "Wonder why she didn't take you out?"

He and the dog limped through the house. The ankle was stiff in the morning, but limbered up as the day progressed.

He sniffed the air. Coffee was on. Thank goodness. But no sign of Larissa.

"Maybe she took a swim."

Outside, he placed Coco on the ground to do her business and went toward the pool house.

Larissa wasn't there, either.

For a minute, he stood in the yard, thinking.

Had she mentioned going anywhere this morning?

With Coco in tow, he returned to the kitchen for much needed coffee. There he found a note stuck to the coffeepot.

"Mother's decorator is coming this morning. She needs my input. Back by noon."

"Should have guessed," he groused.

He had work to do in the darkroom anyway, though

Larissa's company down there was way better than the teenage Ryan's. But Ryan wasn't coming, either. He had school.

"Just me and you, girl," he said. Coco's response was a baleful stare that made him chuckle.

The morning flew by. He developed photos, talked to his agent, sorted kid pictures that he thought might work in this book idea of hers.

That whole thing freaked him out, but it was good, too. With books in the works, he'd have an income regardless of what happened with the vision.

And the books would make Larissa happier, too. He could stay home more. He'd never been in one spot very long, and wasn't sure how he would feel in the long run. But being here with Larissa all this time had settled him in a way he hadn't thought possible. He loved waking up to her. Truth be told, he didn't trust his eyes enough to travel much right now.

At noon, he went upstairs to grab a bite. He was creating the world's fattest sandwich when the phone rang. Expecting Larissa, he grabbed for it.

"Hello."

An unfamiliar masculine voice said, "Is this Drew?"

Cradling the phone between shoulder and ear, he smeared mayo on a slice of bread. "In the flesh. Who am I talking to?"

There was an eerie pause.

Telemarketer, Drew thought and started to hang up.

"Drew." The man sounded choked. "This is Collin."

The knife in Drew's hand clattered against the jar. "Collin?" He could barely whisper. "Collin who?"

But he knew. Even after all this time, he knew. There were thousands of men named Collin but this was the one.

"Your brother. I've found Ian, too. He's on his way here now."

All the air whooshed out of Drew's lungs. He stumbled to a bar stool and collapsed. "My brother. Where? How? Oh, man. Is it really you?"

A soft chuckle reassured him. "Yeah, it's me, you little twerp. Where have you been hiding?"

It was his big brother all right. And Drew didn't know how to act. "It's been twenty years."

"More than that. I'm sorry to catch you by surprise like this. I was actually calling to speak to Larissa, but when I heard your voice, I couldn't wait any longer."

Elbow on the breakfast bar, Drew leaned his head on one palm. His mind swam, as jumbled as his emotions. "Why would you want to talk to my wife?"

Another long pause. "She didn't tell you."

"Tell me what?"

"That she and I talked yesterday. Between the two of us we figured out the truth, that you're my long missing, presumed dead brother."

"Larissa knows?" All of a sudden, her strange behavior last night came into focus. She *knew*.

That's why she hadn't welcomed his massage. That's why she'd hardly talked to him at the play. That's why she'd turned her back and pretended to be asleep when he whispered his love.

The sense of loss engulfed him. In finding his brothers, he was losing his wife. This time the rift would be too big to mend.

He could never repair the damage he'd done by marrying her under false pretenses. And now she knew. At least part of it. Now, it was only a matter of time until she discovered the rest.

"As I said, Ian is on his way here now," Collin was saying. "We want to come to Tulsa and meet you. We've got a lot of catching up to do."

Drew sat bolt upright. "No. Not here. I mean, where are you? I'll come there."

"Works for me. I'm in Oklahoma City."

Oklahoma City. All this time his brother was less than two hours away. Reeling from the information, he couldn't think straight. One thing kept coming back to him. Larissa knew. She knew he was nothing. She knew he was a fraud and a fake.

Everything in him screamed denial. He'd tried so hard to keep the ugliness away, only to have it return in the form of a brother he loved.

How did he reconcile the two?

The fact was, he couldn't.

The world he'd created was coming to an end. Larissa knew about him, and their life together was over. Oh, she'd deny that his background made a difference, but her actions last night told the tale. She'd never accept his life of lies.

With a mix of joy and sadness, he made arrangements to meet his brothers.

Slowly, he replaced the receiver and sat staring at it. His sandwich waited on the counter, but his appetite was gone. Like a man in a trance, he put away the food and went to pack his clothes.

His instincts had been right after all. He never should have come back here.

Might as well make the break and save the humiliation of being ordered to get out.

As he pulled jeans and boots from the closet, Coco managed to leave her basket and toddle into the bedroom, tags jingling. She cocked her head at him as if to say, "Are you leaving again?"

"Daddy's gotta go, girl." The word daddy choked him.

Larissa wanted kids. Once he was out of her life, she could find someone else, a man who wasn't afraid to give her the babies she wanted so badly.

He sat down on the side of the bed, his whole being screaming against the decision. Larissa with someone else? He'd thought he had that all settled in his head months ago. He'd been wrong. The notion tore him apart.

Back to square one. She deserved far better than a throwaway kid with bad genes and a worse track record. Now that his identity had been revealed, the rest of the story would soon come out.

He wouldn't saddle her with a convict.

He glanced at the clock—already past noon and Larissa's promised return time. Not that he was surprised. A trip to her demanding mother's was never as short or as simple as she planned.

And then again, maybe she was avoiding him now that she knew.

In too short a time, he was packed. He traveled light. Mostly his camera equipment and a few clothes. When the smoke cleared, he'd send word for her to give his other things to Goodwill.

For now, he'd head to the city for a few days, get reacquainted with his brothers. By then he'd have a job. As scared as he was to travel, he was more afraid to stay. Afraid to face Larissa. Afraid that a restless wanderer couldn't survive in an eight-by-ten cell.

He wasn't much else, but he was a survivor.

Backpack slung over one shoulder, he picked up his duffel bag and headed to the kitchen. He couldn't just walk out without at least scribbling a note. Larissa would worry. No matter what she thought of him, his sweet wife would still worry.

His lips twisted bitterly. What did a man write at a time like this?

He started and stopped several times, ending up with wads of paper, before scratching out a quick note.

"That'll have to do." He stuck the note on her pillow then reshouldered his bag.

Coco tried to follow him to the door. He picked her up, pressed the warm, soft little body to his face. "Take care of her, girl."

As he walked out into the clear spring afternoon, closing the door of the only home he'd ever known, the wound in Drew's soul reopened and started to bleed.

He checked into a small hotel off Interstate 40 before driving to meet his brothers. Sick to his stomach with emotion, he couldn't eat, so he stopped at a convenience store for antacids and a bottle of water.

Finding Collin and Drew had always been in the back of his mind, but he'd wanted to do it on his time and in his way. Not like this. Not when opening the door to the past cost him so dearly.

Directions to Collin's farm on the seat beside him, he made the trip west of the city where the houses grew farther apart and dirt roads took the place of pavement. The countryside was in bloom, a gorgeous feast for a photographer's eyes.

He could imagine Collin out here in the country.

The phone call had been such a shock he'd failed to learn much about his brothers' lives. He hoped they had both been happy.

When he spotted the half-finished house surrounded by animal pens and a big new barn, he knew this had to be Collin's place.

A grin broke over his face.

His big brother hadn't changed. He'd always provide for an animal first and himself second.

As soon as the thought came, he sobered. Collin had provided for Ian and him first, as well. He'd been the best big brother any boy could ever have, and Drew was truly sorry they'd spent all these years apart.

He pulled next to a late-model SUV and killed the engine. Palms clammy against the steering wheel, he licked dry lips. He was literally scared spitless.

What did he say to two brothers who were strangers? Would they be angry that he'd never searched for them? Would he have the nerve and the faith in their brothers' bond to tell them the reason?

The front door opened. A shaggy little dog with three legs bounded from the house, pink tongue bobbing.

"Might as well get out, Michaels," he muttered, and then shook his head. What would Collin and Ian say to the name change?

Behind the small, delighted dog, a tall, dark man came into view. A man with an uncanny resemblance to himself.

Drew's heart lurched. *Collin.*

Every cell in his body cried out. This was his brother. His flesh and blood. So different, but still the same.

He pushed the car door open and managed to move forward, though he was wobbly enough to collapse.

"You grew up," he said.

"Makes two of us." Collin crossed the space between

them and the two men stood taking each other's measure. "After Larissa told me about the explosion, I expected the worst. You look good, little brother. Real good."

They clasped firm handshakes, then clapped each other on the back, each uncertain how to behave but hungry to reclaim the lost years. To Drew's way of thinking, his brothers were now all he would have.

"Come on in. Ian's on the phone with his lady." Collin shot him a sideways grin. "The reporter in New Orleans who did the story."

Drew blinked, confused. "What story?"

"The news story Larissa saw. The one on Ian and me. None of us ever dreamed it would have this impact. But God knew what He was up to."

"I didn't know." When Collin turned to look at him, he clarified. "About the story. I didn't see it."

"Didn't you talk to Larissa before driving down here?"

Drew shook his head, not ready to go there.

"Well, come on in. We'll fill you in on everything." He held the storm door open. "It may take all night."

"Fine with me." The only place he had to go was a hotel room.

The three-legged dog whined and pushed against Collin's legs.

"This little annoyance is Happy," Collin said affectionately, bending to stroke the shaggy little animal.

Remembering Coco's sad eyes, Drew added a pat to

the friendly head and stepped inside to meet his baby brother.

Ian came from the kitchen carrying a plate filled with pastries and three glasses of milk. He quickly plunked them onto a makeshift coffee table and grabbed Drew's hand.

"Man, it's good to see you," he said.

His open, friendly face was wreathed in smiles, and even as an adult he reminded Drew of a puppy. A good-looking puppy with gentle blue eyes and an aura of peace. Drew liked him all over again.

For the next two hours the three brothers renewed a long dormant relationship while they munched goodies from the Carano Bakery. The Caranos, he discovered, would soon be Collin's in-laws.

As they reminisced about crazy antics and good times, Drew was amazed at how good he felt to let the memories out again. For so long, he'd kept his brothers locked away in the back of his mind, afraid to go there.

He learned that Ian had been adopted into a happy home and now ran a mission for runaways in New Orleans. Collin, like him, grew up in the system, and now was not only an Oklahoma City police officer but also ran a rehab ranch for wounded and abandoned animals.

The avocation fit. It was the vocation that struck Drew as funny. It also terrified him.

"I still can't believe you're a cop." Drew shook his head at Collin. "After all the food we stole out of stores and gardens, I figured you'd be on the other side of the law." *Like me.*

Collin chuckled. "God has a sense of humor. That's for certain."

"And you, a preacher," he said to Ian. "I can see that. You were always the good one."

They all three chuckled. Collin said, "You were the one we figured would end up in jail. For years, I kept expecting to arrest you at any time."

The joke would have been funny if it wasn't so close to the truth. He couldn't even think of a clever come-back.

He stuffed his mouth with a cherry Danish, chewing thoughtfully. His brother was a cop. In all his search-ing for Drew and Ian, had Collin never looked into the records of the fire? Did he not know of Drew's crime? And if he did, would he feel duty bound to turn in his own brother?

A shiver of dread snaked up Drew's spine. His past was rapidly closing in on him. He definitely needed to make a quick exit out of the country.

The notion hurt like sticking his hand to a hot stove. This time, he didn't want to go. But he had to.

"So," he said, eager to change the subject before he broke down like a fool and confessed everything. "Tell me about these ladies you're engaged to."

Blue eyes twinkling, Ian rubbed his hands together with an eager excitement that was so like the little boy Drew remembered.

"I'm engaged to Gretchen, the most incredible, hard-headed, smart and sassy woman in New Orleans." While his brothers laughed at the description, he added, "She's the reporter who nagged us into doing that re-union story."

"I still haven't seen it," Drew admitted. That tiny segment had changed his life and he wanted to watch it for more reasons than one. He hoped the story didn't include anything that could lead Larissa to his worst nightmare. She didn't deserve the humiliation of know-ing she'd loved a murderer. "Do you have the tape?"

"Are you kidding?" Ian asked. "Gretchen is so proud of that piece. She stuck three copies in my suitcase. I'll give you one to take home."

Home. Wherever that was.

But he only said, "That would be great. I appreciate it." He looked at Collin. "What about you? You engaged to a reporter, too?"

"Worse." Collin aimed a chocolate éclair at him, one eyebrow quirked exactly the way Drew recalled. The memory was sweet and unexpected. "Prepare yourself. This is gonna hurt. My lady, Mia, is a social worker."

Drew nearly choked on his Danish. When he'd man-aged to swallow the chunk, he said, "You have to be joking."

As kids, they had, all three, feared and despised so-cial workers, seeing them as an enemy who would sepa-rate them. In the end, that's exactly what had happened.

"Nope. No joke at all. She's the best thing, after the

Lord, that ever happened to me. Mia Carano. Kind, generous, beautiful, even if she is a social worker. I'm crazy about her." He chomped down onto the éclair. Mouth full, he muttered, "Terrific cook, too."

"Can't argue with that." Drew gulped a swig of milk and then helped himself to another sweet roll. "I'd like to meet them both."

And he meant it, too. Before he hit the road again, he wanted to know more about his brothers' lives, including the women who'd captured their hearts.

"Hey, we can arrange a meeting anytime," Collin said. "All you have to say is 'get-together,' and Mia and her big Italian family will whip into action, rustle up more food than anyone can eat, and invite us all to a three-day celebration."

The glow in Collin's dark eyes said he loved every minute of it, just as he loved his fiancée. Drew was glad. Truly. Collin deserved someone special to love him. Even if Mia Carano *was* a social worker, Drew liked her already.

"I see a big family reunion in our very near future," Ian said. "Gretchen is already talking about it. And she wants to report *that* story, too."

Collin groaned. "I figured as much."

"Hey, she's responsible for getting us three back together. Giving her another warm and fuzzy story is the least we can do."

"Just joking," Collin said. "I thank God for your

nosey reporter fiancée. Without her, we'd never have found Drew."

They thanked God to have found him? The idea was humbling to say the least, and he hoped neither lived to regret the enthusiasm.

He was amazed that both of his brothers had somehow ended up as Christians. They sure hadn't learned about Jesus as kids. But now here they were talking about God the way Larissa did. Funny how that didn't make him uncomfortable. In fact, he wanted to know more.

For Larissa being a Christian was easy. She was already good. But how did men loaded down with their ugly baggage reconcile with a holy God?

"We're anxious to meet your wife, too," Ian said, bringing Drew back to the conversation.

The icing on his donut turned bitter. He gazed down at the maple glaze, the ache in his gut starting up again. "That's not going to be possible, guys. Sorry."

Collin narrowed his eyes, cop instinct flashing from him like a neon sign. "Why not?"

Drew sat there for a long moment, unsure of what to say. Should he blow off the question or tell the truth? Well, as much of the truth as he could. Collin was his big brother, but he was still a cop. Besides, Drew had no intention of laying something as heavy as the fire on his newly found siblings. The situation with Larissa was heavy enough.

Heavy enough to break him in two.

Today had been a mixture of joy and grief. Right now, the grief was back.

Careful to keep the worst to himself, he admitted he was divorcing Larissa.

"I'm not even who I claimed to be. I'm nobody, married to a blue blood."

"What difference does that make?" Collin growled, his face intense.

Drew tossed the donut onto a napkin. "Don't you get it, Collin? I lied. I never told her who I really am. Even my name is false. She thought she married some hotshot photographer."

"She did."

He made a disparaging noise. "You of all people know better than that."

"You're not the same wild kid, Drew. That's obvious." Ian leaned forward, his earnest expression one of a both a minister and brother. "You've made a decent life for yourself. Don't blow it now just because Larissa found out about your sorry childhood."

"It's not just the lies I've told. She wants kids. A family. She wants me to settle down, stay home more."

"Pretty normal stuff for a married couple to want."

"She wants it. I don't." But as soon as he spoke, he knew the words were no longer true.

"Last night, she made it pretty clear that I was history. I didn't know why then. Now I do. Finding out that I have an ugly past must have been a big blow. Her father's a congressman. Skeletons in the closet are not acceptable."

Pinching his bottom lip, Ian leaned forward, elbows on his thighs. "Maybe. But did you ever think she might be struggling with how to tell you that your long-lost brother had called? You kept it secret. She had to wonder why. She had to wonder if you would be upset."

He hadn't considered that perspective.

His face must have said so, because Collin pressed the advantage. "She *was* worried about how you would take the news."

"Nice try, guys, but I don't think so. I'm a fake, a fraud. Larissa doesn't even carry my real name."

"Changing your name is no sin," Ian said. "I did it."

Drew made a disparaging noise. "You were adopted. No choice there. I took my name from a British rock star."

Collin laughed. Here Drew was bleeding all over the place and his brother laughed at him. Some things didn't change.

No, not true. Some things did change. As a kid, he would have jumped up and punched Collin in the nose. Today, he saw the humor, too.

"I've made a mess of things. She's better off without me." He shook his head. "There are other problems."

"What kind of problems? If you need money..."

Ian's offer didn't surprise him at all, but he waved him off. "Money's not the issue. At least not at this point. But there are other reasons. Several of them. Too many and too serious to overcome."

Regardless of shared blood, these men were virtual strangers. He couldn't tell them about the crime and he wasn't ready to talk about his eyesight. He shifted gears. "Suffice it to say, I'm not good enough for her. I'm getting out of her life so she can be happy."

Ian's quiet eyes studied him. "Have you talked to Larissa about this?"

"Don't need to."

"Women always need to talk." One side of Collin's mouth jerked up in self-mockery. "I found *that* out the hard way."

"Maybe I'll call her later," Drew said. He wouldn't. No point in prolonging the inevitable.

Ian got up and crossed the narrow space between the couch and chair. His movements were quiet and carried with them a gentle assurance.

"Drew," he said, going down on one knee. "I remember the time we were walking on hot pavement. I was barefoot and my feet were burning, so you carried me on your back." Voice dropping to a hush, he touched Drew's shoulder. "But you didn't have any shoes, either."

Drew swallowed hard, uncomfortable with his brother's emotion. What did a childhood memory have to do with his shattered life?

Ian squeezed Drew's shoulder. "You're my brother. I love ya, man. Always have. Always will. I think I have a right to pry into your personal business. So, don't be offended, but here goes."

"We've been prying into each others' business all evening," Drew answered. Not that he'd told them everything, but these two knew more about him than anyone else on the planet.

"Yeah, well this is real personal. Collin and I believe God brought us all back together. We give him the glory and praise for that."

"He was pretty slow about it."

"God's timing never suits me either, but the point is He does what He's promised." Ian took out his key chain and turned the silver fish on its back. He rubbed his finger across the words emblazoned on all their hearts. "A long time ago, He promised never to leave or forsake three terrified little boys. He kept that promise. Now we've come full circle, back together again."

"I'm not sure what this has to do with Larissa."

"Everything. Collin and I both had to deal with some issues from our childhood. Hurts, rejections, abandonment. God healed those."

Ian glanced at Collin who nodded his agreement.

"He'll heal yours, too, Drew. We were wounded kids. All of us. Wounded kids become wounded adults unless they get help. The best helper you'll ever find is Jesus Christ."

Drew had to agree with one thing. He was one messed up dude.

"I want to pray with you, bro. Can we do that?"

Drew's eyes flashed to Collin. His big brother rose from the chair to join Ian on the hardwood floor.

The sight of two grown men, both of them about as manly as a man could be, on their knees, did something funny to Drew's insides.

It made him envious. They were so at peace. So certain they'd found the answers.

He wanted what his brothers and his wife had found.

"I'm not sure I know how," he admitted. "I mean, I've tried to pray. Larissa's a Christian, goes to church and all that stuff, but I don't know how to be one."

"Do you want to?" Ian's kind face was radiant. He must be a humdinger of a preacher. "Knowing Jesus is the easiest thing in the world."

"Tell me what to do and I'll do it."

"Just believe, brother. Just believe." And then Ian led him in a simple prayer, asking Jesus to come into his heart, to forgive his sins, to help him live a changed life.

As the words fell from his trembling lips, an incredible joy burst inside his soul. Light brighter than the sunrise filled his being.

When the prayer ended, he looked up. The room was the same. His brothers were the same. Except for the holy joy on their faces.

But he was different.

"Larissa talked about the light. I didn't know what she meant," he said in awe.

"The entire book of John talks about it, too. Jesus is the light. When you ask Him into your life, His light fills you. Five minutes ago, you were a child of darkness. Now you have come into God's marvelous light. You are heir to everything in God's kingdom, all the promises, including the right to ask Him to restore your marriage."

As reality tumbled back with a vengeance, Drew swallowed hard. Even though he was different on the inside, his exterior problems hadn't disappeared. "Marriage to me isn't the best thing for Larissa."

"You should let God decide that."

"Being a Christian doesn't change the mistakes I've made."

"No, but God has forgiven you. Maybe you should forgive yourself."

He wasn't sure if he could. Giving his heart to God was one thing. Living with his past was something entirely different. God couldn't erase what he'd done.

Though he didn't tell his brothers, his decision was the same. Larissa was better off without him.

Chapter Fourteen

Larissa couldn't imagine where Drew was.

She glanced out the bay window in the living room toward the garage. His truck was gone, but he'd not said a word about being out this late.

She thought about calling the Radcliffs to ask Ryan, but was too embarrassed. What kind of wife didn't know where her husband was?

This was so unlike him. He always phoned or left a note. She checked the refrigerator, the back door, the table, and a dozen other places.

In the bedroom, she looked on the dresser. Nothing.

Coco lay curled on her pillow, staring up with big eyes.

"How did you get up there, little girl?" she asked, but was too concerned about Drew to give much thought to Coco's renewed ability to jump up on the bed.

A trip down the stairs to the basement proved just as unfruitful.

"Okay, maybe he's out getting night photos."

Her few hours at Mother's had extended to late evening, as usual. She'd called a couple of times, but Drew hadn't answered. Her messages, one offering to bring home a pizza, were still on the machine. Just as the pizza was still on the kitchen counter.

Knowing Drew, he'd gone somewhere with his camera and had become enthralled with some aspect of light that normal people didn't even see. He was probably patiently waiting for the perfect shot. It wouldn't be the first time he'd gotten lost in his work.

She chalked up her disquiet to the conversation yesterday with Collin. Perhaps she'd made a mistake by not telling Drew right away. He had a right to know his brothers were looking for him.

Back in the kitchen, Larissa settled at the bar with a plate of spicy pepperoni and mushroom pizza.

She was tired to the bone. A day with Mother and one of her projects always wore her out. She'd been so tempted to blurt out how wrong they'd been about Drew. The only thing her husband had hidden was a heartbreaking past.

But it was his past and he should make the decision about how much her parents learned. They'd never shown him much sympathy, so she didn't expect that to change. If anything Mother would call him white trash and turn up her snobby nose.

With a weary sigh, she peeled a slice of pepperoni from the crust. Maybe she'd take a long bubble bath and read until Drew came home.

He'd be here soon. It was after eight. Drew loved to shoot at sunset, but that time had come and gone.

Tossing the half-eaten slice back in the box, she rolled her head from side to side, stretching the tired muscles. Then she headed for the tub.

Half an hour later, feeling relaxed and refreshed, she went into the bedroom.

Drew still wasn't home. She gnawed the side of her fingernail. Maybe she should call Ryan, just to be sure. If Drew would carry a cell phone, she wouldn't worry. What if he was driving and his vision blacked out? She shuddered at the thought. He could be in another accident.

Sitting on the side of the bed, she reached for the phone and disturbed Coco in the process. The Yorkie struggled up from the pillow.

As Larissa reached to help the dog down onto the floor, her gaze fell on a wadded, wrinkled piece of paper.

She frowned and picked it up. "What is this?"

But she recognized Drew's scrawling cursive.

"What a weird place for a note."

And then she began to read.

Sorry for everything. I'll file for divorce so you won't have to. Be happy. I will love you always.
Drew

Stunned, as if shot with a Taser gun, she sat there and stared at the note, reading the horrible message over and over again. With each reading, the crack in her heart expanded.

"What is he talking about? He'll always love me, but he still wants a divorce?" And he wanted her to be happy about it. What kind of sense did that make?

She thought they were working things out, that their relationship had grown stronger and better. What could have happened?

With a moan, she lay down on the bed and tried to think.

He'd promised to try. He'd even promised to consider babies. He was going to stay home more, work on the book, let his eyes heal. Why had he walked out this way?

Her mind went back over the last couple of days, searching, thinking. Finally, she settled on the only thing that made any sense at all. An assignment. His work had separated them over and over again. He must have been offered a terrific job, and knowing she would ask him to keep his promise of staying longer, had chosen the work over her again.

All his talk of staying home more, even of having a family, had been lies to keep the peace until his wounds healed.

Hard, cold reality settled in. He'd left this way because he didn't want to tell her face-to-face. He didn't want her to know where he was going.

This time he was gone forever.

And she'd never had a chance to tell him about Collin's phone call.

A tidal wave of hurt and grief welled up, threatening to send her over the edge. She cried until her eyes ached and her throat hurt. She cried until Coco's wet nose pushed at the hair over her ear, trying in vain to comfort her.

When the flood of tears finally subsided, she crawled beneath the covers, a wad of tissues in hand, and lay staring into the darkness. The words of the note rolled over and over inside her head.

She did the only thing she knew to do. She prayed.

"He loves me, Lord. He said so. I *know* so. What happened? Where is he? I'm so confused by this. Please take care of him. Show me what to do."

After a while, unable to sleep, she sat up, clicked on the lamp, and reached for her Bible.

The phone on the bedside table jangled.

"Drew," she whispered. Heart in her throat, she lifted the receiver. "Hello."

"Larissa. Collin here. Drew's brother."

As if she could forget, especially now when she must confess that Drew was gone and the opportunity for a reunion had gone with him.

Hiding the disappointment, she said, "I'm sorry I didn't get back to you sooner."

"Drew was here tonight."

"What? Where?"

"Oklahoma City. My house. Ian's here, too. We had

a nice long talk." He hesitated and she could hear him moving around. "Look, I don't know how to say this. I guess I should put Ian on the phone. He's better at talking than I am."

"Just tell me," she said, and then, to her embarrassment, her voice broke. "Drew left me, Collin. He's gone."

"I know. He told us."

"I'm sorry. I feel so foolish telling this to a complete stranger."

"We aren't strangers. We're family."

And with those simple words, the dam broke and Larissa's flood of emotions poured out. "Do you know where he's going? Did he say anything about why he left? I just don't understand any of this. I thought we had worked things out, but he wants a divorce."

"No, he doesn't. According to our brother, you won't want him now that you know about his past. Is that true?"

"Of course not. I love the man Drew has become. I don't care about the rest."

"We tried to tell him that. But Drew thinks he's not good enough for you. He made the break so you wouldn't have to."

"That's crazy."

"Yeah, well, Drew always was the crazy one. But he needs you, Larissa. Any fool could see that."

"I don't even know where he is."

"I do." He rattled off a hotel address. "I need to tell

you something else, too. Some good news for a change. Drew accepted the Lord tonight."

"Oh, Collin." She closed her eyes in gratitude. "That's wonderful."

If she wasn't so distressed she'd jump for joy. At least, Drew now had Jesus to watch over him no matter what happened.

"I agree, but he's got some cockamamie idea about heading to Indonesia."

"I don't understand this. With his vision problems, he isn't ready to be alone on assignment."

There was a subtle pause. "What vision problems?"

"Since the accident, his vision comes and goes. Sometimes everything goes black."

"Oh, man. He didn't tell us. Our poor, idiotic brother is in worse shape than we thought. And we'd already decided he was a mess. Look, Larissa, he needs you badly. Any fool could see he's dying inside. If you love him, go to him and make him understand that he's worth it. Love never fails to do what two brothers can't."

Stunned to hear Collin repeat the verse she'd clung to for months, she whispered, "What did you just say?"

"Love never fails, Larissa. Never. It may fail to do what we wanted it to at the time we expected, but love will never fail. Even if Drew is pushing you away, he's dying for you to make him stay. He has God's love, but he needs yours, too."

And through the mouth of her husband's brother, God confirmed what Larissa already suspected. She'd made mistakes, too. Her love *had* failed. It had failed because it had been a selfish love. Her own wants and needs and selfish desires had stood in the way. She'd tried to manipulate Drew into staying home, into having a baby, into being the husband she wanted. All for her own agenda.

Fearful of driving Drew away, she'd never fully trusted her marriage to the Lord. She'd been trying to control things on her own.

But no more.

Drew reclined on the brown hotel bedspread, still fully dressed, hands stacked behind his head.

In his need to think about everything that occurred, he'd returned to the hotel over Collin's protestations. Overwhelmed, overloaded, stunned. He couldn't think of enough adjectives to describe his emotions. This had been the strangest day of his life.

He was alternately filled with joy and then despair. His brothers, both incredibly fine men, were back in his life. He didn't even know how to begin thanking God for that miracle.

God.

He touched the ichthus at his throat. Pure, radiant light surrounded him. God had always been here, just as He'd promised. Drew only wished he hadn't taken so long to let the Lord be a real part of his life.

"Lord, I sure wish I'd known you before everything fell apart with Larissa."

Just saying her name brought heat and pressure to the back of his eyes. Angry, he slashed at them. The decision was made. No amount of talking by his brothers would change his mind. They didn't know all the facts, and when they did, they'd agree. Larissa was better off without him.

All this time, he'd prayed for God to change her. Change her mind about his work. Change her mind about having kids. All along, he was the needy one, the one in the wrong. Now that it was too late, he would give up *everything* to change his past and become the good husband Larissa deserved.

He tossed restlessly, full of donuts and milk, a jumble of thoughts.

Tomorrow he'd call Shelby, accept the book deal with instructions to look for other opportunities as well. He'd phone National Geographic himself.

Or maybe he'd wait a few days, spend some time with Collin and Ian. Man, it was good to be with them again.

Rolling to his side, he checked the standard issue alarm clock. Midnight had long since come and gone.

He flipped on the lamp, blinking in the sudden burst of illumination. His equipment bag lay on the tiny round table. In all the stress and excitement, he'd forgotten to take any pictures of his brothers. Very uncharacteristic. Tomorrow he'd rectify the oversight. Next to the bag was Ian's video.

Needing the distraction and curious about the news

story that had changed his life, he rose and started toward the table.

The room faded to black.

Struck with fear, he fumbled in the darkness, bumped into a chair, scraped it back and sat.

He waited, hoping, praying the darkness would dissipate as usual.

Stress brought this on. He was sure of it. He took slow, deep breaths, fighting for calm. He could control his mind. Hadn't the doctors said so?

Fingertips pressed to his eyelids, he concentrated on turning the inner lights back on.

What would he do if that didn't happen?

The air-conditioning snicked into action, and cool, slightly musty air whooshed through the room.

Nothing wrong with the rest of his senses.

Maybe a good night's sleep would restore the vision. No doubt he was overtired and stressed to the max.

Moving around in the unfamiliar room was tricky, but he felt his way to the bed. Flickers of light flashed behind his eyes.

He shook his head. Once. Twice.

The flickers came again, brighter, longer.

"Come on. Come on."

In the next instant, he realized what he'd forgotten. He wasn't alone anymore. He had Someone to help him through life's darkest places. Carefully, he slipped to his knees beside the bed.

"Lord, I don't know the right way to ask You for

things. But the way I figure it, You created eyes in the first place, so if You would please, I need my sight back. I'm a photographer. You probably know that."

Then an overwhelming sense of regret and remorse took hold of him. He began to pray anew, for his messed-up life, for Larissa, for the terrible sin he'd committed all those years ago.

Though he knew next to nothing of prayer, he figured God understood anyway. The words poured out for a long time. How long he couldn't say. He couldn't see the clock.

Finally, he murmured, "Well, that's all, I guess. Thanks for listening."

He opened his eyes, disappointed to still be in the dark. And then a powerful realization swelled inside him. He might be physically blind forever, but spiritual darkness was a choice. He would never be completely free of the dark past until he faced it head-on. Tonight he'd done that in part by meeting with his brothers. But the deeper issue still hung over him like a noose.

Memories of that terrible night rolled through him. Memories that had shaped his entire life and crippled him in a way the roadside bomb never could.

Smoking in the attic. Falling asleep, only to awaken to screams. The flames shooting high into the night sky, consuming everything and everyone.

For years, he'd blocked the visions, but now he let them come. He saw the dying faces. Heard the moans and screams. Tasted the acrid smoke that had left him hoarse for days.

Sweat popped out over his body. But he watched the movie inside his head.

He'd committed this atrocity. He'd killed those boys with his careless disregard of authority.

It was time to stand up and face the consequences of his actions. No more running. No more hiding. He was a man now, not a scared runaway with nowhere to turn.

First thing in the morning he'd call the Oklahoma City police department and turn himself in. Not to Collin. That was too heavy a burden to place on his older brother. The only person he would lean on was himself—and God.

Unless his vision cleared, the cops would have to come for him. He could deal with that.

Blood pounding against his temples, both scared and relieved, he rested back on the pillow to await the morning.

Some time later, he heard footsteps in the hallway. Then someone tapped softly at the door.

He sat upright, listening hard.

A visitor in the middle of the night? Housekeeping? A guest gone astray? Burglars?

"Go away," he called. "The room is occupied."

"Drew. Honey."

His heart slammed against his rib cage. His beautiful wife, the love of his life stood outside in the hallway.

Not knowing what else to do, he got up and felt his way to the door. "Go home, Larissa."

If she saw him now, blind and scared, she'd force him back to Tulsa. He couldn't do that to her.

"Open the door, Drew. I'll stand out here all night if you don't." When he didn't respond, she pecked on the door again. "It's a long drive up here. I'm really tired. Please let me in."

The woman didn't play fair. He'd let her in, but he would not let her stay.

He felt for the security lock, struggling to work the chain through the hole.

"Drew?"

Frustrated, he bit out, "One minute."

Was this what he had to look forward to?

As metal rattled against metal, the chain fell away and he reached for the deadbolt, finally opening the heavy door.

And there she stood, as clear as the morning sun.

His mouth must have gaped. He could see her. For a second, he sagged, mentally screaming thank-you to the God of the universe.

Larissa never needed to know what he'd just gone through.

As soon as he had his wits about him, he said, "What are you doing here?"

She pushed inside. "Don't play tough guy with me. I know what you're trying to do."

"Yeah?" He turned his back to her. If he was rude,

maybe she would leave before he collapsed at her feet and cried like a baby. "I'm trying to get some sleep."

"Then why was the light on?"

He rubbed a hand over his eyes, refusing to go there.

"Why are you here, Larissa? What do you want?" He stared at a picture on the wall, grateful to see it.

Larissa swept around in front of him, blocking the sight. He couldn't complain. She was far more beautiful than the abstract slash of blues and greens. "I love you, and I won't let you go."

"You don't have a choice. I'm leaving. Again. Just like always. Nothing's changed."

"Liar," she said softly, but tears gathered in the corners of her violet eyes and nearly brought him to his knees. "I talked to Collin. He told me about your past. Your childhood. How hard it was."

Bitter gall rose in his throat. She knew too much. "Collin's got a big mouth."

"I'm thankful, Drew. At last I can understand what makes you do the things you do. All this time I thought you loved your cameras and your travel more than me. But now I know better."

She'd just arrived and already he was losing ground. "Go home, Larissa."

But his gentle wife had a relentless side. She shook her head, gold hoops peeking through long, silky hair. "You run because you're afraid."

"I'm a disaster photographer. I'm not afraid of anything."

"Yes, you are. You're afraid of me. Afraid to let someone love you. Afraid of being rejected again. Afraid to trust. So you run."

The issue was far more complicated than she could know. He wasn't running anymore. But he wasn't about to saddle the woman he loved with a convict. Knowing Larissa she would stand by her man until the bitter end. He could live with his punishment. He couldn't live with knowing he'd ruined her life.

"A bunch of psychobabble nonsense."

"Really?" Head to one side, she perched hands on her hips. "Then why did you hide your past from me? Why did you change your name and create an entirely new identity?"

Humiliation added fuel to his pretend anger. "Collin does have a big mouth."

"Collin didn't tell me. My father did."

"Your father?"

"He had you investigated." When he opened his mouth to give his opinion of that little invasion of privacy, she held up a palm. "Hear me out. I've already said all the things you're thinking. I told my parents, essentially, to stay out of our relationship because I know the real you. An investigation did not change my feelings."

Jaw tight, he said, "It should have."

"The investigation didn't. But the Lord did."

The admission stabbed him through the heart. So she'd finally come to her senses. Good. He just wished it didn't hurt so much.

Then she shocked him by saying, "I need your for-giveness, Drew. The Lord showed me how selfish I've been in our marriage. I wanted everything my way. I wanted to force you into the mold of my making. I've tried to change you, to make you do things my way. Instead of easing your fear and distrust, I added to it."

Oh, man. His walls began to crumble.

"You don't know what you're talking about," he growled.

"Your past makes you who you are, Drew. And I love the man you've become. You're incredible."

"I'm a loser. If you're smart you'll be the one who runs—as fast as you can away from me."

She shook her head and moved closer. Her sweet perfume wafted over him like a summer breeze. He stepped back.

"Listen to me, Drew. I know you better than you know yourself. You took a terrible childhood and turned it into a successful life."

"Yeah, right. Name one good thing I've ever done."

"I can name dozens. You give children in dire situa-tions a voice with your pictures. You mentored a trou-bled kid that no one else could stand having around." Love glimmered in the big violet eyes. "You slept on the floor with my dog because I was so worried about her."

He sniffed. "Big deal."

She touched his arm. Though he should shake her off, he couldn't. Her touch was like a salve to an open wound. "You have my heart, Drew. If you leave, you take it with you. No matter what happens, I'll still love you. Love, God's kind of love, never fails. Never."

He heard the hope in her words, saw it in her eyes. Refusing her was the hardest thing he'd ever had to do.

Like a battered prize fighter rising for one last round, he managed to say, "There are things you don't know. Things that will make you hate me. I can't go back to Tulsa because—" Emotion clogged the back of his throat. He had to say the words and drive her away. "Tomorrow morning I'm going to jail."

She blinked. Once. Twice. Dear Lord, he loved her.

"What are you talking about?" she whispered, and the trembling voice tore him up.

"A long time ago, before I became Drew Michaels, I did something terrible." He sucked in a gulp of stale hotel air. He'd tell her and then send her home. "It's time I faced the consequences."

"I don't understand."

"Well here it is. I killed some people."

She gasped, hand pressed to her lips. "You did not."

"People thought I died in a house fire." He grabbed both her arms and pulled her close, grim and determined. "I didn't die, but lots of others did. And it was my fault. I killed those kids."

He expected her to jerk away in revulsion, but she didn't. His amazing, incredible wife walked straight into his chest and wrapped her arms around him. He stood there, arms at his side, lost in the beauty of her love.

"Didn't you hear me?" he choked out, desperate now.

She only shook her head, then began to rock him back and forth, back and forth, holding him in a grip that refused to let go.

"Oh, my Drew," she murmured. "Let me hold you. Let me love the little boy who needed someone, and no one was there. Let me be here for you now. And forever."

Drew squeezed his eyes tight against the piercing sweet emotion. Her tears dampened his shirt, adding to his guilt.

"Listen to me," he pled. "I killed those kids. I caused that fire."

She leaned back, face wet with tears, still refusing to release him. "Tell me everything. Everything."

"If I do, will you go? Will you walk away and never look back? Will you start again and pretend you never knew me?"

"No." She touched the ichthus at his throat. "Jesus will never leave you nor forsake you. I won't either."

"Oh, God," he moaned, looking up at the ceiling. "Please make her see."

His ugly sin hung in the air between them. Clinging to one last chance to set her free, he tugged her down to the side of the bed.

Then he told her everything.

"You already know I was a wild teenager. Angry. Bucking authority. There wasn't much I wouldn't or didn't do." He sucked in a shuddering breath. "Another kid and I hid cigarettes in the attic. After the house parents were asleep, we'd sneak up there and smoke. We thought we were cool."

He shook his head, so sorry for the pain and sorrow he'd caused. "We were so stupid."

Her hand rubbed up and down his arm, soothing. "What happened?"

"I fell asleep. The next thing I knew people were screaming and running, and the house was full of smoke." Vivid memories flashed in his head, cruel but useful. "I jumped out the window and ran. Too scared to come back and face the music, I hid out. The next morning, the paper said everyone died. Including me. I knew if I went back, I'd end up in some institution for the emotionally disturbed or worse, in prison. So I let Drew Grace die in that fire along with everyone else."

"Oh, Drew." Larissa fell against him. He caught her in his arms and held on, letting some of his shame flow out. Several silent moments ticked by while his wife embraced him for the last time.

Suddenly, Larissa sat bolt upright and gripped his arms. "Wait a minute. Wait just a minute." She gave him a little shake. "Drew, listen to me. I don't think you caused that fire."

Hope died hard in this lady. "Well, think again. I was there."

"Where? Tell me again exactly where you were inside that house."

For whatever good it would do, he humored her. "In

the attic. The house mother was—" his mouth quirked "—chubby. She couldn't climb the ladder. It was the perfect hiding place, filled with old boxes and books and used furniture. Add cigarettes and matches and you have a recipe for disaster."

Her eyes danced with an excitement he couldn't comprehend. "That's it, then. Drew, you didn't cause that tragedy. The fire started in the kitchen."

A flicker of hope trembled in his chest. "How could you possibly know that?"

"The TV report. Collin talked about a kitchen fire. Not an attic fire."

Could it be true? "Are you sure?"

"I recorded the segment. Let's go home and watch it."

"No need." He got up and went to the table, hoisting the videotape. "Ian gave me a copy. I rented a VCR downstairs but hadn't gotten around to watching."

Being blind put a damper on watching TV. More hopeful than he'd been in years, he slid the tape into the machine. His hands, so steady with a camera, trembled.

Five minutes later he was a free man.

He looked at his wife. Her face glowed with happiness.

"You didn't cause that fire," she said in wonder.

"I didn't kill those kids," he whispered, hardly able to take it in. All these years of self-loathing and fear, all the lies and hiding.

"I'm free." Tears prickled the back of his eyes, but these were tears of release and happiness. "I'm free."

He pulled her into his arms, this time as a man with the right to love a good woman. Though he'd never deserve her loyalty and love, he could now accept it. And give the same in return.

"I love you, Larissa," he murmured against her hair. "I'm sorry for all the times I've hurt you."

"No more talk of divorce?" she murmured, her soft breath tickling his ear.

"I never wanted a divorce. It was a lie concocted to scare you away. Will you forgive me?"

"If you'll forgive me, too, and promise never to keep secrets again."

There in the tiny hotel room, he pulled her to her feet. They held hands, facing one another as they had when they'd exchanged wedding vows.

"No more secrets." Later, he'd share the vision problems. Right now, he wanted to bask in the moment of release and freedom. "When problems arise, we'll talk them out."

"If you want to travel with your job, I won't whine. Military wives handle the separations. So can I."

"I'll be home more. I want to be."

"I won't nag about a family until you're ready."

Nearing overload, he swallowed the lump of emotion. "I think I am."

"What?"

He loved putting the joy in her eyes. "You. Me. A little rug rat or two. Sounds pretty good."

"I love you so much."

"The feeling, Mrs. Michaels, is mutual."

They stared into one another's eyes for several long, sweet, healing seconds. And then, in one movement, Drew grabbed Larissa around the waist and hoisted her high. He whirled her round and round until they both were laughing with joy and relief.

When the euphoria subsided, he set her on her feet and said, "Ready to go home?"

Her smile was beautiful.

"Right after you kiss me."

Feeling strong and confident and a little cocky, he grinned. "I think I can handle that."

And he did.

Epilogue

On a quiet side street in Oklahoma City, on a typical Saturday in July, a not-so-typical celebration occurred.

Drew, Collin and Ian, the three Grace brothers were together again as a family. Only this time, the family had increased so much Drew could hardly take it in. In fact, he'd already taken four rolls of film and was working on a fifth.

He breathed a lungful of oregano-scented air. The smell was pure contentment, a new and unexpected bonus of finding his brothers and a life in Christ.

Next to him at the long, food-laden table was Larissa, the woman who had never given up even when leaving would have been more sensible and much easier. He squeezed her hand and was rewarded with her gentle smile.

"Good, huh?" she murmured.

"Better than good."

Drew gazed around the big, crowded dining room. His brothers sat across the table with their own ladies.

Rounding out the group was the Carano family along with Ian's feisty adoptive mother, Margot Carpenter. The lady, who'd traveled with Ian and Gretchen from Louisiana, was a blend of genteel Southern belle and solid steel. Her devotion to Ian—and the woman he'd chosen as his wife—was evident. And what could he say about the exuberant Carano family? They were as warm as the Oklahoma summer.

Though he was a bit overwhelmed, Drew liked them all.

The Carano house was older, comfortable, a place that welcomed visitors like family. A place that embraced the noise and mess of kids. A place where love was as abundant as pastries, and every bit as sweet.

This was the kind of family life the Grace brothers had only dreamed about. But the Lord always knew where the long, broken road would lead.

Drew had never imagined Collin, the tough loner, as part of a huge Italian family, either. But here he was all smiles and jokes with his fiancée's gaggle of brothers, Nic, Adam, and Gabe who were giving him a hard time about marrying their sister.

All afternoon, the women had perused bridal magazines and made to-do lists in preparation for the double wedding of Ian to Gretchen and Collin to Mia. The date was set for Christmas, a fitting time, Drew thought, for a glorious celebration of love.

For now, the meal was essentially over, but the dining table seemed the perfect spot for conversation. So the adults remained, talking, sipping tea, munching Mama Carano's chocolate biscotti.

Mia, who never seemed to stop talking or waving her expressive hands somehow managed to wave everyone to silence.

"I asked Ian to bring his saxophone for a special reason. By the grace of God, the Grace brothers are all back together again. And not only have they found each other, they've found us!" Her wide mouth stretched in a happy grin as everyone chuckled. "I think there is something wonderfully significant about all that grace. So I've asked Ian to play a special song."

She nodded toward his baby brother who was just returning from the other room with his saxophone in hand. Drew hadn't even known his brother was a musician. He supposed they'd be learning things about each other for a long time to come.

Ian lifted the gleaming instrument and music flowed out like rough honey. Almost immediately, the listeners picked up the melody, first in low, murmuring voices, but soon the lyrics swelled in thanksgiving and wonder.

"Amazing grace, how sweet the sound that saved a wretch like me. I once was lost but now I'm found. Was blind but now I see…"

Drew had never given the song much thought before, but now he listened with every cell in his body. Whoever had written the words had lived them. So had he.

He'd been blind, spiritually and emotionally, but God had turned on the lights. The light to a relationship with the Lord and to a strong marriage. And even if the light of his vision was forever extinguished, the other two would shine bright enough to sustain him.

When the last notes died away, he pulled his wife against his side and nuzzled her hair.

"I love you," he whispered. "And I thank God every day for the amazing grace that brought us to this point."

Her radiant smile washed over him. "Me, too."

"Everything would be perfect if..."

"Your vision?" She frowned, the action drawing her perfect eyebrows together in a way that made him want to smooth a finger over them. He never wanted Larissa to frown or cry or be sad again.

"No. Not even that." His agent had sold the book proposal for a lot of money with an option for more. And there was talk of him teaching a photography class in Tulsa. "I hope my vision is back for good, but if not—" he shrugged, amazed to really believe his words "—we'll be okay. God will take care of us."

"Yes. I believe that with all my heart. But why did you say everything would be perfect *if?*"

"Your parents. You love them. They hate me. I'm sorry about that." More sorry than he could ever say. "I know how important family is, especially now. I don't want to take yours from you. I'd do about anything to mend fences with them."

A sweet secret smile tipped his wife's full, lush mouth. "I think you already have."

He tilted his head, puzzled.

Larissa went on, her violet eyes glowing. "I have a secret that may do the trick."

He offered a mock scowl. "We promised not to keep secrets, remember?"

"That's why I'm about to reveal all." Around them, the assembled group chattered and laughed, paying them no mind. Larissa leaned in to whisper, "Mother and Dad have wanted grandchildren for a long time."

The air above Drew buzzed with energy and sucked his breath away. Was she saying what he thought she was saying? "Are you—?"

His heart beat so hard, he thought he'd have a heart attack. And it wasn't caused by overindulging on Mama Carano's lasagna.

"I mean, Daddy Drew, you and I are going to have a baby."

Drew had expected to be scared, but he wasn't. Not at all. He was ecstatic. Adrenaline rushed to his head. Without stopping to remember where they were, he cried, "Yes!" and bolted from the chair.

The clatter of forks died away. A dozen pairs of eyes stared in astonishment. Drew didn't care. He tenderly pulled his beautiful, pregnant wife up into his arms and kissed her.

A half dozen catcalls circled the room. When the kiss

ended, Drew draped an arm around Larissa and turned
to blurt, "We're having a baby."

The noise started up again. This time congratulations and hugs were in order. Collin and Ian pounded
his back until he feared they'd rebreak his ribs. Larissa
glowed as the women huddled around to ask due dates
and discuss the mysteries of childbirth.

And as the circle of family surrounded him, Drew
lifted a silent prayer of thanksgiving to Heaven. For his
wife, the new extended family, the tiny blend of himself and Larissa that would join them early next year.
And of course, for his brothers.

As Gretchen's news report so beautifully phrased it,
he, Ian and Collin were separated as boys, but reunited
as men. But the bond that had brought them together
again was more than a bond of blood. It was a bond of
family. A bond of love.

A gift of God.

Larissa turned to him with one of her smiles.

Yes, a gift of God. And he would never, ever again
take that gift for granted.

* * * * *

Dear Reader,

Thank you for choosing *The Heart of Grace,* the
final book in The Brothers' Bond trilogy. I hope you
have enjoyed reading about the Grace brothers as
much as I have enjoyed writing about them. I must
confess to a mix of joy and sadness in bringing their
stories to a close. Somewhere out there are three
little boys who first inspired this series. I hope and
pray that they, too, have found a happy ending.

As always, I enjoy hearing from readers and value
their thoughts on my stories. You may contact me
at www.lindagoodnight.com or at Linda Goodnight,
c/o Love Inspired Books, 233 Broadway, Suite
1001, New York, NY 10279.

God bless the needy children of the world. And
God bless you, as well.

Linda Goodnight

celebrating
**15
YEARS**

This holiday season enjoy four heartfelt stories
of kindness and love from two fan-favorite
Love Inspired® authors!

Discover hope, love and the holiday spirit in

A FAMILY-STYLE CHRISTMAS and
YULETIDE HOMECOMING

by Carolyne Aarsen

And sweet small-town romances in

A BRIDE FOR DRY CREEK and
SHEPHERDS ABIDING IN DRY CREEK

by Janet Tronstad

Get two happily-ever-afters for the price of one!

Available in December 2012 wherever books are sold.

REQUEST YOUR FREE BOOKS!

2 FREE INSPIRATIONAL NOVELS
PLUS 2
FREE
MYSTERY GIFTS

YES! Please send me 2 FREE Love Inspired® novels and my 2 FREE mystery gifts (gifts are worth about $10). After receiving them, if I don't wish to receive any more books, I can return the shipping statement marked "cancel." If I don't cancel, I will receive 6 brand-new novels every month and be billed just $4.49 per book in the U.S. or $4.99 per book in Canada. That's a saving of at least 22% off the cover price. It's quite a bargain! Shipping and handling is just 50¢ per book in the U.S. and 75¢ per book in Canada.* I understand that accepting the 2 free books and gifts places me under no obligation to buy anything. I can always return a shipment and cancel at any time. Even if I never buy another book, the two free books and gifts are mine to keep forever.

105/305 IDN FEGR

Name	(PLEASE PRINT)	
Address		Apt. #
City	State/Prov.	Zip/Postal Code

Signature (if under 18, a parent or guardian must sign)

Mail to the **Reader Service:**
IN U.S.A.: P.O. Box 1867, Buffalo, NY 14240-1867
IN CANADA: P.O. Box 609, Fort Erie, Ontario L2A 5X3

Not valid for current subscribers to Love Inspired books.

**Are you a subscriber to Love Inspired books
and want to receive the larger-print edition?
Call 1-800-873-8635 or visit www.ReaderService.com.**

* Terms and prices subject to change without notice. Prices do not include applicable taxes. Sales tax applicable in N.Y. Canadian residents will be charged applicable taxes. Offer not valid in Quebec. This offer is limited to one order per household. All orders subject to credit approval. Credit or debit balances in a customer's account(s) may be offset by any other outstanding balance owed by or to the customer. Please allow 4 to 6 weeks for delivery. Offer available while quantities last.

Your Privacy—The Reader Service is committed to protecting your privacy. Our Privacy Policy is available online at www.ReaderService.com or upon request from the Reader Service.

We make a portion of our mailing list available to reputable third parties that offer products we believe may interest you. If you prefer that we not exchange your name with third parties, or if you wish to clarify or modify your communication preferences, please visit us at www.ReaderService.com/consumerschoice or write to us at Reader Service Preference Service, P.O. Box 9062, Buffalo, NY 14269. Include your complete name and address.

LIREG11B

*When a baby is left on the doorstep of an Amish house,
Sheriff Nick Bradley comes face-to-face with his past.*

*Read on for a preview of A HOME FOR HANNAH
by Patricia Davids.*

The farmhouse door swung open before Sheriff Nick Bradley
could knock. A woman with fiery auburn hair and green eyes
stood glaring at him. "There has been a mistake. We don't
need you here."

The shock of seeing Miriam Kauffman standing in front
of him took him aback. He struggled to hide his surprise.
It had been eight years since he'd laid eyes on her. A life-
time ago.

"Good morning to you, too, Miriam."

After all this time, she wasn't any better at hiding her
opinion of him. She looked ready to spit nails. Proof that
she hadn't forgiven him.

"Miriam, don't be rude," her mother chided. Miriam
reluctantly stepped aside. He entered the house.

His cousin Amber sat at the table. "Hi, Nick. Thanks for
coming. We do need your help."

Ada Kauffman sat across from her. The room was bathed
in soft light from two kerosene lanterns hanging from hooks
on the ceiling.

He glanced at the three women facing him. Ada Kauffman
was Amish, from the top of her white prayer bonnet to the
tips of her bare toes poking out from beneath her plain
dress. Her daughter, Miriam, had never joined the church,
choosing to leave before she was baptized. Her arms were
crossed over her chest.

Amber served the Amish and non-Amish people of Hope Springs, Ohio, as a nurse midwife. Exactly what was she doing here?

He said, "Okay, I'm here. What's so sensitive that I had to come instead of sending one of my perfectly competent deputies?"

"This is why we called you." Amber gestured toward the basket. He took a step closer and saw a baby swaddled in the folds of a quilt.

"You called me here to see a new baby? Congratulations to whomever."

"Exactly," Miriam said.

He looked at her closely. "What am I missing?"

Amber said, "It's more about what we are missing."

"And that is?" he demanded.

Ada said, "A mother to go with this baby."

He shook his head. "You've lost me."

Miriam rolled her eyes. "I'm not surprised."

Her mother scowled at her, but said, "Someone left this baby on my porch."

Will Nick and Miriam get past their differences to help little Hannah?

Pick up A HOME FOR HANNAH by Patricia Davids, available August 2012 from Love Inspired Books.